John Hewitt Jellett, James MacCullagh

The collected Works of James MacCullagh

John Hewitt Jellett, James MacCullagh

The collected Works of James MacCullagh

ISBN/EAN: 9783337218645

Printed in Europe, USA, Canada, Australia, Japan

Cover: Foto ©Andreas Hilbeck / pixelio.de

More available books at **www.hansebooks.com**

DUBLIN UNIVERSITY PRESS SERIES.

THE COLLECTED WORKS

OF

JAMES MAC CULLAGH, LL.D.,

FELLOW OF TRINITY COLLEGE,

AND

PROFESSOR OF NATURAL PHILOSOPHY IN THE UNIVERSITY OF DUBLIN.

EDITED BY

JOHN H. JELLETT, B.D.,

AND

SAMUEL HAUGHTON, CLK., M.D.

DUBLIN: HODGES, FIGGIS, & CO., GRAFTON-STREET.
LONDON: LONGMANS, GREEN, & CO., PATERNOSTER-ROW.
1880.

DUBLIN:
PRINTED AT THE UNIVERSITY PRESS.

PREFACE.

THE present volume contains a complete collection of the scientific works of the late Professor Mac Cullagh. They have been reprinted for the most part from the *Proceedings* and *Transactions* of the Royal Irish Academy, in which they originally appeared. Some few have been taken from the *Philosophical Magazine*.

Prof. Mac Cullagh's most important contributions to Science were made in the departments of Physical Optics and Geometry—the first class being very much the larger. The discrepancy is not, however, as great as might at first sight appear. A considerable part of his Optical researches, more especially those of earlier date, really belong to the domain of Geometry; and, if they were so classed, the inequality between the classes would be much reduced. Such a classification, however, involving the separation of the purely geometrical propositions from their physical applications, would be exceedingly inconvenient, and these propositions have been allowed to remain in the connexion in which the author placed them.

In his earlier Optical Memoirs, Prof. Mac Cullagh aimed chiefly at elucidating, by means of geometrical theorems, the physical theory of Fresnel. This is the principal object of the Memoirs I.–IV. in the present volume. In V. occurs the first notice of a problem which subsequently occupied so large a space in Prof. Mac Cullagh's researches, namely, the investigation of the laws according to which polarized light is reflected and refracted at the surface of a crystalline medium. This problem is discussed at length in XI. and XIV. In the former of these memoirs he deduces a solution of the problem from certain assumed physical principles. In the second he seeks to establish the theory upon a strictly mechanical basis by means of the general dynamical equation of Lagrange. These, which are the principal memoirs treating of the general question, are supplemented by Memoirs XVI.–XIX., in which the same problem is discussed. Two other important questions, namely, metallic reflexion and the double refraction of quartz, which required a peculiar mode of treatment, are considered in Memoirs VI., VII., XV., XVII., XXI.

Prof. Mac Cullagh's contributions to pure Geometry, excluding, as has been said, all those theorems which have been introduced by the author as auxiliary to his Optical researches, form the second Part of the present volume. The first of these is a Memoir on the Rectification of the Conic Sections, which (with his first Optical Memoir) was communicated to the Royal Irish Academy shortly after he obtained his B. A. degree. This was followed, many years afterwards, by an elaborate memoir, which may, indeed, be fairly called a treatise: " On Surfaces of the Second Order." In this memoir a new definition is given for this class of surfaces analogous to the well-known mode of defining curves of the second order by means of a focus and directrix.

The articles contained in the third and fourth parts of the present volume were not published during the lifetime of the author. They are records of Courses of Lectures on the subjects of Rotation and Attraction, given by Prof. Mac Cullagh. These records were preserved by Professors Haughton and Allman, and communicated by them to the Royal Irish Academy.

Two short Papers on Egyptian Chronology, which, like most of Prof. Mac Cullagh's writings, were originally communicated to the Royal Irish Academy, have been printed at the end of this volume.

CONTENTS.

PART I.

PHYSICAL OPTICS.

PART II.

GEOMETRY.

PART III.

ROTATION.

PART IV.

ATTRACTION.

SUPPLEMENT.

EGYPTIAN CHRONOLOGY.

I.—ON THE DOUBLE REFRACTION OF LIGHT IN A CRYSTALLIZED MEDIUM, ACCORDING TO THE PRINCIPLES OF FRESNEL.

[*Transactions of the Royal Irish Academy*, Vol. xvi.—Read June 21, 1830.]

THE mathematical difficulties under which the beautiful and interesting theory of Fresnel has hitherto laboured are well known, and have been regarded as almost insuperable. He tells us, in his Memoir (see the *Memoirs of the Royal Academy of Sciences of Paris*, tom. vii. p. 136), that the calculations, by which he assured himself of the truth of his construction for finding the surface of the wave, were so tedious and embarrassing, that he was obliged to omit them altogether. A direct demonstration has since been supplied by M. Ampere (*Annales de Chimie et de Physique*, tom. xxxix. p. 113) ; but his solution is excessively complicated and difficult.

Judging from the simplicity and elegance of the results that there must be some simple method of arriving at them, I have been led to consider the subject with the attention which it merits, and have succeeded in discovering a method by which the whole may be explained with that simplicity which is characteristic of every theory that is founded in nature.

In the following Paper I shall give a brief view of this method, sufficient to enable those who are acquainted with the mechanical principles laid down in the original memoir of Fresnel, to trace, at a glance, the connexion between the several parts of his theory. For this purpose it will be convenient to premise the following Geometrical Lemmas :—

. 1. If a, b, c, be the semiaxes of an ellipsoid, and a, β, γ, the angles which they make with a perpendicular from the centre on a tangent plane, the square of the perpendicular will be equal to

$$a^2 \cos^2 a + b^2 \cos^2 \beta + c^2 \cos^2 \gamma.$$

Let a plane through the point of contact Q, and one of the semiaxes OA, intersect the ellipsoid in the ellipse AON, and the tangent plane in the tangent QL, and draw QM perpendicular to OA; then OA is a semiaxis of the ellipse AON, and therefore is a mean proportional between OM and OL; whence $OL = \dfrac{a^2}{x}$, denoting OM by

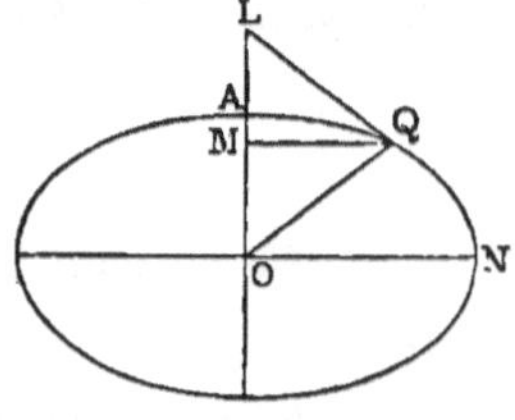

Fig. 1.

x. But if p denote the length of the perpendicular from the centre O on the tangent plane at Q, the cosine of the angle which it makes with OA will be equal to $\dfrac{p}{OL}$, and therefore

$$\cos a = \frac{px}{a^2}, \text{ and } a \cos a = \frac{px}{a}.$$

Similarly,

$$b \cos \beta = \frac{py}{b}, \text{ and } c \cos \gamma = \frac{pz}{c}.$$

Hence

$$a^2 \cos^2 a + b^2 \cos^2 \beta + c^2 \cos^2 \gamma = p^2 \left(\frac{x^2}{a^2} + \frac{y^2}{b^2} + \frac{z^2}{c^2} \right) = p^2.$$

Cor.—Since x, y, z, are as the cosines of the angles which OQ makes with the semiaxes, it appears from the demonstration that the cosines of the angles which the perpendicular to a tangent plane makes with the semiaxes are, with respect to each other, directly as the cosines of the angles which the semidiameter through the point of contact makes with the semiaxes, and inversely as the squares of the semiaxes themselves.

2. If the semiaxes a, b, c, and a', b', c', of two concentric

ellipsoids coincide in direction, and be reciprocally proportional, so that $aa' = bb' = cc' = k^2$; and if a semidiameter OR of the one be cut perpendicularly in P by a plane which touches the other, then will OR be inversely as OP, so that $OP \times OR$ will be always equal to k^2.

Let OR be a semidiameter of the ellipsoid whose semiaxes are a', b', c' ; and let a, β, γ, be the angles which it makes with them ; then if x, y, z, be the co-ordinates of R, we have

$$\frac{x^2}{a'^2} + \frac{y^2}{b'^2} + \frac{z^2}{c'^2} = 1,$$

and therefore

$$\frac{1}{OR^2} = \frac{\cos^2 a}{a'^2} + \frac{\cos^2 \beta}{b'^2} + \frac{\cos^2 \gamma}{c'^2}$$

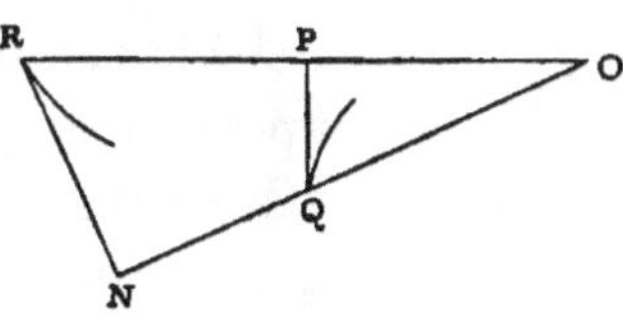

Fig. 2.

$$= \frac{1}{k^4} \left(a^2 \cos^2 a + b^2 \cos^2 \beta + c^2 \cos^2 \gamma. \right)$$

But by the preceding lemma, since OP is perpendicular to the tangent plane at Q, we have

$$OP^2 = a^2 \cos^2 a + b^2 \cos^2 \beta + c^2 \cos^2 \gamma.$$

Hence

$$\frac{1}{OR^2} = \frac{OP^2}{k^4},$$

and therefore

$$OP \times OR = k^2.$$

3. If through the point of contact Q the straight line OQ be drawn to meet in N the tangent plane at R, it will meet it at right angles.

For the cosines of the angles made by OP with the semi-axes are directly as the cosines of the angles made by OQ with them, and inversely as the squares of a, b, c (Lem. 1, *Cor.*) ; and the cosines of the angles made with the semiaxes, by a perpendicular to the tangent plane at R, are directly as the cosines of the angles made with them by OP, and inversely as the squares of a', b', c', or as the same cosines and the squares of a, b, c, directly ; that is, simply, as the cosines of the angles made by OQ

with the semiaxes.   Hence OQ coincides with the perpendicular to the tangent plane at R.

4. If a perpendicular at O to the plane POQ meet the surface of the ellipsoid abc in q, then will OQ and Oq be the semiaxes of the section QOq made by a plane passing through them.

For the tangent plane at Q and the plane QOq are perpendicular to POQ, and therefore the intersection of the two former, which is a tangent to the ellipse QOq at Q, is perpendicular to OQ; whence OQ is one semiaxis, and Oq the other.

If the perpendicular Oq meet the other ellipsoid in r, then OR and Or will be the semiaxes of the section ROr made by a plane passing through them; for (by lem. 3), the straight line OQN is perpendicular to the tangent plane at R.

5. In a straight line, at right angles to any diametral section QOq of the ellipsoid abc, let OT and OV be taken equal to OQ and Oq, the semiaxes of the section, and imagine the double surface which is the locus of all the points T and V; then if OS be perpendicular to the plane which touches this surface in T, and OP to that which touches the ellipsoid in Q, the lines OP and OS will be equal and perpendicular to each other, and the four, OP, OQ, OS, OT, will lie in the same plane, which will be at right angles to Oq.

By the preceding lemma it is evident that Oq is perpendicular to the plane POQ; and since OT is perpendicular to the plane QOq, it follows that OP, OQ, OT, are in the same plane at right angles to Oq.   In the surface which is the locus of T, and in the plane TOq, let a point $T_{,}$ be taken indefinitely near to T; then the plane of the section at right angles to $OT_{,}$ will pass through OQ, and will have one of its semiaxes (that to which $OT_{,}$ is equal) indefinitely near to OQ, and therefore differing from OQ by an indefinitely small quantity of the second order, adopting, for brevity, the language of

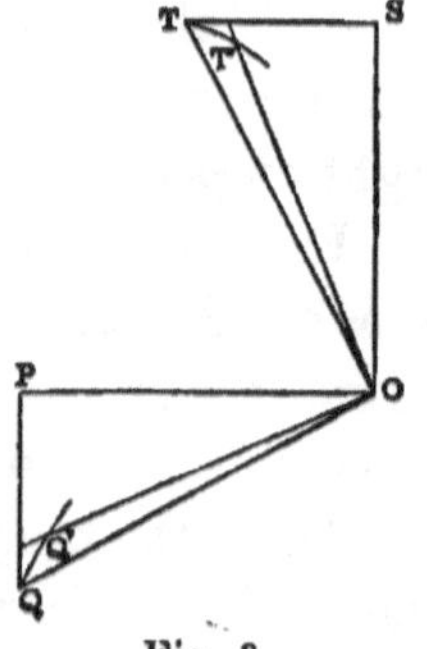

Fig. 3.

infinitesimals.   To see this, it is only necessary to recollect that, by the property of maxima and minima, the semiaxis differs from any semidiameter indefinitely near to it, such as OQ, by an indefinitely small quantity of the second order.   Hence, since OT is equal to OQ, and $OT_{,}$ to the above-mentioned semiaxis, it follows that OT and $OT_{,}$ differ by an indefinitely small quantity of the second order, and that therefore the angle $OTT_{,}$ is ultimately a right angle : consequently the tangent to the curve in which the plane TOq intersects the locus of T is perpendicular to the plane $PQOT$.   But the tangent plane at T passes through this tangent, and therefore the perpendicular OS to the tangent plane must lie in the plane $PQOT$.

Again, let a point T' indefinitely near to T, and in the plane $PQOT$, be taken in the surface which is the locus of T, and let the plane of the section which is perpendicular to OT'' intersect the plane $PQOT$ in the straight line OQ' which meets the ellipsoid in Q'.   Then that semiaxis of the section to which OT'' is equal will be indefinitely near to OQ', and will therefore differ from it by an indefinitely small quantity of the second order.   Hence, since OT is equal to OQ, the angle OTT' will be ultimately equal to OQQ' ; and therefore, TS and QP being tangents, the angles OTS and OQP are equal.   But $OT = OQ$, and the angles P and S are right; therefore $OS = OP$, and the angle $SOT = POQ$; whence $SOP = TOQ = $ a right angle.

Similarly, if one perpendicular be let fall from O on a plane touching the locus in V, and another on the plane touching the ellipsoid in q, it may be proved that the two perpendiculars are equal and at right angles to each other, and that, with the lines OV and Oq, they lie in a plane at right angles to OQ.

6. An ellipsoid being cut by any plane through its centre, the difference between the squares of the reciprocals of the semi-axes of the section is proportional to the rectangle under the sines of the angles which the plane of the section makes with the planes of the two circular sections of the ellipsoid.—(*See* Fresnel's *Memoir*, p. 150.)

Let the plane which cuts the ellipsoid intersect its circular sections in the lines OR', OS', and let the principal section AOC of the ellipsoid cut the circular sections in OR and OS; then OR, OS, OR', OS', will be all equal to the mean semiaxis OB, and hence the semiaxes OA', OC' of the section $A'OC'$ will bisect the acute and obtuse angles made by OR' and OS'. Let a plane through OB and OA' intersect the principal plane ACO in the line OT. Then, by the nature of the ellipse, we have, in the ellipse $A'OC'$,

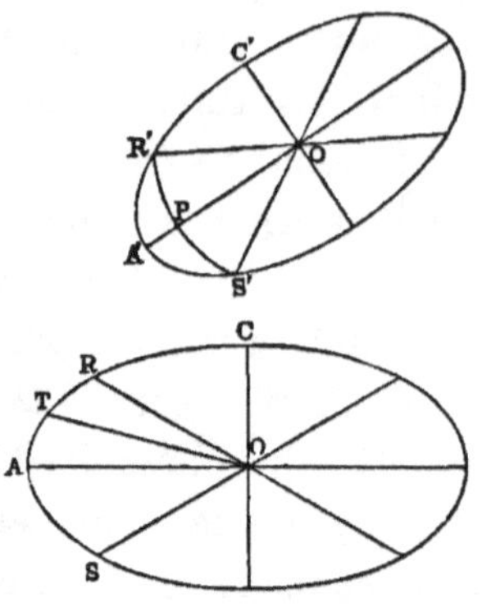

Fig. 4.

$$\frac{1}{OR'^2} - \frac{1}{OA'^2} = \left(\frac{1}{OC'^2} - \frac{1}{OA'^2}\right)\sin^2 A'OR';$$

and in the ellipse BOT,

$$\frac{1}{OB^2} - \frac{1}{OA'^2} = \left(\frac{1}{OB^2} - \frac{1}{OT^2}\right)\sin^2 BOA'.$$

Hence, observing that OB and OR' are equal, we have

$$\frac{1}{OC'^2} - \frac{1}{OA'^2} = \left(\frac{1}{OB^2} - \frac{1}{OT^2}\right)\frac{\sin^2 BOA'}{\sin^2 A'OR'}.$$

But the ellipse OAC gives

$$\frac{1}{OR^2} - \frac{1}{OT^2} = \left(\frac{1}{OC^2} - \frac{1}{OA^2}\right)(\sin^2 AOR - \sin^2 AOT)$$

$$= \left(\frac{1}{OC^2} - \frac{1}{OA^2}\right) \times \sin ROT \sin SOT.$$

Therefore

$$\frac{1}{OC'^2} - \frac{1}{OA'^2} = \left(\frac{1}{OC^2} - \frac{1}{OA^2}\right)\frac{\sin^2 BOA}{\sin^2 A'OR}\sin ROT \sin SOT,$$

because OB and OR are equal.

Imagine a sphere described from the centre O with a radius equal to OB, and passing through R' and S', and cutting $A'O$ in P. The sides BP and PR' of the spherical triangle BPR' subtend the angles BOA' and $A'OR'$ at the centre; and its angle PBR' is equal to the angle ROT; whence the sines of the sides being proportional to the sines of the opposite spherical angles, it follows that

$$\frac{\sin BOA'}{\sin A'OR'}, \sin ROT$$

is equal to the sine of the spherical angle $BR'P$, which is the angle made by the section $A'OC'$ with the plane of the circular section BOR. Similarly, by means of the spherical triangle BPS', it may be shown that

$$\frac{\sin BOA'}{\sin A'OS'}, \sin SOT$$

is equal to the sine of the angle made by the plane $A'OC'$ with the plane of the circular section BOS. Therefore, since the angles $A'OR'$ and $A'OS'$ are equal, it follows that

$$\frac{1}{OC'^2} - \frac{1}{OA'^2} \text{ is equal to } \frac{1}{OC^2} - \frac{1}{OA^2}$$

multiplied by the product of the sines of the angles which the plane $A'OC'$ makes with the planes of the two circular sections.

I shall now demonstrate a geometrical construction for finding the magnitude and direction of the elastic force arising from a displacement in any direction—a construction which, with the help of the preceding lemmas, will lead us immediately to all the conclusions established by Fresnel.

Let O be the position of a point in the medium when quiescent, and let three rectangular axes passing through it, and fixed in space, be taken for the axes of co-ordinates. For a small displacement in the direction of x, let the elastic forces, excited in the directions of x, y, z, be a, b, c; for an equal displacement in the direction of y let the forces be a', b', c'; and for the same in the direction of z let them be a'', b'', c''. Then, if a point receive an equal displacement in a direction OI making with OX, OY, OZ, the angles a, β, γ, the forces in the direction of x, y, z (denoting then by X, Y, Z, respectively), will be

$$X = a \cos a + a' \cos \beta + a'' \cos \gamma,$$

$$Y = b \cos a + b' \cos \beta + b'' \cos \gamma,$$

$$Z = c \cos a + c' \cos \beta + c'' \cos \gamma,$$

as follows from considering (*see* Fresnel's *Memoir*, p. 82) that the force arising from a displacement in any direction is the resultant of the forces arising from the three displacements in the directions of x, y, z, which are the statical components of that displacement. But since (p. 90) the force in the direction of one of the axes, arising from a displacement in the direction of another, is equal to the force in the direction of the latter, arising from an equal displacement in the direction of the former, it follows that $a' = b$, $a'' = c$, $b'' = c'$; and hence

$$X = a \cos a + b \cos \beta + c \cos \gamma,$$

$$Y = b \cos a + b' \cos \beta + c' \cos \gamma,$$

$$Z = c \cos a + c' \cos \beta + c'' \cos \gamma.$$

Let $ax^2 + b'y^2 + c''z^2 + 2c'yz + 2czx + 2bxy = 1$ be the equation of a surface of the second order. Let OI intersect it in I, the co-ordinates of I being x', y', z'; then the equation of the tangent plane at I will be, by the known formulæ

$$(ax' + by' + cz') x + (bx' + b'y' + c'z') y + (cx' + c'y' + c''z') z = 1.$$

Put $OI = r$, and let the tangent plane intersect OX, OY, OZ, in the points P, Q, R; then from this equation we have

$$\frac{1}{OP} = ax' + by' + cz' = r\,(a \cos a + b \cos \beta + c \cos \gamma) = rX,$$

$$\frac{1}{OQ} = bx' + b'y' + c'z' = r\,(b \cos a + b' \cos \beta + c' \cos \gamma) = rY,$$

$$\frac{1}{OR} = cx' + c'y' + c''z' = r\,(c \cos a + c' \cos \beta + c'' \cos \gamma) = rZ.$$

Now if p be the length of the perpendicular let fall from O on the tangent plane, the cosines of the angles which this perpendicular makes with the axes of co-ordinates will be equal to

$$\frac{p}{OP}, \quad \frac{p}{OQ}, \quad \frac{p}{OR},$$

respectively, that is, to prX, prY, prZ; and since the sum of the squares of these cosines is equal to unity, we have

$$pr \sqrt{X^2 + Y^2 + Z^2} = 1.$$

Hence it appears that the perpendicular let fall from O on the tangent plane is parallel to the direction of the resultant elastic force, and that the magnitude of the resultant is expressed by $\dfrac{1}{pr}$.

From this conclusion we may, with the greatest facility, deduce several corollaries.

1°. Since the elastic force is supposed finite, whatever be the *direction* of the displacement, it is manifest that the above-mentioned surface of the second order must be an ellipsoid, and that when the displacement is in the direction of any of the three axes of the ellipsoid, the elastic force excited will be in the direction of the same axis, because the tangent plane will be perpendicular to it. Hence the remarkable consequence, that *there are always three axes of elasticity at right angles to each other.—(Memoir*, p. 93.) Also the elasticities arising from equal displacements in the directions of the three axes are inversely as the squares of the axes; and hence, the positions of the axes and the elasticities in their respective directions being given, the ellipsoid may be constructed.

2°. The ellipsoid being thus constructed, the direction of the elastic force, arising from a displacement in the direction of any of its semidiameters, will be parallel to the normal at the extremity of that semidiameter; and for equal displacements the magnitude of the force will be inversely as the rectangle under the semidiameter and the perpendicular from the centre on the tangent plane at its extremity. If the displacements are proportional to the semidiameters, the elastic forces will be both parallel and proportional to the normals; for the normal, terminated by any of the principal planes, is inversely as the perpendicular on the tangent plane.

3°. If the elastic force be resolved into two, one parallel and the other perpendicular to the direction of the displacement, the former will be inversely as the square of the semidiameter in the direction of the displacement.

4°. If the ellipsoid be cut by a plane through its centre, and if the elastic force arising from a displacement in the direction of either axis of the section be resolved parallel and perpendicular to that axis, the part perpendicular to the axis will also be perpendicular to the plane of the section. For (by Lem. 4) the plane passing through one axis and the perpendicular to the tangent plane at its extremity, is perpendicular to the other axis, and therefore to the plane of the section. But if the displacement be in the direction of any other diameter of the section, the elastic force, resolved perpendicularly to that diameter, will be oblique to the plane of the section.

To apply these things to the double refraction of light in a crystallized medium, imagine the ellipsoid to be described as above, and let it be cut through its centre by a plane parallel to that of a *plane* wave of light incident on the crystal ; then if the vibrations of the light be parallel to either of the axes of the section, the plane containing the direction of the vibrations and that of the elastic force arising from them will be perpendicular to the plane of the wave (No. 4, preceding) ; and therefore, according to Fresnel's theory, the direction of the vibrations will remain parallel to itself, while the wave is propagated. But if the light be common light, or if it be polarized, and the plane of polarization be not perpendicular to either of the axes of the section, the wave will be divided into two others having the directions of their vibrations parallel to the semiaxes of the elliptic section, and their planes of polarization perpendicular to them : their velocities of propagation—measured in a direction perpendicular to their plane—will be different, and will be in the sub-duplicate ratio of the elasticities in the direction of their respective vibrations, and therefore (by No. 3) inversely as the semiaxes of the section to which those vibrations are parallel.

If a wave be propagated *in all directions* from an origin O within a crystal, its surface will at each instant be touched by the simultaneous position of a plane wave which passed through O at the instant when the former began to be propagated (*Memoir*, p. 127). Hence, to find the surface of the double wave in a crystal, let the above-mentioned ellipsoid be cut by any plane through its centre O, and imagine two other planes parallel to this section, and at distances from it which are third proportionals to its semiaxes, OR, Or, and any given line k: the double surface which touches these planes in all their positions will be the surface of the wave.

Now conceive another concentric ellipsoid, having the directions of its semiaxes the same, but their lengths a, b, c, inversely proportional to those of the former, so that the rectangle under any coinciding pair of semiaxes is equal to k^2: then if a plane, touching this second ellipsoid in Q, cut OR perpendicularly in P, the line OP will be a third proportional to OR and k (Lem. 2); and if Or intersect the second ellipsoid in q, the semiaxes of the section QOq will be OQ and Oq (Lem. 4). Draw OT perpendicular to QOq and equal to OQ, and conceive the surface which is the locus of the point T to be described, and a tangent plane, to which the line OS is drawn perpendicular, to be applied at the point T. Then OS will be perpendicular to the plane ROr and equal to OP (Lem. 5): and hence the point T always lies in the surface of the wave. Similar things may be proved with respect to the other semiaxis Or of the ellipse ROr. Hence we deduce the following construction for the surface of the wave :—

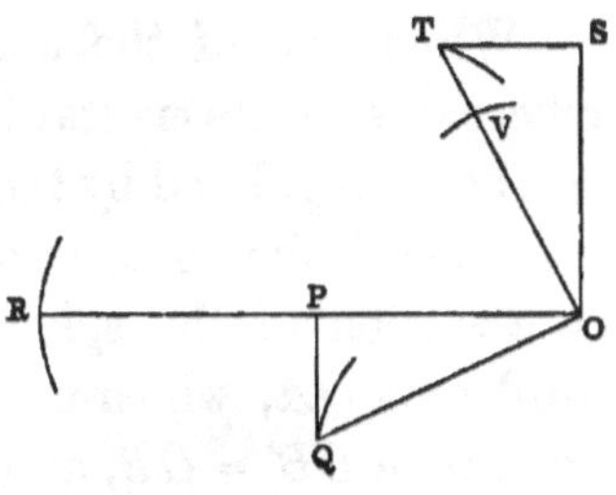

Fig. 5.

" Describe an ellipsoid whose axes are in the directions of the axes of elasticity, the squares of their lengths being *directly* as the elasticities in their respective directions ; cut the ellipsoid by a plane through its centre, as QOq, and in a perpendicular to that plane take two portions OT and OV equal to the semiaxes OQ and Oq of the section. The double surface which is the locus of the points T and V is the surface of the wave."

As to the planes of polarization of the rays belonging to the two parts of the wave, Fresnel has shown how to find them by means of a surface which he calls the surface of elasticity. But it is desirable to be able to find them by means of the same ellipsoid which serves to find the surface of the wave. Now TS, parallel to OR, is the direction of the vibrations of the ray OT, and the tangent plane at Q is perpendicular to OR, and therefore parallel to the plane of polarization of the ray OT. In like manner the plane of polarization of the ray OV is parallel to the tangent plane at q. Hence the planes of polarization of two different rays, having a common direction, are parallel to the planes which touch the ellipsoid at the extremities of the semiaxes of the diametral section perpendicular to their common direction.

When two of the axes are equal, the ellipsoid becomes a spheroid, and the crystal is said to be uniaxal, the double refraction being regulated by the third axis which is perpendicular to their plane. Let AOB be a section of the spheroid through the third axis OA, which is its axis of revolution ; take $OB' = OB$, and $OA' = OA$, and let the ellipse $A'OB'$ and the circle BOB' revolve about OB' as an axis ; they will describe a surface compounded of a spheroid and sphere, which will in this case be the surface of the double wave. For if OM be the direction of a ray, and if a plane perpendicular to OM cut the ellipse AOB in OQ, and the equator of the spheroid in Oq, the lines OQ and Oq, of which the latter is equal to OB, will be the semiaxes of the section

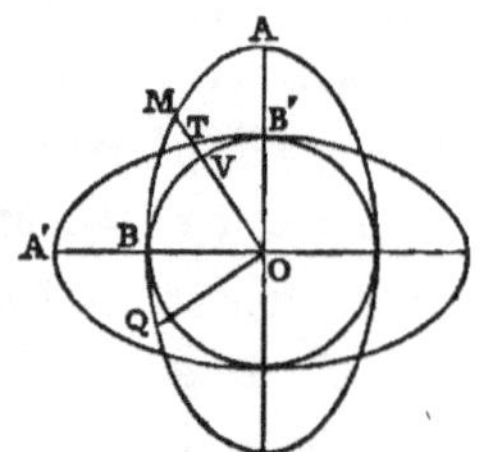

Fig. 6.

QOq. Taking, therefore, OT and OV equal to OQ and OB, the locus of V will evidently be the circle BOB'; and the locus of T will be the ellipse $A'OB'$, since the angle $B'OT'$ is equal to the angle BOQ.

In the general case, OT and OV, which are equal to OQ and Oq, represent the velocities of the two different sorts of rays having a common direction in the crystal; and two right lines, which lie in the plane of the greatest and least axes of the ellipsoid, and are perpendicular to its two circular sections, are called the optic axes. It appears, therefore, by the 6th Lemma, that the difference of the squares of the reciprocals of the velocities of the two rays, having a common direction in the crystal, is proportional to the product of the sines of the angles which that direction makes with the optic axes. This is the celebrated law of M. Biot, to which he was led by analogy, and which he afterwards found to agree with that previously laid down by Dr. Brewster.

Such, in their simplest form, are the principal features of the Mechanical Theory of Double Refraction, invented by the late M. Fresnel—a theory which would do honour to the sagacity of Newton, and which gives us ample reason to regret that the life of its author was not longer spared, to enrich with further discoveries his favourite science. Of him it may be said, as Newton said of Cotes—and apparently with much greater reason— that if he had lived longer, we should have known something at last of the laws of nature.

II.—ON THE INTENSITY OF LIGHT WHEN THE VIBRATIONS ARE ELLIPTICAL.

[*Edinburgh Journal of Science, April,* 1831.]

ACCORDING to the opinions commonly received, the intensity of light, in the undulatory hypothesis, is proportional to the *vis viva*, which again is proportional to the square of the greatest velocity. Now the greatest velocity will be the same in an ellipse and a right line which have the same period, if the greater axis of the former be equal to the whole extent of the latter; so that in elliptic vibrations the intensity would be independent of the minor axis, which is far from being true. I would propose the integral $Sv^2 dt$—so remarkable for its mechanical properties—as the measure of the intensity, the integral being extended to the whole time of a vibration. This gives precision to the notion of *vis viva*, and leads, moreover, to an elegant result; for if a and b denote the semiaxes of the ellipse, and T the time of vibration, the integral, by an easy calculation, will be found equal to $\dfrac{2\pi^2}{T}(a^2 + b^2)$, showing that for the same colour the intensity is proportional to the sum of the squares of the semiaxes, and that for different colours it increases with the rapidity of the vibrations, as it would be natural to suppose *à priori.*

This theorem assigns very simply the reason why two portions of light polarized at right angles do not interfere; but to show this it will be necessary to lay down the following general rule for compounding rectilinear vibrations having the same period, whatever be the difference of their origin and direction :—

Let *AA′* and *BB′* (Fig. 7), bisecting each other at *O*, represent in extent and direction the vibrations to be compounded, and suppose *C* and *D* to be two simultaneous positions of the moving molecule, which it would have in virtue of each vibration singly. Complete the parallelograms *OE* and *OP*, and through *P* describe an ellipse having *O* for its centre, and touching the sides of

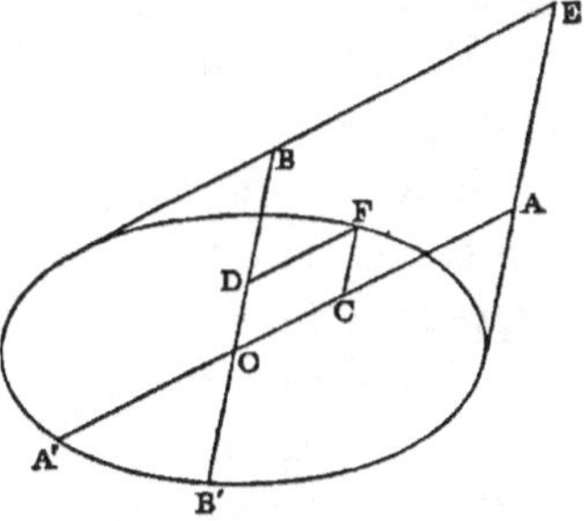

Fig. 7.

the parallelogram *OE*; this ellipse will represent the resulting vibration; it will have the same period as the compound one, and equal areas will be described in equal times about its centre.

To apply this construction to the case proposed, it is necessary to show that when *OA* and *OB* are constant and at right angles to each other, the intensity of the elliptic vibration, or the sum of the squares of the semiaxes, is independent of the difference of origin, or of the position of the points *C* and *D*.

Now in an ellipse, when a perpendicular from the centre on a tangent makes an angle ϕ with the major axis, the square of its length is equal to $a^2 \cos^2 \phi + b^2 \sin^2 \phi$. If ϕ be the angle which the major axis makes with *OA*, it will make its complement with *OB*, and we shall have

$$OA^2 = a^2 \cos^2 \phi + b^2 \sin^2 \phi,$$

$$OB^2 = a^2 \sin^2 \phi + b^2 \cos^2 \phi,$$

and therefore

$$OA^2 + OB^2 = a^2 + b^2.$$

Hence the intensity is independent of the difference of origin, and therefore the rays do not interfere.

This remarkable circumstance is commonly accounted for by

observing, that since the component velocities are at right angles to each other, the square of the actual velocity must be the sum of their squares; but this proves the proposition only when the greatest velocities are simultaneous, which happens only in the cases of a complete accordance or of a difference of a semi-undulation in the interfering portions.

It may be observed also, that the method usually given for finding the intensity of the vibration resulting from two or more rectilinear vibrations proceeds upon no certain grounds. All the vibrations may be reduced to two in rectangular directions, the expression for the square of the velocity in each of their directions consisting of two parts, one of which is constant, and the other depends on the cosine of an arc increasing proportionally to the time: the square of the resultunt velocity, therefore, consists also of a constant part, and a part depending similarly on the time; and it is assumed that the intensity of the resulting vibration is proportional to the former, which is true only in the very particular cases just mentioned, if the intensity be measured by the square of the greatest velocity.

This assumption, however, gives a correct result; and the reason that it does so is obvious from the principle laid down in the commencement; for if the expression for the square of the velocity be multiplied by the differential of the time and integrated, the variable parts will vanish when the integral is extended to the whole time of a vibration.

III.—NOTE ON THE SUBJECT OF CONICAL REFRACTION.

[*From the Philosophical Magazine*, Vol. III., 1833.]

WHEN Professor Hamilton announced his discovery of Conical Refraction, he did not seem to have been aware that it is an obvious and immediate consequence of the theorems published by me, three years ago, in the *Transactions* of the Royal Irish Academy, vol. xvi., pt. ii., p. 65, &c. The indeterminate cases of my own theorems, which, optically interpreted, mean conical refraction, of course occurred to me at the time; but they had nothing to do with the subject of that Paper; and the full examination of them, along with the experiments they might suggest, was reserved for a subsequent essay, which I expressed my intention of writing. Business of a different nature, however, prevented me from following up the inquiry.

I shall suppose the reader to have studied the passage in pp. 75, 76, of the volume referred to. He will see that when the section of either of the two ellipsoids employed there is a *circle*, the semiaxes—answering to OR, Or, and to OQ, Oq, in the general statement*—are *infinite* in number, giving of course an infinite number of corresponding rays. And this is *conical refraction*. I shall add a few words on the two cases :—

1. When ROr is a circle, any two of its rectangular radii may be taken for OR and Or. The line OS and the tangent plane perpendicular to it at S are fixed; but the point of con-

---

* The right line Oqr is perpendicular to the plane of the figure, and intersects the two ellipsoids in q and r.

tact T is variable, for the plane ROS in which it lies changes
with OR. Thus we get a curve
of contact on the tangent plane
of the wave surface, and a cone
of rays OT derived from the same
incident ray. The vibrations of
any ray OT are in the line TS
passing through the fixed point S,
as follows from a general remark
in the place referred to.

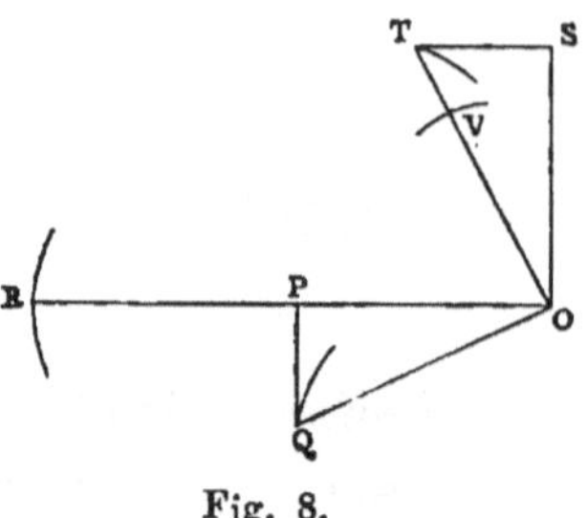

Fig. 8.

The three right lines OQ, Or, OT, are at right angles to each
other, and a geometer will observe that the first two of them are
confined to given planes. For Or is always in the plane of the
circle ROr; and the point Q must be in a given plane, because
the line OP, perpendicular to the plane that touches the ellipsoid in Q, is in a given plane ROr.

2. When QOq is a circle, the points T and V coincide in a
nodal point n, where the two sheets of the wave surface cross
each other. At this point there are an infinite number of tangent planes, for OQ and Oq are now indeterminate. The same
refracted ray On may therefore be derived from any one of an
infinite number of incident rays, and its polarization will differ
accordingly; for the vibrations are in the line nS drawn from
the node to the foot of the perpendicular OS on the tangent
plane. The ray On, however, is always accompanied by another,
but variable, refracted ray.

The lines, OP, Oq, OS, are at right angles to each other, and
the first two of them are confined, as before, to given planes.
For Oq is in the plane of the circle QOq; and OP, being perpendicular to the tangent plane at Q, must lie in a given plane.
These given planes are parallel to two principal tangent planes
passing through n, and touching the circle and ellipse that compose the wave section in the plane of the nodes: whence it is
easy to see that every nodal tangent plane intersects the two
principal tangent planes in lines that are constantly at right
angles; for these lines are parallel to OP and Oq.

The examination of both cases is completed by the following theorem :—

When three right lines at right angles to each other pass through a fixed point, in such a manner that two of them are confined to given planes, the plane of these two, in all its positions, touches the surface of a cone whose sections parallel to the given planes are parabolas ; while the third right line describes another cone, whose sections parallel to the same planes are circles.

The application is obvious. We see that the curve of contact in the first case is a circle. The points S in the second case are also in a circle.

Note on the above, addressed by Professor Mac Cullagh to the Editors of the Philosophical Magazine.—Vol. iii. 1833.

The introductory part of my Note which appeared in your last Number was written in haste, and I have reason to think it may not be rightly understood. You will therefore allow me to add a few observations that seem to be wanting.

The principal thing pointed out in the Paper published some time ago in the *Transactions* of the Royal Irish Academy is a very simple relation between the tangent planes of Fresnel's *Wave Surface* and the sections of two reciprocal ellipsoids. Now this relation depends upon the *axes* of the sections, and therefore naturally suggested to me the peculiar cases of circular sections in which every diameter is an axis. Thus a new inquiry was opened to my mind. And accordingly, without caring just then to obtain final results, which seemed to be an easy matter at any time, I expressed in conversation my intention of returning to the subject of Fresnel's theory in a supplementary Paper. The design was interrupted, and I was prevented from attending to it again, until I was told that Professor Hamilton had discovered cusps and circles of contact on the wave surface. This reminded me of the cases of circular section, and the details given in my last note were immediately deduced.

IV.—GEOMETRICAL PROPOSITIONS APPLIED TO THE WAVE THEORY OF LIGHT.

[*Transactions of the Royal Irish Academy*, Vol. XVII.—Read June 24, 1833.]

PART I.—GEOMETRICAL PROPOSITIONS.

1. THEOREM I.—Conceive a curved surface B to be generated from a given curved surface A in the following manner: having assumed a fixed origin O, apply a tangent plane at any point Q of the given surface, and perpendicular to this plane draw a right line OPR cutting the plane in P, and terminated in R, so that OP and OR may be reciprocally proportional to each other, their rectangle being equal to a

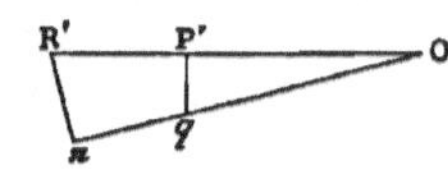

Fig. 9.

constant quantity k^2, and let all the points R taken according to this law generate the second surface B. *Then the relation between these two surfaces, and between the points Q and R, will be reciprocal;* that is to say, if a tangent plane be applied at the point R of the second surface, a perpendicular ON to this plane will pass through the point Q of the first surface, and ON and OQ will be reciprocally proportional to each other, the rectangle under them being also equal k^2.

2. To prove this theorem, take a point q, in the tangent plane of the surface A, and near the point of contact Q (Fig. 9). Through q let several other planes be drawn touching the surface A in points Q', Q'', Q''', &c., and draw the perpendiculars $OP'R'$, $OP''R''$, $OP'''R'''$, &c., according to the same law as OPR. The points R, R', R'', R''', &c., will thus be upon the second surface B, and they will moreover be all in the same

plane ; for from any one of them R' let $R'n$ be drawn perpendicular to the right line Oq and meeting Oq in n ; then, on account of the similar right-angled triangles $OP'q$ and OnR', the rectangle nOq will be equal to the rectangle $R'OP'$, or to the constant quantity k^2, so that the point n, or the foot of the perpendicular let fall upon Oq, will be the same for all the points $R, R', R'', R''',$ &c., and consequently all these points will lie in a plane cutting the right line Oqn perpendicularly in n, so as to make the rectangle nOq equal to k^2. Now, while the point Q remains fixed, let the point q approach to it without limit in the tangent plane at Q ; and the points $R', R'', R''',$ &c., will in like manner approach without limit to the fixed point R ; the plane which contains all those neighbouring points having for its limiting position the tangent plane at R. Also the point n will ultimately coincide with N. It follows, therefore, that the tangent plane at R cuts the right line OQ perpendicularly in N, so as to make the rectangle NOQ equal to k^2.

3. *Corollary.*—If any point Q upon the surface A should be a point of intersection, where the surface admits an infinite number of tangent planes, the perpendiculars from O upon these planes will form a conical surface having O for its vertex. In OQ take, as before, a point N, so that $ON \times OQ = k^2$, and let a plane passing through N at right angles to OQ cut the conical surface. The intersection will be a certain curve. From the preceding demonstration it is evident that every point of this curve belongs to the surface B, and that the plane which touches this surface at any point of the curve cuts OQ perpendicularly in N ; or, in other words, that *the same plane touches the surface B through the whole extent of the curve.*

4. Two surfaces related to each other like A and B in the preceding theorem may be called *reciprocal surfaces*, and points like Q and R *reciprocal points ;* the *radii OQ and OR* may likewise be termed reciprocal. A familiar example of such surfaces is afforded, as I have shown on a former occasion,* by two ellip-

---

* *Transactions* of the Royal Irish Academy, Vol. xvi., pt. ii., pp. 67, 68.—*Supra*, p. 3.

soids having a common centre at the point O, and their semi-axes coincident in direction, and connected by the relation $aa' = bb' = cc' = k^2$; where a, b, c, are semiaxes of one ellipsoid in the order of their magnitude, a being the greatest; and a', b', c', those of the other ellipsoid, a' being the least. The mean semi-axes b and b' coincide, and the circular sections of both ellipsoids pass through the common direction of b and b'.

5. It has also been shown with regard to those ellipsoids, that if Q and R be reciprocal points on the surfaces of abc and $a'b'c'$ respectively, and if a right line Oqr, perpendicular to the plane QOR, cut the first ellipsoid in q and the second in r, the lines OQ and Oq will be the semiaxes of the section made in the ellipsoid abc by a plane passing through them; and the lines OR and Or, in like manner, will be the semiaxes of the section made in the other ellipsoid a' b' c' by the plane in which they lie.

6. It may further be remarked, that if the radius OQ in one of the reciprocal ellipsoids describe a plane, the corresponding radius OR will describe another plane. For the planes touching the ellipsoid abc in the points Q will all be parallel to a certain right line, and therefore the perpendiculars OR to these tangent planes will all lie in a plane perpendicular to that right line. These two planes, containing the reciprocal radii, may, for brevity, be called *reciprocal planes*.

When two reciprocal radii lie in a principal plane, at right angles to a semiaxis of the ellipsoids, it is evident that two planes intersecting in this semiaxis, and passing through the reciprocal radii, are reciprocal planes.

7. THEOREM II.—If three right lines at right angles to each other pass through a fixed point O, so that two of them are confined to given planes, the plane of these two, in all its positions, touches the surface of a cone whose sections parallel to the given planes are parabolas; while the third right line describes another cone, whose sections parallel to the given planes are circles.

Let the plane of the figure (Fig. 10), supposed parallel to one of the given planes, be intersected by the other given plane in the right line MN; and let OQ be perpendicular to the latter plane, while OP is perpendicular to the former and to the plane of the figure, so that PQ being joined will meet MN at right angles in R. Let OA, OB, OC, be the three perpendicular lines, of which OA is parallel to the plane of the figure; this plane will be intersected by the plane of OA and OB in a right line BT parallel to OA, and therefore perpendicular to both OB and OP, and to the plane BOP, and to the line BP. Thus the angle PBT is always a right angle, and therefore BT always touches the parabola whose focus is P and vertex R; or, which

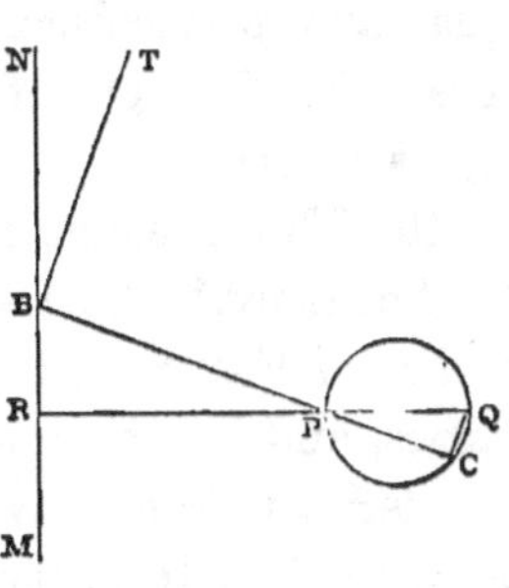

Fig. 10.

comes to the same thing, the plane $AOBT$ always touches the cone which has O for its vertex, and the parabola for its section.

Again, since OB, OP, OC, are all at right angles to OA, they are in the same plane, and therefore the points B, P, C, are in the same straight line; and as BOC is a right angle, the rectangle under BP and PC is equal to the square of the perpendicular OP; but QOR is also a right angle, and therefore $QP \times PR = OP^2$; whence $BP \times PC = QP \times PR$, and therefore the points B, R, C, Q, are in the circumference of a circle, so that the angle at C is a right angle, being in the same segment with the angle at R. Thus the point C describes the circle whose diameter is PQ, and OC describes the cone of which this circle is the section.

8. Of the two right lines OP and OQ perpendicular to the given planes, one is also perpendicular to the plane of the section. That one is OP. Its extremity P is the focus of the parabola. The extremities of both are the extremities of the diameter PQ of the circle. The vertex of the parabola is the point R, where the diameter of the circle intersects that given plane to which the plane of section is *not* parallel.

9. THEOREM III.—In a straight line at right angles to any diametral section QOq of an ellipsoid abc whose centre is O, let OT and OV be taken respectively equal to OQ and Oq, the semi-axes of the section, and imagine the double surface which is the

locus of all the points T and V; then if OS be perpendicular to the plane which touches the surface in T, and OP to the plane which touches the ellipsoid in Q, the lines OP and OS will be equal and perpendicular to each other, and the four straight lines OP, OQ, OS, OT, will lie in the same plane at right angles to Oq

10. This theorem is taken from a former communication to the Academy.* The surface to which it relates, being the *wave surface* of Fresnel, is one of frequent occurrence in optical inquiries, and it is therefore desirable to give it a distinctive name not derived from any physical hypothesis. I shall call it a *biaxal surface*, from the circumstance implied in its construction, and adopted as the definition on which the preceding theorem is founded—namely, that any pair of its coincident diameters are equal to the *two axes* of a central section made in the *generating ellipsoid abc*, by a plane perpendicular to the common direction of the two diameters. The name, perhaps, may appear the more appropriate, as it reminds us of the place which the surface holds in the optical theory of biaxal crystals.

11. Theorem IV.—The biaxal surfaces generated by two reciprocal ellipsoids are themselves reciprocal.

For if Q and R (Fig. 11) be reciprocal points on the two ellipsoids, abc and $a'b'c'$, a tangent plane at Q will cut OR perpendicularly in P; a tangent plane at R will cut OQ perpendicularly in N; and the rectangles ROP and NOQ will be equal to each other and to k^2 (Art. 4). Also if the straight line Oqr, at right angles to the plane of the figure, cut the first ellipsoid in q and the second in r, then (5) the elliptic section QOq will have OQ and Oq for its semiaxes, and the lines OR and Or

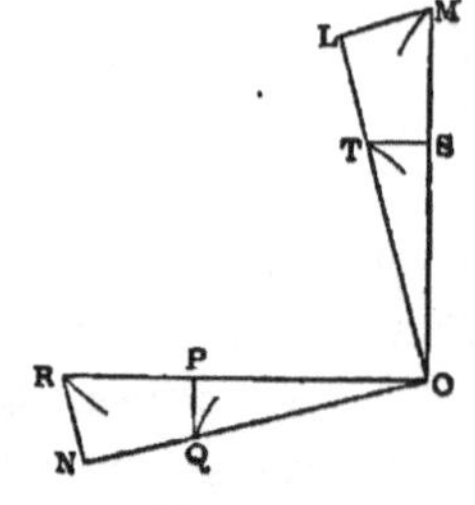

Fig. 11.

will be the semiaxes of the other section ROr. Draw, therefore, in the plane of the figure, the right lines OTL and OSM perpendicular to the right lines OQN and OPR, making OT, OL,

* *Transactions* of the Royal Irish Academy, Vol. xvi., pt. ii., pp. 67, 68.—*Supra*, p. 4.

OS, OM, equal to OQ, ON, OP, OR, respectively; the angles. at S and L being of course right angles. Then it is evident that the point T is on the biaxal surface generated by the ellipsoid abc, because OT is perpendicular to the plane of the ellipse QOq and equal to the semiaxis OQ; and by Theorem III. it appears that OS is perpendicular to the tangent plane at T. In like manner, the point M is on the biaxal surface generated by the other ellipsoid $a'b'c'$, and OL is perpendicular to the tangent plane at M. Moreover, the rectangles MOS and LOT, being equal to the rectangles ROP and NOQ, are each equal to k^2. Hence the proposition is manifest.

12. As the ellipsoid whose semiaxes are a, b, c, may be called the ellipsoid abc, so the biaxal surface generated by this ellipsoid may be called the biaxal abc; and that which is generated by the ellipsoid $a'b'c'$ may be called the biaxal $a'b'c'$.

13. PROPOSITION V.—To find what properties of biaxal surfaces are indicated by the cases wherein one of the two sections QOq, ROr, in the preceding theorem, is a circle.

Case 1.—When QOq is a circular section of the ellipsoid abc, the points T and V (9), in the description of the biaxal surface abc, coincide in a single point n. At this point there are an infinite number of tangent planes; because the semiaxes of the circular section QOq being indeterminate, any two perpendicular radii of the circle may take the place of OQ, Oq, in the general construction. The point n is therefore a point of intersection (3), where the two biaxal sheets cross each other, and it may be called a *nodal point*, or simply a *node*. As OQ always lies in the plane of the circle QOq, the line OR, which is reciprocal to OQ, must lie (6) in a given plane reciprocal to the plane of the circle. And as Oq lies in the plane of the circle, we have three right lines OR, Oq, OS, which are at right angles to each other, and of which the first two are confined to given planes. Therefore by Theorem II. the third line OS describes a cone whose sections parallel to the given planes are circles. Now, TS—or in the present case nS—is parallel to the fixed plane which contains OR, and therefore the point S describes a circle; or, in other words, the feet of the perpendiculars OS, let fall from O on the nodal tangent planes, occupy the circumference of a circle passing (8) through the nodal point.

14. Parallel to the plane of the circle and to its reciprocal plane, conceive two planes passing through the node, and call them the *principal tangent planes* at n. The plane of the circle and its reciprocal plane are intersected in the right lines Oq, OR, by the plane qOR, which is parallel to a tangent plane at n. Consequently this tangent plane at n intersects the two principal tangent planes in lines that are parallel to Oq, OR; and as Oq, OR are perpendicular to each other, it follows that every nodal tangent plane intersects the two principal tangent planes in lines that are at right angles.

Hence again, the nodal tangent planes touch (7) the surface of a cone whose sections, parallel to the principal tangent planes, are parabolas. As this cone touches the biaxal surface all round the point n, it may be called the *nodal tangent cone*.

15. *Case 2.*—When ROr is a circular section of the ellipsoid $a'b'c'$, any two perpendicular radii of the circle may be taken for OR, Or: and because $OR = b'$, and $OR \times OP = k^2 = bb'$, we have OP or OS equal to b, the mean semiaxis of the ellipsoid abc. Hence OS is given both in position and length; for it is perpendicular to the fixed plane ROr, and it is equal to b. Now, a plane cutting OS perpendicularly at S is a tangent plane to the biaxal abc; and we have just seen that this tangent plane remains the same, whatever pair of rectangular radii are taken for OR, Or. But the point of contact T is variable, for the plane ROS in which it lies changes with OR. Therefore as OR revolves, the point T describes a *curve of contact* on the tangent plane of the biaxal abc.

The lines OR, Or, are in the fixed plane ROr; and as OQ is reciprocal to OR, it lies in a fixed plane reciprocal to the plane Ror (6). Therefore the first two of the three perpendicular right lines Or, OQ, OT, are confined to fixed planes. Hence the third line OT describes a cone, whose sections parallel to these planes are circles. But the tangent plane is parallel to the fixed plane

ROr, and its intersection with *OT* describes the curve of contact. Therefore the curve of contact is a circle passing (8) through the point *S*.

16. We have examined the two cases of circular section with reference only to the biaxal *abc*. If we examine the same cases with regard to the second biaxal $a'b'c'$, we shall find that their indications are reversed; the supposition which gives a node upon one biaxal, giving a circle of contact on the other : and that the node and the circle, thus corresponding, are so related, that a line drawn from *O* to the node passes through the circumference of the circle, cutting the plane of the circle perpendicularly; whilst every line drawn from *O* through the circumference of the circle is perpendicular to some nodal tangent plane.

These things are evident on looking at the figure. For when *ROr* is a circle, it is plain that the point *M* is a node of the biaxal $a'b'c'$, since *OM* is perpendicular to the plane of the circle *ROr* and equal to its radius *OR*. But we have already seen (15) that when *ROr* is a circle, the other biaxal *abc* has a circle of contact, whose plane is perpendicular to *OM* at the point *S* of its circumference. The line *OTL* is perpendicular, in general (11), to a tangent plane at *M*, and therefore perpendicular, in the present case, to a nodal tangent plane ; whilst the point *T*, through which it passes, is on the circle of contact. It is also evident that $OT \times OL = k^2$.

We have here an example of the general remark in the corollary of Theorem I.

17. The section made in the biaxal surface *abc*, by any of the principal planes of its generating ellipsoid, consists of an ellipse and a circle.

For, let the plane *QOq* pass through one of the semiaxes, *a*, and let it revolve round this semiaxis, while the right line *OTV* (9), perpendicular to the plane *QOq*, revolves about *O* in the plane of the semiaxes *b*, *c*. Then the semiaxis *a* of the ellopsoid will always be one of the semiaxes of the ellipse *QOq*; and if *OT* be equal to this semiaxis, the point *T* will describe a circle with the radius *a* about the centre *O*. The other semiaxis of the ellipse QOq is that semidiameter of the principal ellipse bc which lies in the intersection of the plane bc with the plane QOq; and as OV is equal and perpendicular to this semidiameter, the point V describes an ellipse equal to bc, but turned round through a right angle, so that the greater axis of the ellipse described by V coincides in direction with the less axis of the ellipse bc. As the radius a of the circle is greater (4) than both the semiaxes b, c, of the ellipse, the circle will lie wholly without the ellipse.

In like manner, the section made in the biaxal surface by the plane ab consists of a circle with the radius c, and an ellipse with the semiaxes a, b; and as the radius of the circle is less than both the semiaxes of the ellipse, the circle lies wholly within the ellipse.

18. But when the section lies in the plane of the greatest and least semiaxes a, c, the circle and ellipse, of which it is composed, intersect each other. For the radius b of the circle is less than one semiaxis of the ellipse ac and greater than the other. Leaving the ellipse ac in the position which it has as a section of the ellipsoid abc, if we describe the circle b with the centre O and radius b, the ellipse and the circle will cut each other in four points at the extremities of two diameters; and planes, passing through these diameters and through the semiaxis b of the ellipsoid, will evidently be the planes of the two circular sections of the ellipsoid. Now, turning the ellipse ac round through a right angle (17), the circle and the ellipse in its new position will constitute the section of the biaxal surface, and will cut each other (Fig. 12) in four points n at the extremities of two diameters nOn, nOn, which are perpendicular to the two former diameters, and therefore perpendicular to the planes of the two circular sections. Consequently, the biaxal surface has four nodes at the four

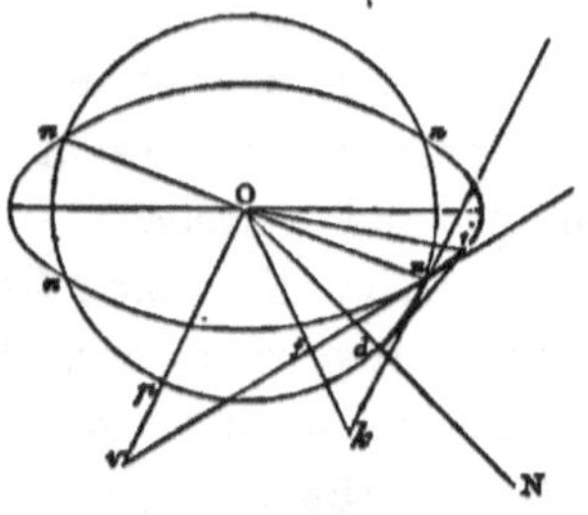

Fig. 12.

points n. These nodes, it is manifest, are alike in all their properties; and they are the only points common to the two biaxal sheets, since the points T and V (9), in the description of the biaxal surface, cannot coincide unless the section QOq, perpendicular to OTV, be a circle.

19. The plane of the greatest and least semiaxes, a, c, of the generating ellipsoid, may be called the plane of the nodes; and the two diameters nOn, nOn, passing through the nodes, may be called the *nodal diameters*.

At one of the nodes n (Fig. 12) draw tangents nf, nk, to the ellipse and the circle that compose the biaxal section; and through O draw Op perpendicular to On, cutting the circle in p. Then as On is perpendicular to the plane of a circular section of the ellipsoid abc, this circular section will have Op for its radius, and its circumference will cross that of the ellipse ac (belonging to the ellipsoid) in the point p. A line touching the ellipse ac at p will be parallel to every plane that touches the ellipsoid in a point of the circular section, and will therefore (6) be perpendicular to the plane which is reciprocal to the plane of the circular section. But the tangent at p is perpendicular to the tangent nf, since the two tangents would coincide if the ellipse ac were turned round (18) through a right angle, the point p then falling upon n. Hence the circular section and its reciprocal plane are parallel to the tangents nk, nf; and therefore two planes perpendicular to the plane of the figure, and passing through these tangents, are the planes that we have called (14) the principal tangent planes at n.

20. Produce Op to meet nf in v, and conceive a parabola having its focus at O, its vertex at v (8), and its plane perpendicular to the plane of the figure. A cone, with its vertex at n and this parabola for its section, is (14) the nodal tangent cone.

Draw Of perpendicular to nf at f, and meeting nk in k. The perpendiculars let fall from O upon the nodal tangent planes form a cone, of which the circles described in planes perpendicular to the figure upon the diameters nf, nk, are sections (8). On the other biaxal surface $a'b'c'$ there is (16) a circle of contact whose plane is perpendicular to On. This circle of contact is (16) another section of the cone last mentioned.

21. To the circle b and to the principal section ac of the ellipsoid abc conceive a common tangent $d'i'$ to be drawn, in a quadrant adjacent to that which contains the node n, and let it touch the circle in d' and the ellipse ac in i'. A radius Od', drawn through the point d' to meet the ellipsoid $a'b'c'$ in the point d'', will be reciprocal to the radius Oi', because it is perpendicular to a tangent at i', and it will be equal in length to b', because $Od'' \times Od' = k^2 = bb'$, and $Od' = b$; whence $Od'' = b$. Therefore Od'' is in a circular section of the ellipsoid $a'b'c'$. Two planes perpendicular to the plane of the figure, and passing through the reciprocal radii Od'', Oi', are (6) reciprocal planes, and we have seen that the first of them makes a circular section in the ellipsoid $a'b'c'$. They are therefore (15) the fixed planes in the second case of Prop. V.

22. Now draw di a common tangent to the circle b and ellipse ac composing the biaxal section, and let it touch the circle in d and the ellipse in i. The lines Od, Oi, are of course perpendicular to the lines Od', Oi', and therefore perpendicular to the fixed planes just mentioned. Hence the line Od and the point d are the same as the fixed line OS and the point S in the second case of Prop. V. The plane of the circle of contact is therefore perpendicular to Od at the point d (15) ; and the points d and i, where its plane intersects the right lines Od, Oi, perpendicular to the fixed planes, are (8) the extremities of a diameter.

These things agree with the obvious remark, that the points of contact d and i must be points of the circle of contact; and that di must be a diameter, because the plane of the circle is perpendicular to the plane of the figure, and this latter plane divides the biaxal surface symmetrically.

As the circle and ellipse may have a common tangent opposite to each node, there are four circles of contact in planes perpendicular to the plane of the nodes.*

23. The biaxal surface belongs to a class that may be called

* The curves of contact on biaxal surfaces, and the conical intersections or nodes, were lately discovered by Professor Hamilton, who deduced from these properties a theory of conical refraction, which has been confirmed by the experiments of

apsidal surfaces, from the manner in which they are conceived to be generated.

Let G be a given surface, and O a fixed origin or pole. If a plane passing through O cut the surface G, the curve of intersection will in general have several apsides A, A', A'', &c., where the lines OA, OA', OA'', &c., are perpendicular to the curve. Through the point O conceive a right line perpendicular to the plane of the curve, and on this perpendicular take from O the distances Oa, Oa', Oa'', &c., respectively equal to the apsidal distances OA, OA', OA'', &c. Imagine a similar construction to be made in every possible position of the intersecting plane passing through O, and the points a, a', a'', &c., will describe the different sheets of an *apsidal surface*.

The apsidal surface has a centre at the point O, because the lengths Oa, Oa', Oa'', &c., may be measured on the perpendicular at either side of the intersecting plane.

Referring* to the demonstration of Theorem III., it will be seen to depend only on the supposition that the point Q is an apsis of the section made by the plane QOq; or, which is the same thing, that OQ is a position wherein the radius vector from O to the curve of section is a *maximum* or a *minimum*. Hence we have the following general theorem :—

24. PROP. VI. THEOREM.—If tangent planes be applied at corresponding points A, a, on the surface G and the apsidal surface which it generates, these tangent planes will be perpendicular to each other and to the plane of the points O, A, a.

This is equivalent to saying that perpendiculars from O on the tangent planes are equal to each other, and lie in the plane of the lines OA, Oa.

25. If Q and R be reciprocal points on two reciprocal surfaces, of which Q is the fixed origin or pole, the tangent plane at Q

Professor Lloyd. See *Transactions* of the Royal Irish Academy, Vol. xvii., part i., pp. 132, 145; and the present Paper, Art. 55–58.

The indeterminate cases of circular section—at least the case of the nodes—had occurred to me long ago; but having neglected to examine the matter attentively, I did not perceive the properties involved in it (13).

* *Transactions* of the Royal Irish Academy, Vol. xvi., part ii., p. 68.

will be (1) perpendicular to *OR* and to the plane *QOR*. Let a plane also perpendicular to the plane *QOR* pass through *OQ*, cutting the surface to which the point *Q* belongs in a certain curve, and the tangent plane at *Q* in a tangent to this curve. The tangent is evidently perpendicular to *OQ*, and therefore the point *Q* is an apsis of the curve.

In like manner, the point *R* is an apsis of the section made in the other surface by a plane passing through *OR* and perpendicular to the plane *QOR*.

26. From these observations, and from Prop. VI., it appears that if the points *Q*, *R*, in the figure of Theorem IV., be reciprocal points on *any* two reciprocal surfaces, and if the same construction be supposed to remain, the points *T* and *M* will be points on the apsidal surfaces generated by these reciprocal surfaces, and the tangent planes at *T* and *M* will be perpendicular to the lines *OM* and *OT* respectively. Also the rectangles *LOT* and *MOS* will be equal to k^2. Hence we have another general theorem :—

PROP. VII. THEOREM.—The apsidal surfaces generated by two reciprocal surfaces are themselves reciprocal.

27. A very simple example of apsidal surfaces, with nodes and circles of contact, may be had by supposing the generatrix *G* to be a sphere, and the pole *O* to be within the sphere, between the surface and the centre *C*.

It is evident that the apsidal surface in this case will be one of revolution round the right line *OC* as an axis. Therefore taking for the plane of the figure (Fig. 13) a plane passing through *OC* and cutting the sphere in a great circle of which the radius is *CS*, let a plane at right angles to the figure revolve about *O*, cutting the circle *CS* in the points *A*, *A'*. The section of the sphere made by the revolving plane will have only two apsides *A*, *A'*, with respect to the point *O*, except when the plane is perpendicular to *OC*.

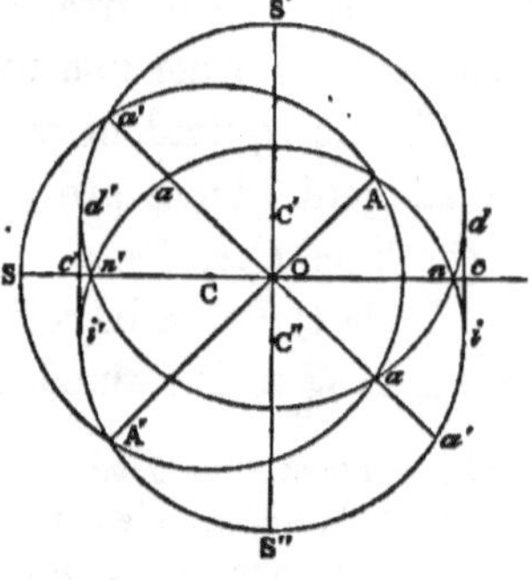

Fig. 13.

Hence, if we draw the right line Oaa' perpendicular to AOA', taking Oa, Oa', always equal to OA, OA', the points a, a', will describe a section of the apsidal surface. This section will evidently consist of two circles $C'S'$, $C''S''$, equal to the circle CS, and having their centres C', C'', on the opposite sides of O in a right line $C'OC''$ perpendicular to OC; the distances OC, OC', OC'' being equal. The circles $C'S'$, $C''S''$, intersect in two points n, n', on the line OC, and have two common tangents di, $d'i'$, which are bisected at right angles by OC in the points c, c'.

28. Now let the circles $C'S'$, $C''S''$, with their common tangents, or only one of the circles with the half tangents, revolve about the axis OC, and we shall have the apsidal surface with nodes at n, n', and with circles of contact described by the radii cd, $c'd'$.

The section of the sphere, by a plane passing through O at right angles to On, is a circle of which O is the centre. If therefore we suppose that the point n answers to a in Prop. VI., the apsis A corresponding to n will be indeterminate, and the position of the tangent plane at n will also be indeterminate, which ought to be the case at a node.

The surface reciprocal to the sphere, the pole being at O, is evidently a surface of revolution about the axis OC (it is easily shown to be a spheroid having a focus at O) ; and the section of this reciprocal surface, by a plane perpendicular to the axis at O, is a circle of which O is the centre. This circumstance indicates (15) that on the apsidal surface there is a curve of contact, whose plane is parallel to the plane of circular section; which agrees with what we have already seen.

29. When the point O is without the sphere, the axis OC will pass between the circles $C'S'$, $C''S''$, without intersecting either of them. The apsidal surface, described by the revolution of one of these circles about OC, will be a circular ring. The nodes have disappeared; but the circles of contact still exist, as is evident.

Part II.—On the Wave Theory of Light.

30. Some of the foregoing propositions lead to a simple transformation of the theory of light.

In this theory, the *surface of waves*, or the *wave surface*, is a geometrical surface used to determine the directions and velocities of refracted or reflected rays, being the surface of a sphere in a singly refracting medium; a double surface, or a surface of two sheets, in a doubly refracting medium; a surface of three sheets on the supposition of triple refraction; and having always a centre O round which it is symmetrical. The radii of the wave surface, drawn from its centre O in different directions, represent the velocities of rays to which they are parallel.

31. We shall consider particularly the case of a doubly refracting crystal, with two plane faces parallel to each other, and surrounded by a medium of the common kind wherein the constant velocity is V: supposing, for the sake of clearness, that the crystal refracts more powerfully than the surrounding medium, so that the velocities in the crystal are less than the velocity V.

A ray $S'O$, falling on the first surface of the crystal at the point O, is partly reflected according to the common law of reflection, and partly refracted. The two refracted rays pass on to the second surface, where each of them is divided by internal reflection into a pair, the two reflected pairs being parallel to each other; while the two emergent rays—one from each refracted ray—are parallel to each other and to the incident ray $S'O$. The directions of the rays within the crystals are usually found by the following construction :—

32. Describe a wave surface of the crystal, having its centre at O the point of incidence. By the nature of the wave surface, a right line OTU, drawn from the point O, will in general cut this surface in two points T, U, on the same side of O; and a ray passing through the crystal in a direction parallel to OTU will have one of the two velocities represented by the radii OT,

OU, taking a line of a certain length k to represent the uniform velocity V in the external medium. With the centre O and a radius OS equal to this line k describe a sphere. As the velocities in the crystal are supposed to be less than V, the wave surface will lie wholly within this sphere. Let the plane of the figure (Fig. 14) be the plane of incidence, perpendicular to the parallel faces of the crystal, and intersecting the first face in the right line FA. Through the point S, where the incident ray $S'O$, produced through the crystal, cuts the surface of the sphere, draw SI at right angles

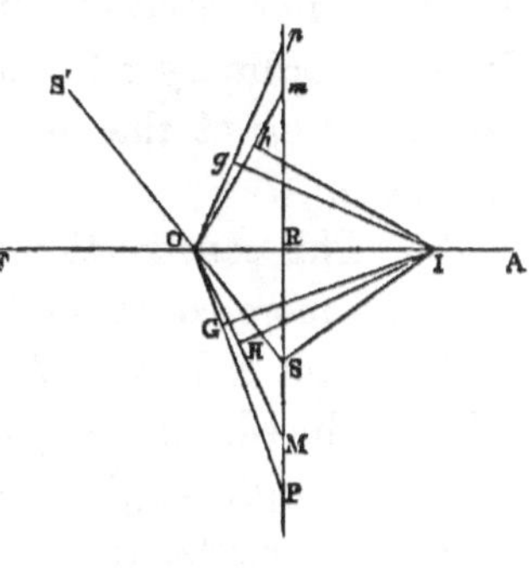

Fig. 14.

to OS and meeting FA in the point I. A right line perpendicular to the plane of the figure, and passing through this point I, we shall call the right line I.

33. Through the right line I draw two planes touching the two sheets of the wave surface, on the side remote from the incident light, in the points T, T', which will lie within the sphere (32); then the incident plane wave, perpendicular to OS, will be refracted into two plane waves parallel to these two tangent planes; and the lines OT, OT', will be the directions of the refracted rays along which the refracted waves are propagated. The lengths OT, OT', represent the velocities with which the light moves along the rays; and of course the normal velocities, which are the velocities of the refracted waves, are represented by the perpendiculars OG, OH, let fall from O on the two tangent planes at T, T'. These two perpendiculars OG, OH, evidently lie in the plane of the figure; but the points T, T', in general, do not lie in this plane.

34. Again, through the right line I draw two other planes touching the wave surface, at the side of the incident light, in the points t, t'. The rays OT, OT', arriving at the second surface of the crystal, will each be divided by internal reflection into two rays parallel to Ot, Ot'; and these four reflected rays,

arriving at the first surface, will each be divided, by a new reflection, into two rays parallel to OT, OT'; and so on, for any number of reflections. Any of the rays emerging at the first surface, after internal reflections, is parallel to the ray Os produced by ordinary reflection at the point of incidence; and any ray emerging at the second surface is parallel to the incident ray $S'OS$.

35. This construction may be changed into another that will be found more convenient both in theory and practice.

Through S draw SR perpendicular to OI, and meeting OG, OH, produced, in the points P, M. Then as the angles at G and R are right angles, the points I, R, G, P, are in the circumference of a circle, and therefore $OP \times OG = OI \times OR = OS^2 = k^2$; and similarly, $OM \times OH = k^2$. If then we take O for the fixed origin, or pole, and k^2 for the constant rectangle (Theorem I.), and describe the surface which is reciprocal to the wave surface, it is evident that the points P and M will be points of the surface so described, and that OT, OT', will coincide in direction with perpendiculars let fall from O on planes touching the surface at P and M, and will be inversely proportional to these perpendiculars. It follows in the very same manner, that if perpendiculars Og, Oh, let fall from O on the tangent planes at t, t', be produced to meet SR in the points p, m, these points will also be on the surface reciprocal to the wave surface.

In the present case, it is manifest that this reciprocal surface lies wholly without the sphere OS.

36. The surface reciprocal to the wave surface, the pole being at O, we shall call the *surface of refraction*.

It is hardly necessary to observe that the surface of refraction has a centre at the point O, round which it is symmetrical; that it is a sphere in a singly refracting medium, a double surface in a doubly refracting medium, and a surface of three sheets if we suppose a case of triple refraction.

37. In the case that we are considering, let the figure (Fig. 15) represent a section made in the double surface of refraction and its attendant sphere by the plane of incidence.

Through the point S, where the incident ray $S'O$, prolonged, cuts the circular section of the sphere, draw SR perpendicular to the face of the crystal, or to FA ; and let SR, produced, cut the circle again in the point s.   Then Os is the direction of the ray given by ordinary reflection at the first surface of the crystal.

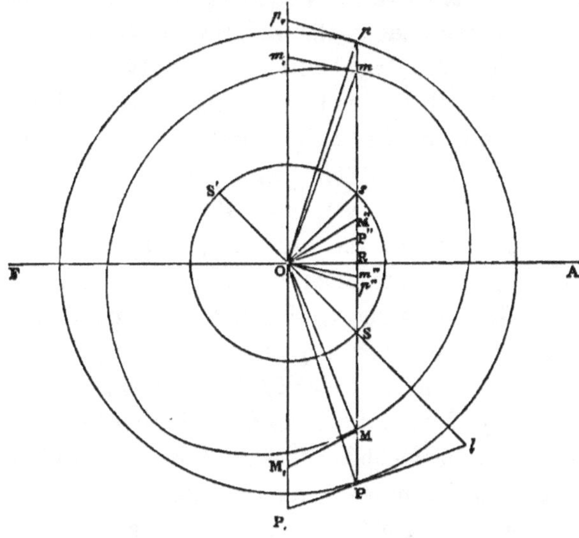

Fig. 15.

Produce the right line SRs both ways, to cut the surface of refraction in the points P, M, behind the crystal, and in the points p, m, before it ; and conceive planes to touch the surface of refraction at the points P, M, p, m.   Suppose also that perpendiculars OP', OM', Op', Om', are let fall from O upon these tangent planes, and that they intersect the planes in the points P', M', p', m', respectively.

Then from the preceding observations (33, 34, 35), it is manifest that OP', OM', are the directions of the rays into which $S'O$ is divided by refraction ; that each of these refracted rays, on arriving at the second surface of the crystal, is divided by internal reflection into two rays parallel to Op', Om' ; and that each of the four reflected rays, on arriving at the first surface, is again divided by reflection into two rays parallel to OP', OM', and so on. In general, every ray going into the crystal from the first surface, whether after refraction or after any even number of internal reflections, is parallel either to OP' or to OM'; and every ray returning from the second surface of the crystal after any odd number of internal reflections, is parallel either to Op' or to Om'. Thus the direction of every ray in the interior of the crystal is the same as the direction of some one of the four lines OP', OM', Op', Om'; and the velocity of the ray is inversely as the length of this line ; so that the velocity of the ray OM', for example, or of any ray parallel to OM', is to the velocity V as OS is to OM'. The little plane waves that, keeping always parallel to themselves, move along these rays, are respectively perpendicular to the lines OP, OM, Op, Om; and the lengths of these lines are inversely as the velocities of the waves estimated in directions perpendicular to their planes; so that the velocity of the wave which moves along the ray OM', or along any parallel ray, is to the velocity V as OS is to OM.

38. The ray OP', and all the rays parallel to it, are perpendicular to the plane which touches at P the surface of refraction ; and the waves which move along these rays are perpendicular to the right line OP. Any ray of this set may be called a *ray P*, and any of the waves a *wave P*. In like manner, the *rays M, p, m*, are rays that are perpendicular to the tangent planes at the points M, p, m, respectively; and the *waves M, p, m*, are the waves that belong to these rays, and that have their planes respectively perpendicular to the right lines OM, Op, Om. The rays P, M, all come from the first surface of the crystal ; the rays p, m, from the second.

As the ordinates RP, Rp, are greater than the ordinates RM, Rm, so the rays P, p, are more refracted or more reflected than the rays M, m. The former rays may therefore be said to be *plus refracted*, or *plus reflected*, and the latter to be *minus refracted*, or *minus reflected*. Or—for the convenience of naming— the rays P, p, may be called *plus rays ;* and the rays M, m, *minus rays*. The waves P, p, in like manner, may be termed *plus waves*, and the waves M, m, *minus waves*.

For a medium of the common kind, or a singly refracting medium, we may use the letters S and s. Thus the incident ray $S'OS$, or any ray emerging parallel to OS from the second surface of the crystal, may be marked by the letter S; while the ray Os produced by common reflection, or any ray emerging parallel to Os from the first surface, may be denoted by the letter s.

39. The course of a ray through the crystal may now be easily expressed. A ray $SMps$, for example, is a ray (S) incident on the crystal, undergoing minus refraction (M) at the first surface, plus reflection (p) at the second, and emerging (s) from the first surface in a direction parallel to Os. Of this ray the part within the crystal is Mp. A ray SPS is a ray plus refracted, and then emerging in a direction parallel to that of incidence. A ray $SPpMS$ is a ray plus refracted at the first surface, then plus reflected at the second surface, then minus reflected at the first surface, and finally emerging from the second surface in a direction parallel to that of incidence. Its path within the crystal is PpM.

These examples indicate the general method of expressing the path of a ray.

Suppose light to be moving in the same direction and with the same velocity along two proximate parallel rays, so that it is at the point A in one ray when it is at the point B in the other ; and through the points A and B conceive two planes perpendicular to the common direction of the rays. These planes are either coincident, or maintain a constant distance. In the first case, the rays are said to be in complete accordance. In the second case, the constant distance between the planes is called the *interval* between the portions of light composing the rays, or the interval between the waves that move along the rays.

We proceed to find the lengths of these intervals in the case of rays emerging parallel to each other, at either side of the crystal that we have been hitherto considering.

41. Let the tangent planes at P, M, p, m, intersect the plane of the figure (Fig. 15) in the right lines $PP_{,\prime}$, $MM_{,\prime}$, $pp_{,\prime}$, $mm_{,\prime}$, which of course are tangents to the section of the surface of re-

fraction represented in the figure; let a perpendicular at O to the face of the crystal cut these tangents in the points $P_{,}, M_{,}, p_{,}, m_{,}$; and let the lines OP'', OM'', Op'', Om'', respectively parallel to $PP_{,}, MM_{,}, pp_{,}, mm_{,}$, cut the line SRs in the points P'', M'', p'', m''.

The length of the path which a ray P describes within the crystal is equal to the thickness Θ of the crystal divided by the cosine of the angle $P'OP_{,}$ which the path of the ray makes with a perpendicular to the faces of the crystal; and the velocity of P is equal to $V \times \dfrac{OS}{OP'}$ (37): dividing therefore the length of the path by the velocity, we find that the time in which a ray P crosses the crystal is equal to

$$\frac{\Theta \times OP'}{V \times OS \times \cos P'OP_{,}}.$$

But as OP' is perpendicular to the tangent plane at P, we have

$$\frac{OP'}{\cos P'OP_{,}} = OP_{,} = PP''.$$

Therefore the time is equal to $\dfrac{\Theta \times PP''}{V \times OS}$. Similarly, the times in which rays M, p, m, pass from one surface of the crystal to the other are equal to

$$\frac{\Theta \times MM''}{V \times OS}, \quad \frac{\Theta \times pp''}{V \times OS}, \quad \frac{\Theta \times mm''}{V \times OS}, \quad \text{respectively.}$$

42. Now suppose the path of a ray P to be projected perpendicularly on a right line having any proposed direction in space. Through O conceive a right line OL parallel to the proposed direction, and meeting in L the tangent plane at P. The length of the projection is equal to the length of the path multiplied by the cosine of the angle $P'OL$ which the ray P makes with OL; that is, the projection is equal to $\Theta \dfrac{\cos P'OL}{\cos P'OP}$. But because OP' is perpendicular to the tangent plane at P, we have

$$\cos P'OL = \frac{OP'}{OL}, \text{ and } \cos P'OP_{,} = \frac{OP'}{OP_{,}} = \frac{OP'}{PP''};$$

therefore

$$\frac{\cos P'OL}{\cos P'OP,} = \frac{PP''}{OL}.$$

Hence the projection is equal to $\Theta \dfrac{PP''}{OL}$.

If the path of a ray P be projected on the incident-ray OS, then producing OS to meet $PP,$ in l, we see, by what has just been proved, that the length of the projection is equal to

$$\Theta \frac{PP''}{Ol} = \Theta \frac{SP''}{OS},$$

by similar triangles. In like manner, the projections of the paths of rays M, p, m, on the direction of the incident ray OS, are equal to

$$\Theta \frac{SM''}{OS}, \quad \Theta \frac{Sp''}{OS}, \quad \Theta \frac{Sm''}{OS},$$

respectively.

43. Let each rectilinear path be measured in the direction in which the light moves along it ; and according as the direction so measured makes an acute or an obtuse angle with the direction OS, measured from O to S, let the projection of the path on OS be reckoned positive or negative. Then if $SPmMpMS$ be any ray entering the crystal at O, and emerging from its second surface at E, and if a perpendicular EI be let fall from E upon OS, meeting OS in I, the distance OI, from O to the foot of this perpendicular, will evidently be equal to the algebraic sum of the projections of the paths P, m, M, p, M, contained within the crystal, taking each projection with its proper sign. It is obvious that the projections of the P and M rays are always positive. And as the lines Op', Om'—the directions of the rays p, m—lie in planes which are respectively perpendicular to $pp,$, $mm,$, or to Op'', Om'', it is easy to see that these directions make acute or obtuse angles with OS, according as the points p'', m'', lie below the point S or above it ; that is, the projections are positive or negative according as the points p'', m'', lie without the circle OS towards P, M, or within the

circle.   Therefore the distance OI, in the case of the figure, i
equal to

$$\frac{\Theta}{OS}\,(SP'' - Sm'' + SM'' - Sp'' + SM'').$$

44. If the paths of rays P, M, p, m, be projected on th
direction Os of the ordinarily reflected ray, the lengths of thei
projections will be

$$\Theta\,\frac{sP''}{OS},\quad \Theta\,\frac{sM''}{OS},\quad \Theta\,\frac{sp''}{OS},\quad \Theta\,\frac{sm''}{OS},$$

respectively.   The projections upon Os of the rays p, m, will b
always positive; and the projections of the rays P, M, will b
positive or negative according as the points P'', M'', lie abov
the point s or below it; that is, according as the points P'', M''
lie without the circle OS towards p and m, or within the circle
So that if $SPmMps$ be a ray entering the crystal at O anc
emerging from the first surface at e, and if a perpendicula
ei be let fall from e upon Os, the distance Oi, from the point C
to the foot of this perpendicular, or the algebraic sum of th
projections of the paths P, m, M, p, contained within th
crystal, will be equal to

$$\frac{\Theta}{OS}\,(- sP'' + sm'' - sM'' + sp''),$$

in the case of the figure.

45. Let us imagine that the light in the incident ray $S'O$,
instead of being interrupted at O by the crystal, had continued
to move with the same velocity V in the same right line OS,
leaving the point O at the moment when the refracted light
enters the crystal at O.   Comparing the light in this imaginary
ray with that in a ray emerging parallel to it from the second
surface of the crystal, after an even number of internal reflections, we shall find that the emergent is behind the imaginary
ray, and that the interval between them (40)—or the retardation of the former—may be derived very easily from the
letters that designate that ray.   Let $SPmMpMS$ be any such

ay. The sum of the distances of the point S from each of the points marked by the letters $(PmMpM)$ that denote (39) the part of the ray contained within the crystal, is proportional to he interval of retardation, that interval being equal to

$$\frac{\theta}{OS}\,(SP + Sm + SM + Sp + SM).$$

For if from the point E, where the last internal ray M merges from the second surface of the crystal, a perpendicular EI be let fall upon OS, meeting OS in I, the time of describing OI with the velocity V would (43) be

$$\frac{\theta}{V \times OS}\,(SP'' - Sm'' + SM'' - Sp'' + SM'').$$

But (41) the actual time of describing the broken path $PmMpM$ s

$$\frac{\theta}{V \times OS}\,(PP'' + mm'' + MM'' + pp'' + MM'') \;;$$

nd, on inspecting the figure, this time is seen to be greater han the time of describing OI, by

$$\frac{\theta}{V \times OS}\,(SP + Sm + SM + Sp + SM),$$

r by the time in which the line

$$\frac{\theta}{OS}\,(SP + Sm + SM + Sp + SM)$$

rould be described with the velocity V. Consequently, at the moment when the light in the ray $SPmMpMS$ emerges at the oint E from the second surface of the crystal, the light in the maginary uninterrupted ray OS will have passed the point I y an interval equal to the line just mentioned ; and as the two ays afterwards have the same velocity and parallel directions, his interval is the retardation of the emergent ray.

46. The rays emerging from the first surface after any odd umber of internal reflections are to be compared with the

ordinarily reflected ray Os to which they are parallel, the lig
in Os, which moves with the velocity V, being supposed to lea
O at the moment when the refracted light enters the crystal
O. The mode of proceeding in this case is exactly similar
that in the last, and the interval is determined in the same wa
using s in place of S; the retardation of the ray $SPmMps$,
example, of which the part $PmMp$ is contained within 1
crystal, being equal to

$$\frac{\theta}{OS}\,(sP + sm + sM + sp).^*$$

47. It is remarkable that the preceding demonstration in 1
wise depends upon the supposition that the planes perpendicu
to the rays P, M, p, m, are tangent planes to the surface
refraction at the points P, M, p, m. If we had supposed a
planes—different from the plane of the figure—to pass throu
the points P, M, p, m, and the rays to coincide in the directi
with perpendiculars let fall from O upon these planes, and
have velocities inversely proportional to the lengths of 1
perpendiculars, the intervals of retardation would have remair
unchanged. Hence the retardations are the same as if the li
OP, OM, Op, Om, were the directions of the rays in passi
through the crystal, as will appear by conceiving the pla1
that we have spoken of to be perpendicular to these lines.

If the incident ray $S'O$ were refracted in the ordinary w
with an index equal to $\dfrac{OP}{OS}$, it would take the direction OP;

it were refracted, in like manner, with the index $\dfrac{OM}{OS}$, it wou

take the direction OM; and if the two rays, thus ordinar
refracted, were to emerge from the second surface of the crys
in directions parallel to OS, it is evident, from what has be
said, that they would be in complete accordance, respective
with the rays SPS and SMS.

---

* The *change of phase*, which may take place at a surface of the crystal, is
here considered as affecting the intervals.

If the surface of refraction should happen to have a node N, which is a point of intersection where it admits an infinite number of tangent planes (3), let the direction of the incident ray $S'OS$ be chosen, so that the right line RS perpendicular to the face of the crystal, being produced below S, may pass through N, and we shall have a cone of refracted rays formed by the perpendiculars let fall from O upon the tangent planes at N; all of which rays, on emerging parallel to OS from the second surface of the crystal, will be in complete accordance with one another. For we have just seen that if the ray $S'OS$ were supposed to emerge after being refracted in the ordinary ray with an index equal to $\dfrac{ON}{OS}$, it would be in complete accordance with any ray of the cone.

48. The interval between any two rays emerging at the same side of the crystal is the difference of their retardations. In taking the difference, the letters that are common to the names of the two rays may be left out. Thus the ray $SPmMS$ is behind the ray SPS by the interval

$$\frac{\Theta}{OS}\,(Sm + SM) = \frac{\Theta}{OS}\,Mm.$$

The line $\dfrac{\Theta}{OS}\,Pp$ is the interval between the rays SMS and $SMpPS$, or between the reflected ray Os and the ray $SPps$, and so on.

49. The retardations of the two refracted rays SPS and SMS, emerging without internal reflection, are $\dfrac{\Theta}{OS}\,SP$ and $\dfrac{\Theta}{OS}\,SM$ respectively. The difference of these is $\Theta\,\dfrac{PM}{OS}$. Consequently, when the two refracted rays have emerged from the second surface in directions parallel to the incident ray, the light in the plus emergent ray is behind the light in the minus emergent ray by an interval equal to $\dfrac{\Theta \times PM}{OS}$. Or, in other words, the incident plane wave, perpendicular to OS, produces

two emergent waves parallel to each other and to the incide
wave, moving along the emergent rays with equal velocities
and preserving the distance $\dfrac{\Theta \times PM}{OS}$ between their planes, t
minus wave being foremost. If OS, the radius of the sphere,
taken for unity, PM will be a number—generally a very sm
fraction—and the interval will be the thickness of the crys
multiplied by this number.

50. Suppose the right line PMR, remaining always perpe
dicular to the face of the crystal, to describe a cylindrical si
face, with the condition that the part PM, intercepted betwe
the two sheets of the surface of refraction, shall remain of a cc
stant length; the point R will then describe, on the surface
the crystal, a curve whose radii OR are the sines (to the radi
OS) of the angles of incidence of a cone of rays; and every r
$S'O$ of this cone, when refracted by the crystal, will afford t
emergent rays, or two waves, having the same given interv
between them. Lines drawn from the eye parallel to the sic
of this cone are the emergent rays belonging to a ring, wh
rings are made to appear, in any of the usual ways, on trar
mitting polarized light through the plate of crystal. In nomir
conformity to this, we see that the line PM describes a ring
constant breadth between the two sheets of the surface of refr
tion. The ring described by supposing pm to remain consta
corresponds to the interval between two rays p and m reflect
at the same point of the second surface of the crystal, and th
emerging at the first. The other intercepts Pp, Mm, Pm, M
are proportional (48) to intervals like those in Newton's rings
to the intervals, namely, between the reflected ray Os and t
rays $SPps$, $SMms$, $SPms$, $SMps$, emerging at the first surfa
after one reflection within the crystal; or to the intervals betwe
rays that are twice reflected in the crystal and the rays trar
mitted without reflection.

51. The general investigation of the figure of a geometric
ring does not distinguish between the different intercepts, ar
will therefore include all the rings PM, pm, Pp, Mm, Pm, M

so that it will be sufficient to contemplate any one of them, as *PM*, of which the breadth *PM* is equal to a given line *I*.

The points *P* and *M* describe, in general, similar and equal curves of double curvature, which may be called *ring-edges*, as being the edges of the ring; and if we imagine the surface of refraction, carrying these curves along with it, to be shifted either way, in a direction parallel to *PM*, through a distance equal to *I*, it is clear that the new position of one of the ring-edges will exactly coincide with the first position of the other, and that therefore the curve of the latter ring-edge will be given by the intersection of the two equal surfaces in these two positions. Let $U = 0$—where U is a function of x, y, z, and given quantities—be the equation of the surface of refraction in its original position ; and, the axes of co-ordinates being fixed, suppose that by the shifting of the surface the co-ordinates of a point assumed on it are diminished by the given lines f, g, h, which are the projections of the given line I on the axes of x, y, z, respectively. Then the equation of the surface in its new position will be had by substituting $x + f$, $y + g$, $z + h$, for x, y, z, in the equation $U = 0$, which will thus become $U + V = 0$, where V is the increment of U produced by the substitution. These two equations combined are equivalent to the equations $U = 0$, $V = 0$, which are therefore the equations of one of the ring-edges. If the surface had been shifted the opposite way, in a direction·parallel to *PM*, the intersection would have been the other ring-edge, whose equations are therefore deducible from those already found, by changing the signs of f, g, h.

52. If the equation of the surface of refraction be transformed, so that the plane of xy may coincide with the face of the crystal, and the axis of z be perpendicular to it, the origin of co-ordinates being at the centre O, no change will be produced in x or in y by the motion of the surface, because *PM*, the direction of the motion, is now parallel to the axis of z ; but z will be diminished or increased by I; and, accordingly, if $U' = 0$ be the equation of the surface in its first position, when the centre is at O, and if U' become $U' + V'$ when z becomes $z + I$, the

equation of the surface in its second position, when the centre has moved through a distance equal to I along the axis of z, will be $U' + V' = 0$; and these two equations combined will give $U' = 0$, $V' = 0$, for the equations of one of the ring-edges. The equations of the other ring-edge are deduced from these by changing the sign of I.

The projection of each of the ring-edges on the plane xy is the curve traced by the point R on the surface of the crystal (50). This curve may be called a *ring-trace*. Its equation is obtained by eliminating z between the equations of a ring-edge; and as the result must be the same whether I be taken positive or negative, the equation of the ring-trace, when found by this general method, will contain only even powers of I. The radii drawn from O to the points R of the ring-trace are (50) the sines (to the radius OS) of the angles of incidence or emergence of the rays that form an optical ring, the rays that come from this ring to the eye being parallel to the sides of the cone described by the right line $S'OS$, while the point R describes the ring-trace.

53. It is evident that tangents to the ring-edges, at the points P and M, are parallel to each other, and therefore parallel to the intersection of two planes touching the surface of refraction at P and M, because these tangent planes pass through the tangents. But the directions OP', OM', are perpendicular to the tangent planes, and therefore the plane $P'OM'$, containing the two rays, is perpendicular to the intersection of the tangent planes, and of course perpendicular to the parallel tangents. Hence the plane $P'OM'$ intersects the face of the crystal in a right line perpendicular to the projection of the parallel tangents on the face of the crystal. As this projection is a tangent to the curve described by R, it follows that the normal to the ring-trace at the point R is parallel to the line joining the points in which the two refracted rays cut the second surface of the crystal.

In like manner, taking any two consecutive rays (P and m), having a common extremity on one surface of the crystal, the line joining the points where these rays cut the other surface is parallel to the normal at the point R of the ring-trace which is described when the intercept (Pm) between the letters that mark the rays is supposed to remain constant.

54. In all that precedes we have made no supposition about the surface of refraction except that it is a surface of two sheets; and if we supposed it to have three sheets, the conclusions would be easily extended to this hypothesis.

In the theory of FRESNEL, the wave surface is[*] a biaxal whose generating ellipsoid has its centre at the point O, and its semiaxes parallel to the three principal directions of the crystal, the length of each semiaxis being equal to OS divided by one of the principal indices of refraction. The surface of refraction is reciprocal to the wave surface, and is (11) therefore another biaxal generated by an ellipsoid reciprocal to the former, having its centre at the same point O, and the directions of its semiaxes the same as before, the rectangle under each coincident pair of semiaxes being equal to k^2 or OS^2. Hence the semiaxes of the ellipsoid which generates the biaxal surface of refraction are equal in length to OS multiplied by each of the three principal indices. This biaxal surface is of course to be substituted for the surface of refraction in the preceding observations.

55. When the line RS, produced below S, passes through a node N of the biaxal surface of refraction, the points P, M, coincide in the point N, and the interval PM vanishes. At the point N there are an infinite number of tangent planes, and the perpendiculars from O on these tangent planes give a cone of refracted rays whose sections we have already shown how to determine (20). All the rays in this cone, on arriving at the second surface of the crystal, emerge parallel to the incident ray OS; and if the rays in the emergent cylinder be cut by a plane perpendicular to their common direction, they will all arrive at this plane at the same instant, because the interval PM vanishes. *See* Art. 47.

56. Suppose fig. 12 to be a section of the wave surface. The

---

[*] *Transactions* of the Royal Irish Academy, VOL. XVI., p. 76 (*supra*, p. 11).

right line Od will pass through N; and the circle of contact, described on the diameter di in a plane perpendicular to the right line OdN, will be a section of the refracted cone. Now it will be recollected* that, in general, the vibrations of a ray OT, which goes to any point T of the wave surface, are parallel to the line which joins the point T with the foot of the perpendicular let fall from O on the tangent plane at T. In the present case, the perpendicular is the same for all the rays of the refracted cone, and its extremity coincides with the point d: so that the line dT, drawn from d to any point T of the circle of contact, is parallel to the vibrations of the ray OT which passes through T. Conceive, therefore, a plane perpendicular to ON at the nodal point N. This plane will cut the refracted cone in a circle whose circumference will pass through N; and a line NT', drawn from the node to any other point T' of the circumference, will be the direction of the vibrations in a ray OT' which crosses the circle at this point. The plane of polarization is perpendicular to the direction of the vibrations.

57. The transverse section of the emergent cylinder is always a very small ellipse, affording a hollow pencil of parallel rays in complete accordance (55). If the crystal be thin, this ellipse will be of evanescent magnitude. Hence the line OS will be the direction of a line drawn from the eye to the centre of the rings commonly observed (50) with polarized light; or it will be what is called the apparent direction of one of the *optic axes*. The diameter passing through N will be the direction of the optic axis within the crystal. There are therefore two optic axes, parallel to the two nodal diameters (19) of the surface of refraction.

As ON is equal to the mean semiaxis of the generating ellipsoid, or to the mean index of refraction, when OS is unity, it follows that the apparent direction of an optic axis is the direction of an incident ray, which, if refracted in the ordinary way, with an index equal to the mean index of refraction, would pass along a nodal diameter of the surface of refraction.

---

* *Transactions* of the Royal Irish Academy, Vol. XVI., p. 76 (*supra*, p. 12).

58. We have seen (15) that there is a circle of contact on the biaxal surface of refraction. If an incident ray $S'OS$ be taken, cutting the sphere in S, so that the line RS produced may pass through the circumference of this circle, it is manifest that the direction of the refracted ray will be the same through whatever point Π of the circumference the line RS may pass, because that direction is perpendicular to the tangent plane at Π, which is in fact the plane of the circle itself. If, therefore, the line RS move parallel to itself along the circumference of the circle, cutting the sphere in a series of points S, every incident ray $S'OS$ which passes through a point S so determined will be refracted into two rays, of which one will have a fixed direction in the crystal, being perpendicular to the plane of the circle of contact, and therefore coinciding (16) with nOn, one of the nodal diameters of the wave surface. But though the direction On of the refracted ray is fixed, its polarization changes with the incident ray from which it is derived; for if Π be the point in which the line RS, corresponding to any position of the incident ray, crosses the circle of contact, the vibrations of the refracted ray On will be contained in the plane of the lines On, $O\Pi$, and will be perpendicular to $O\Pi$. Conceive a circle described on the diameter nf in a plane perpendicular to the figure (Fig. 12). This circle, and the circle of contact on the surface of refraction, are (20) sections of the same cone. Let Π' therefore be the point at which $O\Pi$, in any position of the incident ray, crosses the circumference of the circle nf; and the line Πn, drawn to the node of the wave surface, will be the corresponding direction of the vibrations in the ray On.

59. With regard to the general law of polarization in the theory of FRESNEL, it may be observed, that if the ellipsoid abc which generates the biaxal surface of refraction be cut by a plane perpendicular to OP, the vibrations of the ray P will be parallel to the greater axis of the section, and therefore the plane of polarization will pass through OP and the less axis; whence it is easy to show that the plane of polarization of a ray P bisects one of the angles made by two planes intersecting in OP and

passing through the nodal diameters of the surface of refraction ; the bisected angle being that which contains the least semiaxis c of the generating ellipsoid. The plane of polarization of the ray p is found in like manner. But for the rays M, m, the angle to be bisected is that which contains within it the greatest semiaxis a.

If OP' be perpendicular to a tangent plane at P, the vibrations of the ray P will be perpendicular to OP, and will lie in the plane POP'. A similar remark applies to the rays M, p, m.

60. When two semiaxes a, b, of the ellipsoid abc become equal, it changes into a spheroid aac described by the revolution of the ellipse ac about the semiaxis c ; and the biaxal aac, generated by this spheroid, is* composed of a sphere whose radius is a, and a concentric spheroid acc described by the revolution of the ellipse ac about the semiaxis a ; so that, the diameter of the sphere being equal to the axis of revolution of the spheroid, the two surfaces touch at the extremities of the axis. This combination of a sphere and a spheroid is the surface of refraction for uniaxal crystals. In these crystals, therefore, the refracted ray whose direction is determined by the intersection of the right line RS with the surface of the sphere follows the ordinary law of a constant ratio of the sines, and is called the *ordinary* ray ; whilst the other, whose variable refraction is regulated by the intersection of RS with the spheroid, is called the *extraordinary* ray. And hence uniaxal crystals are usually divided into the two classes of positive and negative, according to the character of the extraordinary ray ; being called *positive* when it is the *plus* ray, and *negative* when it is the *minus* ray. The first case evidently happens when the spheroid is oblate, and therefore lies without the sphere described on its axis ; the second, when the spheroid is prolate, and therefore lies within the sphere. The second case (which is that of Iceland spar) may be supposed to be represented in the figure (Fig. 15), where the elliptic section of the spheroid, made by a plane of incidence oblique to the axis, lies

* *Transactions* of the Royal Irish Academy, Vol. XVI., p. 77 (*supra*, p. 12).

within the circular section of the sphere, and the minus ray is of course the extraordinary one.

61. Let PM, preserving a constant length I, move parallel to itself between the surfaces of the uniaxal sphere and spheroid, so as to form a ring (50). Then supposing the spheroid, with the ring-edge described on it by the point M, to remain fixed, imagine the sphere, carrying the ring edge P along with it, to move parallel to PM, from P towards M, through a distance equal to I, and the two ring-edges will exactly coincide.

Hence the *uniaxal ring-edge* is the intersection of a sphere and a spheroid, the diameter of the sphere being equal to the axis of revolution of the spheroid, and the line joining their centres being perpendicular to the faces of the crystal and equal to the breadth I of the ring. And the projection of this intersection, on a plane perpendicular to the line joining the centres of the sphere and the spheroid, is the *uniaxal ring-trace*.

62. The *biaxal ring-edge* is (51) the intersection of two equal biaxal surfaces similarly posited, the line joining their centres being perpendicular to the faces of the crystal and equal to the breadth of the ring. And the projection of this intersection, on a plane perpendicular to the line joining the centres of the surfaces, is the *biaxal ring-trace.**

* In applying the general theory (51, 52) to biaxal rings, it is necessary to know the equation of a biaxal surface, which may be found in the following manner :—Let r, r', r'', be three rectangular radii of the generating ellipsoid abc, the two latter being the semiaxes of the section made by a plane passing through them; so that if from the centre O two distances OT, OV, equal to r', r'', be taken on the direction of r, the points T and V will belong (9) to the biaxal surface; and let a plane parallel to the plane of r', r'', and touching the ellipsoid, cut the direction of r at the distance p from the centre. Then if r make the angles α, β, γ, with the semiaxes a, b, c, we shall have, by the nature of the ellipsoid,

$$\frac{1}{r^2} = \frac{\cos^2 \alpha}{a^2} + \frac{\cos^2 \beta}{b^2} + \frac{\cos^2 \gamma}{c^2},$$

$$p^2 = a^2 \cos^2 a + b^2 \cos^2 b + c^2 \cos^2 \gamma.$$

Now, since the sum of the squares of the reciprocals of three rectangular radii of an ellipsoid is constant, as well as the parallelopiped described on three conjugate semidiameters, we have the equations

$$\frac{1}{r^2} + \frac{1}{r'^2} + \frac{1}{r''^2} = \frac{1}{a^2} + \frac{1}{b^2} + \frac{1}{c^2},$$

$$p^2 \, r'^2 \, r''^2 = a^2 \, b^2 \, c^2 \,;$$

or,

$$\frac{1}{r'^2} + \frac{1}{r''^2} = \frac{1}{a^2} + \frac{1}{b^2} + \frac{1}{c^2} - \left(\frac{\cos^2 \alpha}{a^2} + \frac{\cos^2 \beta}{b^2} + \frac{\cos^2 \gamma}{c^2} \right) = M,$$

$$\frac{1}{r'^2 \, r''^2} = \frac{a^2 \cos^2 \alpha + b^2 \cos^2 \beta + c^2 \cos^2 \gamma}{a^2 \, b^2 \, c^2} = N.$$

Whence it appears that r', r'', are the values of ρ in the equation

$$\frac{1}{\rho^4} - \frac{M}{\rho^2} + N = 0,$$

in which ρ denotes indifferently either semidiameter, OT or OV, of the biaxal surface. Therefore putting for M and N their values, and writing $\frac{x}{\rho}, \frac{y}{\rho}, \frac{z}{\rho}$, instead of $\cos \alpha$, $\cos \beta$, $\cos \gamma$, and $x^2 + y^2 + z^2$ instead of ρ^2, we obtain, for the equation of the biaxal surface,

$$(x^2 + y^2 + z^2)(a^2 x^2 + b^2 y^2 + c^2 z^2) - a^2 (b^2 + c^2) x^2 - b^2 (a^2 + c^2) y^2$$

$$- c^2 (a^2 + b^2) z^2 + a^2 b^2 c^2 = 0.$$

This is the equation of the surface of refraction for a biaxal crystal in which a, b, c, are (54) the three principal indices of refraction, taking OS the radius of the sphere to be unity. The left-hand member of the equation is therefore the expression supplied by FRESNEL for the function U in Art. 51.

When the faces of the crystal are parallel to any of the principal planes of the ellipsoid—to the plane of xy for example—the nature of the ring-trace may be found very easily. For if the difference of the two values of z, deduced from the preceding equation of the surface of refraction, be put equal to a constant quantity I, the result, when cleared of radicals, will be an equation of the fourth degree in x and y, which will be the equation of the corresponding ring-trace. This is a case that occurs frequently in practice; the crystal being often cut with its faces perpendicular to the axis of x or of z, because these lines bisect the angles made by the optic axes.

V.—A SHORT ACCOUNT OF SOME RECENT INVESTIGATIONS CONCERNING THE LAWS OF REFLEXION AND REFRACTION AT THE SURFACE OF CRYSTALS.

[*Fifth Report of the British Association*, 1835.]

To understand the nature of the general problem which a complete theory of double refraction requires to be solved, let it be supposed that a ray of light is reflected and refracted at the separating surface of an ordinary medium and a doubly refracting crystal, the light passing out of the former medium into the latter. This limited view of the subject is taken merely for the sake of clearness of conception; since we might suppose that both media are crystallized, without increasing the difficulty of the problem. The question, it is obvious, naturally divides into two distinct heads. The first relates to the laws of the *propagation* of light in the *interior* of either of the two media, before or after it has passed their separating surface; and this part of the subject has been fully treated, according to their different methods, by MM. Fresnel and Cauchy. The second division of the subject had been left completely untouched. It relates to the more complex consideration of what takes place at the separating surface of the media, the laws according to which the light is there divided between the reflected and refracted rays, including a determination of the attendant circumstances indicated by the wave theory, with regard to the vibrations in the reflected and refracted rays. In the case above mentioned, when the incident light is polarized, there are four things to be determined, namely, the *magnitude* and *direction* of the reflected vibration, with the *magnitudes* of the two refracted vibrations. The four conditions necessary for this determination are furnished by two new laws, which could not be easily stated without entering too much into detail. The results applied to determine the polarizing angle of a crystal, in different azimuths of the plane of reflexion, agree very closely with the admirable experiments of Sir David Brewster on Iceland spar. In the course of these experiments it was observed that the polarizing angle remained the same when the crystal was turned half round (through an angle of 180°) ; although the inclination of the refracted rays to the axis of the crystal was thereby greatly changed. This remarkable fact is a consequence of theory. After some complicated substitutions in the primary equations, the value of the polarizing angle is found to contain only *even* powers of the sine or cosine of the azimuth of the plane of reflexion, and therefore a change of 180° in the azimuth produces no change in the polarizing angle.

The two new laws above mentioned, on which the theory depends, occurred to the author in the beginning of last December; but, owing to an oversight in forming one of the equations, they were not fully verified until the beginning of June.

In this theory it is supposed that the vibrations are parallel to the plane of polarization, according to the opinion of M. Cauchy. This is contrary to the views of Fresnel, whose theory of double refraction obliged him to adopt the hypothesis that the vibrations are perpendicular to the plane of polarization. It is further supposed that the density of the vibrating ether is the same in both media ; and the hypothesis of a constant density in different media, which was found necessary for the theory, seems to accord, better than the supposition of a varying density, with the phenomena of astronomical aberration.

If we conceive the three principal indices of refraction for the crystal to become equal, we shall obtain the solution of a very simple case of the general problem with which we have been occupied—the case of an ordinary refracting medium such as glass. This simple case, it is well known, was solved by Fresnel. The foregoing theory leads to a simple law, expressing all the particulars of the case, but differing with regard to the *magnitude* of the refracted vibration from the formulæ of Fresnel. The law may be stated by saying that *the refracted vibration is the resultant of the incident and reflected vibrations;* the first vibration being the diagonal of a parallelogram, of which the other two vibrations are the sides, just as in the composition of forces. The plane of the parallelogram is the plane of polarization of the refracted ray. It is to be remembered, that the vibrations in each ray are perpendicular to the ray itself, and parallel to its plane of polarization.

This simple case has been considered by M. Cauchy in a short Paper inserted in the *Bulletin Universel,* tom. xiv. ; but it does not seem to have been observed by anyone that his solution is erroneous. His formula for light polarized parallel to the plane of reflexion is that which belongs to light polarized perpendicular to the plane of reflexion, and *vice versâ.*

VI.—LAWS OF REFLEXION FROM METALS.

[*Proceedings of the Royal Irish Academy*, Vol. I., p. 2.—Read Oct. 24, 1836.]

THE author observes that the theory of the action of metals upon light is among the *desiderata* of physical optics, whatever information we possess upon this subject being derived from the experiments of Sir David Brewster. But, in the absence of a real theory, it is important that we should be able to represent the phenomena by means of empirical formulæ; and, accordingly, the author has endeavoured to obtain such formulæ by a method analogous to that which Fresnel employed in the case of total reflexion at the surface of a rarer medium, and which, as is well known, depends on a peculiar interpretation of the sign $\sqrt{-1}$. For the case of metallic reflexion, the author assumes that the velocity of propagation in the metal, or the reciprocal of the refractive index, is of the form

$$m \left(\cos \chi + \sqrt{-1} \, \sin \chi \right) ;$$

without attaching to this form any physical signification, but using it rather as a means of introducing two constants (for there must be two constants, m and χ, for each metal) into Fresnel's formulæ for ordinary reflexion, which contain only one constant, namely, the refractive index.

Then if i be the angle of incidence on the metal, and i' the angle of refraction, we have

$$\sin i' = m \left(\cos \chi + \sqrt{-1} \, \sin \chi \right) \sin i, \tag{1}$$

and therefore we may put

$$\cos i'' = m' (\cos \chi' - \sqrt{-1} \sin \chi') \cos i, \tag{2}$$

if

$$m'^4 \cos^4 i = 1 - 2m^2 \cos 2\chi \sin^2 i + m^4 \sin^4 i, \tag{3}$$

and

$$\tan 2\chi' = \frac{m^2 \sin 2\chi \sin^2 i}{1 - m^2 \cos 2\chi \sin^2 i}. \tag{4}$$

Now, first, if the incident light be polarized in the plane of reflexion, and if the preceding values of sin i'', cos i'', be substituted in Fresnel's expression

$$\frac{\sin (i - i'')}{\sin (i + i'')}, \tag{5}$$

for the amplitude of the reflected vibration, the result may be reduced to the form

$$a (\cos \delta - \sqrt{-1} \sin \delta),$$

if we put

$$\tan \psi = \frac{m}{m''}, \tag{6}$$

$$\tan \delta = \tan 2\psi \sin (\chi + \chi'), \tag{7}$$

$$a^2 = \frac{1 - \sin 2\psi \cos (\chi + \chi')}{1 + \sin 2\psi \cos (\chi + \chi')}. \tag{8}$$

Then, according to the interpretation, before alluded to, of $\sqrt{-1}$, the angle δ will denote the *change of phase*, or the retardation of the reflected light; and a will be the amplitude of the reflected vibration, that of the incident vibration being unity. The values of m', χ', for any angle of incidence, are found by formulæ (3), (4), the quantities m, χ, being given for each metal. The angle χ' is very small, and may in general be neglected.

Secondly, when the incident light is polarized perpendicularly to the plane of reflexion, the expression

$$\frac{\tan (i - i')}{\tan (i + i')},$$

treated in the same manner, will become

$$a' (\cos \delta' - \sqrt{-1} \sin \delta'), \tag{9}$$

if we make

$$\tan \psi' = mm', \tag{10}$$

$$\tan \delta' = \tan 2\psi' \sin (\chi - \chi'), \tag{11}$$

$$a'^2 = \frac{1 - \sin 2\psi' \cos (\chi - \chi')}{1 + \sin 2\psi' \cos (\chi - \chi')}; \tag{12}$$

and here, as before, δ' will be the retardation of the reflected light, and a' the amplitude of its vibration.

The number $M = \dfrac{1}{m}$ may be called the *modulus*, and the angle χ the *characteristic* of the metal. The modulus is something less than the tangent of the angle which Sir David Brewster has called the maximum polarizing angle. After two reflexions at this angle a ray originally polarized in a plane inclined 45° to that of reflexion will again be plane-polarized in a plane inclined at a certain angle ϕ (which is 17° for steel) to the plane of reflexion ; and we must have

$$\tan \phi = \frac{a'^2}{a^2}. \tag{13}$$

Also, at the maximum polarizing angle we must have

$$\delta' - \delta = 90°. \tag{14}$$

And these two conditions will enable us to determine the constants M and χ for any metal, when we know its maximum polarizing angle and the value of ϕ ; both of which have been found for a great number of metals by Sir David Brewster. The following Table is computed for steel, taking $M = 3\frac{1}{2}$, $\chi = 54°$.

i	δ	δ'	a^2	a'^2	$\frac{1}{2}(a^2 + a'^2)$
0°	27°	27°	0·526	0·526	0·526
30	23	31	0·575	0·475	0·525
45	19	38	0·638	0·407	0·522
60	13	54	0·729	0·308	0·518
75	7	98	0·850	0·240	0·545
85	2	152	0·947	0·491	0·719
90	0	180	1·000	1·000	1·000

The most remarkable thing in this Table is the last column, which gives the intensity of the light reflected when common light is incident. The intensity *decreases* very slowly up to a large angle of incidence (less than 75°), and then increases up to 90°, where there is total reflexion. This singular fact, that the intensity decreases with the obliquity of incidence, was discovered by Mr. Potter, whose experiments extend as far as an incidence of 70°. Whether the subsequent increase which appears from the Table indicates a real phenomenon, or arises from an error in the empirical formulæ, cannot be determined without more experiments. It should be observed, however, that in these very oblique incidences Fresnel's formulæ for transparent media do not represent the actual phenomena for such media, a great quantity of the light being stopped, when the formulæ give a reflexion very nearly total.

The value $\delta' - \delta$, or the difference of phase, increases from 0° to 180°. When a plane-polarized ray is twice reflected from a metal, it will still be plane-polarized if the sum of the values of $\delta' - \delta$ for the two angles of incidence be equal to 180°.

It appears from the formulæ that when the characteristic χ is very small, the value of δ' will continue very small up to the neighbourhood of the polarizing angle. It will pass through 90°, when $mm' = 1$; after which the change will be very rapid, and the value of δ' will soon rise to nearly 180°. This is exactly the phenomenon which Mr. Airy observed in the diamond.

Another set of phenomena to which the author has applied his formulæ are those of the coloured rings formed between a glass lens and a metallic reflector; and he has thus been enabled to account for the singular appearances described by M. Arago in the *Memoires d'Arcueil*, tom. iii., particularly the succession of changes which are observed when common light is incident, the intrusion of a new ring, &c. But there is one curious appearance which he does not find described by any former author. It is this. Through the last twenty or thirty degrees of incidence the first dark ring, surrounding the central spot, which is comparatively bright, remains constantly of the same magnitude; although the other rings, like Newton's rings formed between two glass lenses, dilate greatly with the obliquity of incidence. This appearance was observed at the same time by Professor Lloyd. The explanation is easy. It depends simply on this circumstance (which is evident from the Table), that the angle $180° - \delta'$, at these oblique incidences, is nearly proportional to $\cos i$.

As to the index of refraction in metals, the author conjectures that it is equal to $\dfrac{M}{\cos \chi}$.

VII.—ON THE LAWS OF THE DOUBLE REFRACTION OF QUARTZ.

[*Transactions of the Royal Irish Academy*, Vol. xvii.—Read Feb. 22, 1836.]

THE singular laws of the double refraction of quartz, which have been discovered by the successive researches of Arago, Biot, Fresnel, and Airy, are known merely as so many independent facts ; they have not been connected by a theory of any kind. I propose, therefore, to show how these laws may be explained hypothetically, by introducing differential coefficients of the third order into the equations of vibratory motion.

Suppose a plane wave of light to be propagated within a crystal of quartz. Let the co-ordinates x, y, z, of a vibrating molecule be rectangular, and take the axis of z perpendicular to the plane of the wave, and the axis of y perpendicular to the axis of the crystal. Let us admit that the vibrations are accurately in the plane of the wave, and of course parallel to the plane of xy. Then, using ξ and η to denote, at any time t, the displacements parallel to the axes of x and y respectively, we shall assume the two following equations for explaining the laws of quartz :—

$$\frac{d^2\xi}{dt^2} = A\frac{d^2\xi}{dz^2} + C\frac{d^3\eta}{dz^3}, \tag{1}$$

$$\frac{d^2\eta}{dt^2} = B\frac{d^2\eta}{dz^2} - C\frac{d^3\xi}{dz^3}. \tag{2}$$

The peculiar properties of this crystal depend on the constant C. When $C = 0$, the third differentials disappear, and the equations are reduced to the ordinary form, in which state they ought to agree with the common equations for uniaxal crystals. Hence, putting a for the reciprocal of the ordinary index, b for the reciprocal of the extraordinary, and ϕ for the angle made by the axis of z with the axis of the crystal, we must have

$$A = a^2, \quad B = a^2 - (a^2 - b^2) \sin^2 \phi, \tag{3}$$

supposing the velocity of propagation in air to be unity.

Now, from the nature of equations (1) and (2), the vibrations must be elliptical. In fact, if we put

$$\xi = p \cos \left\{ \frac{2\pi}{l} (st - z) \right\}, \quad \eta = q \sin \left\{ \frac{2\pi}{l} (st - z) \right\} \tag{4}$$

where p, q, s, l are constant quantities, the differential equations will be satisfied by assigning proper values to s and to the ratio $\dfrac{q}{p}$. For, after substituting in equations (1) and (2) the values of the partial differential coefficients obtained by differentiating formulæ (4), we shall find that every term of each equation will have the same sine or cosine for a factor : omitting therefore, the common factors, and making $\dfrac{q}{p} = k$, we shall get the following equations of condition :—

$$s^2 = A - \frac{2\pi}{l} Ck, \tag{5}$$

$$s^2 = B - \frac{2\pi}{l} \frac{C}{k}. \tag{6}$$

Subtracting these, we have

$$A - B + \frac{2\pi C}{l} \left(\frac{1}{k} - k \right) = 0, \tag{7}$$

which, by formulæ (3), becomes

$$k^2 - \frac{l}{2\pi C} (a^2 - b^2) \sin^2 \phi . k = 1. \tag{8}$$

Let us now interpret these results. It is obvious, from formulæ (4), that s is the velocity of propagation for a wave whose length is l, and that each vibrating molecule describes a little ellipse whose semiaxes p and q are parallel to the directions of x and y.   But the number k, expressing the ratio of the semiaxes, has two values, one of which is the negative reciprocal of the other, as appears by equation (8) ; and each value of k has a corresponding value of s determined by equation (5) or (6).   Hence there will be two waves elliptically polarized, and moving with different velocities, the ratio of the axes being the same in both ellipses ; but the greater axis of the one will coincide with the less axis of the other.   The difference of sign in the two values of k shows that if the vibration be from left to right in one wave, it will be from right to left in the other.   These laws were discovered by Mr. Airy.

The law by which the ellipticity of the vibrations depends on the inclination ϕ, and on the colour of the light, is contained in equation (8).   The value of the constant C will be determined presently.   In the mean time we may observe, that C denotes a line, whose length is very small, compared with the length of a wave.

When $\phi = 0$, the light passes along the axis of the crystal. In this case we have $k^2 = 1$, and $k = \pm 1$; which shows that there are two rays, circularly polarized in opposite directions.   The value of s for each ray may be had from equation (5) or (6), by putting $+ 1$ and $- 1$ successively for k.   Calling these values s' and s'', we find

$$s'^2 = a^2 - 2\pi \frac{C}{l}, \qquad s' = a\left(1 - \frac{\pi C}{a^2 l}\right); \qquad (9)$$

$$s''^2 = a^2 + 2\pi \frac{C}{l}, \qquad s'' = a\left(1 + \frac{\pi C}{a^2 l}\right). \qquad (10)$$

Suppose a plate of quartz to have two parallel faces perpendicular to the axis, and conceive a ray of light, polarized in a given plane, to fall perpendicularly on it.   The incident rectilinear vibration may be resolved into two opposite circular vibrations,

F

which will pass through the crystal with different velocities; and which, after their emergence into air, will again compound a rectilinear vibration, whose direction will make a certain angle ρ with that of the incident vibration: so that the plane of polarization will appear to have been turned round through an angle equal to ρ, called the angle of rotation. This angle may be determined by means of the preceding formulæ. Putting θ for the thickness of the crystalline plate, the circularly polarized wave whose velocity is s' will pass through it in the time

$$\frac{\theta}{s'} = \frac{\theta}{a}\left(1 + \frac{\pi C}{a^2 l}\right);$$

and the wave whose velocity is s'' in the time

$$\frac{\theta}{s''} = \frac{\theta}{a}\left(1 - \frac{\pi C}{a^2 l}\right).$$

Therefore, if δ be the difference of the times, we have

$$\delta = \frac{2\pi C\theta}{a^3 l}. \tag{11}$$

But, since the velocity of propagation in air is supposed to be unity, the time and the space described are represented by the same quantity; and therefore δ, which is evidently a line, denotes the distance between the fronts of the two circularly polarized waves, when they emerge into air. The waves being at this distance from each other, if we conceive, at the same depth in each of them, a molecule performing its circular vibration, and carrying a radius of its circle along with it, the two radii will revolve in contrary directions, and will always cross each other in a position parallel to the incident rectilinear vibration. Now let two series of such waves be superposed, so as to agitate every molecule by their compound effect, and it is evident that, when the radius vector of one component vibration attains the position just mentioned, the radius vector of the other will be separated from it by an angle equal to $\dfrac{2\pi\delta}{\lambda}$, where λ is the length of a wave in air. The resultant rectilinear vibration will bisect this angle; and therefore ρ, the angle of rotation, will be equal to $\dfrac{\pi\delta}{\lambda}$. Hence, substituting for δ its value, and observing that l, the length of a wave in quartz, is equal to $a\lambda$, we find

$$\rho = \frac{2\pi^2 C\theta}{a^4\lambda^2}\,;\tag{12}$$

which gives the experimental law of M. Biot, that the angle of rotation is directly as the thickness of the crystal, and inversely as the square of the length of a wave for any particular colour. By changing the sign of C, we should have an equal rotation in the opposite direction. And here we may remark, that C may be made negative in all the preceding equations, its magnitude remaining. There are two kinds of quartz, the right-handed and left-handed, distinguished by the sign of C.

The angle of rotation, 'for a given colour and thickness, is known from M. Biot's experiments. We can therefore find the value of C by means of the last formula; and substituting this value in equation (8), we shall be able to compute k when ϕ and l are given. Now it happens that Mr. Airy,* by a very ingenious method of observation, has determined the values of k in red light for two different values of ϕ; and of course we must compare these observed values of k with the independent results of theory. As Mr. Airy's experiments were made upon red light, we shall select, for the object of our calculations, the red ray which is marked by the letter C in the spectrum of Fraunhofer. For this ray, Fraunhofer has given the length λ, which, expressed in parts of an English inch, is equal to ·0000258; and M. Rudberg has found $a = $ ·64859, $b = 64481$. Moreover, from the experiments of M. Biot, we may collect that the arc of rotation, produced by the thickness of a millimetre, is something more than 19 degrees for the ray we have chosen; so that the fraction $\frac{1}{3}$ may be taken to express nearly the length of that

* *Transactions* of the Cambridge Philosophical Society, Vol. IV., p. 205.

arc in a circle whose radius is unity. We have, therefore, $\theta = \cdot 03937$ inch, and $\rho = \cdot 333$. Substituting these values in the formula

$$\frac{l}{2\pi C} = \frac{\pi \theta}{a^3 \lambda \rho}$$

derived from (12), we find

$$\frac{l}{2\pi C} = 52710 ;$$

from which it appears that C is about twenty thousand times less than the millionth part of an inch.

Again, since $a^2 - b^2 = \cdot 00489$, we have

$$\frac{l}{2\pi C} (a^2 - b^2) = 258,$$

so that equation (8) becomes

$$k^2 - 258 \sin^2 \phi \,.\, k = 1. \tag{13}$$

The results of this formula are compared with Mr. Airy's experiments in the following Table, in which the less root is taken for k, and its sign is neglected.

Values of ϕ.	Values of k.	
	Observed.	Calculated.
6° 15′	tan 16° 38′ = ·2897	·2980
8° 54′	tan 8° 56′ = ·1582	·1579

The angles ϕ, in the first column, are deduced from the observed inclinations of the rays in air to the axis of the crystal; and as k was observed to be somewhat different for the ordinary and extraordinary rays, its mean values are given in the second column. The exact coincidence between these and the calculated values is, perhaps, in some degree accidental; but a less perfect agreement would be sufficient to confirm the theory.

The magnitude of k varies considerably with the colour of the light, increasing from the red to the violet, while the coefficient of $\sin^2\phi \cdot k$, in formula (13) diminishes. If we take the violet ray H, for example, this coefficient will be 159. But it would be useless to make any more calculations, as we have no experiments with which they might be compared.

The figure of the wave surface yet remains to be examined.

Eliminating k between formulæ (5) and (6), we obtain the equation

$$(s^2 - A)(s^2 - B) = 4\pi^2 \frac{C^2}{l^2}, \tag{14}$$

which expresses the nature of the surface, s being a perpendicular from the origin on a tangent plane. From this equation it follows that the two values of s can never become equal in quartz, as they do in other crystals; for if we solve the equation for s^2, and put the radical equal to zero, we shall get the condition

$$(A - B)^2 + 16\pi^2 \frac{C^2}{l^2} = 0,$$

which cannot be fulfilled, since the quantity which ought to vanish is the sum of two squares. The two sheets, or *nappes*, of the wave surface are therefore absolutely separated.

It is commonly assumed that one of the rays is refracted according to the ordinary law; but this is not the case, since neither of the values of s is constant. However, the ray which has the greater velocity (a being greater than b) may still, for convenience, be called the ordinary ray. Of the two roots of equation (8), the one, k_o, whose numerical value (supposing ϕ not to vanish) is less than unity, corresponds to this ray. When C is positive, k_o is negative; and when C is negative, k_o is positive: therefore in both kinds of quartz, by formulæ (5) and (6), we have $s_o^2 > A$, and $s_e^2 < B$; denoting by s_o and s_e the respective velocities of propagation of the ordinary and extraordinary waves. Hence, if we conceive a sphere of the radius a, with its centre at the origin, and a concentric prolate spheroid, whose semiaxis of revolution is also equal to a, and parallel to the axis of the crystal, while the radius of its equator is equal to b, the ordinary *nappe* of the wave surface will fall entirely without the sphere, and the extraordinary *nappe* entirely within the spheroid, whether the crystal be right-handed or left-handed. With respect to the little ellipse in which the vibrations are performed, and of which the semiaxes parallel to x and y are represented by p and q respectively, it is evident that $p > q$ for the ordinary wave, since $k_0 < 1$; and that $p < q$ for the extraordinary wave. When C vanishes, the minor axis of each ellipse also vanishes, and the rays become plane-polarized, the ordinary vibrations being then parallel to the direction of x, and the extraordinary parallel to that of y. This is exactly what ought to happen on the supposition that the vibrations of a plane-polarized ray* are parallel to its plane of polarization—a supposition which was kept in view in framing the fundamental equations (1) and (2).

To show, with precision, how the two kinds of quartz are to be distinguished by the sign of C, we must give definite directions to the axes of co-ordinates. To this end, let us imagine the plane of xy to be horizontal, and a circle to be described in it with the origin O for its centre; and let the north, east, and south points of this circle be marked respectively with the letters N, E, S. Let the direction of $+x$ be eastward, from O to E; that of $+y$ northward, from O to N; and that of $+z$ vertically downwards; the progress of the light through the crystal being

---

* On this point there are two very different opinions. Fresnel supposed, as is well known, that the vibrations of a plane-polarized ray are perpendicular to its plane of polarization; whereas, according to M. Cauchy, whom I have followed, they are parallel to that plane. I am induced to adopt the latter supposition, because I have succeeded, by means of hypotheses which are grounded on it, in discovering the laws of reflexion from crystallized surfaces; laws which include, as a particular case, those discovered by Fresnel for ordinary media. The hypotheses alluded to, along with some of their results, are published in the *London and Edinburgh Philosophical Magazine*, Vol. VIII., p. 103, in a letter to Sir David Brewster (*supra*, pp. 75, *et seq.*) *See also* Vol. VII., p. 295, of the same Journal (*supra*, pp. 55, *et seq.*) I hope soon to offer the Academy a detailed account of my researches on this subject.

also downwards, and the plane of the wave moving parallel, as before, to the plane of xy. Then the crystal will be right-handed or left-handed, according as C is positive or negative. For, if C be positive, k_0 will be negative, and formulæ (4) will become, by exhibiting the sign of k_0,

$$\xi = p \cos \left\{ \frac{2\pi}{l} (st - z) \right\}, \quad \eta = - k_0\, p \sin \left\{ \frac{2\pi}{l} (st - z) \right\}, \quad (15)$$

for the ordinary vibration; and

$$\xi = k_0\, q \cos \left\{ \frac{2\pi}{l} (st - z) \right\}, \quad \eta = q \sin \left\{ \frac{2\pi}{l} (st - z) \right\}, \quad (16)$$

for the extraordinary vibration. Now if we suppose the arc $\frac{2\pi}{l} (st - z)$ either to vanish, or to be a multiple of the circumference, the molecule will be at the east point of its vibration; and upon increasing the time a little, the value of η will become negative in (15), and positive in (16), so that the movement will be towards the south in the first case, and towards the north in the second. Therefore, when C is positive, the ordinary vibration takes place in the direction NES, or from left to right, and the extraordinary in the direction SEN, or from right to left, supposing a spectator to look in the direction of the progress of the light. It may be shown, in like manner, that when C is negative, the ordinary and extraordinary vibrations are in the directions SEN and NES, or from right to left and from left to right respectively. Now if a plane-polarized ray be transmitted along the axis of the crystal, the plane of polarization will be turned in the direction of the ordinary vibration, because this vibration, being propagated more quickly, will be in advance of the other, upon emerging from the crystal. Hence, the rotation is from left to right when C is positive, and from right to left when C is negative; and the crystal is called right-handed in the first case, and left-handed in the second.

We have all along supposed that C is a constant quantity, and the agreement of our results with experiment proves that this supposition is at least very nearly true in the neighbourhood of the axis. It is probable, however, not only that C varies with ϕ, but that it becomes different in equations (1) and (2) ; that is to say, it is probable that the following equations

$$\frac{d^2\xi}{dt^2} = A \frac{d^2\xi}{dz^2} + C \frac{d^3\eta}{dz^3},$$

$$\frac{d^2\eta}{dt^2} = B \frac{d^2\eta}{dz^2} - C' \frac{d^3\eta}{dz^2},$$

(17)

in which C' is a little different from C, would be more correct than those which we have assumed. Indeed Mr. Airy's experiments seem to indicate that C' is greater than C; for he found, as we have already said, that the ratio of the axes of the little ellipse described by a vibrating molecule is somewhat different for the two rays, being more nearly a ratio of equality for the ordinary than for the extraordinary ray. Now if we set out from equations (17), instead of (1) and (2), and proceed in all respects as before, we shall arrive at the formula

$$k^2 - \frac{l}{2\pi C} (a^2 - b^2) \sin \phi . k = \frac{C'}{C}$$

(18)

instead of formula (8). The quantity $\frac{C'}{C}$ will be greater than unity, if C' be greater than C, and the value of k_0 will be greater than before. This seems to be the explanation of the difference between the ratios observed by Mr. Airy.

It may be proper to state briefly the considerations which led to the foregoing theory. Beginning with the simple case of a ray passing along the axis, the first thing to be explained was the law of M. Biot, that the angle of rotation varies inversely as the square of l or of λ. Now it was remarked by Fresnel, who first resolved the phenomena of rotation into the interference of two circularly polarized waves, that the interval δ between these waves, at their emergence from the crystal, must be inversely as l, if the angle of rotation be inversely as the square of l. This remark suggested* to me the idea of adding, to the equations of the common theory, terms containing the third differential coefficients of the displacements ; for it was evident that such additional terms would give, in the value of s^2, a part inversely proportional to l. It was also evident that the third differential coefficient of ξ should be combined with the second differential coefficients of η, and the third of η with the second of ξ, in order that, after substitutions such as we have indicated in deducing formulæ (5) and (6), the sines or cosines might disappear by division, and that thus the value of s^2 might be independent of the time, as it ought to be.   This kind of reasoning led me to assume the equations

$$\frac{d^2\xi}{dt^2} = a^2 \frac{d^2\xi}{dz^2} + C \frac{d^3\eta}{dz^3}, \tag{19}$$

$$\frac{d^2\eta}{dt^2} = a^2 \frac{d^2\eta}{dz^2} + D \frac{d^3\xi}{dz^3}, \tag{20}$$

for the case of a ray passing along the axis of quartz ; and then, substituting in these equations the values of the differential co-efficients obtained by differentiating the formulæ

$$\xi = p \cos \left\{ \frac{2\pi}{l} (st - z) \right\}, \quad \eta = \pm p \sin \left\{ \frac{2\pi}{l} (st - z) \right\},$$

which express a circular vibration (from right to left, or from left to right, according to the sign of the second p), the result was

$$s^2 = a^2 \mp \frac{2\pi}{l} C$$

from (19), and

$$s^2 = a^2 \pm \frac{2\pi}{l} D$$

* " The singular relation between the interval of retardation [δ] and the length of the wave [l] seems to afford the only clue to the unravelling of this difficulty."— " Report on Physical Optics," by Professor Lloyd (" Fourth Report of the British Association," p. 409).   It was in reading this Report that Fresnel's remark, about the relation between δ and l, first came to my knowledge.

from (20) ; which showed that $D = - C$, since the values of s, corresponding to the same circular vibration, ought to be equal. The transition from this simple case to that of a ray inclined at a given angle ϕ to the axis was easily made, by taking into account the doubly refracting structure of the crystal. This was done by supposing ξ and η parallel to the principal directions in the plane of the wave, and by changing a^2, in equation (20), into $a^2 - (a^2 - b^2) \sin^2\phi$; and thus the fundamental equations (1) and (2) were obtained.

VIII.—ON THE LAWS OF REFLEXION FROM CRYSTAL-LIZED SURFACES.

[From the *Philosophical Magazine*, VOL. VIII., 1835.]

To SIR DAVID BREWSTER.

DEAR SIR—I have great pleasure in sending you an account of the laws by which I conceive that the vibrations of light are regulated when a ray is reflected and refracted at the separating surface of two media; especially as the only guide which I had, in my inquiry after these laws, was your Paper on the action of crystallized surfaces upon light, published in the *Philosophical Transactions* for the year 1819. The observation which I found there, that the polarizing angle was the same for a given plane of incidence, " whether the obtuse angle of the rhomb [of Iceland spar] was nearest or furthest from the eye, or whether it was to the right or left hand of the observer," disappointed me at first, being contrary to what I had anticipated from principles analogous to those which had been employed by Fresnel in the problem of reflexion from ordinary media. I then sought other principles, and the observation is now a result of theory.

Assuming, as a basis for calculation, that Fresnel's law of double refraction is rigorously true, I have been obliged to make an essential change in his physical ideas. Conceive an ellipsoid whose semiaxes are parallel to the three principal directions of the crystal, and equal respectively to its three principal indices of refraction, and let a central section of the ellipsoid be made by a plane parallel to the plane of a wave passing through the crystal. The section will be an ellipse, and the wave will be polarized by the crystal in a plane parallel to either semiaxis of this ellipse, the index of refraction for the wave being equal to the other semiaxis. This is Fresnel's law of double refraction; and the theory which led him to it makes it necessary to admit that the vibrations of the wave are perpendicular to its plane of polarization; whereas, according to the views which I have adopted, the vibrations of the wave are parallel to its plane of polarization, and to one semiaxis of the elliptic section, while its index of refraction is equal to the other semiaxis. These views nearly agree with the theory of M. Cauchy, according to whom the vibrations of polarized light are parallel to its plane of polarization, but inclined at small angles to the plane of the wave in crystallized media, instead of being exactly parallel to the latter plane, as I have supposed them to be. Besides, the theory of M. Cauchy, founded on the six equations of pressure in a crystallized medium, implies the existence of a third ray of feeble intensity, and for the other two rays gives a law somewhat different from that of Fresnel. Being obliged, in order to account for your experiments, to abandon the physical ideas of Fresnel, and to approximate towards those of M. Cauchy, I was embarrassed by this third ray; and wishing to get rid of it, as well as of the slight deviations from the symmetrical law of Fresnel, I adopted the expedient of altering the equations of pressure, in such a way as to make them afford only two rays, and give a law of refraction exactly the same as Fresnel's. The equations which I found to answer this purpose are the following :—

$$A = -2\,c^2\left(\frac{d\eta}{dy} + b^2\frac{d\zeta}{dz}\right)V^2\,\rho,$$

$$B = -2\left(a^2\frac{d\zeta}{dz} + c^2\frac{d\xi}{dx}\right)V^2\,\rho,$$

$$C = -2\left(b^2\frac{d\xi}{dx} + a^2\frac{d\eta}{dy}\right)V^2\,\rho,$$

$$D = a^2 \left(\frac{d\eta}{dz} + \frac{d\zeta}{dy} \right) V^2 \rho,$$

$$E = b^2 \left(\frac{d\zeta}{dx} + \frac{d\xi}{dz} \right) V^2 \rho,$$

$$F = c^2 \left(\frac{d\xi}{dy} + \frac{d\eta}{dx} \right) V^2 \rho.$$

In these equations, the axes of co-ordinates are perpendicular to each other, and parallel to the principal directions of the crystal; x, y, z are the co-ordinates of a vibrating molecule at the time t; ξ, η, ζ are the components of the displacement of the same molecule at the same time; a, b, c are the three principal indices of refraction out of the crystal into an ordinary medium in which the velocity of light is equal to V; and ρ is the density of the ether, which density I suppose to be the same in all media. The quantities A, F, E are the components, parallel to the axes of x, y, z, respectively, of the pressure upon a plane perpendicular to the axis of x; F, B, D are the components of the pressure upon a plane perpendicular to the axis of y; and E, D, C the components of the pressure upon a plane perpendicular to the axis of z. The values of D, E, F are the same as those given by M. Cauchy; but the values of A, B, C are different from his, and much simpler. By introducing into the equations of M. Cauchy the condition that the vibrations shall be performed without any change of density, the resulting values of A, B, C might be shown to agree nearly with those given above. The six pressures, A, B, C, D, E, F, being known, it is easy to find the pressure upon a plane making any given angles with the axes of co-ordinates.

These things being premised, it is time to mention the laws, or rather hypotheses, which I have imagined for discovering the relations that exist, as to direction and magnitude, among the vibrations in each ray, when reflexion and refraction take place at the separating surface of two media, whether crystallized or not. In stating the two very simple laws that have occurred to me for this purpose, it will be convenient, when the first medium is an ordinary one, to suppose that the incident light is polarized. Then, by the first law, *the vibrations in one medium are equivalent to those in the other;* that is to say, if the incident and reflected vibrations be compounded, like forces acting at a point, their resultant will be the same, both in length and direction, as the resultant of the refracted vibrations similarly compounded. By the second law, *the lateral pressure upon the separating surface is the same in both media;* the lateral pressure being understood to mean the pressure in a direction perpendicular to the plane of incidence.

As it would engage us too long to follow these laws into detail, I shall merely state some of the results which I have obtained from them, for the case of a uniaxal crystal into which the light passes out of an ordinary medium.

Imagine the surface of the crystal to be horizontal, and call the point of incidence I. With the centre I and any radius, conceive a sphere to be described, cutting in the point Z a vertical line IZ drawn through the centre, and let a radius IP, parallel to the axis of the crystal, meet the surface of the sphere in P. Let the great circle ZOE be the plane of incidence, containing both the direction IO of the ordinary refracted ray produced backwards, and the direction IE of a normal to the extraordinary wave;

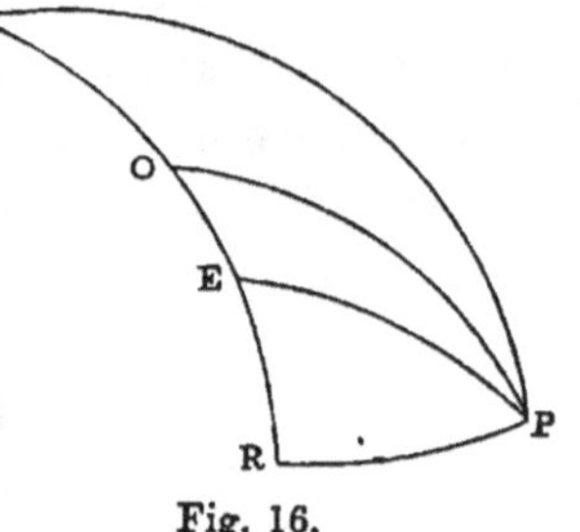

Fig. 16.

and draw the great circles PZ, PO, PE. The angle Z will be the azimuth of the plane of incidence. Let $ZO = \phi$, $ZE = \phi'$, $PO = \psi$, $PE = \psi'$, the angle $ZOP = \theta$, and the angle $ZEP = \theta'$. Call the angle of incidence i, and suppose b to be the reciprocal of the ordinary refractive index and a the reciprocal of the extraordinary.

Each of the refracted rays, in turn, may be made to disappear, by polarizing the incident ray in a certain direction assigned by theory. When the extraordinary ray disappears, the reflected ray is polarized in a plane inclined to the plane of incidence at an angle β determined by the formula

$$\tan \beta = \cos (i + \phi) \tan \theta + 2 (a^2 - b^2) \sin \theta \sin \psi \cos \psi \frac{\sin^2 i}{\sin (i - \phi)}. \quad (2)$$

When the ordinary ray disappears, the plane of polarization of the reflected ray is inclined to the plane of incidence at an angle β determined by the formula

$$- \tan \beta' = \cos (i + \phi') \cotan \theta'$$
$$+ (a^2 - b^2) \frac{\cos 2\theta'}{\sin \theta'} \sin \psi' \cos \psi' \frac{\sin^2 i}{\sin (i - \phi')}. \quad (3)$$

And when the angles β, β', become equal, the plane of polarization of the reflected ray becomes independent of the plane of polarization of the incident ray ; and the angle of incidence i, at which this equality takes place, is the polarizing angle of the crystal. Hence we have the equation of condition

$$\left.\begin{array}{l} \cos (i + \phi) \tan \theta + 2 (a^2 - b^2) \sin \theta \sin \psi \cos \psi \dfrac{\sin^2 i}{\sin (i - \phi)} \\[2ex] + \cos (i + \phi') \cotan \theta' + (a^2 - b^2) \dfrac{\cos 2\theta'}{\sin \theta'} \sin \psi' \cos \psi' \dfrac{\sin^2 i}{\sin (i - \phi')} \end{array}\right\} = 0 \quad (4)$$

to be fulfilled at the polarizing angle.

Since $i + \phi$, in this equation, is nearly equal to a right angle, put $i + \phi = \frac{\pi}{2} + \delta$, and δ will be a small quantity. Draw PR an arc of a great circle perpendicular to ZOE, and let $ZR = p$, $PR = q$. Then we shall find from equation (4), after various substitutions and reductions,

$$\delta = K \cos^2 q \,(\cos^2 \phi - \cos^2 p) \,; \text{ where } K = \frac{(a^2 - b^2) \,(1 + b^2)}{2b \,(1 - b^2)}. \quad (5)$$

In deducing this value of δ, the approximations were made with a tacit reference to the case of reflexion in air from a common rhomb of Iceland spar. The coefficient K, in this case, is equal to about nine degrees, and the resulting numerical values of the polarizing angles in various azimuths agree very well with your experiments. You will perceive that the value of δ is the same in supplementary azimuths, which explains the observation, cited in the beginning of my letter, relative to the equality of the polarizing angles at opposite sides of the perpendicular IZ in a given plane of incidence.

When the point R falls upon O, we have $\delta = 0$, and $i + \phi$ equal to a right angle. Hence, when the cotangent of ZR is equal to the ordinary index, the tangent of the polarizing angle is equal to the same index. This theorem, though deduced from an approximate equation, might be shown to be exact.

When the axis of the crystal lies in the plane of incidence, we may obtain an exact expression for the polarizing angle. The condition of polarization then becomes

$$\cos (i + \phi') - (a^2 - b^2) \sin \psi' \cos \psi' \frac{\sin^2 i}{\sin (i - \phi')} = 0 ; \qquad (6)$$

from which, by the proper substitutions, we obtain the following expression :—

$$\sin^2 i = \frac{1 - a^2 \cos^2 \lambda - b^2 \sin^2 \lambda}{1 - a^2 \, b^2} ; \qquad (7)$$

where λ denotes the complement of ZP, or the inclination of the axis to the face of the crystal, and i is the polarizing angle. This formula, in a shape somewhat different, was communicated, above a year ago, to Professor Lloyd, who has noticed it, in connexion with your Paper, in his "Report on Physical Optics." When a and b become equal, the formula gives your law of the tangent for ordinary media.

The foregoing results show that, when a ray is polarized by reflexion from a crystal, the plane of polarization deviates from the plane of incidence, except when the axis lies in the latter plane ; and that the deviation may be made very great by placing the crystal in contact with a medium whose refractive power is nearly equal to that of the crystal itself ; for when i is nearly equal to ϕ or to ϕ', the divisor $\sin (i - \phi)$ or $\sin (i - \phi')$ is very small, and therefore $\tan \beta$ or $\tan \beta'$ is very great. But this remark is of no value whatever in explaining the very singular phenomena which you have observed in the extreme case just mentioned; nor can I imagine any reason why there should be a deviation, as there was in some of your experiments, when the axis lies in the plane of incidence, since everything is then alike on both sides of this plane. Indeed the whole of this subject, which occupies the latter part of your Paper of 1819, is very extraordinary and interesting; and I was glad to hear that you had resumed the investigation of it, and made many experiments which have not been published.

I wish you would publish them. They seem to be of great importance in the present state of optical science.

I am, dear Sir, ever truly yours,

J. Mac Cullagh.

Trin. Coll., Dublin, *Dec.* 22, 1835.

IX.—ON THE PROBABLE NATURE OF THE LIGHT TRANS-MITTED BY THE DIAMOND AND BY GOLD LEAF.

[*Proceedings of the Royal Irish Academy*, Vol. I. p. 27.—Read Jan. 9, 1837.]

PROFESSOR MAC CULLAGH made a verbal communication on the probable nature of the light transmitted by the diamond and by gold leaf. He conceives that as there is a change of phase caused by reflexion from these bodies, so there is also a change of phase produced by refraction ; the change being different according as the incident light is polarized in the plane of incidence, or in the perpendicular plane. Consequently, if the incident ray be polarized in any intermediate plane, the refracted ray should be elliptically polarized ; and on examining the light transmitted by gold leaf, this was found to be the case. Of course the same thing is true of the light which enters the other metals, and which is subsequently absorbed. The same remark explains the appearance of double refraction in specimens of the diamond which give only a single image; and it is likely that other precious stones will be found to possess similar properties. Mr. Mac Cullagh has obtained a general formula for the difference of phase between the two component portions of the refracted light—one polarized in the plane of incidence, and the other perpendicular to it. He finds from this formula, that the difference of phase, which is nothing at a perpendicular incidence, increases until it becomes equal to the *characteristic* at an incidence of 90°; and when the light emerges into air, the difference of phase is doubled. The formula has not yet been submitted to the test of experiment.

X.—ON THE LAWS OF CRYSTALLINE REFLEXION.

[*From the Philosophical Magazine*, Vol. x., 1837.]

In a Number of Poggendorff's *Annalen* (No. 6, for 1836), which reached Dublin late in November, there are some remarks by M. Seebeck on a Paper of mine which appeared in the last February Number of this Journal (vol. viii. p. 103). That Paper contains a general theory of reflexion at the surfaces of crystallized media; and M. Seebeck, in comparing the results with his own experiments, has fully confirmed some of my formulæ, while he has shown that others are defective. I have therefore been obliged to revise my theory, and I have ascertained that it was vitiated by the introduction of a certain relation among the quantities denominated pressures, which, following the example of M. Cauchy, I had supposed to be concerned in the problem. This relation I had observed to hold in the case of singly refracting media, and I concluded, without any other reason, that it would hold good generally. But though it led to the correct formula for the polarizing angles in different azimuths, it was nevertheless arbitrary and unfounded; and therefore it is now banished entirely from the investigation, the place which it occupied being supplied by the natural and simple law of the preservation of *vis viva*, while everything else remains as before. I hope the imperfection of my first essay will be excused, when it is considered that the erroneous proposition bears but a small proportion to the whole theory; and, moreover, that the general problem, which I undertook to resolve, is one that has not been attempted by any other person, although the want of a solution has long been felt. The difficulties which we have to deal with, in entering upon this problem, are not mere mathematical difficulties, but difficulties arising from the want of first principles; and, in physical questions of this kind, where we must, at the outset, have recourse to conjecture, in order to supply the very principles of our reasoning, it can hardly be expected that the whole truth should be divined at once. I think, however, that I have now obtained a true mechanical theory; and if so, it will help to decide, not only the question immediately before us, but also the other much-disputed, though more elementary, questions concerning the density of the ether in different media, and the direction of the vibrations in polarized light. In fact, a particular supposition respecting each of the latter questions is included in my theory, the several principles of which, making the single alteration that has been mentioned, I shall here enumerate :—

1. The density of the ether is the same in all media.

2. The vibrations of plane-polarized light are parallel to the plane of polarization.

3. The *vis viva* is preserved.

4. The vibrations are equivalent at the common surface of two media.

To these may be added the definition of the polarizing angle of a crystal; namely, the angle of incidence at which the plane of polarization of the reflected ray becomes independent of the plane of polarization of the incident ray. At the polarizing angle, the former plane does not, in general, coincide with the plane of reflexion, but makes with it a small angle which may be called the *deviation*.

It is curious that, about a year and a half ago, I employed these four principles, precisely as I have now enumerated them, in deducing Fresnel's well-known laws of reflexion for ordinary media; but I did not then apply the law of *vis viva* to crystals, because my mind was preoccupied by the notion that there existed some relation among the pressures. This notion I had taken up from reading a little Paper, by M. Cauchy, in the *Bulletin des Sciences Mathématiques* for July 1830; and by combining such a relation with the three conditions afforded by my own law of *equivalent vibrations*, I had actually obtained, for the polarizing angles in different azimuths, a formula (that marked (5) in my former Paper), which I found to agree very well with Sir David Brewster's experiments, and which M. Seebeck has found to agree still better with his own.

The formula for the polarizing angle is obtained by equating two values of the deviation; and it is remarkable that the very same formula comes out in my present theory, although the values of the deviation are entirely different. Referring, for brevity, to the notation of my former Paper, I find, for the case of a uniaxal crystal,

$$\tan \beta = \cos (i + \phi) \tan \theta, \quad \dots\dots\dots\dots\dots\dots\dots\dots \quad (a)$$

$$-\tan \beta' = \cos (i + \phi') \cotan \theta' + (a^2 - b^2) \frac{\sin \psi' \, \cos \psi' \sin^2 i}{\sin \theta' \sin (i - \phi')}. \quad (b)$$

These equations (a) and (b) are to be substituted for equations (2) and (3),* which are the equations that M. Seebeck found to be at variance with his experiments.

By means of formula (5), equation (a) becomes

$$\beta = \frac{K}{2} \sin 2 q \sin (p - \phi), \quad \dots\dots\dots\dots\dots \quad (c)$$

from which the deviation in any azimuth may be readily calculated. The azimuth (as M. Seebeck reckons it) begins when $\theta = 0$, and p is then positive. This formula (c) perfectly represents the experiments of M. Seebeck on Iceland spar. The corresponding expressions for biaxal crystals may be easily deduced, and will be given in a Paper which I am preparing to lay before the Royal Irish Academy.

At the time of my last communication I was not aware that the case in which the plane of incidence is a principal section of the crystal (or the azimuth = 0) had been solved by M. Seebeck, and that formula (7),† which I regarded as my own, had been obtained by him long before.

* Supra, p. 79.   † Supra, p. 80.

It remains to say a word respecting the new principle of equivalent vibrations, the most important, perhaps, of all, as it is certainly the simplest that can be imagned. If we conceive an ethereal molecule situated at the common surface of two media, it would seem that its motion ought to be the same, whether we regard the molecule as belonging to the first medium or to the second. Now the incident and reflected vibrations are superposed in the first medium, and the refracted vibrations in the second; and therefore we may infer (when the phase is not changed by reflexion or refraction), that *if the incident and reflected vibrations be compounded, like forces acting at a point, their resultant will be the same, both in length and direction, as the resultant of the refracted vibrations similarly compounded.* This is the law of equivalent vibrations, and it gives, at once, three equations. A fourth equation is afforded by Fresnel's law of the *vis viva;* and thus we have the four conditions necessary for a general solution of the problem. From the principle of equivalent vibrations, as we have stated it, it follows that the vibrations resolved parallel to the separating surface are equivalent in the two media; and, in fact, this part of the general principle was assumed by Fresnel; but the other part, namely, that the vibrations perpendicular to the separating surface are equivalent, was not assumed by him, nor is it by any means true in his theory. It appears then that three conditions only are afforded by the hypotheses which Fresnel successfully employed in solving the problem of reflexion from ordinary media. These hypotheses, therefore, are not sufficient when applied to crystals; except, indeed, in the case before alluded to, where the azimuth = 0, which has been solved by M. Seebeck. It should be observed, that though the reasons which I have assigned for the principle of equivalent vibrations are extremely simple, yet it was not by such simple reasoning that I was led to it originally.

TRINITY COLLEGE, DUBLIN, *December* 13, 1836.

XI.—ON THE LAWS OF CRYSTALLINE REFLEXION AND REFRACTION.

[*Transactions of the Royal Irish Academy*, Vol. xviii.—Read Jan. 9, 1837.]

WHEN a ray of light, which has been polarized in a given plane, suffers reflexion and refraction at the surface of a transparent medium, the rays into which it is divided are found to be polarized in certain other planes; and it becomes a question to determine the positions of these planes, as well as the relative intensities of the different rays; or, in theoretical language, to find the direction and magnitude of the reflected and refracted vibrations, supposing those of the incident vibration to be given. The transparent medium may be either a singly-refracting substance, such as glass, or a doubly-refracting crystal, like Iceland spar. When the medium is of the first kind, the problem is comparatively simple, being, in fact, nothing more than a particular case of the problem which we have to consider when the medium is supposed to be of the second kind. In the progress of knowledge it was natural that the simpler question should be first attended to; and accordingly Fresnel, during his brief and brilliant career, found time to solve it. But the general problem, relative to doubly-refracting media, had not been attempted by anyone, when, in the year 1834, my thoughts were turned to the subject. I then recollected a conclusion to which I had been led some years before, and which, on this occasion, proved of essential service to me. Being fond of geometrical constructions, I amused myself, when I first became acquainted with Fresnel's theories, by throwing his algebraical expressions, whenever I could, into a geometrical form ; and treating in this way the well-known formulæ in which he has embodied his solution of the problem just alluded to, I obtained a remarkable result, which gave me the first view of the principle that I have since employed under the name of the *principle of the equivalence of vibrations.* In order to state this result briefly, I will take leave to introduce a new term for expressing a right line drawn parallel to the plane of polarization of a ray, and perpendicular to the direction of the ray itself. Calling such a right line the *transversal* of the polarized ray, I found, from the formulæ of Fresnel, that when polarized light falls upon a singly-refracting medium, the transversals of the incident, of the reflected, and of the refracted rays are all parallel to the same plane, which is the plane of polarization of the refracted ray ; and that the magnitudes of the vibrations, or the greatest excursions of the ethereal molecules, in the incident and the reflected rays, are to each other inversely as the sines of the angles which the respective transversals of those rays make with the transversal of the refracted ray. I was struck by the strong analogy which these relations among the transversals bore to the composition of forces or of small vibrations in mechanics ; but it happened unfortunately that, in the theory of Fresnel, the vibrations of light were supposed to take place, not in the direction of the transversals, but perpendicular to them, so that there was no physical circumstance to support the analogy, there being no motion in the direction of the transversals ; while, on the other hand, no such analogy existed among the vibrations themselves in the directions which Fresnel had assigned to them. It was therefore with some interest that I afterwards learned, upon the publication of the tenth volume of the *Memoirs of the Institute,* that M. Cauchy* had actually inferred, from mechanical principles, that the vibrations of polarized light are in the

* *Mémoires de l'Institut,* tome x. p. 304.

direction of the transversals; but this inference was to be received with caution, as being contrary to the hypothesis of Fresnel; and besides, I had in the meantime contrived a way of adapting my analogy, in some degree, to that hypothesis, by supposing *areas* to be compounded instead of vibrations; so that I hesitated which of the two opinions to prefer. Taking, however, the opinion of M. Cauchy as that which fell in more naturally with the aforesaid analogy, I was led to the conclusion, that the vibration in the refracted ray is probably the resultant of the incident and reflected vibrations; and I saw that if this principle were true for singly-refracting media, it should also, from its very nature, be true, when properly generalized, for doubly-refracting crystals; so that in such crystals the resultant of the two refracted vibrations would be the same, both in length and direction, as the resultant of the incident and reflected vibrations.

This was the principle of *equivalent vibrations.* But I had no sooner begun to regard it as probable, than an objection started up against it. In the case of a ray ordinarily refracted out of a rarer into a denser medium, the magnitude of the refracted vibration, as deduced from this principle, was greater than that which came out from the theory of Fresnel, in the proportion of the sine of the angle of incidence to the sine of the angle of refraction. Consequently, assuming with Fresnel that the ether is more dense in the denser medium, the law of the preservation of *vis viva* was violated.

There was another embarrassment which I felt in my early efforts to find out the laws of crystalline reflexion. Taking for granted the hypothesis of Fresnel, that the density of the ether in an ordinary medium is inversely as the square of its refractive index, I was at a loss what hypothesis to make, in this respect, for doubly-refracting crystals, wherein the refractive index changes with the direction of the ray. For the density, being independent of direction, could not be conceived to vary with the refractive index. About two years ago I got over this difficulty, by supposing the density of the ether to be the same in all media.* At the same time I was compelled to employ the principle of equivalent vibrations, in order to have a sufficient number of conditions, though for a while I overlooked the perfect agreement which now subsisted between this principle and the law of *vis viva:* it happened, in fact, that the new hypothesis of a constant density made the *vis viva* of the refracted ray exactly the same as in the theory of Fresnel.†

But to see why it was necessary to assume the principle of equivalent vibrations, we must observe, that when a polarized ray is incident on a crystal there are four things to be determined, namely, the direction and magnitude of the reflected vibration, and the magnitudes of the two refracted vibrations. Hence we must have four conditions, or we must have relations affording so many equations. But the hypotheses of Fresnel, by which he solved the problem of reflexion for ordinary media, afford only three conditions. We will state his hypotheses at length :—

1st. The vibrations of polarized light are in the plane of the wave, and *perpendicular* to the plane of polarization.

2nd. The density of the ether is inversely as the square of the refractive index of the medium.

3rd. The *vis viva* is preserved.

4th. The vibrations parallel to the separating surface of two media are equivalent; that is, the refracted vibration parallel to the surface is the resultant of the incident and reflected vibrations parallel to the same.

We see that the fourth hypothesis gives two conditions, and the law of *vis viva* gives a third.

Let us now take the more general principle of equivalent vibrations, in place of the fourth hypothesis of Fresnel, altering

---

* This hypothesis is maintained by Mr. Challis; and certainly it falls in extremely well with the astronomical phenomenon of the aberration of light.—See, on this subject, Professor Lloyd's Report on Physical Optics, "Fourth Report of the British Association for the Advancement of Science," pp. 311, 313.

† *Supra*, p. 100, *note*.

the first hypothesis in the way that we have shown to be necessary in order to suit that principle, and making the ethereal density constant. Then, if we retain the law of *vis viva*, our new hypotheses will be these :—

1st. The vibrations of polarized light are in the plane of the wave, and *parallel* to the plane of polarization; which may be expressed in a word, by saying that the vibrations are *transversal*, according to the peculiar sense in which I use the term.

2nd. The density of the ether is the same in all bodies as in *vacuo*.

3rd. The *vis viva* is preserved.

4th. The vibrations in two contiguous media are equivalent; that is, the resultant of the incident and reflected vibrations is the same, both in length and direction, as the resultant of the refracted vibrations.

It is evident that the last hypothesis affords three equations, by resolving the vibrations parallel to three axes of co-ordinates; and the law of *vis viva* supplies a fourth equation. Thus we have the requisite number of conditions.

The hypotheses that we have last enumerated are those which will be employed in the present Paper. They have been made to include the law of *vis viva*, because I lately found that this law must necessarily accompany the rest; but at first I neglected it, and even made considerable progress without it; for, by the help of another hypothesis, I obtained formulæ which represented such experiments as I was aware of at the time. This other hypothesis I took up from reading an article by M. Cauchy in the *Bulletin des Sciences Mathématiques,** in which he arrives, by a peculiar process, at the formulæ of Fresnel for the case of ordinary reflexion. The hypotheses

* " Sur la Réfraction et la Réflexion de la Lumière," *Bulletin des Sci. Math.*, Juillet, 1830. In this Paper the vibrations of polarized light must be supposed perpendicular to the plane of polarization, though the Paper was published immediately after the author had promulged the contrary opinion. The latter opinion, which I adopted from him because it harmonized with my analogy before mentioned, he has formally renounced of late, and has returned to the

which he chiefly employs are relations among certain quantities called pressures; and it was such a relation that I adopted
instead of the law of *vis viva*. I supposed that, at the confines
of two media, the pressure on the separating surface, in a direction perpendicular to the plane of incidence, ought to be the
same, whether it be considered as resulting from the vibrations
in the first medium or in the second. This hypothesis I conceived to be true in general, because I found it to be true for
ordinary media; but I could never assign any better reason for
it. Combining it, however, with the principle of equivalent
vibrations, I deduced several expressions for uniaxal crystals,
and among others a formula for the polarizing angles in different azimuths of the plane of reflexion. When this formula was
compared with the experiments of Sir David Brewster* on the
polarizing angles of Iceland spar, the accordance was so satisfactory as to leave no doubt upon my mind that I had arrived
at the true formula for these angles; and though the truth of
the conclusion did not allow me to argue that the premises

hypothesis of Fresnel. M. Cauchy supposed too, in the above Paper, that the
ethereal density is the same in different media; but he has found cause to abandon
this hypothesis also. *See* his notes addressed to M. Libri, in the *Comptes rendus
des Séances de l'Académie des Sciences*, Séance du 4 Avril, 1836, where he gives the
reasons for his present opinions. He says, "Ainsi Fresnel a eu raison de dire,
non-seulement que les vibrations des molécules éthérées sont généralement com-
prises dans les plans des ondes, mais encore que les plans de polarisation sont
perpendiculaires aux directions des vitesses ou des déplacements moléculaires.
J'arrive au reste à cette dernière conclusion d'une autre manière, en établissant
les lois de la réflexion et de la réfraction à l'aide d'une nouvelle méthode qui
sera développée dans mon mémorie...... [cette méthode] ne m'oblige plus à
supposer, comme je l'avais fait dans un article du *Bulletin des Sciences*, que la
densité de l'éther est la même dans tous les milieux. Mes nouvelles recherches
donnent lieu de croire que cette densité varie en général quand on passe d'un
milieu à un autre." More lately, in his *Nouveaux Exercices de Mathématiques*,
7ᵉ Livraison, M. Cauchy states positively that his principles do not permit him
to adopt the hypothesis that the density of the ether is the same in all media. He
also gives the differential equations which, as he has found by his new method,
ought to subsist at the separating surface of two media, and from which he has
obtained the formulæ of Fresnel for ordinary reflexion. But these equations do
not include the laws of crystalline reflexion.

  * *Phil. Trans.*, 1819, p. 150.

were true, yet the presumption in their favour was very strong, insomuch that, upon remarking, as I did soon after, that the law of *vis viva* harmonized with my other hypotheses, I did not think it worth while* to try what would be the consequence of using this law, instead of the relation which I had put in its place. In this state of my theory, I gave an account of it at the meeting of the British Association† in Dublin, in August, 1835; and the leading steps and results were afterwards published in a letter to Sir David Brewster.‡

Now we are to observe, that when common light is polarized by reflexion at the surface of a doubly-refracting crystal, the polarization does not, in general, coincide with the plane of reflexion, as in the case of ordinary media, but is inclined to it at a certain angle, which may be called the *deviation;* and it was by equating two values of the deviation that I obtained the formula above mentioned for the polarizing angle. This formula, as we have seen, was correct; but it happened, singularly enough, that the expressions for the deviation, which were

---

* I had, besides, an objection to the law of *vis viva*, on the ground that it would give an equation of the second degree; and I wished to have all my equations linear, lest, in the seemingly complicated question of crystalline reflexion, they should give two answers when the nature of the question required but one. This has actually happened, since the present Paper was read, in applying my hypotheses to the case of *internal* reflexion at the second surface of a uniaxal crystal. Supposing an ordinary ray to emerge after double reflexion, and putting θ for the angle which the emergent transversal makes with the plane of incidence, I found, for determining θ, an equation of the form

$$A + B \tan \theta + C \tan^2\theta = O,$$

wherein A is very small, but does not vanish; so that the equation gives two roots, one very small, the other about the proper value. It is clear, therefore, that there is a want of adjustment somewhere: but I am now inclined to think that the fault is not in the principle of *vis viva*. Possibly our laws of the propagation of light in doubly refracting media are not quite accurate. Whatever supplementary law shall be found to remedy this untoward result will probably, at the same time, account for the extraordinary phenomena observed by Brewster, in reflexion at the *first* surface when the crystal is in contact with a medium of nearly equal refractive power.

† *London and Edinburgh Philosophical Magazine*, Vol. VII. p. 295.

‡ *Ibid.*, Vol. VIII. p. 103; February, 1836. (*Supra*, p. 75.)

used in obtaining the formula, were erroneous. It is to M. Seebeck
that I am obliged for pointing out this curious circumstance.
In Poggendorff's *Annals*,* he gave an abstract of my letter to
Sir David Brewster, and compared my results with his own
numerous and accurate experiments, both on the polarizing
angles of Iceland spar and on the angles of deviation. He
found that my formula represented the former class of experiments as well as could be wished; but the theoretical
values of the deviations did not at all agree with his experimental measures. These measures of the deviation he published on this occasion; and, with their assistance, I traced
the error to its source, which was the relation among the pressures. The principle of *vis viva* was therefore introduced, instead
of that relation, and the theory became much simpler by the
change. I now obtained, for the deviation, a new expression,
which agreed with the experiments of M. Seebeck; but the
formula for the polarizing angle came out the very same as
before. This correction was made on the 6th of December,
and was published in the *Philosophical Magazine†* on the first
of the present month.

In the interval I have arrived at very elegant geometrical
laws, which can be easily remembered, and which embrace the
whole theory of crystalline reflexion. In enunciating these, it
will be convenient to draw our transversals always through the
same origin O, which we shall suppose to be the point of incidence, as this point is common to all the rays, whether incident,
reflected, or refracted; and we may imagine wave planes to be
drawn through the origin, parallel to the plane of each wave,
so that every transversal will lie in its own wave plane. The
incident and reflected wave planes will be perpendicular to the
incident and reflected rays, but the two refracted wave planes
will in general be oblique to their respective rays. In the latter
case, a right line drawn through the origin perpendicular to

* *Annalen der Physik und Chemie*, Vol. xxxviii. p. 276.

† *London and Edinburgh Philosophical Magazine*, Vol. x. p. 43.   (*Supra*, p. 84.)

the wave plane is called the wave normal. It is scarcely
necessary to remark, that all the four wave planes intersect
the surface of the crystal in the same right line which is perpendicular to the plane of incidence; and that the angles of
refraction are the angles which the refracted wave normals
make with a perpendicular to that surface. The index of
refraction is the ratio of the sine of the angle of incidence to
the sine of the angle of refraction, just as in ordinary media;
but here it is a variable ratio, and has different values for the
same angle of incidence. I have elsewhere* shown how to find
the refracted rays and waves when the incident ray is given.

As we suppose the ethereal molecules to vibrate parallel to
the transversals, we may take the lengths of the transversals
proportional to the magnitudes or amplitudes of the vibrations;
these lengths being always measured from the common origin
O. Then, in virtue of our fourth hypothesis, the transversals
will be compounded and resolved exactly by the same rules as
if they were forces acting at the point O.

We must now conceive a wave surface of the crystal, with
its centre at O, the point of incidence. As the velocities of rays which traverse the crystal in directions
parallel to the radii of its wave surface are represented by those radii, so let a concentric sphere be
described with a radius OS, which shall represent,
on the same scale, the constant velocity of light in
the medium external to the crystal. At any point
T on the wave surface apply a tangent plane, on
which let fall, from O, a perpendicular OG, meeting
the plane in G. On this perpendicular take the length
OP from towards G, so that OP shall be a third proportional
to OG and the constant line OS. Then, while the point T
describes the wave surface, the point P will describe another
surface reciprocal† to the wave surface. This other surface may

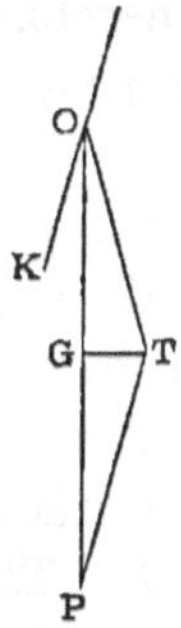

Fig. 17.

* Irish Academy *Transactions*, Vol. xvii. p. 252.

† For the general theory of reciprocal surfaces, *see* Irish Academy *Transactions*,
Vol. xvii. p. 241.

very properly be called the *index surface*,* because its radius
OP is the refractive index of the ray whose velocity is *OT*, or
rather of the wave *TG*, which belongs to that ray; for if we
conceive an incident wave, touching the sphere, to be refracted
into the wave *TG*, touching the wave surface in *T*, the sine
of the angle of incidence will be to the sine of the angle of
refraction as *OS* to *OG*, or as *OP* to *OS;* so that, taking the
constant *OS* for unity, the index of refraction will be represented by *OP*. The wave surface and the index surface will
thus be reciprocal to each other, every point *T* on the one
having a point *P* reciprocally corresponding to it on the other.

It is remarkable that the transversal of the ray *OT* is perpendicular to the plane *OPT*; for in the theory of Fresnel, as
I formerly proved,† the direction of the vibrations is the right
line *TG*; and as I suppose the transversal to be perpendicular
to the vibrations of that theory, and to be, at the same time, in
the wave plane, which is perpendicular to *OP*, it follows that
the transversal must be perpendicular to both the right lines
TG and *OP*, and therefore perpendicular to their plane *OPT*.
Therefore conceiving the transversal to be drawn through *O*
at right angles to the plane *OPT*, the plane of polarization
of the ray *OT* must needs pass through it. But there is
nothing else to fix the position of this last plane. We may
make it pass through the ray itself *OT*, as an ordinary media,
or we may draw it through the wave normal *OP* with Fresnel.
Or, instead of drawing it through either of these two sides of
the triangle *OPT*, we may make it parallel to the third side
PT. The last is what I should prefer, because the plane so
determined possesses important properties. I shall call it, however, the *polar plane*, because the name, plane of polarization, is
a long one; and the signification of the latter may, if any one

---

* This is the surface which I formerly called (*Trans.*, p. 252) the *surface of
refraction;* a name not sufficiently descriptive. Sir W. Hamilton has called it
the *surface of wave slowness*, and sometimes the *surface of components*. But the
name *index surface* seems to recommend itself, as both short and expressive.

† *Ibid.* Vol. xvi. p. 76. (*Supra*, p. 12.)

chooses, be kept distinct, though in an ordinary medium both terms must mean the same thing. The polar plane then of the ray *OT* is a plane passing through its transversal and parallel to the right line *PT*; so that if *OK* be drawn parallel to *PT*, the polar plane will pass through *OK*. In general, to find the transversals and the polar plane of any ray, we take the point where the ray meets *its own* nappe of the wave surface, and join it with the corresponding point on the index surface, drawing a plane through the origin and the joining line. Then a right line perpendicular to this plane at the origin will be the transversal, and a plane drawn through the transversal parallel to the joining line will be the polar plane.

Now let a polarized ray be incident at *O* upon the crystal. It will in general be divided into two rays. But each of these rays in turn may be made to disappear by polarizing the incident ray in a certain plane. Let us suppose then that there is only one refracted ray *OT*. In what direction must the incident ray be polarised, or, in other words, what must be the position of its transversal, in order that this may be the case? and what will be the corresponding transversal of the reflected ray? The answer is simple—*both transversals will lie in the polar plane of the refracted ray.* Let us pursue this remark a little.

The refracted ray *OT* being given, we can find its polar plane, and thence the intersections of this plane with the incident and reflected wave planes. These intersections will be the positions of the incident and reflected transversals when *OT* is the sole refracted ray. The refracted transversal lies also in the polar plane; and this transversal is, by our fourth hypothesis, the diagonal of a parallelogram, whose sides are the other two transversals, which determines the relative lengths of the three transversals, or the relative amplitudes of the vibrations. The intensities of the reflected and incident rays are, of course, proportional to the squares of their transversals. When the ray *OT* dissappears, we must take the polar plane of the other ray, and proceed as before.

Thus there are, in the incident wave plane, two transversal

directions which give only a single refracted ray. These, as well as the corresponding ones in the reflected wave plane, may be called *uniradial* transversals. They are the intersections of the two refracted polar planes with the incident and reflected wave planes.

When the incident transversal does not coincide with either of the uniradial directions, it is to be resolved parallel to them, and then each component transversal will supply a refracted ray, according to the foregoing rules. The reflected transversals, arising from the component incident ones, are to be found separately by the same rules, and then to be compounded.

In ordinary reflexion, if the incident transversal be in the plane of incidence, or perpendicular to it, the reflected transversal will be so likewise. But this does not hold in crystalline reflexion. The general method just given will, however, enable us to determine the positions and magnitudes of the reflected transversals in these two remarkable cases; and then, if we choose, we can reduce any other case to these two, by resolving the incident transversal in directions parallel and perpendicular to the plane of incidence.

If we conceive a pair of incident transversals, at right angles to each other, to revolve about the origin, it is evident that there will be a position in which the reflected transversals corresponding to them will also be at right angles to each other. There is no difficulty in finding this position, and there will be an advantage in using it when common unpolarized light is incident on the crystal. For, the incident transversals being rectangular, we may suppose the light to be equally divided between them, and then the intensities of the corresponding reflected portions can be found by the preceding rules. As the reflected transversals are also rectangular, the sum of these intensities will be the whole intensity of the reflected light, and their difference will be the intensity of the polarized part of it. This part will be polarized in a plane passing through the greater of the two reflected transversals.

Common light will be completely polarized by reflexion when

the two uniradial directions in the reflected wave plane coincide with each other; that is, when this plane and the two refracted polar planes have a common intersection. For then, if the incident light be polarized, it is manifest that the reflected transversal will lie in that intersection, whatever be the position of the incident transversal; and therefore if common light be incident, with its transversals in every possible direction, the reflected transversals will have but one direction. Thus the reflected light will be completely polarized in a plane passing through the above intersection.

Hence, as the reflected ray is perpendicular to its wave plane, it follows that, *at the polarizing angle of a crystal, the reflected ray is perpendicular to the intersection of the polar planes of the two refracted rays.* The reflected transversal, as we have seen, is this very intersection. This transversal is inclined, in general, to the plane of incidence, and we have had occassion to speak of its inclination under the name of the *deviation.* If we now suppose the double refraction to diminish until it disappears, the intersection of the polar planes will at last coincide* with the refracted ray. There will then be no deviation, and the reflected and refracted rays will be at right angles to each other, agreeably to the law of Brewster, which prevails at the polarizing angle of an ordinary medium.

There is a case in which the construction that we have given for determining the polar plane of a ray becomes useless. It is when the ray OT is a normal to the wave surface; for then OP coincides with OT, and we cannot fix the transversal by our construction. But it is precisely in such a case that the polar plane is most easily ascertained, for it is then nothing more than the plane of polarization of the common theory. For example, if we take the ordinary ray of a uniaxal crystal, its polar plane will pass through the ray itself and the axis of the crystal. Of course in an ordinary medium the polar plane and the plane of polarization are synonymous.

* For the polar planes will become two planes of polarization at right angles to each other.

It may not be amiss to apply our general rules to the case of ordinary reflexion and refraction. Suppose then a polarized ray to fall on the surface of an ordinary medium. Draw a plane through the incident transversal and the refracted ray; this will be the plane of polarization of the refracted ray, and it will intersect the reflected wave plane in the reflected transversal. The refracted transversal will be the diagonal of a parallelogram, whose sides are the other two transversals; hence we have the relative lengths of the transversals, and thus everything is determined.*

* This construction was mentioned at the meeting of the British Association in Dublin.—*See* the Reports of the Association, or *London and Edinburgh Phil. Mag.* vol. vii. p. 295. The following is an extract from the Paper which I read at that meeting :—

"The formulæ given by Fresnel for the same purpose will be found to agree exactly with this rule, in determining the positions of the planes of polarization ; and his expression for the amplitude of the reflected vibration is also in accordance with our construction. But the coincidence does not hold with regard to the *amplitude* of the refracted vibration, though the *vis viva* of the refracted ray is the same in both theories.

"Now it is very remarkable that if we alter the hypotheses of Fresnel where they are at variance with the preceding principles, we shall, from his own equations of condition, deduce formulæ agreeing in every respect, even as to the amplitude of the refracted wave, with the construction which we have accounted for in a different way (*i. e.* by using the relation among the pressures instead of the law of *vis viva*). The requisite alterations are two in number. First, the vibrations are to be supposed parallel to the plane of polarization, and not perpendicular to it, as Fresnel conceived ; and secondly, the density of the ether is to be considered the same in both media, from which it follows, that the corresponding ethereal masses, imagined by Fresnel, are to each other as the sine of twice the angle of incidence to the sine of twice the angle of refraction. Substituting in Fresnel's equations of condition this value of the ratio of the masses, we obtain the formulæ which I am inclined to regard as correct."

The equations spoken of in this extract are those which arise from the principle of *vis viva*, and from the equivalence of vibrations parallel to the separating surface of the two media. But it is worth while to observe, that when the vibrations are all in the same direction, that is, when the light is polarized perpendicular to the plane of incidence, the very same formulæ will come out from Young's remarkable analogy of the two elastic balls, one of which impinges directly on the other, supposed previously at rest, the masses of the balls being to each other in the ratio of the ethereal masses mentioned above. And, perhaps, this consideration affords the simplest possible explanation of Brewster's law relative to the pola-

The reason of this construction will be evident, if we consider that, in an ordinary medium, the polar plane is the same as the plane of polarization; and that, when there is only one refracted ray, the three transversals lie in the polar plane of that ray, according to the general remark with which we set out. We now proceed to show that the theorem asserted in this remark is a consequence of our hypotheses, and we shall afterwards deduce a few results which may be readily compared with experiments.

Let us suppose then that the direction of the incident trans-

rizing angle; for, as there is no reflected motion when the balls are equal, the whole velocity of impact being communicated to the ball that was at first quiescent, so there is no reflected vibration when the ethereal masses are equal; that is, when the sine of twice the angle of incidence is equal to the sine of twice the angle of refraction, or when the angles of incidence and refraction are together equal to a right angle. The whole of the incident vibration then passes into the refracted ray. In general, if ι_1, ι_2 denote the angles of incidence and refraction, the masses of the imaginary balls will be as $\sin 2\iota_1$, to $\sin 2\iota_2$; and, if the velocity of the original impact be taken for unity, the common theory of the collision of elastic bodies will give

$$\frac{\sin 2\iota_1 - \sin 2\iota_2}{\sin 2\iota_1 + \sin 2\iota_2} \quad \text{or} \quad \frac{\tan(\iota_1 - \iota_2)}{\tan(\iota_1 + \iota_2)}, \tag{I.}$$

for the velocity retained by the impinging ball after the impact; and

$$\frac{2\sin 2\iota_1}{\sin 2\iota_1 + \sin 2\iota_2} \quad \text{or} \quad \frac{\sin 2\iota_1}{\sin(\iota_1 + \iota_2)\cos(\iota_1 - \iota_2)}, \tag{II.}$$

for the velocity communicated to the other ball. These expressions (I.) and (II.), are the same as the values of τ_3 and τ_2, which we should deduce from equations (1) and (2), on the next page, by supposing τ_1 to be unity, and the angles θ_1, θ_2, θ_3 to be right angles. The general construction given in the text will lead to the same results, if we find from it the limiting ratios of the transversals, on the supposition that their directions approach each other indefinitely, and ultimately coincide in a right line perpendicular to the plane of incidence.

When the transversals are all in the plane of incidence, or when the light is polarized in that plane, the incident, the reflected, and the refracted transversals are to each other as $\sin(\iota_1 + \iota_2)$, $\sin(\iota_1 - \iota_2)$, and $\sin 2\iota_2$ respectively; because each transversal is proportional to the sine of the angle between the other two; and, in the present case, the angle between any two transversals is equal to the angle between the corresponding rays. Hence, taking the incident transversal for unity, the reflected transversal is

$$\frac{\sin(\iota_1 - \iota_2)}{\sin(\iota_1 + \iota_2)}; \tag{III.}$$

versal is such that there is only one refracted ray. It is evident that, in this case, the three transversals must lie in the same plane, since, by the fourth hypothesis, the refracted vibration is the resultant of the other two vibrations; and, therefore, we have only to prove that the plane of the transversals is the same as the polar plane of the refracted ray. Let τ_1, τ_2, τ_3 be the respective lengths of the incident, refracted, and reflected transversals; let θ_1, θ_2, θ_3 be the angles which they make with the plane of incidence, the angle θ_2 being known from the theory of Fresnel; put ι_1, ι_2, ι_3 for the angles made by the respective wave planes with the surface of the crystal, and m_1, m_2, m_3 for the relative quantities of ether set in motion by each wave. Then our hypotheses will give us the four following equations:—

$$m_1 \tau_1^2 = m_2 \tau_2^2 + m_3 \tau_3^2, \tag{1}$$

$$\tau_1 \sin \theta_1 + \tau_3 \sin \theta_3 = \tau_2 \sin \theta_2, \tag{2}$$

$$\tau_1 \cos \theta_1 \cos \iota_1 + \tau_3 \cos \theta_3 \cos \iota_3 = \tau_2 \cos \theta_2 \cos \iota_2, \tag{3}$$

$$\tau_1 \cos \theta_1 \sin \iota_1 + \tau_3 \cos \theta_3 \sin \iota_3 = \tau_2 \cos \theta_2 \sin \iota_2. \tag{4}$$

The first equation is manifestly the translation of the law of

and the refracted transversal is

$$\frac{\sin 2\iota_1}{\sin (\iota_1 + \iota\ )}. \tag{iv.}$$

It has been already observed that our theory differs from that of Fresnel with regard to the magnitude of the refracted transversals. The expressions (ii.) and (iv.) must, in fact, be multiplied each by $\dfrac{\sin \iota_2}{\sin \iota_1}$ in order to produce the corresponding expressions which result from Fresnel's hypotheses. But the two theories also differ as to the relative directions of the incident and reflected transversals. For, supposing the light to fall upon the denser medium, or ι_1 to be greater than ι_2, our construction indicates that these transversals, when the angle of incidence is small, point in the same direction; whereas Fresnel concludes the contrary to be the case. However, the disagreement in this respect ceases as we approach the limiting incidence of 90°; for then, according to both theories, the incident and reflected transversals point in opposite directions. This last conclusion is conformable to the inference which Professor Lloyd has drawn from his experiments on the interference of direct light with light reflected at a very oblique incidence.—See Irish Acad. *Transactions*, vol. xvii. p. 176.

the preservation of *vis viva ;* the other three are obtained from the principle of equivalent vibrations, by resolving the vibrations, or transversals, in three rectangular directions. In the second equation, the transversals are resolved perpendicular to the plane of incidence; in the fourth, perpendicular to the surface of the crystal; and in the third equation they are resolved parallel to the intersection of these two planes. When the angles θ_1, θ_2, θ_3 begin, the transversals are in the plane of incidence in such a relative position, that, if they were turned round together in that plane through a right angle, they would point each in the direction of its own wave's progress. These angles increase on the same side of the plane of incidence, and range through the whole circumference. The angles ι_1, ι_2, ι_3 are those of incidence, refraction, and reflexion; but, for the sake of symmetry, they are taken to be the angles which the wave normals, drawn from the origin in the direction of each wave's motion, make with the perpendicular to the surface, this perpendicular being directed towards the interior of the crystal. Thus it happens that ι_3 is the supplement of ι_1. Attending to this circumstance, equations (3) and (4) give us

$$\left.\begin{array}{l} \tau_1 \cos\theta_1 - \tau_3 \cos\theta_3 = \tau_2 \cos\theta_2 \dfrac{\cos \iota_2}{\cos \iota_1}, \\[2em] \tau_1 \cos\theta_1 + \tau_3 \cos\theta_3 = \tau_2 \cos{}_2 \dfrac{\sin \iota_2}{\sin \iota_1}; \end{array}\right\} \quad (5)$$

and, by adding and subtracting these, we find

$$\left.\begin{array}{l} \tau_1 = \tau_2 \dfrac{\cos\theta_2}{\cos\theta_1} \dfrac{\sin(\iota_1+\iota_2)}{\sin 2\iota_1}, \\[2em] \tau_3 = \tau_2 \dfrac{\cos\theta_2}{\cos\theta_3} \dfrac{\sin(\iota_2-\iota_1)}{\sin 2\iota_1}; \end{array}\right\} \quad (6)$$

which values if we substitute in equations (1) and (2), observing that $m_3 = m_1$, as is evident, we shall get

$$\frac{\sin^2(\iota_1+\iota_2)}{\cos^2\theta_1} - \frac{\sin^2(\iota_1-\iota_2)}{\cos^2\theta_3} = \frac{m_2}{m_1} \frac{\sin^2 2\iota_1}{\cos^2\theta_2}, \quad (7)$$

$$\sin(\iota_1 + \iota_2)\tan\theta_1 - \sin(\iota_1 - \iota_2)\tan\theta_3 = \sin 2\iota_1 \tan\theta_2. \qquad (8$$

Subtracting from (7) the identity

$$\sin^2(\iota_1 + \iota_2) - \sin^2(\iota_1 - \iota_2) = \sin 2\iota_1 \sin 2\iota_2,$$

there remains

$$\sin^2(\iota_1 + \iota_2)\tan^2\theta_1 - \sin^2(\iota_1 - \iota_2)\tan^2\theta_3$$
$$= \frac{\sin^2 2\iota_1}{\cos^2\theta_2}\left(\frac{m_2}{m_1} - \frac{\sin 2\iota_2}{\sin 2\iota_1}\cos^2\theta_2\right); \qquad (9)$$

and this, by making

$$\frac{m_2}{m_1} = \frac{\sin 2\iota_2 + 2h\sin^2\theta_2}{\sin 2\iota_1}, \qquad (10$$

becomes

$$\sin^2(\iota_1 + \iota_2)\tan^2\theta_1 - \sin^2(\iota_1 - \iota_2)\tan^2\theta_3 = \sin 2\iota_1(\sin 2\iota_2 + 2h)\tan^2\theta_2, \quad (11)$$

which is divisible by equation (8), the quotient being

$$\sin(\iota_1 + \iota_2)\tan\theta_1 + \sin(\iota_1 - \iota_2)\tan\theta_3 = (\sin 2\iota_2 + 2h)\tan\theta_2. \qquad (12)$$

Then, by adding and subtracting equations (8) and (12) we obtain

$$\left.\begin{aligned}
\tan\theta_1 &= \cos(\iota_1 - \iota_2)\tan\theta_2 + \frac{h\tan\theta_2}{\sin(\iota_1 + \iota_2)}, \\[2mm]
\tan\theta_3 &= -\cos(\iota_1 + \iota_2)\tan\theta_2 + \frac{h\tan\theta_2}{\sin(\iota_1 - \iota_2)}.
\end{aligned}\right\} \qquad (13)$$

These equations give the positions of the incident and reflected transversals when h is known.

Now let the directions in which the transversals have been resolved in equations (2), (3), (4), be taken for the axes of z, x, y respectively; so that, the origin being at O, the plane of xy may be the plane of incidence, and the axis of x may lie in the surface of the crystal. And, the reflected ray being conceived to lie within the angle made by the positive directions of x and y, let the initial condition that we have assumed for the angles θ_1, θ_2, θ_3 be satisfied by supposing that, when these angles begin, the transversals τ_1, τ_2 lie between the negative directions of x and y, and the transversal τ_3 between the directions of $+x$ and $-y$. Then if θ_1, θ_2, θ_3 be reckoned towards the positive axis of z, so that each angle may be 90° when the corresponding transversal points in the direction of z positive, the equations of the transversal τ_1 will be

$$\frac{z}{\tan \theta_1} = -\frac{x}{\cos \iota_1} = -\frac{y}{\sin \iota_1} \tag{14}$$

and those of τ_3 will be

$$\frac{z}{\tan \theta_3} = \frac{x}{\cos \iota_1} = -\frac{y}{\sin \iota_1}. \tag{15}$$

Let

$$z + Ax + By = 0 \tag{16}$$

be the equation of a plane passing through the directions of τ_1, τ_2 and τ_3. To determine A and B, let the variables be eliminated from this equation by means of (14) and (15) successively, and we shall get the two equations of condition,

$$\left.\begin{array}{l} \tan \theta_1 - A \cos \iota_1 - B \sin \iota_1 = 0, \\ \tan \theta_3 + A \cos \iota_1 - B \sin \iota_1 = 0; \end{array}\right\} \tag{17}$$

which, by addition and subtraction, give

$$\left.\begin{array}{l} B = \dfrac{\tan \theta_1 + \tan \theta_3}{2 \sin \iota_1}, \\[2ex] A = \dfrac{\tan \theta_1 - \tan \theta_3}{2 \cos \iota_1}; \end{array}\right\} \tag{18}$$

substituting, in these values, the expressions (13) for $\tan \theta_1$, $\tan \theta_3$, we have

$$\left.\begin{array}{l} B = \tan \theta_2 \left(\sin \iota_2 + \dfrac{h \cos \iota_2}{\sin^2 \iota_1 - \sin^2 \iota_2} \right), \\[3ex] A = \tan \theta_2 \left(\cos \iota_2 - \dfrac{h \sin \iota_2}{\sin^2 \iota_1 - \sin^2 \iota_2} \right); \end{array}\right\} \tag{19}$$

whence, by making

$$\tan \kappa = \frac{h}{\sin^2 \iota_1 - \sin^2 \iota_2}, \tag{20}$$

we find

$$\frac{B}{A} = \frac{\tan \iota_2 + \tan \kappa}{1 - \tan \iota_2 \tan \kappa} = \tan(\iota_2 + \kappa). \qquad (21)$$

But if $z = 0$ in (16), we have

$$Ax + By = 0, \qquad (22)$$

for the equation of the right line in which the plane of the transversals intersects the plane of incidence. This right line, lying, like the refracted wave normal, between the directions of $+x$ and $-y$, makes with the direction of $-y$ an angle v which obviously has $\dfrac{B}{A}$ for its tangent; and therefore, by (21),

$$v = \iota_2 + \kappa; \qquad (23)$$

which shows that the intersection of the two planes is inclined to the refracted wave normal at an angle equal to κ.

We must now find the value of h, which depends on the relative ethereal masses put in motion by the incident and refracted waves. Conceiving the incident and refracted rays to be cylindrical pencils, having of course a common section in the plane of xz, which is the surface of the crystal, let each pencil be cut by a pair of planes parallel to its wave plane, and distant a wave's length from each other; then the cylindrical volumes so cut out will represent the corresponding masses, since, by our second hypothesis, the densities are equal. These volumes are to each other in the compound ratio of their altitudes, which are the wave lengths, and of the areas of their bases. The altitudes are evidently as $\sin \iota_1$ to $\sin \iota_2$. The first base is a perpendicular section of the incident pencil; the second base an oblique section of the refracted one, the obliquity being equal to the angle ε at which the wave normal is inclined to the ray. The perpendicular sections are to each other as the cosines of the angles which they make with the common section of the cylinders, or as $\cos \iota_1$ to $\cos \iota_{(2)}$; putting $\iota_{(2)}$ for the angle which the refracted ray makes with the negative direction of y. The second base is greater than the perpendicular section of the refracted pencil in the proportion of unity to $\cos \epsilon$. Therefore, compounding all these ratios, we find

$$\frac{m_2}{m_1} = \frac{\sin \iota_2 \cos \iota_{(2)}}{\sin \iota_1 \cos \iota_1 \cos \epsilon}. \tag{24}$$

The same result may be otherwise obtained by observing that, in a system of waves, the corresponding masses are proportional to the ordinates y of the points where the rays meet their wave surfaces. By a system of waves, I mean an incident wave with all that are derived from it by reflexion or refraction at the same surface of the crystal, or at parallel surfaces. If, at the point where the incident ray intersects its spherical wave surface, we apply a tangent plane intersecting the plane of xz in a right line parallel to z, through which right line other planes are drawn touching the wave surface of the crystal in four points, these tangent planes will be the waves derived from the incident wave which touches the sphere ; and the points of contact, including that on the sphere, will be the points where the rays meet the wave surfaces. Then the corresponding masses will be represented by prisms having a common rectangular base in the plane xz, one side of this rectangle being the distance, on the axis of x, between the origin and the common intersection of the tangent planes; and the triangular face of each prism having the same distance for one side, and a point of contact for the opposite angle. These prisms, as they have a common base, will be proportional to their altitudes, which are the ordinates y of the points of contact, The expression (24) may be easily deduced from this relation.

Let OT, OP, and the negative direction of y meet the surface of the wave sphere (described with the radius OS) in the points $T_{,}$, $P_{,}$, $Y_{,}$; and let the right line, in which the plane of the transversals intersects the plane of incidence, meet the sphere in $L_{,}$. Then the points $Y_{,}$, $P_{,}$, $L_{,}$,

Fig. 18.

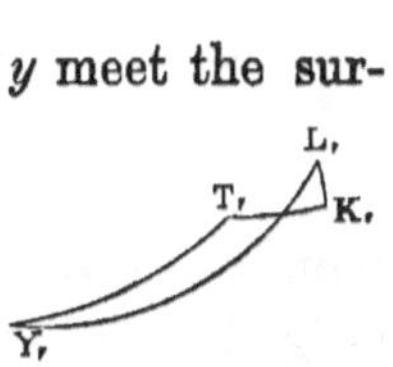

being all in the plane of incidence, will be on the same great circle $Y_{,}P_{,}L_{,}$; and drawing the great circles $T_{,}P_{,}$, $Y_{,}T_{,}$, we shall have $Y_,P_, = \iota_2,\ Y_,T_, = {}_{(\iota_2)}\ T_,P_, = \epsilon,\ Y_,L_, = v = \iota_2 + \kappa,$ by (23); whence $P_,L_, = \kappa.$

As the transversal τ_2 is perpendicular to the plane OTP, or to the plane of the great circle $T_,P_,$, the cosine of the spherical angle $T_,P_,Y_,$ is the sine of θ_2; and therefore, from the triangle $T_,P_,Y_,$, we have

$$\cos \iota_{(2)} = \cos \iota_2 \cos \epsilon + \sin \iota_2 \sin \epsilon \sin \theta_2, \tag{25}$$

which being substituted in (24), gives

$$\frac{m_2}{m_1} = \frac{\sin 2\iota_2 + 2 \sin^2 \iota_2 \sin \theta_2 \tan \epsilon}{\sin 2\iota_1}; \tag{26}$$

and comparing this result with (10), we find

$$h = \frac{\sin^2 \iota_2 \tan \epsilon}{\sin \theta_2}; \tag{27}$$

whence, and from (20), it follows that

$$\tan \kappa = \frac{\sin^2 \iota_2 \tan \epsilon}{(\sin^2 \iota_1 - \sin^2 \iota_2) \sin \theta_2}. \tag{28}$$

Draw the great circle $L_,K_,$ at right angles to $T_,P_,$, and meeting it in $K_,$; then the plane of $L_,K_,$ will be the plane of the transversals, since the latter plane passes through $L_,$, and is perpendicular to $T_,P_,$. But the tangent of $P_,K_,$ is equal to the tangent of $P_,L_,$ multiplied by the cosine of the angle $P_,$ or by the sine of θ_2; therefore, denoting $P_,K_,$ by ϵ_1, and recollecting that $P_,L_, = \kappa$, we find, by (28),

$$\frac{\tan \epsilon_1}{\tan \epsilon} = \frac{\sin^2 \iota_2}{\sin^2 \iota_1 - \sin^2 \iota_2}. \tag{29}$$

Now we have seen that the ratio of OP to OS, or OS to OG (Fig. 17), is the index of refraction; so that $\sin^2 \iota_1$ is to $\sin^2 \iota_2$ as OP to OG. Therefore, by (29),

$$\frac{\tan \epsilon_1}{\tan \epsilon} = \frac{OG}{OP - OG} = \frac{OG}{GP}; \tag{30}$$

but OG is to GP as the tangent of the angle GPT is to the tangent of the angle GOT; and since ϵ is the angle GOT, it follows that ϵ_1 is equal to the angle GPT or KOP. Consequently, OK will meet the surface of the sphere in the point $K_{,}$. Thus we have proved our assertion, that, *when there is only one refracted ray, the plane of the transversals is the polar plane of that ray.*

The sign of the quantity h is always the same as that of the cosine of the spherical angle $T_{,}P_{,}Y_{,}$. But to remove all ambiguity respecting signs, we must make a few additional conventions. Supposing, as we have hitherto done, that the refracted light moves from O to T, and conceiving a right line to be drawn from the origin parallel to GT, and directed from G towards T, let the angle ϑ_2, which this right line makes with the plane of incidence, be reckoned, like θ_1, θ_2, from an initial position comprised between the negative directions of x and y ; and let ϑ_2, like the angles θ_1, θ_2, θ_3, increase on the side of z positive, and range from $0°$ to $360°$. Then ϑ_2 will always be equal either to the angle $P_{,}$ of the spherical triangle $T_{,}P_{,}Y_{,}$, or to the reentrant angle, which is the difference between $P_{,}$ and $360°$. In either case, the cosine of ϑ_2 will be the same, both in magnitude and sign, as the cosine of the angle $T_{,}P_{,}Y_{,}$. Consequently, if, instead of (25), we use the direct trigonometrical formula

$$\cos \iota_{(2)} = \cos \iota_2 \cos \epsilon + \sin \iota_2 \sin \epsilon \cos \vartheta_2, \tag{31}$$

we shall find

$$h = \frac{\sin^2 \iota_2 \tan \epsilon \cos \vartheta_2}{\sin^2 \theta_2} ; \tag{32}$$

showing that the sign h is always the same as the sign of $\cos \vartheta_2$. Now as θ_2 differs from ϑ_2 by a right angle, we will suppose

$$\theta_2 = \vartheta_2 + 90°, \tag{33}$$

and then we shall have $\sin \theta_2 = \cos \vartheta_2$, algebraically as well as numerically. Thus we see that, by adopting these conventions, the value of h in (27) will have the proper sign. Therefore, substituting this value of h in formulæ (13), we obtain

$$\tan \theta_1 = \cos\left(\iota_1 - \iota_2\right)\tan \theta_2 + \frac{\sin^2 \iota_2 \tan \epsilon}{\cos \theta_2 \sin\left(\iota_1 + \iota_2\right)},$$

$$\tan \theta_3 = -\cos\left(\iota_1 + \iota_2\right)\tan \theta_2 + \frac{\sin^2 \iota_1 \tan \epsilon}{\cos \theta_2 \sin\left(\iota_1 - \iota_2\right)}. \qquad (34)$$

These formulæ give the uniradial directions, or the positions of the incident and reflected transversals, when the sole refracted ray is that with which we have been occupied. The like directions, when the other ray exists alone, will be given by the formulæ

$$\tan \theta'_1 = \cos\left(\iota_1 - \iota'_2\right)\tan \theta'_2 + \frac{\sin^2 \iota'_2 \tan \epsilon'}{\cos \theta'_2 \sin\left(\iota_1 + \iota'_2\right)},$$

$$\tan \theta' = -\cos\left(\iota_1 + \iota'_2\right)\tan \theta'_2 + \frac{\sin^2 \iota'_2 \tan \epsilon'}{\cos \theta'_2 \sin\left(\iota_1 - \iota'_2\right)}; \qquad (35)$$

where all the quantities, except ι_1, which remains the same, are marked with accents, to show that they belong to the second refracted ray.

The uniradial directions having been found by these equations, the relative magnitudes of the uniradial transversals are determined by equations (6). When the incident transversal is not uniradial, it is evident, as we said before, that it may be resolved* in the two uniradial directions; that each component

---

* That, if an incident transversal be resolved in any two directions, the reflected and refracted transversals arising from it will be the resultants of those which would arise from each of its components separately, is a principle which appears very evident, insomuch that we can hardly suppose it to be untrue, without doing violence to our physical conceptions. Nevertheless, it is necessary to prove that this principle is not contrary to the law of *vis viva ;* for though the *vis viva* may be preserved by each set of components (as it is when these are uniradial), yet we cannot *therefore* conclude that it will be preserved by their resultants. Here then is a test of the consistency of our theory; for we are bound to show that the law of *vis viva* is not infringed by the adoption of the principle in question. Now it is easy to see that, whatever be the two directions in which the incident transversal is resolved, the final results will always be the same ; because, taking the component in each of these directions separately, the reflected and refracted transversals belonging to it must be obtained, in the first place, by the help of a resolution per-

transversal, as if the other component did not exist, will furnish a refracted ray and a partial reflected transversal uniradial in its direction; and that the total (or actual) reflected transversal will be the resultant of the two partial ones.

When $\theta_3 = \theta'_3$, the partial reflected transversals will coincide, and their resultant will have a fixed direction, independent of the direction of the incident transversal. The angle of incidence at which this takes place is the polarizing angle, and the common value of θ_3 and θ'_3 is the *deviation*. If, at the polarizing angle, the partial reflected transversals be equal in magnitude, and opposite in direction, their resultant will vanish, and the reflected ray will disappear. This will happen when the incident transversal is in the plane of the two refracted transversals, and therefore in the intersection of this plane with the incident wave plane; for, when there is no reflected ray, the incident transversal alone must be equivalent to the two refracted transversals.

Since the reflected transversal can be made to vanish at the polarizing angle, this angle might be found directly by putting the *vis viva* of the incident ray equal to the sum of the *vires vivæ* of the two refracted rays, and by making the incident transversal the resultant of the two refracted transversals. Resolving the transversals parallel to the axes of co-ordinates, these conditions would give four equations, from which we could

formed in the uniradial directions. We need not, therefore, consider any case but that in which the resolution is uniradial throughout.

The incident transversal being denoted by T_1, let T_3 be the reflected transversal determined by the rules given in the text; and let the uniradial components of the former be τ_1, τ'_1, while those of the latter are τ_3, τ'_3. Then will

$$T_1^2 = \tau_1^2 + \tau'^2_1 + 2\tau_1\tau'_1 \cos(\theta_1 - \theta'_1),$$

$$T_3^2 = \tau_3^2 + \tau'^2_3 + 2\tau_3\tau'_3 \cos(\theta_3 - \theta'_3) ;$$

where the signification of θ_1, θ'_1, θ_3, θ'_3 is the same as in the text. The *vis viva* of one refracted ray is $m_1(\tau_1^2 - \tau_3^2)$, and that of the other is $m_1(\tau'^2_1 - \tau'^2_3)$; therefore the *vis viva* of both refracted rays is

$$m_1(\tau_1^2 + \tau'^2_1 - \tau_3^2 - \tau'^2_3),$$

eliminate the two ratios of the three transversals, together with
the angle at which the incident transversal is inclined to the
plane of incidence. In the equation produced by this elimina-
tion, the angle of incidence would be the polarizing angle, and
the other quantities would be known functions of that angle ;
whence the angle itself would be known.

a quantity which ought to be equal to

$$m_1 \left(T_1^2 - T_3^2 \right) \; ;$$

and consequently the equation

$$\tau_1 \tau'_1 \cos (\theta_1 - \theta'_1) = \tau_3 \tau'_3 \cos (\theta_3 - \theta'_3) \tag{v.}$$

ought to be true, This equation, by help of the expressions (6) for τ_1, τ_3, and the
like expressions for τ'_1, τ'_3, becomes

$$\sin (\iota_1 + \iota_2) \sin (\iota_1 + \iota'_2) (1 + \tan \theta_1 \tan \theta'_1)$$

$$= \sin (\iota_1 - \iota_2) \sin (\iota_1 - \iota'_2) (1 + \tan \theta_3 \tan \theta'_3) ; \tag{vi.}$$

which again, by substituting the values (13) and the other similar values, is
changed into

$$\sin (\iota_2 + \iota'_2) \left\{ \cos (\iota_2 - \iota'_2) + \cotan \theta_2 \cotan \theta'_2 \right\} + h + h' = 0, \tag{vii.}$$

where h' denotes for one refracted ray what h denotes for the other, the value of h
being given by formula (27), and that of h' by the same formula with accented
letters. The angle of incidence, we may observe, has disappeared from the
equation.

If, therefore, the laws of reflexion, which we have endeavoured to establish, are
consistent with each other, this last equation must be satisfied by means of the relations which the laws of propagation afford; or rather, the equation must express a
property of the wave surface of the crystal, however strange it may be thought that
such a property should be derived from the laws of reflexion—laws which would
seem, at first sight, to have no connexion at all with the form of the wave surface.
Now I have found that the equation (vii.) really does express a *rigorous* property of the biaxal wave surface of Fresnel; a very curious fact, which not only
shows that the laws of reflexion and the laws of propagation are perfectly adapted
to each other, but also indicates that both sets of laws have a common source in
other and more intimate laws not yet discovered.   Indeed the laws of reflexion are
not independent even among themselves; for the expressions (iii.) and (iv.) in the
note on ordinary reflexion (page 101) have been deduced solely from the principle of
equivalent vibrations, and yet they satisfy the law of *vis viva*. Perhaps the next step
in physical optics will lead us to those higher and more elementary principles by
which the laws of reflexion and the laws of propagation are linked together as parts
of the same system.

It deserves to be remarked, that, at any angle of incidence, if the incident and reflected wave planes be intersected by a plane drawn through the two refracted transversals, the intersections will be corresponding transversal directions; that is to say, if the incident transversal coincide with one intersection, the reflected transversal will coincide with the other. For it is evident, from our fourth hypothesis, that if three of the transversals be in one plane, the fourth transversal must be in the same plane.

We come now to apply our theory to the case of uniaxal crystals; and, in doing so, we shall take the crystal to be of the *negative* kind, like Iceland spar, so that the ordinary refraction will be more powerful than the extraordinary. On the sphere described with the centre O and radius OS, let XY be a great circle in the plane of incidence, the radii OX, OY being the positive directions of the co-ordinate axes of x and y. Suppose the right lines iO and Oi'', intersecting the sphere in i and i', to be the incident and reflected rays; let the ordinary refracted ray and the extraordinary wave normal be produced backwards from O to meet the sphere, at the side of the incident light, in the points o and e respectively; let the right line OA, cutting the sphere in A, be the direction of the axis of the crystal; and draw the great circles Ao, Ae, AY. The points i, e, o, i' are all on the circle XY. The point E, where the extraordinary ray OE produced backwards meets the sphere, will be on the circle Ae; and if, as in the figure, the arc Ae be less than a quadrant, the point e will lie between A and E. The polar plane of the ordinary ray is obviously the plane of the circle Ao; but the polar plane of the other ray must be found by a construction. On the arc AeE

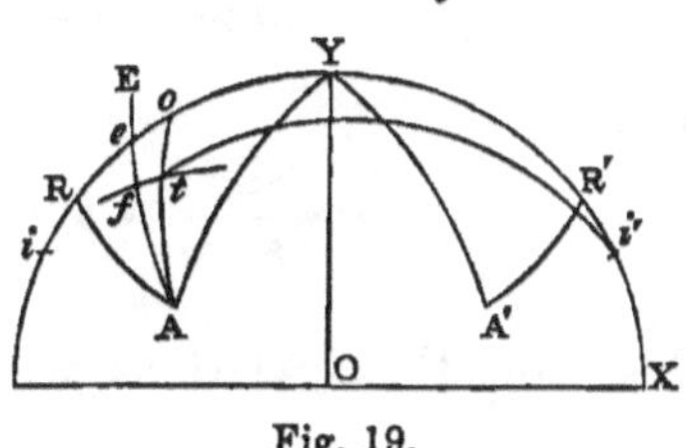

Fig. 19.

take the portion ef, so that the point e may lie between the points E and f, and so that the tangent of ef may be to the tangent of Ee as the square of the sine of the arc eY is to the difference between the squares of the sines of iY and eY. Through f draw the great circle ft perpendicular to the circle AeE; and it is manifest from (29) that the plane of ft is the polar plane of the extraordinary ray. On each circumference Ao and ft, the points which are distant 90° from i and i'', the distances being measured by arcs of great circles, are the points where the uniradial transversals, prolonged from the centre, intersect the sphere. Let Ao and ft intersect each other in t, and let ti'' be an arc of a great circle connecting the point t with the point i''. When the connecting arc ti'' is a quadrant, the two uniradial transversals, belonging to the reflected ray, coincide with each other and with the right line Ot; the angle of incidence is then the polarizing angle; the plane of ti'' is the plane of polarization of the reflected ray; and the angle $ti''Y$ is the deviation.

To find the equations appropriate to uniaxal crystals, we may suppose formulæ (34) to belong to the ordinary, and formulæ (35) to the extraordinary ray. Then will $\epsilon = 0$, and $\epsilon' =$ the arc Ee. Putting θ and θ' for the spherical angles Aoi and Aei, we shall easily see that $\theta_2 = \theta + 180°$, and $\theta'_2 = \theta' + 90°$, if we conceive the point A and the positive axis of z to be both on the upper side of the plane XOY. And if ω' denote the arc Ae, while b and a respectively express the reciprocals of the principal indices, ordinary and extraordinary, the law of Huyghens, for the double refraction of uniaxal crystals, will give us

$$\tan \epsilon' = \frac{a^2 - b^2}{s^2} \sin \omega' \cos \omega', \qquad (36)$$

where

$$s^2 = \frac{\sin^2 \iota'_2}{\sin^2 \iota_1} = b^2 + (a^2 - b^2) \sin^2 \omega'. \qquad (37)$$

Observing these relations, we have, from (34),

$$\begin{aligned} \tan \theta_1 &= \cos (\iota_1 - \iota_2) \tan \theta, \\ \tan \theta_3 &= -\cos (\iota_1 + \iota_2) \tan \theta, \end{aligned} \right\} \qquad (38)$$

for the ordinary ray; and from (35) we get

$$\left.\begin{aligned}
\tan \theta'_1 &= -\cos(\iota_1 - \iota'_2)\cotan\theta' - (a^2-b^2)\frac{\sin\omega'\cos\omega'\sin^2\iota_1}{\sin\theta'\sin(\iota_1+\iota'_2)}, \\[2mm]
\tan \theta'_3 &= \cos(\iota_1 + \iota'_2)\cotan\theta' - (a^2-b^2)\frac{\sin\omega'\cos\omega'\sin^2\iota_1}{\sin\theta'\sin(\iota_1-\iota'_2)},
\end{aligned}\right\} \quad (39)$$

for the extraordinary ray.

The four preceding equations determine the uniradial directions; and the following equation,

$$\cos(\iota_1+\iota_2)\tan\theta + \cos(\iota_1+\iota'_2)\cotan\theta' - (a^2-b^2)\frac{\sin\omega'\cos\omega'\sin^2\iota}{\sin\theta'\sin(\iota_1-\iota'_2)} = O, \quad (40)$$

obtained by putting $\tan\theta_3 = \tan\theta'_3$, is that which determines the polarizing angle.

In making use of this last equation to deduce the law of the polarizing angles in various positions of the axis of the crystal, we shall confine ourselves to the case in which the reflexion from the crystal takes place *in air*, because the angle $\iota_1 - \iota'_2$ will then be considerable, and the quantities $\cos(\iota_1 + \iota_2)$ and $\cos(\iota_1 + \iota'_2)$ will be small, so that it will be easy to arrive at approximate results. For we shall have, in the first place,

$$\cos(\iota_1 + \iota'_2) = \cos(\iota_1 + \iota_2) - (\iota'_2 - \iota_2), \quad (41)$$

nearly, since $\iota_1 + \iota_2$ will not differ much from a right angle; and because

$$\sin\iota_2 = b\sin\iota_1, \quad \sin\iota'_2 = s\sin\iota_1, \quad (42)$$

we shall also have, rigorously,

$$\sin^2\iota'_2 - \sin^2\iota_2 = (s^2-b^2)\sin^2\iota_1 = (a^2-b^2)\sin^2\omega'\sin^2\iota_1, \quad (43)$$

or

$$\sin(\iota'_2 - \iota_2) = (a^2-b^2)\frac{\sin^2\omega'\sin^2\iota_1}{\sin(\iota'_2+\iota_2)}, \quad (44)$$

which may be written

$$\iota'_2 - \iota_2 = (a^2-b^2)\frac{\sin^2\omega'\sin^2\iota_1}{\sin 2\iota_2}, \quad (45)$$

with sufficient accuracy. This value of $\iota'_2 - \iota_2$ having been substituted in (41), the resulting expression for $\cos(\iota_1 + \iota'_2)$ must be substituted in equation (40), which will then become

$$\cos (\iota_1 + \iota_2)(\tan \theta + \cotan \theta) - (a^2 - b^2) \sin^2 \iota_1 \sin \omega \left(\frac{\sin \omega \cotan \theta}{\sin 2\iota_2} \right.$$

$$\left. + \frac{\cos \omega}{\sin \theta \cos 2\iota_2} \right) = 0, \tag{46}$$

if, denoting the arc Ao by ω, we confound ω' with ω, θ' with θ, and write $\cos 2\iota_2$ instead of $\sin (\iota_1 - \iota'_2)$. Multiplying all the terms of (46) by $\sin \theta \cos \theta$, we find

$$\cos (\iota_1 + \iota_2) = (a^2 - b^2) \sin^2 \iota_1 \sin \omega \cos \theta \left(\frac{\sin \omega \cos \theta}{\sin 2\iota_2} + \frac{\cos \omega}{\cos 2\iota_2} \right). \tag{47}$$

From A draw the arc AR meeting the arc iY at right angles in the point R, and put $RY = p$, $AR = q$. Then by means of the values

$$\cos \omega = \cos q \cos (p - \iota_2),$$
$$\sin \omega \cos \theta = \cos q \sin (p - \iota_2), \qquad \left. \right\} \tag{48}$$

afforded by the right-angled triangle ARo, the equation (47) will take the form

$$\cos (\iota + \iota_2) = \frac{(a^2 - b^2) \sin^2 \iota_1}{\sin 2\iota_2 \cos 2\iota_2} \cos^2 q \sin (p - \iota_2) \sin (p + \iota_2), \tag{49}$$

or

$$\cos (\iota + \iota_2) = K \cos^2 q \ (\sin^2 p - \sin^2 \iota_2), \tag{50}$$

where

$$K = \frac{(a^2 - b^2) (1 + b^2)}{2b (1 - b^2)} ; \tag{51}$$

this value of K being found by assuming $\tan \iota_2 = \cotan \iota_1 = b$, which is accurate enough for the purpose.

Thus we have obtained $\iota_1 + \iota_2$, or the sum of the polarizing angle and the angle of ordinary refraction. The former angle itself may be inferred from formula (50) by help of the relation $\sin \iota_2 = b \sin \iota_1$. In this way, if we use ϖ_1 instead of ι_1 to distinguish the polarizing angle from other angles of incidence, and if we put

$$k = \frac{K}{1 + b^2} = \frac{a^2 - b^2}{2b(1 - b^2)}, \tag{52}$$

we shall find

$$\varpi_1 = \varpi - k \cos^2 q \,(\sin^2 p - \sin^2 \iota_2), \tag{53}$$

in which ϖ is the angle whose cotangent is equal to b; in other words, ϖ is the polarizing angle of an ordinary medium whose refractive index is equal to the ordinary index of the crystal.

This result accounts for a remarkable fact observed by Sir David Brewster, who, in the year 1819, led the way in the experimental investigation of the laws of crystalline reflexion. He found that the polarizing angle remains the same when the crystal is turned round through 180°, though one of the angles of refraction is changed, and though the situation of the refracted rays, with respect to the axis of the crystal, becomes quite different from what it was. This circumstance, which surprised me when I first met with it, is an immediate consequence of formula (53); for the effect of a semi-revolution of the crystal is to change the signs of p and q; but the nature of the formula is such that these changes of sign do not alter the value of ϖ_1. Neither is that value altered by turning the crystal until the azimuth, as the spherical angle AYi is usually called, is changed into its supplement; for then the sign of p alone is affected.

Another remark, made by the same distinguished observer, is also a consequence of formula (53). From his experiments it appears that, on a given surface of the crystal, the polarizing angle differs from a constant angle by a quantity proportional to the square of the sine of the azimuth AYi. Now, calling this azimuth a, and putting λ for the acute angle at which the axis of the crystal is inclined to its surface, so that λ may be the complement of the arc AY, we have

$$\sin q = \cos \lambda \sin a, \qquad \tan p = \cotan \lambda \cos a ; \tag{54}$$

and by making these substitutions in formula (53), after having changed $\sin \iota_2$ into $\cos \varpi$, that formula becomes

$$\varpi_1 = \varpi - k \,(\sin^2 \varpi - \sin^2 \lambda) + k \sin^2 \varpi \cos^2 \lambda \sin^2 a, \tag{55}$$

which agrees with the remark of Brewster.

The deviation θ_3 or θ'_3 is found from the second of equations (38), by putting $\dfrac{\tan q}{\sin (p - \iota_2)}$ for $\tan \theta$, and by substituting for $\cos (\iota_1 + \iota_2)$ the value (49) or (50) which it has at the polarizing angle. The result is

$$\theta_3 = \theta'_3 = - \frac{K}{2} \sin 2q \sin (p + \iota_2), \qquad (56)$$

since the small arc θ_3 may be taken for its tangent. This result is easily transformed into

$$\theta_3 = \theta'_3 = - K \sin q \cos \phi, \qquad (57)$$

where ϕ denotes the arc Ai, or the angle which the incident ray makes with the axis of the crystal; and this last expression is equivalent to the following,

$$\theta_3 = \theta'_3 = - K \cos \lambda \sin a (\sin \lambda \cos \varpi + \cos \lambda \sin \varpi \cos a), \qquad (58)$$

which gives the deviation in terms of λ and a.

As an example of the application of our formulæ, we shall make some computations relative to Iceland spar. According to M. Rudberg, the ordinary index of that crystal, for a ray situated in the brightest part of the spectrum, at the boundary of the orange and yellow, is 1·66; and the least extraordinary index for the same ray is 1·487. Dividing unity by each of these numbers, we get $a = ·6725$, $b = ·6024$; whence $\varpi = 58° 56'$; $k = ·1164 = 6° 40'$; $K = ·1587 = 9° 5'$. Having thus determined the constants, we can readily calculate the polarizing angle and the deviation, for any given values of λ and a.

First, let us see how the polarizing angle varies on different faces of the crystal.

1. When $\lambda = 90°$, the face of the crystal is perpendicular to its axis, and ϖ_1 is independent of a. In this case the formula (55) gives

$$\varpi_1 = \varpi + k \cos^2 \varpi = 60° 42',$$

which is the maximun value of the polarizing angle.

2. When $\lambda = 0$, the axis lies in the face of the crystal, and formula (55) becomes

$$\varpi_1 = \varpi - k \sin^2 \varpi \cos^2 a,$$

showing that $\varpi_1 = \varpi$, when a is either 90° or 270°. But when a is 0 or 180°, we have

$$\varpi_1 = \varpi - k \sin^2 \varpi = 54° \, 2',$$

which is the minimum value of the polarizing angle.

3. For the natural fracture-faces of the crystal the value of λ is 45° 23'. Hence, when $a = 0$ or 180°,

$$\varpi_1 = \varpi - k \, (\sin^2 \varpi - \sin^2 \lambda) = 57° \, 26';$$

and when $a = 90°$ or 270°,

$$\varpi_1 = \varpi + k \cos^2 \varpi \sin^2 \lambda = 59° \, 50'.$$

These values of the polarizing angles agree very well with the experiments of Sir David Brewster, and still better with those of M. Seebeck.

If we wish to know in what azimuths ϖ_1 is equal to ϖ, on a given surface of the crystal, it is obvious from (55) that we must make

$$\sin^2 \varpi - \sin^2 \lambda = \sin^2 \varpi \cos^2 \lambda \sin^2 a,$$

whence we have, simply,

$$\cos a = \pm \frac{\tan \lambda}{\tan \varpi}, \tag{59}$$

which shows that the thing is impossible when λ is greater than ϖ; and that, when λ is less than ϖ, there are four such azimuths; as indeed there are, generally speaking, four values of a corresponding to any other particular value of the polarizing angle. If a' be the least of these azimuths, the others will be $180° - a'$, $180° + a'$, and $360° - a'$. On a natural face of the crystal, the value of a', answering to the supposition $\varpi_1 = \varpi$, is found to be 52° 22'.

Next, let us trace the changes which the deviation undergoes in some remarkable cases.

1. When the face of the crystal is perpendicular to its axis there is evidently no deviation.

2. When the axis lies in the face of the crystal the deviation vanishes in the azimuths 0, 90°, 180°, 270°. In the intermediate azimuths, differing 45° from each of these, the deviation is a maximum; for if we put $\lambda = 0$ in formula (55) the result will be

$$\theta_3 = -\frac{K}{2} \sin \varpi \sin 2a \, ;$$

and this quantity (neglecting its sign) is a maximum when $\sin 2a = \pm 1$. The coefficient of $\sin 2a$ is equal to 3° 54′, which is consequently the greatest value of the deviation. According to the experiments of M. Seebeck, the value is 3° 57′.

3. On the fracture-faces of the crystal the deviation vanishes in the azimuths 0 and 180°, as also in two other azimuths for which

$$\cos a = -\frac{\tan \lambda}{\tan \varpi},$$

and in which, therefore, ϖ_1 is equal to ϖ. In the azimuth 45° the deviation is $-3° 35′$; in the azimuth 90° it is $-2° 32′$; and in the azimuth 127° 38′ it vanishes; after which it attains a small maximum with a positive sign, and vanishes again in azimuth 180°. The calculated values of the deviation agree pretty well with the values observed by M. Seebeck.

The sign of the deviation shows at what side of the plane of incidence the plane of polarization lies. But the position of the latter plane is best indicated by that of the transversal of the reflected ray. If this transversal and the axis of the crystal be produced from the origin, towards the same side of the plane of xz, until they intersect the sphere in the points t and A respectively, these points will be on the same side of the great circle XY when the deviation and the sine of the azimuth have unlike algebraic signs; and they will be on opposite sides of that circle when those quantities have like signs. Therefore if the crystal be supposed to revolve in its own plane, beginning at the azimuth 0, the points t and A will lie on the same side of XY until A reaches the position A', where the angle $A'Yi$ is equal to $127°\ 38'$; the point t will then pass over to the side opposite A, at which side it will remain until A arrives at the azimuth $232°\ 22'$. Thenceforward, to the end of the revolution, both points will be found on the same side of the circle XY.

We have seen that the deviation always vanishes when the axis of the crystal lies in the plane of incidence. The reason is, because the crystal is then symmetrical on opposite sides of that plane. In this case the problem of reflexion offers peculiar facilities for solution, since the uniradial directions are obviously parallel and perpendicular to the plane of incidence. Let us, therefore, consider the case at length.

1. In the first place, when the only refracted ray is the ordinary one, the three transversals are in the plane of incidence, and the transversal of each ray is proportional to the sine of the angle between the other two rays. Hence the proportions are

$$\frac{\tau_1}{\sin(\iota_1+\iota_2)} = \frac{\tau_2}{\sin 2\iota_1} = \frac{\tau_3}{\sin(\iota_1-\iota_2)}, \tag{60}$$

the same as in ordinary media.

2. In the second place, when the sole refracted ray is the extraordinary one, the three transversals are perpendicular to the plane of incidence; and, if we use accents to mark the quantities connected with this ray, we have the equations

$$\left.\begin{aligned} \tau'_1+\tau'_3 &= \tau'_2, \\ m_1\tau'^2_1 &= m'_2\tau'^2_2 + m_1\tau'^2_3, \end{aligned}\right\} \tag{61}$$

which give the proportions

$$\frac{\tau'_1}{m_1+m'_2} = \frac{\tau'_2}{2m_1} = \frac{\tau'_3}{m_1-m'_2}, \tag{62}$$

wherein

$$\frac{m'_2}{m_1} = \frac{\sin 2\iota'_2 \pm 2\sin^2\iota'_2\tan\epsilon'}{\sin 2\iota_1} \tag{63}$$

by (26); the upper or lower sign being taken, in the numerator of (63), according as the refracted ray or its wave normal makes the smaller angle with a perpendicular to the face of the crystal.

To find the polarizing angle, we have only to make $m_1 = m'_2$, for then r'_3 will vanish by (62); and therefore, if common light be incident, the whole reflected pencil will be polarized in the plane of incidence. Supposing the crystal to be a negative one, let us conceive the refracted ray to lie within the acute angle made by the axis of the crystal with a perpendicular to its surface. We shall then have to take the positive sign in the numerator of (63), and the polarizing angle will be given by the condition

$$\sin 2\iota_1 = \sin 2\iota'_2 + 2 \sin^2\iota'_2 \tan \epsilon'. \tag{64}$$

But from (36) we have, in general,

$$\sin^2\iota'_2 \tan \epsilon' = (a^2 - b^2) \sin \omega' \cos \omega' \sin^2\iota_1, \tag{65}$$

and in the present instance it is evident that

$$\omega' = 90° - \lambda - \iota'_2,$$

where λ denotes, as before, the angle which the axis of the crystal makes with its surface. Substituting these values in (64), and multiplying all the terms by $\tan \iota'_2$, we get

$$\sin^2\iota'_2 = \sin \iota_1 \cos \iota_1 \tan \iota'_2 - (a^2 - b^2) \sin (\lambda + \iota'_2) \cos (\lambda + \iota'_2) \tan \iota'_2 \sin^2\iota_1.$$

Again, from (37) we have

$$\sin^2\iota'_2 = b^2 \sin^2\iota_1 + (a^2 - b^2) \cos^2 (\lambda + \iota'_2) \sin^2\iota'_1 ; \tag{66}$$

and by equating these two expressions for $\sin^2\iota'_2$, we find

$$\tan \iota'_2 = \frac{a^2 \cos^2 \lambda + b^2 \sin^2 \lambda}{\cotan \iota_1 + (a^2 - b^2) \sin \lambda \cos \lambda}. \tag{67}$$

Then, if this value of $\tan \iota'_2$ be substituted in equation (66), after all its terms have been divided by $\cos^2\iota'_2$, we shall obtain the simple and rigorous formula

$$\sin^2\iota_1 = \frac{1 - a^2 \cos^2 \lambda - b^2 \sin^2 \lambda}{1 - a^2 b^2} = \sin^2\varpi_1, \tag{68}$$

for determining the polarizing angle ϖ_1, when the axis of the crystal lies in the plane of incidence. It is manifest, from the nature of the formula, that this angle is the same, whether the azimuth is 0 or 180°; that is, whether the light is incident at the right or left side of the perpendicular to the surface of the crystal.

This formula might be deduced more briefly by recollecting what we have already proved, that the corresponding masses m_1 and m'_2 are proportional to the ordinates y of the points where the incident ray and the extraordinary refracted ray meet their respective wave surfaces; whence it follows that these ordinates must be equal at the polarizing angle; and thus the question is reduced at once to a geometrical problem. For as both rays are in the plane of incidence, the axis of x will be intersected in one and the same point by right lines touching the wave surfaces, or their sections, at the extremities of the ordinates. Now the sections in the plane of xy are a circle and ellipse with their common centre at the origin, the radius of the circle being unity, and the semiaxes of the ellipse being a and b, of which b is in-clined at the angle λ to the axis of x; and therefore it is required to draw, parallel to the axis of x, a right line intersecting the circle and ellipse, so that if tangents be applied to them at two points of intersection which lie on the same side of the axis of y, these tangents, when produced, may cut each other on the axis of x. The angle which the tangent to the circle makes with the axis of x is then the polarizing angle ϖ_1; and the solution of the problem just stated leads directly and easily to the formula (68). From this way of viewing the matter we see the reason why the polarizing angle is the same in the azimuths 0 and 180°; for if tangents be applied at the two remaining points where the parallel that we have spoken of intersects the circle and ellipse, it is evident that these tangents also will cut each other on the axis of x; since tangents drawn at the ex-tremities of any chord, either of a circle or an ellipse, intersect the parallel diameter at equal distances from the centre.

Let the reflecting surface of the crystal be in contact with a fluid medium whose index of refraction out of vacuo is represented by N, and let B and A respectively denote the ordinary and the principal extraordinary indices of refraction out of vacuo into the crystal. Then putting $\dfrac{N}{A}$ for a, and $\dfrac{N}{B}$ for b, in the preceding formula, and making

$$L^2 = A^2 \sin^2 \lambda + B^2 \cos^2 \lambda,$$

we readily deduce

$$\tan^2 \varpi_1 = \frac{A^2 B^2 - L^2 N^2}{N^2 (L^2 - N^2)}. \tag{69}$$

Hence we perceive that if $L^2 = AB$, that is, if

$$\tan \lambda = \sqrt{\frac{B}{A}}$$

(in which case λ will never be much above or below $45°$), the value of ϖ_1 will be always possible; for then we shall have

$$\tan^2 \varpi_1 = \frac{AB}{N^2}. \tag{70}$$

But if λ be different from this, and of course L^2 not equal to AB, the value of ϖ_1 may become impossible for certain values of N. For it is clear that if N lie *between* the limits L and $\dfrac{AB}{L}$, the numerator and denominator of the fraction (69) will have unlike signs, and the tangent of ϖ_1 will be the square root of a negative quantity. In this case, therefore, if common light be incident, it will "refuse to be polarized," as Brewster expresses it; in other words, it will be impossible to find an angle of incidence at which the reflected pencil will cease to contain light polarized perpendicularly to the plane of incidence, or at which the reflected transversal r'_3 will vanish. With all values of N, except those which are included between the narrow limits L and $\dfrac{AB}{L}$, the polarizing angle is possible. It is zero at the latter limit, and $90°$ at the former. Outside these limits it changes rapidly at first, until N has passed either of them by a quantity considerable in proportion to the interval between them.

From (68) we find $\varpi_1 = \lambda$, when $a = 1$, or $N = A$; and also $\varpi_1 = 90° - \lambda$, when $b = 1$, or $N = B$. In the latter case it is remarkable that no light is reflected when common light is incident at the angle $90° - \lambda$. For then we have $r'_3 = 0$; and because $\iota_1 = \iota_2$, we have likewise $r_3 = 0$. Therefore no light can enter the reflected pencil. But this case deserves that we should consider it more at large, without restricting ourselves to the supposition that the axis of the crystal lies in the plane of incidence.

Assuming then that $N = B$, or that the refractive index of the fluid, which covers the reflecting surface, is equal to the ordinary index of the crystal itself, we may observe that, in this case, every angle of incidence, in every azimuth, has a right to be regarded as a polarizing angle. In fact, common light cannot suffer reflexion at the separating surface of the crystal and the fluid, without becoming completely polarized. For if polarized light be incident, and if r_3 and r'_3 be the uniradial reflected transversals, respectively belonging to the ordinary and to the extraordinary ray, the former transversal must necessarily vanish, for the same reason that no reflexion can take place at the separating surface of two ordinary media whose refractive indices are equal; and thus the actual reflected transversal will always coincide in direction with r'_3, whatever be the direction of the incident transversal. Consequently, if common light be incident, the whole reflected pencil will be polarized in a plane passing through r'_3, and making with the plane of incidence an angle θ'_3 determined by the second of formulæ (39). By putting $\iota_2 = \iota_1$ in that formula, and employing the expression (44), we first obtain

$$\tan \theta'_3 = \frac{\cos(\iota_1 + \iota'_2)\cos\theta'\tan\omega' + \sin(\iota_1 + \iota'_2)}{\sin\theta'\tan\omega'}$$

$$= \frac{\cos(\iota_1 + \iota'_2)\tan(p - \iota'_2) + \sin(\iota_1 + \iota'_2)}{\sin\theta'\tan\omega'};$$

and thence

$$\tan \theta'_3 = \frac{\sin (p + \iota_1)}{\sin \theta' \tan \omega' \cos (p - \iota'_2)} = \frac{\sin (p + \iota_1) \cos \omega'}{\sin q \cos (p - \iota'_2)};$$

and finally,

$$\tan \theta'_3 = \sin (p + \iota_1) \cotan q ; \qquad (71)$$

a result which shows that the plane of polarization of the reflected ray is perpendicular to a plane drawn through the ray itself and the axis of the crystal.

Moreover, we find, from the first of formulæ (39), by proceeding as above,

$$\tan \theta'_1 = - \sin (p - \iota_1) \cotan q = - \cotan \theta ; \qquad (72)$$

and from (38) it is evident that $\theta_1 = \theta$. Therefore all that relates to the case under our consideration may be summed up in the following statement:

When $N = B$, and the incident light is polarized in a plane passing through the axis, the course of the light is unaltered, and there is neither reflexion nor refraction. When it is polarized in the perpendicular plane, all the light which enters the crystal undergoes extraordinary refraction. Whatever light is reflected is always polarized in a plane at right angles to that which passes through the reflected ray and the axis of the crystal; and this is true, whether the incident light is polarized or not.

Here, for the present, we must terminate our deductions from the general theory propounded in this Paper. Several other questions remain to be discussed, such as the reflexion of common light* at the first surface, and the internal† reflexion

---

* The mode of treating the case in which common light is incident has been pointed out at the bottom of p. 100.

† I have since found that the problem of reflexion at the second surface may be reduced to that of reflexion at the first surface by means of a very simple rule. Let us suppose the two surfaces of the crystal to be parallel; and let a ray R_1, uniradially polarized, and incident on the first surface, give the ray R_3 by reflexion, and the single ray R_2 by refraction. Let R_2 be the ray which suffers internal reflexion at the second surface, thereby giving the two reflected rays $R_{,,}$, $R'_{,,}$ and the

at the second surface of a crystal; but these must be reserved for a future communication. It would be easy, indeed, to write down the algebraical solutions resulting from our theory; but this we are not content to do, because the expressions are rather complicated, and, when rightly treated, will probably contract themselves into a simpler form. It is the character of all true

single refracted ray $R_{(1)}$ emerging from the crystal in a direction parallel to R_1. Put τ_1, τ_3, τ_2, and $\tau_{,,}$, $\tau'_{,,}$, $\tau_{(1)}$ for the transversals of the rays in the order in which they have been named. As the transversal τ_2 is supposed to be given in magnitude, the lengths as well as the directions of τ_1 and τ_3 can be found by the construction in page 97.

Now, the direction of τ_3 being changed, and its magnitude retained, let the ray R_3 be turned directly back, so as to be incident again on the crystal, and to suffer reflexion and refraction at the first surface. Then the two refracted rays which it gives will be parallel to $R_{,,}$, $R'_{,,}$ and their transversals will be equal and parallel to $\tau_{,,}$, $\tau'_{,,}$. The reflected ray which it gives will coincide with R_1; and the reflected transversal, when compounded with τ_1, will furnish a resultant equal and parallel to the emergent transversal $\tau_{(1)}$.

Thus the constructions, which have been given for the first surface, may be made available for the second surface, and every question relative to crystalline reflexion may be solved geometrically by means of the polar planes.

The foregoing rule was not, properly speaking, deduced from theory. I first formed a clear conception of what the rule ought to be, and then verified it for the simple case of singly-refracting media, and finally proved it for doubly-refracting crystals. The truth of the rule, in crystals, depends upon the truth of the three following equations:—

$$\left. \begin{aligned} &\sin(\iota_{,,} + \iota'_{,,})\left\{\cos(\iota_{,,} - \iota'_{,,}) + \cotan\theta_{,,}\cotan\theta'_{,,}\right\} + h_{,,} + h'_{,,} = 0, \\ &\sin(\iota_2 - \iota_{,,})\left\{\cos(\iota_2' + \iota_{,,}) - \cotan\theta_2\cotan\theta_{,,}\right\} + h_2 - h_{,,} = 0, \\ &\sin(\iota_2 - \iota'_{,,})\left\{\cos(\iota_2 + \iota'_{,,}) - \cotan\theta_2\cotan\theta'_{,,}\right\} + h_2 - h'_{,,} = 0, \end{aligned} \right\} \quad \text{(VIII.)}$$

in which the notation is intelligible without any explanation. The first equation is the same as equation (VII.) already noticed; and the other two differ from it only in appearance, the change in the signs being occasioned by a change in the relative position of the rays.

When the reflexion is total, I suppose we may follow the example which Fresnel has set us in the case of ordinary media. The general algebraic expression for each reflected transversal will then become imaginary; and by putting it under the form

$$T(\cos\phi + \sqrt{-1}\sin\Phi),$$

we shall have T for the reflected transversal, and Φ for the change of phase.

theories that the more they are studied, the more simple they appear to be. And we may add, that a close examination of such theories always meets with its reward, in the unexpected* consequences which present themselves to view. Nothing can be simpler than the laws of double refraction, as they were delivered by Fresnel; yet the properties of his wave surface still continue to furnish the geometer with beautiful and curious relations. So we may hope that a little more time, devoted to the laws of reflexion, will not be spent in vain. They promise to supply many other theorems, not undeserving of attention, though perhaps not as simple and comprehensive as those that have already been made known.

From the nature of the rules which we have given for treating the question of reflexion at either surface of the crystal, it follows that the final equation, for determining the position of a transversal, is always linear, though the equation of *vis viva* is of the second degree. This result very strongly confirms the theory; but it shows, at the same time, that the law of the preservation of *vis viva* is not to be regarded as an ultimate principle, but rather as a consequence of some elementary law not yet discovered.

It now appears that the conjectures put forward in the note, p. 93, were hasty, and that there was some mistake in the calculations which gave rise to them. It ;s scarcely necessary to mention, that the sheet in which that note is found was printed off before I had obtained the result announced in the subsequent note, p. 111. Various delays occurred while my Paper was going through the press; and I took advantage of them to increase its value, by appending notes on some of the questions which I had overlooked or omitted in the first consideration of the subject.

*As an instance of this, it may be mentioned, that the conclusion arrived at in the note, p. 111, was wholly unexpected. And in verifying the equation (vii.), an unexpected and useful theorem was obtained; for it became necessary to find a manageable expression for the tangent of the angle ϵ which the wave normal makes with the ray. This expression is wanted in applying the formulæ (34) and (35) to biaxal crystals, and therefore I shall make no apology for introducing it here.

Having described a sphere concentric with the wave surface, let the wave normal OP and the two optic axes (which are the nodal diameters of the *index surface*) be produced from the centre O to meet the sphere in the points $P_{,}, A, A_{,}$, respectively, thus marking out the angles of a spherical triangle $P_{,}AA_{,}$. The same wave normal may belong to two different rays; and if we select one of these rays, its transversal must lie in a plane drawn through the wave normal, and bisecting either the internal angle $AP_{,}A_{,}$ of the spherical triangle, or the ex-

If we are asked what reasons can be assigned for the hypotheses on which the preceding theory is founded, we are far from being able to give a satisfactory answer. We are obliged to confess that, with the exception of the law of *vis viva*, the hypotheses are nothing more than fortunate conjectures. These conjectures are very probably right, since they have led to elegant laws which are fully borne out by experiments; but this is all that we can assert respecting them. We cannot attempt to deduce them from first principles; because, in the theory of light, such principles are still to be sought for. It

ternal supplementary angle. By producing the optic axes in the proper directions, we may always make the above plane (which Fresnel calls the plane of polarization) bisect the internal angle. Supposing this to have been done for the ray which was selected, put ω and $\omega_{,}$ for the sides $P_{,}A$ and $P_{,}A_{,}$ of the spherical triangle, and ψ for the contained angle $AP_{,}A_{,}$. Let s be the length of the wave normal from the centre O to the point where it intersects the tangent plane applied at the extremity of the ray, that is, applied at the point where the ray meets its own nappe of the wave surface; and let a and c be the greatest and least semiaxes of the ellipsoid which generates the wave surface. Then we shall have

$$\tan \epsilon = \frac{a^2 - c^2}{2} \sin (\omega - \omega_{,}) \sin \tfrac{1}{2} \psi. \qquad \text{(ix.)}$$

And it is now manifest that if $\epsilon_{,}$ be the angle which the other ray makes with the same wave normal, and $s_{,}$ the length of the wave normal intercepted between the centre and the tangent plane at the extremity of this ray, we shall also have

$$\tan \epsilon_{,} = \frac{a^2 - c^2}{2 s_{,}^{2}} \sin (\omega + \omega_{,}) \cos \tfrac{1}{2} \psi. \qquad \text{(x.)}$$

If a ray is given in direction it will have two wave normals; and then the angles ϵ, $\epsilon_{,}$, which it makes with each normal, may be found from the formulæ

$$\left. \begin{aligned} \tan \epsilon &= \frac{r^2}{2}\left(\frac{1}{c^2} - \frac{1}{a^2}\right) \sin (\omega - \omega_{,}) \sin \tfrac{1}{2} \psi, \\[2ex] \tan \epsilon_{,} &= \frac{r_{,}^{2}}{2}\left(\frac{1}{c^2} - \frac{1}{a^2}\right) \sin (\omega + \omega_{,}) \cos \tfrac{1}{2} \psi, \end{aligned} \right\} \qquad \text{(xi.)}$$

where r and $r_{,}$ are the two radii of the wave surface which are in the direction of the ray; the spherical triangle $P_{,}AA_{,}$, of which the sides and contained angle are expressed by the same letters as before, being now formed by producing the *ray* and the two nodal diameters of the *wave surface*, until they intersect the sphere in the points $P_{,}, A_{,} A_{,}$.

is certain, indeed, that light is produced by undulations, propagated, with transversal vibrations, through a highly elastic ether; but the constitution of this ether, and the laws of its connexion (if it has any connexion) with the particles of bodies, are utterly unknown. The peculiar mechanism of light is a secret that we have not yet been able to penetrate. As a proof of this, we might observe, that some of the simplest and most familar phenomena have never been explained. Not to mention dispersion, about which so much has been fruitlessly written, we may remark, that the very cause of ordinary refraction, or of the retardation which light undergoes upon entering a transparent medium, is not at all understood. Much less can it be said that double refraction has been rigorously explained; its laws alone have been clearly developed by Fresnel. In short, the whole amount of our knowledge, with regard to the propagation of light, is confined to the *laws* of phenomena: scarcely any approach has been made to a mechanical theory of those laws. And if the case of uninterrupted propagation through a continuous medium presents such difficulties, it would be useless to think of accounting for the laws which subsist at the confines of two media, where the continuity is broken.

But perhaps something might be done by pursuing a contrary course; by taking those laws for granted, and endeavouring to proceed upwards from them to higher principles. In this point of view, our second law, or hypothesis, is extremely remarkable; for it seems to be opposed, in some degree, to the notion that the ethereal molecules are strongly attracted or repelled by the particles of bodies. However that may be, it would appear that a true theory must be in accordance with this hypothesis; and that any mechanical ideas, which would make the *mean* density of the ether vary from one medium to another,* cannot be admitted to represent the real state of

---

* Those who maintain that the density of the ether is different in different media, ought to consider the following question :—What function of the three principal indices of a doubly-refracting crystal represents the density of the ether within the crystal ?

things in nature. It is no objection to the hypothesis in question, to say that it increases the difficulty of accounting for refraction; for, as there is positive evidence in favour of the hypothesis, we ought rather to conclude that the common opinion, which attributes refraction to a change of density in the ether, is altogether erroneous.

In the next place we may remark, that our first hypothesis,* concerning the direction of vibrations in polarized light, will be useful in testing any proposed theory; for as it now seems to be certain that the vibrations are parallel to the plane of polarization, and not perpendicular to it, as Fresnel supposed, such a direction of the vibrations ought to be a consequence of the theory which we adopt.

The third hypothesis, or the principle of the preservation of *vis viva*, is the most natural that can be imagined, inasmuch as it implies only this, that the incident light is equal to the sum of the reflected and refracted lights. Yet it is probable that even this principle, like the law of *vis viva* in ordinary mechanics, is a result of simpler laws, and will be shown to be so as soon as the true mechanism of light shall be discovered.

The fourth hypothesis is a very important one, because the whole theory turns upon it; and therefore, in the beginning of this Paper, a particular account has been given of the manner in which it was originally suggested. If we wish to give a reason for this hypothesis, we might say that the motion of a particle of ether, at the common surface of two media, ought to be the same, to whichsoever medium the particle is conceived to belong; and as the incident and reflected vibrations are superposed in one medium, and the refracted vibrations in the other, we might infer that the resultant of the former vibrations ought to be the same, both in length and direction, as the resultant of the latter. At first sight this reasoning appears sufficiently plausible; but it will not bear a close examination. For as the argument is general, it would prove that the principle of

---

* This hypothesis properly belongs to the laws of propagation, as it relates only to what passes within a given medium.

K 2

the equivalence of vibrations is true for metals,* as well as for crystals, which it certainly is not. It is not easy to see why the principle should hold in the one case and not in the other; but it is probably prevented from holding, in the case of metals,

* A few days after this Paper was read, I found reason to persuade myself that in metals the vibrations parallel to the surface are equivalent, but not those perpendicular to it; and that in metals, as well as in crystals, the *vis viva* is preserved. This persuasion was founded on a system of formulæ which I had invented for expressing the laws of metallic reflexion and refraction; and which seem to represent very satisfactorily the experiments of Brewster, *Phil. Trans.*, 1830. As metallic and crystalline reflexion are kindred subjects, and will one day be brought under the same theory, however distinct they may now appear, it will not be out of place to insert the formulæ for metals here. These formulæ are not proposed as true, but as likely to be true; and they will be found to express, at least with general correctness, all the circumstances that have hitherto been regarded as anomalies in the action of metals upon light.

I suppose that for every metal there are two constants, M and χ, of which the first is a number greater than unity, and the second is an angle included between 0 and 90°. The number M I call the *modulus*, and the angle χ the *characteristic* of the metal. Both M and χ vary with the colour of the light, and the ratio $\dfrac{M}{\cos\chi}$ is probably the index of refraction. From Brewster's experiments it appears that M diminishes from the red to the violet; and therefore I should suppose that $\cos\chi$ diminishes in a greater ratio, in order that the index of refraction may increase as in transparent substances.

Put ι_1 for the angle of incidence, and ι_2 for the angle of refraction, so that

$$\frac{\sin\iota_1}{\sin\iota_2} = \frac{M}{\cos\chi};\qquad\qquad\text{(XII.)}$$

and let μ be a variable determined by the condition

$$\mu = \frac{\cos\iota_1}{\cos\iota_2}.\qquad\qquad\text{(XIII.)}$$

These two relations combined will give

$$\frac{1}{\mu^2} = 1 + \left(1 - \frac{\cos^2\chi}{M^2}\right)\tan^2\iota_1,\qquad\qquad\text{(XIV.)}$$

which shows that μ is equal to unity at a perpendicular incidence, and that it vanishes at an incidence 90°, decreasing always during the interval.

Now if plane polarized light be incident on the metal, we must distinguish two principal cases, according as the light is polarized in the plane of incidence, or in the perpendicular plane. In the first case, denoting the reflected and refracted transversals by τ_3 and τ_2 respectively, let us put Δ_3 for the change of phase in

by the same cause, whatever it is, which produces a change of phase in metallic reflexion.

It will be proper to conclude this Essay with a brief sketch of the researches of Sir David Brewster and M. Seebeck, the

the reflected ray, and Δ_2 for the change of phase in the refracted ray. Let the same symbols, marked with accents, be used in the second case with similar significations. Then if the incident transversal be taken for unity, we shall have the following formulæ:

1. When the incident transversal is in the plane of incidence,

$$\begin{aligned}
\tau_3{}^2 &= \frac{M^2 + \mu^2 - 2M\mu \cos \chi}{M^2 + \mu^2 + 2M\mu \cos \chi}, \\[2mm]
\tau_2{}^2 &= \frac{4M^2\mu^2}{M^2 + \mu^2 + 2M\mu \cos \chi}, \\[2mm]
\tan \Delta_3 &= \frac{2M\mu \sin \chi}{M^2 - \mu^2}, \qquad \tan \Delta_2 = \frac{\mu \sin \chi}{M + \mu \cos \chi},
\end{aligned} \qquad \text{(xv.)}$$

2. When the incident transversal is perpendicular to the plane of incidence,

$$\begin{aligned}
\tau'_3{}^2 &= \frac{1 + M^2\mu^2 - 2M\mu \cos \chi}{1 + M^2\mu^2 + 2M\mu \cos \chi}, \\[2mm]
\tau'_2{}^2 &= \frac{4M^2\mu^2}{1 + M^2\mu^2 + 2M\mu \cos}, \\[2mm]
\tan \Delta'_3 &= \frac{2M\mu \sin \chi}{M^2\mu^2 - 1}, \qquad \tan \Delta'_2 = \frac{\sin \chi}{M\mu + \cos \chi}.
\end{aligned} \qquad \text{(xvi.)}$$

When $\chi = 0$, there is no change of phase, and the formulæ become identical with those given in the note, p. 101. When $\chi = 90°$, there is total reflexion at all incidences. The case of pure silver approximates to this. For good speculum metal, χ is about 70°. The value of M ranges from $2\frac{1}{2}$ to 5 in different metals.

When the incident transversal is inclined to the plane of incidence, its components, parallel and perpendicular to that plane, will give two reflected transversals with a difference of phase equal to $\Delta'_3 - \Delta_3$. The reflected vibration will then be performed in an ellipse; and the position and magnitude of the axes of the ellipse may be deduced from the preceding formulæ. The consequences of these formulæ are very simple and elegant, but I cannot dwell upon them here. Suffice it to observe, that every angle of incidence has another angle corresponding to it, which I call its *conjugate* angle of incidence; and that the value of $\Delta'_3 - \Delta_3$ at one of these angles is the supplement of its value at the other, while the ratio $\dfrac{\tau'_3}{\tau_3}$ is the same at both angles; whence it follows that, *ceteris paribus*, the elliptic vibrations, reflected at conjugate angles, are similar to each other, and have their homologous

only other writers who have treated of the subject of crystalline reflexion.

So early as the year 1819, Sir David Brewster published, in the *Philosophical Transactions,* a Paper " On the Action of Crystallized Surfaces upon Light." * In this Paper the Author details a great variety of experiments on the polarizing effects of Iceland spar. He gives the measures of the polarizing angles in different azimuths, when the reflexion takes place in air; but he does not notice the accompanying deviations, which were probably too small to attract his attention. In another instance, however, he obtained very large deviations. He conceived the idea of pushing his experiments into an extreme case, by masking, as it were, the ordinary reflecting action of the crystal, and leaving the extraordinary energy at full liberty to display itself. This was done by dropping on the reflecting surface a little oil of cassia, a fluid whose refractive index is nearly equal to the ordinary index of Iceland spar. When common light, incident at 45°, was reflected at the separating surface of the oil and the spar, the reflected pencil was found to be partially, and sometimes completely, polarized in planes variously inclined to the plane of incidence, the inclination going through all magnitudes from 0 to 180°, as the crystal was turned round in azimuth. This general result is no more than what theory would lead us to expect, when the angle of incidence is nearly equal to one of the angles of refraction ; but to institute a minute comparison of theory with experiment would require troublesome calcula-

---

axes equally inclined to the plane of incidence, but on opposite sides of it. When $\Delta'_3 - \Delta_3 = 90°$, the conjugate incidences are equal, the ratio $\dfrac{\tau'_3}{\tau_3}$ is a minimum, and the axes of the elliptic vibration are parallel and perpendicular to the plane of incidence. When $\Delta'_3 = 90°$, or $M\mu = 1$, the value of τ'_3 is a minimum, and equal to $\tan \frac{1}{2} \chi$.

The foregoing formulæ differ slightly from those which I have given in No. I. of the *Proceedings* of the Royal Irish Academy. The small quantity χ', which occurs in the latter, has been purposely neglected, as its presence interferes with the simplicity of the expressions.

    * *Phil. Trans.* 1819, p. 145.

tions, which I have not had time to make. With the view, however, of showing clearly, from theory, that the range of the deviation is unlimited, I have considered the simple case in which $N = B$, or in which the refractive index of the fluid is *exactly* equal to the ordinary index of the crystal. This case, moreover, is remarkable on its own account; and it might be worth while to try whether it could not be verified by direct experiment. If a fluid could be procured whose refractive index, for some definite ray of the spectrum, should be equal to the ordinary index of the crystal for the same ray, and if common light, incident at any angle and in any azimuth, were reflected at the confines of the fluid and the crystal, then, supposing the theory to be exact, the definite ray aforesaid would, as we have seen, be completely polarized by reflexion, and the plane of polarization would always be perpendicular to a plane drawn through the direction of the reflected ray and the axis of the crystal. This experiment would be an elegant test of the theory in its application to these extreme and trying cases; and if it were successful, no doubt could be entertained* as to the rigorous accuracy of the geometrical laws of reflexion.

* I was at this time in doubt whether the phenomena observed with oil of cassia could be reconciled to theory; and when the note in page 93 was written, I was almost certain that they could not. But I have since, I think, found out the cause of this perplexity. Some of Brewster's experiments were made with *natural* surfaces of Iceland spar; others with surfaces *artificially polished*. I believe (though I have made very few calculations relative to the point) that the former class of experiments will be perfectly explained by the theory; the latter I am certain cannot be so explained, nor ought we to expect that they should. For the process of artificial polishing must necessarily occasion small inequalities, by exposing little elementary rhombs with their faces inclined to the general surface; and the action of these faces may produce the *unsymmetrical* effects which Brewster notices as so extraordinary (Sixth Report of the British Association, Transactions of the Sections, p. 16). If this will not account for such effects, I do not know what will. From an old observation of Brewster (*Phil. Trans.*, 1819), it would appear that imperfect polish does actually produce a want of symmetry in the phenomena; for when common light was reflected between oil of cassia and a badly polished surface *perpendicular* to the axis, he found that the reflected ray was polarized neither in the plane of incidence, nor perpendicular

The experiments with oil of cassia must be very difficult on account of the great feebleness of the reflected light. Sir David Brewster, however, resumed them at different times; and he laid an extensive series of his results before the Physical Section of the British Association at its late meeting in Bristol.

It was not until the latter end of November, 1836, that I became acquainted with the investigation of M. Seebeck, who has contributed greatly to the advancement of the subject. He made very acurate experiments on the light reflected in air from Iceland spar. He detected the deviation, notwithstanding its smallness, and measured it with great care. He also made the first step in the theory of crystalline reflexion; and the remarkable formula (68), which gives the polarizing angle when the axis lies in the plane of incidence, is due to him. The hypotheses which he employed were similar to those of Fresnel, and they enabled him to solve the problem of reflexion in the case just mentioned, but not to attempt it generally. The date of his first Papers* is the year 1831; but he did not publish his experiments on the deviation until a recent occasion, when he was led to compare them † with the theory which I had originally given in my letter to Sir David Brewster. I have already stated the correction which the theory underwent in conse-

---

to it, but 75° out of it. The same surface, when the light was reflected in air, gave the polarizing angle more than two degrees below its proper value.

To show that, in other respects, the general character of the phenomena is in accordance with theory, we may observe that when $N = B$, and $\lambda = 0$ or 90°, if common light be incident at 45° in the plane of the principal section of the crystal, the whole of the reflected light will be polarized perpendicularly to that plane; and therefore if N be *nearly* equal to B, while every thing else remains the same, the reflected pencil will contain some unpolarized light, and will be only partially polarized in a plane perpendicular to the plane of incidence; so that (as Brewster has found by experiment) the crystal will then produce by reflexion the same effect which is produced by ordinary refraction. This (as he also found) will not happen when λ and the angle of incidence are each equal to 45°, because the light is then incident at the polarizing angle.

* Poggendorff's *Annals*, Vol. xxi. p. 290; Vol. xxii. p. 126.

† *Ibid.*, Vol. xxxviii. p. 280.

quence of those experiments, and by which it was brought to its present simple form.*

* Two or three months after this correction had been published in the *Philosophical Magazine*, a notice of it was inserted in Poggendorff's *Annals*, vol. xl. p. 462. Up to that time, I believe, nothing had been published in Germany on the general theory of crystalline reflexion; at least the writer of the notice (whom I take to be M. Seebeck) does not seem to have heard of any other theory, or any other principles than mine. But in the next number of Poggendorff, vol. xl. p. 497, there appeared a letter from M. Neumann, in which the writer speaks of a theory of his own, founded on principles exactly the same as those which I had already announced, and refers to a Paper which he had communicated on the subject to the Academy of Berlin. The Paper has been printed in the *Transactions* of that Academy for the year 1835; and through the kindness of the author I have received a copy of it, just in time to acknowledge it here. On casting my eye over it, I recognize several equations which are familiar to me—in particular, the equations (vii.), (viii.), (ix.), (x.), which I discovered independently in November last. M. Neumann's Paper is very elaborate, and supersedes, in a great measure, the design which I had formed of treating the subject more fully at my leisure; nor can I do better than recommend it to those who wish to pursue the investigations through all their details.

TRINITY COLLEGE, DUBLIN, *March*, 1838.

XII. — ON A NEW OPTICAL INSTRUMENT, INTENDED CHIEFLY FOR THE PURPOSE OF MAKING EXPERIMENTS ON THE LIGHT REFLECTED FROM METALS.

[*Proceedings of the Royal Irish Academy*, April 9, 1838.]

THE instrument consists of two hollow arms or tubes, moveable about the centre, and in the plane, of a large divided circle, each arm being provided with a Nicol's eye-piece, or some equivalent contrivance for polarizing light in a single plane; while in one arm, which is of course crooked, a Fresnel's rhomb is interposed between the eye-piece and the centre of the circle. At this centre is placed a stage for carrying the reflector, with its plane perpendicular to the plane of the circle, and having a motion to and fro for adjustment. Each eye-piece, as well as the Fresnel's rhomb, turns freely about the axis of the arm to which it belongs, and is provided with a small circle for measuring its angle of rotation. When the two arms are set at equal angles with the reflector, and the observer looks through the crooked arm, he will see a light admitted through the straight one; and then, by turning the Fresnel's rhomb, and the eye-piece next his eye, he will be able, by means of their combined movements, to find a position in which the light will entirely disappear. An observation will then have been made; for the light, before its incidence on the metal, is polarized in a given plane by the first eye-piece; but after reflexion from the metal (as we know from Sir David Brewster's experiments) it is elliptically polarized; and our object is to determine the *position* and *species* of the little ellipse in which the reflected vibration is supposed to be performed. Now, the axes of this ellipse are parallel and perpendicular to the principal plane of the rhomb, when it is in the situation above described, where the light completely disappears; and the ratio of the axes is the tangent of the angle which that plane makes with the principal section of the eyepiece next the eye. The angles are read off from the divided circles; and thus, for any angle of incidence, and any plane of primitive polarization, we can at once ascertain the nature of the reflected elliptic vibration. Professor Mac Cullagh mentioned that the instrument was made last year with the view of testing certain formulæ which he has proposed for the case of metallic reflexion, and which have been printed in Vol. xviii. pp. 70, 71, of the *Transactions* of the Academy*; but that he had not yet found leisure to make the various adjustments which are necessary in order to obtain satisfactory results with it. The instrument is beautifully executed by Mr. Grubb, who himself contrived the subordinate mechanism, by which the requisite movements are effected with perfect ease to the observer.

* *Supra*, pp. 132, 133.

XIII.—LAWS OF CRYSTALLINE REFLEXION.—QUESTION OF PRIORITY.

[*Proceedings of the Royal Irish Academy*, Nov. 30, 1838.]

THE President, Sir William R. Hamilton, read the following letter which had been addressed to him by M. Neumann of Königsberg, on some points connected with the history of the Laws of Crystalline Reflexion :—

MONSIEUR,

Le haut prix que j'attache à votre suffrage et à celui de l'illustre Académie, à laquelle vous présidez, et l'honorable mention, que vous avez voulu faire de mon mémoire sur la théorie de la lumière dans la séance de cette Académie du 25 Juin, m'engagent à vous dresser la lettre suivante. Vous avez donné dans cette séance un jugement dans la question de priorité, qui pouvait s'élever entre Mr. Mac Cullagh et moi par rapport à la découverte des lois suivant lesquelles la lumière est reflechie et refractée par des milieux crystallins—j'ai l'honneur de vous communiquer dans ce qui suit quelques faits et quelques reflexions fondées sur ces faits, et qui auraient été peut-être de quelque influence sur ce jugement.

Au commencement de l'année 1833 j'ai communiqué à M. Seebeck de Berlin non seulement l'ensemble des principes de ma théorie tels qu'ils se trouvent imprimés dans le § 2 de mon mémoire, mais j'avais illustré encore ces principes par leur application aux milieux non crystallins. En même tems j'ai annoncé à M. Seebeck, que les résultats tirés de ces principes par rapport aux milieux crystallins étaient parfaitement d'accord avec ses observations sur l'angle de polarisation du kalkspath, et je lui fis part de la formule même, qui exprime l'inclinaison du plan de polarisation du rayon polarisé par réflexion vers le plan de reflexion. Sous la date du 11 Mai, 1833, M. Seebeck m'écrivit, que cette formule aussi s'accordait parfaitement avec ses observations, qu'il n'avait pas encore publiées et qu'il avait la complaisance de me communiquer en manuscrit. Dans le printems de 1834 le manuscrit de mon mémoire tel qu'il a paru depuis allait être achevé; mais un voyage que je fis dans ce tems et qui m'éloigna assez long-tems de Königsberg, m'empêcha de la publier incessamment. Cependant j'avais pris soin d'en faire un abrégé dans lequel je développai complètement les principes de ma théorie et les résultats auxquels elle m'avait conduit par rapport aux crystaux à un axe.

J'envoyai cet extrait en Mai ou Juin, 1834, par la librairie de M. Schropp de Berlin à M. Arago, en le priant de le faire imprimer dans les Annales de Chimie et de Physique, ce savant ayant dans une note publiée dans ce tems marqué un grand intérêt pour l'investigation des lois des intensités du rayon ordinaire et extraordinaire, lois qui se trouvaient parmi les résultats mentionnés. Il n'y a pas de doute que cet extrait ne soit parvenu dans les mains de M. Arago, entre lesquelles il doit se trouver encore à présent. Du reste, M. Jacobi en avait pris une connaissance détaillée, et à Berlin il a été entre les mains de MM. Weiss et Poggendorf.

En passant par Vienne dans l'été de 1834, j'avais le plaisir d'entretenir de mes résultats et de ma méthode M. Ettinghausen, savant très distingué et très versé dans les parties les plus épineuses de l'optique. Antérieurement j'avais enseigné mes doctrines à M. Senff, maintenant professeur à l'Université de Dorpat, pendant le séjour que fit à Koenigsberg ce jeune et habile physicien, qui vient de publier un excellent travail sur les propriétés optiques et crystallographiques du fer sulfaté.

Il suit de tout ce qui précède, que déjà en 1834, mes resultats trouvés par rapport aux lois de reflexion et de refraction des crystaux n'étaient guère inconnus aux physiciens de l'Allemagne, qui s'occupent de l'optique, et si dès lors ils n'ont pas reçu une plus grande publicité, vous voyez, Monsieur, cela tenait aux Annales de Chimie. La publication de mon mémoire a été rétardée par l'espoir que j'avais conçu de pouvoir lui ajouter une partie expérimentale. Mais l'exécution des appareils me faisant attendre trop long tems, j'ai présenté vers la fin de 1835 à l'Académie de Berlin mon ouvrage tel qu'il a été imprimé depuis parmi les mémoires de cette Académie. La partie expérimentale a été publiée en 1837 dans le volume 42 des Annales de M. Poggendorf.

Je vois du discours que vous avez tenu, Monsieur, dans la Séance de votre Académie du 25 Juin passé, et qui vient de m'être communiqué, que c'est déjà en Août, 1835, que Mr. Mac Cullagh a fait à l'Association Britannique une communication sur les lois de reflexion et refraction par les crystaux, et qui a été imprimée dans le Lond. and Edinb. Phil. Mag., Février, 1836. Je crois très volontiers, que Mr. Mac Cullagh est parvenu aux résultats qui se trouvent dans cette publication, par ses propres efforts et sans avoir eu connaisance de mes travaux sur ce même sujet. Toutefois ce ne sont pas ces résultats qui pourraient être l'objet d'une question de priorité. En effet dans une note publiée dans les Annales de M. Poggendorf (vol. xxxviii. 1836), M. Seebeck a montré que les formules auxquelles est parvenu Mr. Mac Cullagh ne sont pas justes, et qu'elles ne représentent pas les lois de reflexion et de refraction par les crystaux. Dans la même note M. Seebeck a exposé, comment les lois de reflexion et de refraction des milieux non crystallins conformes à cette definition du plan de polarisation, à laquelle on est conduit dans la théorie de la double refraction, peuvent être déduites des suppositions faites par Fresnel, avec la seule modification de l'homogénéité de l'éther dans tous les milieux. Mais les suppositions de Fresnel ainsi modifiées forment la base principale de ma méthode, dont j'avais déjà fait part à M. Seebeck depuis plusieurs années. Il est vrai, que dans les deux milieux Fresnel ne suppose que l'égalité de deux composantes parallèles au plan de séparation, mais l'égalité de la troisième n'est qu'une simple conséquence de celle des deux autres et des autres suppositions. Ce sont les suppositions de Fresnel modifiées de la dite manière, qu'a adoptées Mr. Mac Cullagh, après s'être convaincu par la note de M. Seebeck de la faussete des résultats qu'il avait jusque-là obtenus, conviction qui l'engagea à rejeter tout ce qui n'était pas conforme à ces suppositions, et dès lors seulement en 1837, dans le Lond. and Edinb. Phil. Mag., Mr. Mac Cullagh est parvenu aux mêmes lois de reflexion et de refraction que j'avais eues l'honneur de présenter à l'Academie des Sciences de Berlin en 1835.

Vous voyez par tout ceci, Monsieur, que dès 1833 j'ai été en pleine possession de la méthode, et que dès le commencement de 1834 j'ai été en pleine possession des résultats qu'elle fournit, que dans ce même tems j'ai envoyé un abrégé contenant ces résultats et lu en manuscrit par plusieurs savans bien connus à M. le redacteur des Annales de Physique et Chimie pour le publier dans ce recueil, et qu'à la fin de 1835, j'ai présenté l'ouvrage complet à present imprimé à l'Académie de Berlin; vous voyez en même tems, que Mr. Mac Cullagh ayant communiqué à l'Association Britanique en 1835 des lois de réflexion et de refraction crystallin, ces lois ont été demontrées être fautives par M. Seebeck in 1836, et que Mr. Mac Cullagh n'est parvenu en 1837 aux vraies lois qu' après avoir pris connaissance du fondement de ma méthode, et s'en être servi.

De tout cela résulte, Monsieur, que la priorité de la découverte des lois de réflexion et réfraction par des crystaux n'est pas douteuse, et qu'il n'y a pas de simultanéité entre mes travaux et ceux de Mr. Mac Cullagh, dont du reste personne ne peut estimer plus que moi le talent distingué.

Daignez, Monsieur, agréer les assurances de la plus haute considération avec laquelle je suis, &c.,

F. E. NEUMANN.

Königsberg, *5 Octobre*, 1838.

When this letter was read, Professor Mac Cullagh requested permission to make a few remarks. After expressing much regret that his researches in the theory of light should have clashed with those of any other person (though in the present state of science such collisions were perhaps inevitable), he proceeded to say, that he did not think it necessary to detain the Academy with a formal reply to the communication which had just been read; it would be sufficient for him to observe, in general, that the facts brought forward by the writer, with reference to the history of his own investigations, were all, without exception, of a private nature, not one of them being

taken from any published document; that the *first* document
of the kind, which professed to give any account of M. Neumann's "method," or any statement of the principles employed
in it, appeared in the Annals of Poggendorf (Vol. XL. p. 497),
some months after Mr. Mac Cullagh had published his *last*
Paper on the subject in the *Philosophical Magazine* (Vol. x.
p. 43), and even after that Paper had been noticed in the
aforesaid *Annals* (Vol. XL. p. 462); that M. Neumann's Memoir
in the Berlin *Transactions* was not published until a later
period; that, therefore, there could be no question about priority of publication; and that, consequently, if it were to be
imagined for a moment that either author had borrowed from
the other, the presumption must necessarily be against M. Neumann. With respect to M. Seebeck's note, it would be enough
to state, that M. Neumann is not mentioned there at all; that
the principles there given by M. Seebeck are not adequate to
the general solution of the problem; and that such of them
as differ from those of Fresnel had been previously published
by Mr. Mac Cullagh. It was clear, therefore, that Mr. Mac
Cullagh owed nothing on the score of theory to anyone but
Fresnel. He had, indeed, made one alteration in his theory
as it originally stood; for he had at first rejected Fresnel's law
of the *vis viva*, and had been obliged to restore it afterwards,
in order to account for certain experiments of M. Seebeck,
which M. Seebeck himself, from want of sufficient principles,
had not attempted to account for; but the real service which
M. Seebeck had rendered him, and for which he had frequently
acknowledged his obligations, was the communication of these
experiments, and not any suggestion of the law of *vis viva*,
which he knew well enough before. In all this, however, it
was plain that M. Neumann had no concern, unless he chose
to say that he had appropriated to himself Fresnel's law of
the *vis viva*, that he had determined to regard it as the foundation of his method (*le fondement de sa méthode*), and that
thenceforward no one else (however ignorant of such appro-
priation) could have any right to use it.

Having thus endeavoured to prove his claim to priority of publication, and to establish the independence of his own researches, which was all that was necessary for self defence, Mr. Mac Cullagh concluded by saying, that he would there drop the argument, without discussing his claim to priority in the abstract, as he had an objection to disputes of such a kind, and did not wish to pursue them any farther than he was compelled to do. But if anyone thought it worth while to examine the merits of this second question, he would find the circumstances relating to it very fully and clearly stated in the last number of the *Proceedings* of the Academy,* and would thence be enabled to form a judgment for himself.

* Vol. i. p. 217.

XIV.—AN ESSAY TOWARDS A DYNAMICAL THEORY OF CRYSTALLINE REFLEXION AND REFRACTION.

[*Transactions of the Royal Irish Academy*, Vol. xxi.—Read December 9, 1839.]

Sect. I.—Introductory Observations.—Equation of Motion.

NEARLY three years ago I communicated to this Academy* the laws by which the vibrations of light appear to be governed in their reflexion and refraction at the surfaces of crystals. These laws—remarkable for their simplicity and elegance, as well as for their agreement with exact experiments—I obtained from a system of hypotheses which were opposed, in some respects, to notions previously received, and were not bound together by any known principles of mechanics, the only evidence of their truth being the truth of the results to which they led. On that occasion, however, I observed that the hypotheses were not independent of each other; and soon afterwards I proved that the laws of reflexion at the surface of a crystal are connected, in a very singular way, with the laws of double refraction, or of propagation in its interior; from which I was led to infer that "all these laws and hypotheses have a common source in other and more intimate laws which remain to be discovered;" and that "the next step in physical optics would probably lead to those higher and more elementary principles by which the laws of reflexion

* In a Paper "On the Laws of Crystalline Reflexion and Refraction."—*Transactions* of the Royal Irish Academy, Vol. xviii. p. 31. (*Supra*, p. 87.)

and the laws of propagation are linked together as parts of the same system."*   This step has since been made, and these anticipations have been realised. In the present Paper I propose to supply the link between the two sets of laws by means of a very simple theory, depending on certain special assumptions, and employing the usual methods of analytical dynamics.

In this theory, the two kinds of laws, being traced from a common origin, are at once connected with each other and severally explained ; and it may be observed, that the explanation of each, as well as the source of their connexion, is now made known for the first time. For though the laws of crystalline propagation have attracted much attention during the period which has elapsed since they were discovered by Fresnel,† they have hitherto resisted every attempt that has been made to account for them by dynamical reasonings ; and the laws of reflexion, when recently discovered, were apparently still more difficult to reach by such considerations. Nothing can be easier, however, than the process by which both systems of laws are now deduced from the same principles.

The assumptions on which the theory rests are these :—*First*, that the density of the luminiferous ether is a constant quantity; in which it is implied that this density is unchanged either by the motions which produce light or by the presence of material particles, so that it is the same within all bodies as in free space, and remains the same during the most intense vibrations. *Second*, that the vibrations in a plane-wave are rectilinear, and that, while the plane of the wave moves parallel to itself, the vibrations continue parallel to a fixed right line, the direction of this right line and the direction of a normal to the wave being functions of each other. This supposition holds in all known crystals, except quartz, in which the vibrations are elliptical.

Concerning the peculiar constitution of the ether we know

* *Ibid*, p. 53, note. (*Supra*, p. 112.) The note here referred to was added some time after the Paper itself was read.

† These laws were published in his Memoir on Double Refraction—*Mémoires de l'Institut*, tom. vii. p. 45.

nothing, and shall suppose nothing, except what is involved in the foregoing assumptions. But with respect to its physical condition generally, we shall admit, as is most natural, that a vast number of ethereal particles are contained in the differential element of volume; and, for the present, we shall consider the mutual action of these particles to be sensible only at distances which are insensible when compared with the length of a wave.

By putting together the assumptions we have made, it will appear that when a system of plane waves disturbs the ether, the vibrations are transversal, or parallel to the plane of the waves. For all the particles situated in a plane parallel to the waves are displaced, from their positions of rest, through equal spaces in parallel directions; and therefore if we conceive a closed surface of any form, including any volume great or small, to be described in the quiescent ether, and then all its points to partake of the motion imparted by the waves, any slice cut out of that volume, by a pair of planes parallel to the wave-plane and indefinitely near each other, can have nothing but its thickness altered by the displacements; and since the assumed preservation of density requires that the volume of the slice should not be altered, nor consequently its thickness, it follows that the displacements must be in the plane of the slice, that is to say, they must be parallel to the wave-plane. And conversely, when this condition is fulfilled, it is obvious that the entire volume, bounded by the arbitrary surface above described, will remain constant during the motion, while the surface itself will always contain within it the very same ethereal particles which it enclosed in the state of rest; and all this will be accurately true, no matter how great may be the magnitude of the displacements.

Let x, y, z be the rectangular co-ordinates of a particle before it is disturbed, and $x + \xi$, $y + \eta$, $z + \zeta$ its co-ordinates at the time t, the displacements ξ, η, ζ being functions of x, y, z and t. Let the ethereal density, which is the same in all media, be regarded as unity, so that $dxdydz$ may, at any instant, represent indifferently either the element of volume or of mass. Then the equation of motion will be of the form

$$\iiint dx\,dy\,dz \left(\frac{d^2\xi}{dt^2}\,\delta\xi + \frac{d^2\eta}{dt^2}\,\delta\eta + \frac{d^2\zeta}{dt^2}\,d\zeta\right) = \iiint dx\,dy\,dz\,\delta V, \qquad (1)$$

where V is some function depending on the mutual actions of the particles. The integrals are to be extended over the whole volume of the vibrating medium, or over all the media, if there be more than one.

Setting out from this equation, which is the general formula of dynamics applied to the case that we are considering, we perceive that our chief difficulty will consist in the right determination of the function V; for if that function were known, little more would be necessary, in order to arrive at all the laws which we are in search of, than to follow the rules of analytical mechanics, as they have been given by Lagrange. The determination of V will, of course, depend on the assumptions above stated respecting the nature of the ethereal vibrations; but, before we proceed further, it seems advisable to introduce certain lemmas, for the purpose of abridging this and the subsequent investigations.

Sect. II.—Lemmas.

Lemma I.—Let a right line making with three rectangular axes the angles a, β, γ, be perpendicular to two other right lines which make with the same axes the angles a', β', γ' and a'', β'', γ'' respectively, and which are inclined to each other at an angle denoted by θ; then it is easy to prove that

$$\sin\theta\,\cos a = \cos\beta'\,\cos\gamma'' - \cos\beta''\,\cos\gamma',$$

$$\sin\theta\,\cos\beta = \cos\gamma'\,\cos a'' - \cos\gamma''\,\cos a', \qquad (\text{A})$$

$$\sin\theta\,\cos\gamma = \cos a'\,\cos\beta'' - \cos a''\,\cos\beta';$$

supposing the first right line to be prolonged in the proper direction from the origin, in order that the opposite members of any one of these equations may have the same sign, as well as the same magnitude.

If the last two right lines be perpendicular to each other, we have sin $\theta = 1$, and the formulæ become

$$\cos a = \cos \beta' \cos \gamma'' - \cos \beta'' \cos \gamma',$$

$$\cos \beta = \cos \gamma' \cos a'' - \cos \gamma'' \cos a', \qquad \text{(B)}$$

$$\cos \gamma = \cos a' \cos \beta'' - \cos a'' \cos \beta';$$

but in this case the three right lines are perpendicular to each other, and therefore we have, in like manner,

$$\cos a' = \cos \beta'' \cos \gamma - \cos \beta \cos \gamma'',$$

$$\cos \beta' = \cos \gamma'' \cos a - \cos \gamma \cos a'', \qquad \text{(B')}$$

$$\cos \gamma' = \cos a'' \cos \beta - \cos a \cos \beta'';$$

and also

$$\cos a'' = \cos \beta \cos \gamma' - \cos \beta' \cos \gamma,$$

$$\cos \beta'' = \cos \gamma \cos a' - \cos \gamma' \cos a, \qquad \text{(B'')}$$

$$\cos \gamma'' = \cos a \cos \beta' - \cos a' \cos \beta.$$

The last three groups of formulæ will still be true, if we suppose the first right line to make with the axes the angles a, a', a'', the second the angles β, β', β'', and the third the angles γ, γ', γ''

Lemma II.—Let ξ, η, ζ denote, as before, the displacements of a particle whose initial co-ordinates are x, y, z; and after putting

$$X = \frac{d\eta}{dz} - \frac{d\zeta}{dy}, \quad X = \frac{d\zeta}{dx} - \frac{d\xi}{dz}, \quad Z = \frac{d\xi}{dy} - \frac{d\eta}{dx}, \qquad \text{(c)}$$

suppose the axes of co-ordinates, still remaining rectangular, to have their directions changed in space, whereby the quantities X, Y, Z will be changed into X', Y', Z', answering to the new co-ordinates x', y', z', and to the new displacements ξ', η', ζ'; then will the quantities X', Y', Z' be connected with X, Y, Z by the very same relations which connect the co-ordinates x', y', z' with x, y, z, or the displacements ξ', η', ζ' with ξ, η, ζ.

That is to say, if the axes of x, y, z make with the axis of x' the angles a, β, γ, with the axis of y' the angles a', β', γ', and with the axis of z' the angles a'', β'', γ'' respectively, we shall have

$$X = X' \cos a + Y' \cos a' + Z' \cos a'',$$

$$Y = X' \cos \beta + Y' \cos \beta' + Z' \cos \beta'', \qquad \text{(D)}$$

$$Z = X' \cos \gamma + Y' \cos \gamma' + Z' \cos \gamma'',$$

and

$$X' = X \cos a + Y \cos \beta + Z \cos \gamma,$$

$$Y' = X \cos a' + Y \cos \beta' + Z \cos \gamma', \qquad \text{(D')}$$

$$Z' = X \cos a'' + Y \cos \beta'' + Z \cos \gamma'' ;$$

just as we have, for example,

$$\xi = \xi' \cos a + \eta' \cos a' + \zeta' \cos a'',$$

$$\eta = \xi' \cos \beta + \eta' \cos \beta' + \zeta' \cos \beta'', \qquad \text{(d)}$$

$$\zeta = \xi' \cos \gamma + \eta' \cos \gamma' + \zeta' \cos \gamma'',$$

and

$$x' = x \cos a + y \cos \beta + z \cos \gamma,$$

$$y' = x \cos a' + y \cos \beta' + z \cos \gamma', \qquad \text{(d')}$$

$$z' = x \cos a'' + y \cos \beta'' + z \cos \gamma''.$$

For, the change of the independent variables x, y, z into x', y', z' gives us the equations

$$\frac{d\eta}{dz} = \frac{d\eta}{dx'}\frac{dx'}{dz} + \frac{d\eta}{dy'}\frac{dy'}{dz} + \frac{d\eta}{dz'}\frac{dz'}{dz},$$

$$\frac{d\zeta}{dy} = \frac{d\zeta}{dx'}\frac{dx'}{dy} + \frac{d\zeta}{dy'}\frac{dy'}{dy} + \frac{d\zeta}{dz'}\frac{dz'}{dy},$$

in the right-hand members of which we have to substitute the

values of the differential coefficients obtained from (d) and (d').
Thus we get

$$\frac{d\eta}{dz} = \left(\frac{d\xi'}{dx'}\cos\beta + \frac{d\eta'}{dx'}\cos\beta' + \frac{d\zeta'}{dx'}\cos\beta''\right)\cos\gamma$$

$$+ \left(\frac{d\xi'}{dy'}\cos\beta + \frac{d\eta'}{dy'}\cos\beta' + \frac{d\zeta'}{dy'}\cos\beta''\right)\cos\gamma'$$

$$+ \left(\frac{d\xi'}{dz'}\cos\beta + \frac{d\eta'}{dz'}\cos\beta' + \frac{d\zeta'}{dz'}\cos\beta''\right)\cos\gamma'',$$

$$\frac{d\zeta}{dy} = \left(\frac{d\xi'}{dx'}\cos\gamma + \frac{d\eta'}{dx'}\cos\gamma' + \frac{d\zeta'}{dx'}\cos\gamma''\right)\cos\beta$$

$$+ \left(\frac{d\xi'}{dy'}\cos\gamma + \frac{d\eta'}{dy'}\cos\gamma' + \frac{d\zeta'}{dy'}\cos\gamma''\right)\cos\beta'$$

$$+ \left(\frac{d\xi'}{dz'}\cos\gamma + \frac{d\eta'}{dz'}\cos\gamma' + \frac{d\zeta'}{dz'}\cos\gamma''\right)\cos\beta'';$$

and when we subtract these equations, attending to the formulæ
in Lemma I., we find

$$\frac{d\eta}{dz} - \frac{d\zeta}{dy} = \left(\frac{d\eta'}{dz'} - \frac{d\zeta'}{dy'}\right)\cos a + \left(\frac{d\zeta'}{dx'} - \frac{d\xi'}{dz'}\right)\cos a'$$

$$+ \left(\frac{d\xi'}{dx'} - \frac{d\eta'}{dx'}\right)\cos a'',$$

or simply,

$$X = X'\cos a + Y'\cos a' + Z'\cos a'',$$

which is the first of formulæ (D). And in like manner the others
may be proved.

The same things will obviously hold with respect to quantities derived from X, Y, Z in the same way that these are derived
from ξ, η, ζ. That is, if we put

$$X_{,} = \frac{dY}{dz} - \frac{dZ}{dy}, \qquad Y_{,} = \frac{dZ}{dx} - \frac{dX}{dz}, \qquad Z_{,} = \frac{dX}{dy} - \frac{dY}{dx};$$

and then suppose the axes of co-ordinates to be changed, the formulæ for the transformation of the quantities $X_{\prime}$, $Y_{\prime}$, $Z_{\prime}$, will be similar to those for the transformation of the co-ordinates themselves.   The like will be true of the quantities $X_{\prime\prime}$, $Y_{\prime\prime}$, $Z_{\prime\prime}$, if we put

$$X_{\prime\prime} = \frac{dY_{\prime}}{dz} - \frac{dZ_{\prime}}{dy}, \quad Y_{\prime\prime} = \frac{dZ_{\prime}}{dx} - \frac{dX_{\prime}}{dz}, \quad Z_{\prime\prime} = \frac{dX_{\prime}}{dy} - \frac{dY_{\prime}}{dx}$$

and so on successively.

It is to be observed that, in this Lemma, the displacement is not limited by any restriction whatever.   Each of its components may be any function of the co-ordinates.   But the displacements produced by a system of plane waves are restricted by our definition of such waves; they must be the same for all particles situated in the same wave plane.   If the waves be parallel, for instance, to the plane of x', y', the quantities ξ', η', ζ' will be independent of the co-ordinates x', y', and will be functions of z' only.   This consideration reduces formulæ (D) to the following :

$$X = \frac{d\eta'}{dz'} \cos a - \frac{d\xi'}{dz'} \cos a',$$

$$Y = \frac{d\eta'}{dz'} \cos \beta - \frac{d\xi'}{dz'} \cos \beta', \qquad \text{(E)}$$

$$Z = \frac{d\eta'}{dz'} \cos \gamma - \frac{d\xi'}{dz'} \cos \gamma',$$

in which it is remarkable that the normal displacement ζ' does not appear.   If $\xi' = 0$, these formulæ become

$$X = \frac{d\eta'}{dz'} \cos a, \quad Y = \frac{d\eta'}{dz'} \cos \beta, \quad Z = \frac{d\eta'}{dz'} \cos \gamma ; \qquad \text{(F)}$$

or if $\eta' = 0$, then we have

$$X = -\frac{d\xi'}{dz'} \cos a', \quad Y = -\frac{d\xi'}{dz'} \cos \beta', \quad Z = -\frac{d\xi'}{dz'} \cos \gamma'. \qquad \text{(F')}$$

Lemma III.—If, in an ellipsoid whose semiaxes are equal to a, b, c, there be two rectangular diameters, one making with the semiaxes the angles a, β, γ, and the other the angles a', β', γ', such as to satisfy the condition

$$\frac{\cos a \cos a'}{a^2} + \frac{\cos \beta \cos \beta'}{b^2} + \frac{\cos \gamma \cos \gamma'}{c^2} = 0, \qquad \text{(G)}$$

these diameters will be the axes of the ellipse in which their plane intersects the ellipsoid.

For, the above condition expresses that either diameter is parallel to the tangent plane at the extremity of the other; they are therefore conjugate diameters of the elliptic section; and hence, as they are at right angles to each other, they must be its axes.

If the semiaxes of the ellipsoid be represented by $\dfrac{1}{a}, \dfrac{1}{b}, \dfrac{1}{c}$, the equation of condition will become

$$a^2 \cos a \cos a' + b^2 \cos \beta \cos \beta' + c^2 \cos \gamma \cos \gamma' = 0. \qquad \text{(G')}$$

Lemma IV.—Let s, s' be the lengths of perpendiculars let fall from the centre of an ellipsoid upon any two tangent planes, and r, r' the lengths of radii drawn to the respective points of contact. Then putting ω for the angle between the directions of r and s', and ω' for the angle between the directions of r' and s, we shall have

$$rs \cos \omega = r's' \cos \omega'.$$

For if the semiaxes of the ellipsoid, having their lengths denoted by a, b, c, make with the direction of s the angles a, β, γ, and with that of s' the angles a', β', γ'; with the direction of r the angles a_0, β_0, γ_0, and with that of r' the angles a_1, β_1, γ_1, there will exist the relations

$$a^2 \cos a = rs \cos a_0, \quad b^2 \cos \beta = rs \cos \beta_0, \quad c^2 \cos \gamma = rs \cos \gamma_0,$$

$$a^2 \cos a' = r's' \cos a_1, \quad b^2 \cos \beta' = r's' \cos \beta_1, \quad c^2 \cos \gamma' = r's' \cos \gamma_1,$$

by one set of which the quantity

$$a^2 \cos a \cos a' + b^2 \cos \beta \cos \beta' + c^2 \cos \gamma \cos \gamma'$$

will be converted into

$$rs \,(\cos a_0 \cos a' + \cos \beta_0 \cos \beta' + \cos \gamma_0 \cos \gamma') = rs \cos \omega,$$

and by the other set into

$$r'\,s'\,(\cos a_1 \cos a + \cos \beta_1 \cos \beta + \cos \gamma_1 \cos \gamma) = r'\,s' \cos \omega';$$

so that we shall get

$$rs \cos \omega = r'\,s' \cos \omega' = a^2 \cos a \cos a' + b^2 \cos \beta \cos \beta'$$
$$+ \; c^2 \cos \gamma \cos \gamma'. \qquad \text{(H)}$$

Corollary.—When the condition

$$a^2 \cos a \cos a' + b^2 \cos \beta \cos \beta' + c^2 \cos \gamma \cos \gamma' = 0 \qquad \text{(I)}$$

is satisfied, each of the angles ω, ω' is a right angle. Let us suppose, at the same time, that the direction of s is perpendicular to that of s'. Then will the directions of s and r' coincide with the axes of the ellipse in which their plane intersects the ellipsoid; for s is perpendicular to r' and parallel to the tangent plane at its extremity. The directions of s' and r, in the same manner, will coincide with the axes of another elliptic section.

Sect. III.—Determination of the Function on which the Motion depends. Principal Axes of a Crystal.

We come now to investigate the particular form which must be assigned to the function V, in order that the formula (1) may represent the motions of the ethereal medium. For this purpose conceive the plane of $x'\,y'$ to be parallel to a system of plane waves whose vibrations are entirely transversal and parallel to the axis of y', so that $\xi' = 0$, $\zeta' = 0$. Imagine an elementary parallelepiped $dx'\,dy'\,dz'$, having its edges parallel to the axes of x', y', z', to be described in the ether when at rest, and then all its points to move according to the same law as the ethereal particles which compose it. The faces of the parallelepiped which are perpendicular to the edge dz' will be shifted, each in its own plane, in a direction parallel to the axis of y'; but their displacements will be unequal, and will differ by $d\eta'$, so that the edges connecting their corresponding angles will no longer be parallel to the axis of z', but will be inclined to it at an angle κ whose tangent is $\dfrac{dn'}{dz'}$.

Now the function V can only depend upon the directions of the axes of x', y', z' with respect to fixed lines in the crystal, and upon the angle κ, which measures the change of form produced in the parallelepiped by vibration. This is the most general supposition which can be made concerning it. Since, however, by our second assumption, any one of these directions, suppose that of x', determines the other two, we may regard V as depending on the angle κ and on the direction of the axis of x' alone. But from the equations (F) it is manifest that the angle κ and the angles which the axis of x' makes with the fixed axes of x, y, z are all known when the quantities X, Y, Z are known. Consequently V is a function of X, Y, Z.

Supposing the angle κ to be very small, the quantities X, Y, Z will also be very small; and if V be expanded according to the powers of these quantities, we shall have

$$V = K + AX + BY + CZ + DX^2 + EY^2 + FZ^2$$
$$+ GYZ + HXZ + IXY + \&c.,$$

the quantities K, A, B, C, D, &c., being constant. But in the state of equilibrium the value of δV ought to be nothing, in whatever way the position of the system be varied; that is to say, when the displacements ξ, η, ζ, and consequently the quantities X, Y, Z, are supposed to vanish, the quantity

$$\delta V = A\delta X + B\delta Y + C\delta Z + 2DX\delta X + \&c.,$$

ought also to vanish independently of the variations $\delta\xi$, $\delta\eta$, $\delta\zeta$, or, which comes to the same thing, independently of δX, δY, δZ. Hence* we must have $A = 0$, $B = 0$, $C = 0$; and therefore, if we neglect terms of the third and higher dimensions, we may conclude that the variable part of V is a homogeneous function

* See the reasoning of Lagrange in an analogous case, *Mécanique Analytique*, tom. I. p. 68.

of the second degree, containing, in its general form, the squares and products of X, Y, Z, with six constant coefficients.

Of these coefficients, the three which multiply the products of the variables may always be made to vanish by changing the directions of the axes of x, y, z. For this is a known property of functions of the second degree, when the co-ordinates are the variables; and we have shown, in Lemma II., that the quantities X, Y, Z are transformed by the very same relations as the co-ordinates themselves. Therefore, in every crystal there exist three rectangular axes, with respect to which the function V contains only the squares of X, Y, Z; and as it will presently appear that the coefficients of the squares must all be negative, in order that the velocity of propagation may never become imaginary, we may consequently write, with reference to these axes,

$$V = -\tfrac{1}{2}(a^2 X^2 + b^2 Y^2 + c^2 Z^2), \tag{2}$$

omitting the constant K as having no effect upon the motion.

The axes of co-ordinates, in this position, are the *principal axes* of the crystal, and are commonly known by the name of *axes of elasticity*. Thus the existence of these axes is proved without any hypothesis respecting the arrangement of the particles of the medium. The constants a, b, c are the three principal velocities of propagation, as we shall see in the next section.

Having arrived at the value of V, we may now take it for the starting point of our theory, and dismiss the assumptions by which we were conducted to it. Supposing, therefore, in the first place, that a plane wave passes through a crystal, we shall seek the laws of its motion from equations (1) and (2), which contain everything that is necessary for the solution of the problem. The laws of propagation, as they are called, will in this way be deduced, and they will be found to agree exactly, so far as *magnitudes* are concerned, with those discovered by Fresnel; but the *direction* of the vibrations in a polarized ray will be different from that assigned by him. In the second place, we shall investigate the conditions which are fulfilled when light passes out of one medium into another, and we shall thus obtain the laws of reflexion and refraction at the surface of a crystal.

SECT. IV.—PROPAGATION OF LIGHT IN A CRYSTALLIZED ME-
DIUM.—LAWS OF FRESNEL.—ALTERATION REQUIRED TO BE
MADE IN THEM.— WAVE-SURFACE, INDEX-SURFACE, AND
THEIR PROPERTIES.

The principal axes of the crystal being the axes of x, y, z,
we have, by equation (2),

$$- \delta V = a^2 X \delta X + b^2 Y \delta Y + c^2 Z \delta Z ; \qquad (3)$$

or, by taking the variations from formulæ (c), and interchanging
the characteristics d and δ,

$$- \delta V = a^2 X \left(\frac{d\delta\eta}{dz} - \frac{d\delta\zeta}{dy} \right) + b^2 Y \left(\frac{d\delta\zeta}{dx} - \frac{d\delta\xi}{dz} \right) + c^2 Z \left(\frac{d\delta\xi}{dy} - \frac{d\delta\eta}{dx} \right) ;$$

and if we substitute this value in equation (1), and then integrate by parts the right-hand member, in order to get rid of the
differential coefficients of the variations, we shall obtain

$$\iiint dx\,dy\,dz \left(\frac{d^2\xi}{dt^2} \delta\xi + \frac{d^2\eta}{dt^2} \delta\eta + \frac{d^2\zeta}{dt^2} \delta\zeta \right)$$

$$= \iint dy\,dz \, (c^2 Z \delta\eta - b^2 Y \delta\zeta) + \iint dx\,dz \, (a^2 X \delta\zeta - c^2 Z \delta\xi)$$

$$+ \iint dx\,dy \, (b^2 Y \delta\xi - a^2 X \delta\eta) \qquad (4)$$

$$+ \iiint dx\,dy\,dz \left\{ \left(c^2 \frac{dZ}{dy} - b^2 \frac{dY}{dz} \right) d\xi + \left(a^2 \frac{dX}{dz} - c^2 \frac{dZ}{dx} \right) \delta\eta \right.$$

$$\left. + \left(b^2 \frac{dY}{dx} - a^2 \frac{dX}{dy} \right) \delta\zeta \right\} .$$

But as the variations $\delta\xi$, $\delta\eta$, $\delta\zeta$ are arbitrary and independent,
this equation cannot hold unless the double integrals, which re-
late to the limits of the system, reduce themselves to zero, leaving the equality to subsist, independently of the variations,
between the triple integrals alone. Equating, therefore, the

coefficients of the corresponding variations in the triple integrals, we get

$$\frac{d^2\xi}{dt^2} = c^2 \frac{dZ}{dy} - b^2 \frac{dY}{dz},$$

$$\frac{d^2\eta}{dt^2} = a^2 \frac{dX}{dz} - c^2 \frac{dZ}{dx}, \qquad (5)$$

$$\frac{d^2\zeta}{dt^2} = b^2 \frac{dY}{dx} - a^2 \frac{dX}{dy},$$

which are the equations of propagation, giving the expression for the accelerating force parallel to each axis of co-ordinates.

When there is a single medium extending indefinitely on all sides, the conditions relative to the limits are of no importance, and we have only to consider the equations (5), from which we shall now deduce the laws by which a system of plane waves is propagated.

Supposing the waves to be parallel to the plane of $x'\,y'$, the displacements will be functions of z' only; and if ψ be any function of the displacements, we shall have, by formulæ (d'),

$$\frac{d\psi}{dx} = \frac{d\psi}{dz'}\frac{dz'}{dx} = \frac{d\psi}{dz'}\cos a'', \quad \frac{d\psi}{dy} = \frac{d\psi}{dz'}\cos \beta'', \quad \frac{d\psi}{dz} = \frac{d\psi}{dz'}\cos \gamma'',$$

so that the equations (5) may be written

$$\frac{d^2\xi}{dt^2} = c^2 \frac{dZ}{dz'}\cos \beta'' - b^2 \frac{dY}{dz'}\cos \gamma'',$$

$$\frac{d^2\eta}{dt^2} = a^2 \frac{dX}{dz'}\cos \gamma'' - c^2 \frac{dZ}{dz'}\cos a'',$$

$$\frac{a^2\zeta}{dt^2} = b^2 \frac{dY}{dz'}\cos a'' - a^2 \frac{dX}{dz'}\cos \beta'';$$

and when we combine these with the following,

$$\frac{d^2\xi'}{dt^2} = \frac{d^2\xi}{dt^2}\cos a + \frac{d^2\eta}{dt^2}\cos \beta + \frac{d^2\zeta}{dt^2}\cos \gamma,$$

$$\frac{d^2\eta'}{dt^2} = \frac{d^2\xi}{dt^2}\cos\alpha' + \frac{d^2\eta}{dt^2}\cos\beta' + \frac{d^2\zeta}{dt^2}\cos\gamma',$$

$$\frac{d^2\zeta'}{dt^2} = \frac{d^2\xi}{dt^2}\cos\alpha'' + \frac{d^2\eta}{dt^2}\cos\beta'' + \frac{d^2\zeta}{dt^2}\cos\gamma'',$$

attending to the relations (B), (B'), we find

$$\frac{d^2\xi'}{dt^2} = -\left(a^2\frac{dX}{dz'}\cos\alpha' + b^2\frac{dY}{dz'}\cos\beta' + c^2\frac{dZ}{dz'}\cos\gamma'\right),$$

$$\frac{d^2\eta'}{dt^2} = a^2\frac{dX}{dz'}\cos\alpha + b^2\frac{dY}{dz'}\cos\beta + c^2\frac{dZ}{dz'}\cos\gamma,$$

$$\frac{d^2\zeta'}{dt^2} = 0;$$

from which it appears that there is no accelerating force in the direction of a normal* to the wave, and consequently no vibration in that direction. Introducing now the values of X, Y, Z from formulæ (E), the first two of these equations become

$$\frac{d^2\xi'}{dt^2} = (a^2\cos^2\alpha' + b^2\cos^2\beta' + c^2\cos^2\gamma')\frac{d^2\xi'}{dz'^2}$$
$$- (a^2\cos\alpha\cos\alpha' + b^2\cos\beta\cos\beta' + c^2\cos\gamma\cos\gamma')\frac{d^2\eta'}{dz'^2},$$

$$\frac{d^2\eta'}{dt^2} = (a^2\cos^2\alpha + b^2\cos^2\beta + c^2\cos^2\gamma)\frac{d^2\eta'}{dz'^2}$$
$$- (a^2\cos\alpha\cos\alpha' + b^2\cos\beta\cos\beta' + c^2\cos\gamma\cos\gamma')\frac{d^2\xi'}{dz'^2}.$$

$$(6)$$

But as the axes of x', y' are arbitrarily taken in the plane of $x'y'$ we may subject their directions to the condition

$$a^2\cos\alpha\cos\alpha' + b^2\cos\beta\cos\beta' + c^2\cos\gamma\cos\gamma' = 0; \quad (7)$$

---

* In the ingenious, but altogether unsatisfactory theory, by which Fresnel has endeavoured to account for his beautiful laws, the direction of the elastic force brought into play by the displacement of the ethereal molecules is, in general, inclined to the plane of the wave. He supposes, however, that the force normal to that plane does not produce any appreciable effect, by reason of the great resistance which the ether offers to compression.—*Mémoires de l'Institut*, tom. vii. p. 78.

and then, if we put

$$s^2 = a^2 \cos^2 \alpha + b^2 \cos^2 \beta + c^2 \cos^2 \gamma,$$

$$s'^2 = a^2 \cos^2 \alpha' + b^2 \cos^2 \beta' + c^2 \cos^2 \gamma', \tag{8}$$

the equations (6) will be reduced to the well-known form

$$\frac{d^2 \xi'}{dt^2} = s'^2 \frac{d^2 \xi'}{dz'^2}, \qquad \frac{d^2 \eta'}{dt^2} = s^2 \frac{d^2 \eta'}{dz'^2}. \tag{9}$$

This result shows that, when the directions of x' and y' fulfil the condition (7), the vibrations ξ' and η' are propagated independently of each other, the former with the velocity of s', the latter with the velocity s. The vibrations must therefore be parallel exclusively to one or other of these directions, else the system of waves will split into two systems, one vibrating parallel to x', the other parallel to y'.

When the plane of the wave is parallel to one of the principal axes, it is easy to infer that the vibrations must be either parallel or perpendicular to that axis; and that, in the latter case, the velocity of propagation is constant, being equal to a, b, or c, according as the wave is parallel to the axis of x, y, or z. These constants are therefore called the principal velocities of propagation; and we now perceive the reason of the negative sign in equation (2); for if any of the terms in the right-hand member of that equation were positive, the corresponding velocity would be imaginary.

According to Fresnel, the wave which is propagated with the velocity a has its vibrations not perpendicular to the axis of x, but parallel to it; and it is to be observed that a difference of the same character distinguishes his views, throughout, from the results of the present theory. It will appear in fact, by what immediately follows, that the equations (7), (8), (9), express exactly the laws of Fresnel, provided the quantities ξ' and η', in the equations (9), be interchanged. To make these laws agree with our theory, it is therefore necessary to alter them in one particular, and in one only; it is necessary to suppose that the direction of the vibrations is always perpendicular to that assigned by Fresnel. And since, in order to make his views agree with the phenomena, Fresnel was obliged to say that, in an ordinary medium, the vibrations of a ray polarized in a certain plane are *perpendicular* to that plane, it is clear that, on the present principles, we must come to a different conclusion, and say that the vibrations of a polarized ray are *parallel* to its plane of polarization.

Conceive an ellipsoid with its centre at O, the common origin of the co-ordinates x, y, z, x', y', z' ; and let its semiaxes be parallel to x, y, z, their lengths being equal to $\dfrac{1}{a}, \dfrac{1}{b}, \dfrac{1}{c}$ respectively. From the identity of the condition (7) with that marked (G') in Lemma III., it is evident that the directions of x' and y', when they are the two directions of vibration, coincide with the axes of the ellipse in which the plane of $x'y'$ intersects the ellipsoid ; and if the right line OR, meeting the ellipsoid in R, be the direction of x', we have

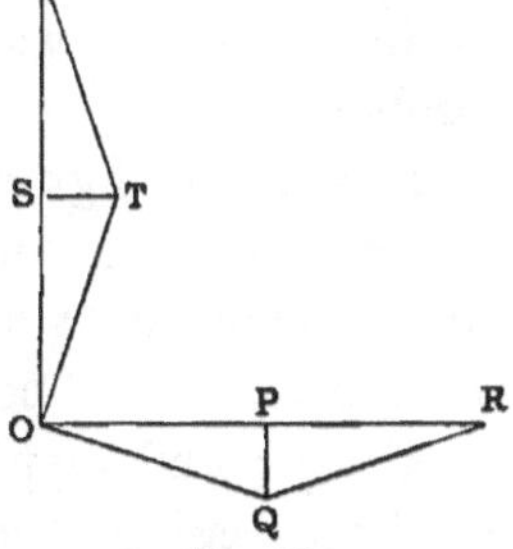

Fig. 20.

$$\frac{1}{(OR)^2} = a^2 \cos^2 a + b^2 \cos^2 \beta + c^2 \cos^2 \gamma,$$

or, by (8),

$$\frac{1}{OR} = s,$$

so that OR is the reciprocal of the velocity with which the vibrations parallel to y' are propagated. Thus we see that the vibrations parallel to either semiaxis of the elliptic section are propagated with a velocity which is measured by the reciprocal of the other semiaxis.

Again, conceive an ellipsoid with its centre at O, and its semiaxes parallel to x, y, z, as before, but equal to a, b, c respectively. Let this ellipsoid be touched in the point Q by a plane which cuts OR perpendicularly in P, and draw the right lines OP, PQ. Then as the condition (7) is identical with that marked (1) in the corollary to Lemma IV., it follows that Oy' (if we so call the direction of y') is perpendicular to OQ, and also that Oy' and OQ coincide with the axes of the elliptic section made in this ellipsoid by the plane QOy', just as Oy' and OR coincide with the axes of the section ROy' in the first ellipsoid. The plane QOR is therefore perpendicular to Oy' and to the plane of the wave. Moreover, we have

$$(OP)^2 = a^2 \cos^2\alpha + b^2 \cos^2\beta + c^2 \cos^2\gamma = s^2,$$

so that OP is the reciprocal of OR, and is equal to the velocity s with which the wave is propagated when its vibrations are parallel to Oy'.

Now let the figure $TOSM$ be equal in all respects to $QOPR$, but in a position perpendicular to it, so that if $QOPR$ were turned round in its own plane through a right angle, the point O being fixed, the points Q, P, R would fall upon T, S, M respectively ; and supposing the wave-plane ROy' to take various positions passing through O, imagine a construction similar to the preceding one to be always made by means of the two ellipsoids. Then while the points R and Q describe the ellipsoids, the points M and T describe two biaxal* surfaces reciprocal to each other, the latter surface being touched† in the point T by a plane which cuts OM perpendicularly in S. But this plane is parallel to the central wave-plane ROy', and distant from it by an interval OS (= OP) which represents the velocity of the wave ; and as the surface whose tangent planes possess this property is, by definition, the *wave-surface* of the crystal, it is obvious that the point T describes the wave-surface. The radius OT, drawn to the point of contact, is then, by the theory of waves, the direction of the *ray* which belongs to the wave ROy', and the length OT represents the velocity of light along the ray. As to the surface described by the point M, it is that

---

* See *Transactions* of the Royal Irish Academy, Vol. xvii. p. 244 (*supra*, p. 24).
† *Ibid.* Vol. xvi. p. 6 (*supra*, p. 4).

which I have called the *surface of indices*, or the *index-surface*,[*] because its radius OM, being the reciprocal of OS, represents the index of refraction, or the ratio of the sine of the angle of incidence to the sine of the angle of refraction, when the wave ROy', to which OM is perpendicular, is supposed to have passed into the crystal out of an ordinary medium in which the velocity of propagation is unity. The angles of incidence and refraction are understood to be the angles which the incident and refracted waves respectively make with the refracting surface of the crystal.

The wave-surface and the index-surface have the same geometrical properties since they are both biaxal surfaces. Let us consider the former, which is generated by the ellipsoid whose semiaxes are a, b, c; and let us conceive this ellipsoid to be intersected by a concentric sphere of which the radius is r. Then the equations of the ellipsoid and the sphere being respectively

$$\frac{x^2}{a^2} + \frac{y^2}{b^2} + \frac{z^2}{c^2} = 1, \quad \frac{x^2 + y^2 + z^2}{r^2} = 1,$$

we get, by subtracting the one from the other,

$$x^2 \left(\frac{1}{a^2} - \frac{1}{r^2} \right) + y^2 \left(\frac{1}{b^2} - \frac{1}{r^2} \right) + z^2 \left(\frac{1}{c^2} - \frac{1}{r^2} \right) = 0, \qquad (10)$$

for the equation of the cone A which has its vertex at O, and passes through the curve of intersection. If OQ be equal to r, it will be a side of this cone; and a plane touching the cone along OQ will make in the ellipsoid a section of which OQ will be a semiaxis; so that OT will be perpendicular to that plane, and equal in length to r. Therefore, as OQ describes the cone A, the right line OT describes another cone B reciprocal to A, and the point T describes the curve in which the wave-surface is intersected by the sphere above mentioned; this curve being a *spherical ellipse*, reciprocal to that which the point Q describes on

---

[*] See *Transactions* of the Royal Irish Academy, Vol. XVIII. p. 38 (*supra*, p. 96). I had previously called it the *surface of refraction*, Vol. XVII. p. 252 (*supra*, p. 36).

the surface of the ellipsoid. The equation of the cone B is found from that of A, by changing the coefficients of the squares of the variables into their reciprocals, and is therefore

$$\frac{a^2 x^2}{r^2 - a^2} + \frac{b^2 y^2}{r^2 - b^2} + \frac{c^2 z^2}{r^2 - c^2} = 0, \tag{11}$$

which, of course, is also the equation of the wave-surface, if r be supposed to be the radius drawn from O to the point whose co-ordinates are x, y, z. Combining this equation with that of the sphere, we have

$$\frac{x^2}{r^2 - a^2} + \frac{y^2}{r^2 - b^2} + \frac{z^2}{r^2 - c^2} = 1, \tag{12}$$

which represents a hyperboloid passing through the common intersection of the sphere, the cone B, and the wave-surface.

Since the differences between the coefficients of the squares of the variables in the equation (10) are the same as the corresponding differences in the equation of the ellipsoid, the cone A has its planes of circular section coincident with those of the ellipsoid. The cone B, being reciprocal to A, has therefore its focal lines perpendicular to the circular sections of the ellipsoid. These focal lines are consequently the *nodal diameters** of the wave-surface, that is, the diameters which pass through the points where the two sheets of that surface intersect each other.

If the direction of OT cut the other sheet of the wave-surface in T', and if two radii of constant lengths, equal to OT and OT' respectively, revolve within the surface, the cones B and B' described by these radii will intersect each other at right angles, since they have the same focal lines. And supposing the axis of y to be the mean axis of the ellipsoid, so that the nodal diameters lie in the plane of xz, the axis of x will lie within one of the cones, as B, and the axis of z within the other cone B'. Now the angle contained by the two sides of either

---

* See *Transactions* of the Royal Irish Academy, Vol. xvii. p. 247 (*supra*, p. 29).

cone, which lie in the plane of xz, is given by the angles θ and θ' which the direction of the right line OTT' makes with the nodal diameters; because the angles which any side of a cone makes with its focal lines have a constant sum, or a constant difference, according to the way in which they are reckoned. But if the angles θ and θ' be reckoned (as they may be) so that their sum shall be equal to the angle contained by the two sides of the cone B which are in the plane of xz, their difference will be equal to the angle contained by the two sides of the cone B' which are in the same plane; the contained angle, in each case, being that which is bisected by the axis of x. Therefore, the lengths OT and OT', which we denote by r and r', are equal to two radii of the ellipse whose equation is

$$\frac{x^2}{a^2} + \frac{z^2}{c^2} = 1,$$

these radii making with the axis of z the angles $\frac{1}{2}(\theta + \theta')$ and $\frac{1}{2}(\theta - \theta')$ respectively. Hence

$$\frac{1}{r^2} = \frac{\sin^2\frac{1}{2}(\theta + \theta')}{a^2} + \frac{\cos^2\frac{1}{2}(\theta + \theta')}{c^2} = \frac{1}{2}\left(\frac{1}{a^2} + \frac{1}{c^2}\right)$$
$$- \frac{1}{2}\left(\frac{1}{a^2} - \frac{1}{c^2}\right)\cos(\theta + \theta'),$$

$$\frac{1}{r'^2} = \frac{\sin^2\frac{1}{2}(\theta - \theta')}{a^2} + \frac{\cos^2\frac{1}{2}(\theta - \theta')}{c^2} = \frac{1}{2}\left(\frac{1}{a^2} + \frac{1}{c^2}\right)$$
$$- \frac{1}{2}\left(\frac{1}{a^2} - \frac{1}{c^2}\right)\cos(\theta - \theta').$$

$$(13)$$

These formulæ give the two velocities of propagation along a *ray* which makes the angles θ, θ' with the nodal diameters. Subtracting them, we have

$$\frac{1}{r^2} - \frac{1}{r'^2} = \left(\frac{1}{a^2} - \frac{1}{c^2}\right)\sin\theta\sin\theta'. \qquad (14)$$

All the preceding equations, relative to the wave-surface,

may be transferred to the index-surface, by changing the quantities a, b, c into their reciprocals. For example, if the normal to a wave make the angles θ_0, θ_1 with the nodal diameters of the index-surface, the formulæ (13) give

$$s^2 = \tfrac{1}{2}(a^2 + c^2) - \tfrac{1}{2}(a^2 - c^2)\cos(\theta_0 + \theta_1),$$

$$s'^2 = \tfrac{1}{2}(a^2 + c^2) - \tfrac{1}{2}(a^2 - c^2)\cos(\theta_0 - \theta_1);$$

$$\text{(15)}$$

observing that s and s', the two normal velocities of propagation, are the reciprocals of the radii of this surface which coincide with the wave-normal. Subtracting these expressions, we get

$$s^2 - s'^2 = (a^2 - c^2)\sin\theta_0 \sin\theta_1. \qquad (16)$$

As the position of the tangent plane, at any point T of a biaxal surface, depends on the position of the axes of the section QOy' made in the generating ellipsoid by a plane perpendicular to OT, it is obvious that when this section is a circle, that is, when the point T is a node of the surface, the position of the tangent plane is indeterminate, like that of the axes of the section; and it is easy to show that the cone which that plane touches in all its positions is of the second order. Again, when the section ROy' of the reciprocal ellipsoid is a circle, the right line OS is given both in position and length; and the tangent plane, which cuts OS in S, is fixed; but the point of contact T is not fixed, since the semiaxis OR, to which the right line ST is parallel, may be any radius of the circle ROy'. In this case, the point T describes a curve in the tangent plane, and this curve is found to be a circle. But both these cases have been fully discussed elsewhere.*

---

* See *Transactions* of the Royal Irish Academy, Vol. xvii. pp. 245, 260 (*supra*, pp. 25-7, 49-51).

Sect. V.—Conditions to be satisfied when Light passes out of one Medium into another.—Remarkable Circumstances connected with them.—Relations among the Transversals of the Incident, Reflected, and Refracted Rays.

Now let light pass out of one medium into another—suppose out of an ordinary into a doubly-refracting medium ; and taking the origin of rectangular co-ordinates x_0, y_0, z_0 at a point O on the surface which separates the two media, let this surface be the plane of $x_0 y_0$. Then if the components of the displacement of a particle whose initial co-ordinates are x_0, y_0, z_0 be denoted by ξ'_0, η'_0, ζ'_0 when the particle is in the first medium, and by ξ_0'', η_0'', ζ_0'' when it is in the second, the equation (1), adapted to the present case, will be

$$\iiint dx_0\, dy_0\, dz_0 \left(\frac{d^2\xi'_0}{dt^2}\, \delta\xi'_0 + \frac{d^2\eta'_0}{dt^2}\, \delta\eta'_0 + \frac{d^2\zeta'_0}{dt^2}\, \delta\zeta'_0 \right)$$

$$+ \iiint dx_0\, dy_0\, dz_0 \left(\frac{d^2\xi''_0}{dt^2}\, \delta\xi''_0 + \frac{d^2\eta''_0}{dt^2}\, \delta\eta''_0 + \frac{d^2\zeta''_0}{dt^2}\, \delta\xi''_0 \right)$$

$$= \iiint dx_0\, dy_0\, dz_0\, \delta V' + \iiint dx_0\, dy_0\, dz_0\, \delta V'' ; \qquad (17)$$

wherein $\delta V'$ and $\delta V''$ are the respective values of δV for the two media, which are conceived to extend indefinitely on each side of the plane of $x_0 y_0$; that plane being an upper limit of the integrations relative to one medium, and a lower limit of the integrations relative to the other. Each medium is conceived to be occupied by systems of plane waves—the first by incident and reflected waves, the second by refracted waves; and, except where they are bounded by the plane of $x_0 y_0$, these waves are regarded as unlimited in extent.

For the ordinary medium, if we put

and suppose the velocity of propagation to be unity, we have[*]

$$-\delta V' = X'_0\left(\frac{d\delta\eta'_0}{dz_0} - \frac{d\delta\zeta'_0}{dy_0}\right) + Y'_0\left(\frac{d\delta\zeta'_0}{dx_0} - \frac{d\delta\xi'_0}{dz_0}\right) + Z'_0\left(\frac{d\delta\xi'_0}{dy_0} - \frac{d\delta\eta'_0}{dx_0}\right).$$

For the crystallized medium, if its principal axes be those of x, y, z, the value of $\delta V''$ will be the same as that of δV in formula (3) ; but instead of the variations of ξ, η, ζ, we must use those of ξ''_0, η''_0, ζ''_0. Denoting the cosines of the angles which the principal axes respectively make with the axis of x_0 by l, m, n ; with the axis of y_0 by l', m', n' ; with the axis of z_0 by l'', m'', n'' ; and putting

$$X''_0 = \frac{d\eta''_0}{dz_0} - \frac{d\zeta''_0}{dy_0}, \quad Y''_0 = \frac{d\zeta''_0}{dx_0} - \frac{d\xi''_0}{dz_0}, \quad Z''_0 = \frac{d\xi''_0}{dy} - \frac{d\eta''_0}{dx_0},$$

$$\delta X'' = \frac{d\delta\eta''_0}{dz_0} - \frac{d\delta\zeta''_0}{dy_0}, \quad \delta Y''_0 = \frac{d\delta\zeta''_0}{dx_0} - \frac{d\delta\xi''_0}{dz_0}, \quad \delta Z''_0 = \frac{d\delta\xi''_0}{dy_0} - \frac{d\delta\eta''_0}{dx_0} ;$$

we have

$$\delta X = l\delta X''_0 + l'\delta Y''_0 + l''\delta Z''_0,$$

$$\delta Y = m\delta X''_0 + m'\delta Y''_0 + m''\delta Z''_0,$$

$$\delta Z = n\,\delta X''_0 + n'\delta Y''_0 + n''\delta Z''_0.$$

These expressions for δX, δY, δZ having been written in formula (3), the resulting value of $\delta V''$, as well as the above value of $\delta V'$, is to be substituted in the equation (17), and then the right-hand member of that equation is to be integrated by parts, in order to get rid of the differential coefficients of the variations. When this operation is performed, the triple integrals on one side of the equation will be equal to those on the other ; and by equating the coefficients of the corresponding variations

---

[*] It is assumed here, and in what follows, that when there are two or more coexisting waves in a given medium, the form of the function V is the same as for a single wave, provided the displacements which enter into the function be the resultants of the displacements due to each wave separately. This, however, ought evidently to be the case, in order that the principle of the superposition of vibrations may hold good.

in each medium, we should get the laws of propagation in each. But we are not now considering these laws, and we need only attend to the double integrals produced by the operation aforesaid. The double integrals are together equal to zero; but we are concerned only with that part of them which relates to the common limit of the media, the plane of $x_0 y_0$; and this part must be separately equal to zero, since the conditions to be fulfilled at the plane of $x_0 y_0$ are independent of anything that might take place at other limiting surfaces, if such were supposed to exist. Collecting therefore the terms produced by integrating with respect to z_0, and observing that a negative sign must be interposed between those which belong to different media, we get

$$\iint dx_0\, dy_0 \left(Y'_0\, \delta\xi'_0 - X'_0\, \delta\eta'_0\right) - \iint dx_0\, dy_0 \left(Q\delta\xi''_0 - P\delta\eta''_0\right) = 0, \quad (18)$$

where

$$P = a^2 lX + b^2 mY + c^2 nZ, \qquad Q = a^2 l'X + b^2 m'Y + c^2 n'Z. \quad (19)$$

In each of these equations it is understood that $z_0 = 0$. But when $z_0 = 0$, we have obviously

$$\xi'_0 = \xi''_0, \qquad \eta_0 = \eta''_0, \qquad (20)$$

and therefore

$$\delta\xi'_0 = \delta\xi''_0, \qquad \delta\eta'_0 = \delta\eta''_0 ;$$

so that the equation (18) becomes

$$\iint dx_0\, dy_0 \left\{ (Y'_0 - Q)\, \delta\xi'_0 - (X'_0 - P)\, \delta\eta'_0 \right\} = 0,$$

which, as the variations $d\xi'_0$ and $d\eta'_0$ are arbitrary and independent, is equivalent to the two equations

$$X'_0 = P, \qquad Y'_0 = Q. \qquad (21)$$

Thus, to find the relations which subsist among the vibrations incident, reflected, and refracted, at the common surface of two media, we have four conditions, expressed by the equations (20) and (21); and these conditions are sufficient to determine the reflected and refracted vibrations, when the incident vibration is given. But though, by the nature of the question, four conditions only are required for its solution, there remains another condition which ought to be satisfied; for we ought evidently to have

$$\zeta'_0 = \zeta''_0, \quad \text{when } z_0 = 0. \tag{22}$$

This condition is apparently independent of the rest; but it cannot really be so, if the preceding theory is consistent with itself. We shall accordingly see, in what follows, that the last condition is included in the other four; which is a remarkable circumstance, and a singular confirmation of the theory.*

As the incident and reflected waves coexist in the first medium, and two sets of refracted waves in the second, the resolved displacements, and all the quantities which depend upon them, are composed of two parts, due to the coexisting waves. Let the point O be, for each set of waves, the origin of a system of rectangular co-ordinates, which we shall call x_1, y_1, z_1 for the incident, and x'_1, y'_1, z'_1 for the reflected wave, the axes of z_1 and z'_1 being perpendicular to the respective waves, and their positive directions being those of propagation. Let the displacements in these waves be parallel to y_1, y'_1, and be denoted by η_1, η'_1, respectively. Then if the axes of x_0, y_0, z_0 make with the axis of x_1 the angles a_1, β_1, γ_1, and with the axis of x'_1 the angles $a'_1, \beta'_1, \gamma'_1$, we have, by the formulæ (F),

$$X'_0 = \frac{d\eta_1}{dz_1} \cos a_1 + \frac{d\eta'_1}{dz'_1} \cos a'_1, \quad Y'_0 = \frac{d\eta_1}{dz_1} \cos \beta_1 + \frac{d\eta'_1}{dz'_1} \cos \beta'_1. \tag{23}$$

Again, let the co-ordinates x_2, y_2, z_2 have reference to one set of refracted waves, and x'_2, y'_2, z'_2 to the other, the axes of z_2 and z'_2 being perpendicular to the respective waves, and their positive directions being those in which the waves are propa-

---

* In considering the question of reflexion at the common surface of two ordinary media (*Mémoires de l' Institut*, tom. ix. p. 396), Fresnel assumes the conditions (20); but his other suppositions violate the condition (22). In fact, this last condition is inconsistent with the supposition that, in a polarized ray, the direction of the vibrations is perpendicular to the plane of polarization. See the *Transactions* of the Royal Irish Academy, Vol. xviii. p. 32 (*supra*, p. 88).

gated. Suppose the displacements to be parallel to y_2, y'_2, and to be denoted by η_2, η'_2 respectively. Then if the axes of x, y, z make with the axis of x_2 the angles $\alpha_{(2)}$, $\beta_{(2)}$, $\gamma_{(2)}$, and with the axis of x'_2 the angles $\alpha'_{(2)}$, $\beta'_{(2)}$, $\gamma_{(2)}$, we have, by the formulæ (F),

$$X = \frac{d\eta_2}{dz_2} \cos \alpha_{(2)} + \frac{d\eta'_2}{dz'_2} \cos \alpha'_{(2)},$$

$$Y = \frac{d\eta_2}{dz_2} \cos \beta_{(2)} + \frac{d\eta'_2}{dz'_2} \cos \beta'_{(2)},$$

$$Z = \frac{d\eta_2}{dz_2} \cos \gamma_{(2)} + \frac{d\eta'_2}{dz'_2} \cos \gamma'_{(2)};$$

and thence, by the relations (19),

$$P = \frac{d\eta_1}{dz_2} \left(a^2 l \cos \alpha_{(2)} + b^2 m \cos \beta_{(2)} + c^2 n \cos \gamma_{(2)} \right)$$

$$+ \frac{d\eta'_2}{dz'_2} \left(a l^2 \cos \alpha'_{(2)} + b^2 m \cos \beta_{(2)} + c^2 n \cos \gamma'_{(2)} \right),$$

$$Q = \frac{d\eta_2}{dz_2} \left(a^2 l' \cos \alpha_{(2)} + b^2 m' \cos \beta_{(2)} + c^2 n' \cos \gamma_{(2)} \right)$$

$$+ \frac{d\eta'_2}{dz'_2} \left(a^2 l' \cos \alpha'_{(2)} + b^2 m' \cos \beta'_{(2)} + c^2 n' \cos \gamma'_{(2)} \right).$$

Suppose the ellipsoid which generates the wave-surface of the second medium to have its centre at O, and to be touched in the points Q and Q' by two planes which cut the axes of x_2 and x'_2 perpendicularly in the points P and P'; the lengths OP and OP' being expressed by s, s', and the lengths OQ and OQ' by r, r'. Let the axes of x_0, y_0, z_0 make with the direction of OQ the angles α_2, β_2, γ_2, and with the direction of OQ' the angles α'_2, β'_2, γ'_2. Then, from the equation (H) in Lemma IV., it is manifest that

$$a^2 l \cos \alpha_{(2)} + b^2 m \cos \beta_{(2)} + c^2 n \cos \gamma_{(2)} = rs \cos \alpha_2,$$

$$a^2 l \cos \alpha'_{(2)} + b^2 m \cos \beta'_{(2)} + c^2 n \cos \gamma'_{(2)} = r's' \cos \alpha'_2,$$

$$a^2 l' \cos \alpha_{(2)} + b^2 m' \cos \beta_{(2)} + c^2 n' \cos \gamma_{(2)} = rs \cos \beta_2,$$

$$a^2 l' \cos \alpha'_{(2)} + b^2 m' \cos \beta'_{(2)} + c^2 n' \cos \gamma'_{(2)} = r's' \cos \beta'_2.$$

Hence,

$$P = \frac{d\eta_2}{dz_2}\, rs\, \cos a_2 + \frac{d\eta'_2}{dz'_2}\, r's'\, \cos a'_2,$$

$$Q = \frac{d\eta_2}{dz_2}\, rs\, \cos \beta_2 + \frac{d\eta'_2}{dz'_2}\, r's'\, \cos \beta'_2.$$

$$(24)$$

The quantities s, s' are, as appears by the last section, the normal velocities with which the two sets of refracted waves are propagated. The velocity with which the incident and reflected waves are propagated is taken as unity. Therefore, if r_1, r'_1 be the transversals, or amplitudes of vibration in the incident and reflected waves, and r_2, r'_2 the transversals of the refracted waves, the lengths of the latter waves being denoted by λ_2, λ'_2, and the length of an incident or reflected wave by λ_1, and if we put

$$\phi_1 = \frac{2\pi}{\lambda_1}\, (t - z_1 + \nu_1), \qquad \phi'_1 = \frac{2\pi}{\lambda_1}\, (t - z'_1 + \nu'_1),$$

$$\phi_2 = \frac{2\pi}{\lambda_2}\, (st - z_2 + \nu_2), \qquad \phi'_2 = \frac{2\pi}{\lambda'_2}\, (s't - z'_2 + \nu'_2),$$

where ν_1, ν'_1, ν_2, ν'_2 are constants, and π is the ratio of the circumference to the diameter of a circle, we may write

$$\eta_1 = r_1 \cos \phi_1, \quad \eta'_1 = r'_1 \cos \phi'_1, \quad \eta_2 = r_2 \cos \phi_2, \quad \eta'_2 = r'_2 \cos \phi'_2. \quad (26)$$

By means of these values the formulæ (23) and (24) become

$$X'_0 = \frac{2\pi}{\lambda_1}\, (r_1 \cos a_1 \sin \phi_1 + r'_1 \cos a'_1 \sin \phi'_1),$$

$$Y'_0 = \frac{2\pi}{\lambda_1}\, (r_1 \cos \beta_1 \sin \phi_1 + r'_1 \cos \beta'_1 \sin \phi'_1),$$

$$P = 2\pi \left(\frac{rs}{\lambda_2}\, r_2 \cos a_2 \sin \phi_2 + \frac{r's'}{\lambda'_2}\, r'_2 \cos a'_2 \sin \phi'_2 \right),$$

$$Q = 2\pi \left(\frac{rs}{\lambda_2}\, r_2 \cos \beta_2 \sin \phi_2 + \frac{r's'}{\lambda'_2}\, r'_2 \cos \beta'_2 \sin \phi'_2 \right).$$

$$(27)$$

The angles ϕ_1, ϕ'_1, ϕ_2, ϕ'_2 are the phases of vibration in the different waves at the time t. To see how they depend on the co-ordinates x_0, y_0, z_0, conceive the axis of z_0 to be directed from O towards the interior of the second medium, and the axis of x_0 to lie in the plane of incidence, so that the positive directions of z_1, z_2, z'_2 may lie within the angle made by the positive directions of x_0 and z_0, while the positive direction of z'_1 lies within the angle made by the positive direction of x_0 and the negative direction of z_0. Let i_1 be the angle of incidence, and i_2, i'_2 the angles of refraction; then

$$z_1 = x_0 \sin i_1 + z_0 \cos i_1, \qquad z'_1 = x_0 \sin i_1 - z_0 \cos i_1,$$
$$z_2 = x_0 \sin i_2 + z_0 \cos i_2, \qquad z'_2 = x_0 \sin i'_2 + z_0 \cos i'_2. \tag{28}$$

These values are to be written in the expressions (25). They show that the phases, and therefore the displacements, are independent of y_0.

Since the conditions relative to the plane of $x_0 \, y_0$ must hold at every instant of time, and for every point of that plane, the co-efficients of t, as well as those of x_0, in the values of the different phases, must be identical; so that we must have

$$\frac{1}{\lambda_1} = \frac{s}{\lambda_2} = \frac{s'}{\lambda'_2}, \qquad \frac{\sin i_1}{\lambda_1} = \frac{\sin i_2}{\lambda_2} = \frac{\sin i'_2}{\lambda'_2} \tag{29}$$

Therefore, when $z_0 = 0$, the supposition

$$\nu_1 = \nu'_1 = \nu_2 = \nu'_2 \tag{30}$$

renders the phases identical, independently of t and x_0. And, from the form of the equations of condition, it is easy to see that this supposition is necessary; because the equations (20), when the values (26) are substituted in them, contain only the cosines of the phases; and the equations (21), when the values (27) are substituted in them, contain only the sines of the phases. Making the latter substitution, and attending to the relations just mentioned, we find

$$\tau_1 \cos \alpha_1 + \tau'_1 \cos \alpha'_1 = r\tau_2 \cos \alpha_2 + r'\tau'_2 \cos \alpha'_2,$$

$$\tau_1 \cos \beta_1 + \tau'_1 \cos \beta'_1 = r\tau_2 \cos \beta_2 + r'\tau'_2 \cos \beta'_2. \tag{31}$$

In these equations, the angles by whose cosines each transversal is multiplied are the angles which a plane, passing through the directions of that transversal and of the corresponding *ray*, makes with the planes of $y_0 z_0$ and $x_0 z_0$. This is evident with regard to the incident and reflected rays. And if we refer to the diagram in the preceding section, it will also be evident with regard to the refracted rays; for OQ is perpendicular to the transversal τ_2, and to the right line OT, which is the direction of the corresponding ray.

Taking O for the point of incidence, let right lines proceeding from it represent the different rays; and let the length of each ray, measured from O in the direction of propagation, be assumed proportional to the velocity with which the light is propagated along it. Through the extremity of each ray conceive its transversal to be drawn, and let the transversals so drawn have their *moments* taken, with respect to the point O, as if they represented forces applied to a rigid body. The length of the incident or reflected ray being considered as unity, the lengths of the refracted rays (as appears by the last Section) are r and r' respectively. Hence, as each transversal is perpendicular to its ray, the moments of the incident and reflected transversals are proportional to τ_1, τ'_1, and the moments of the refracted transversals to $r\tau_2$, $r'\tau'_2$ respectively. The equations (31) therefore signify that when the moments are projected, either upon the plane of $y_0 z_0$, or upon the plane of $x_0 z_0$, the total projected moments are the same for the two media; or that, if the transversals themselves be projected on either of these planes, the moments of the projections of the incident and reflected transversals are together equal to the moments of the projections of the refracted transversals.

But the second of the equations (31) has another signification. For if the transversals applied at the extremities of the refracted rays be projected on the plane of $x_0 z_0$, which is the plane of incidence, and contains the axes of z_2 and z'_2, the projections will be perpendicular to these axes, since the transversals themselves are perpendicular to them; and the distances of the projections from the point O will be proportional to s and s', or, by the relations (29), to $\sin i_2$ and $\sin i'_2$; so that if θ_2 and θ'_2 be the angles which the transversals make with the plane of incidence, the moments of the projections will be represented by $\tau_2 \cos \theta_2 \sin i_2$ and $\tau'_2 \cos \theta'_2 \sin i'_2$. At the same time, if θ_1 and θ'_1 be the angles which the incident and reflected transversals make with the plane of incidence, the moments of the corresponding projections of these transversals will evidently be represented by $\tau_1 \cos \theta_1 \sin i_1$, and $-\tau'_1 \cos \theta'_1 \sin i_1$; the latter quantity being taken with a negative sign, because the extremity of the reflected ray, where the transversal τ'_1 is applied, lies in the first medium, while the extremities of the incident and refracted rays lie in the second, and it is supposed that when any of the angles θ_1, θ'_1, θ_2, θ'_2 is zero, the direction of the corresponding transversal makes an acute angle with the axis of x_0. Hence we have

$$\tau_1 \cos \theta_1 \sin i_1 - \tau'_1 \cos \theta'_1 \sin i_1 = \tau_2 \cos \theta_2 \sin i_2 + \tau'_2 \cos \theta'_2 \sin i'_2;$$

an equation which expresses that if each transversal be projected upon the axis of z_0, the sum of the projections of the incident and reflected transversals will be equal to the sum of the projections of the refracted transversals. Therefore, since the phases of the different vibrations are identical when $z_0 = 0$, the condition (22) is fulfilled, as it ought to be.

On account of this identity of phases, it follows from the conditions (20) and (22), that if the transversals be drawn through the point O, and those which belong to each medium be compounded like forces acting at a point, their resultants will be the same; that is, the resultant of the incident and reflected transversals will be the same as the resultant of the refracted transversals.

Hence, recollecting what has been proved respecting the moments of the transversals applied at the extremities of the rays, we have the following theorem:

Supposing the length of each ray, measured from the point of incidence and in the direction of propagation, to be taken proportional to the velocity with which the light is propagated along it, and its transversal to be drawn through the extremity of this length, the incident and reflected transversals having their proper directions, but the refracted transversals having their directions reversed; if all the transversals so drawn be compounded like forces applied to a rigid body, their resultant will be a couple, lying in a plane parallel to the plane which separates the two media.

This theorem affords a complete solution of the question of reflexion and refraction.* Expressed analytically it gives five equations, of which four are independent.

To apply the preceding results to a simple case, suppose the second medium, as well as the first, to be an ordinary one. We have then only one refracted ray, and one refracted transversal τ_2.

1°. When the incident ray is polarized in the plane of incidence, the transversals are all in that plane; and as they are perpendicular to the rays, and the refracted transversal is the resultant of the other two, we have evidently

$$\tau'_1 = \tau_1 \frac{\sin (i_1 - i_2)}{\sin (i_1 + i_2)}, \qquad \tau_2 = \tau_1 \frac{\sin 2i_1}{\sin (i_1 + i_2)}. \qquad (32)$$

2°. When the incident ray is polarized perpendicularly to

---

* The same theorem applies to the other case of reflexion and refraction, when a ray which has entered the crystal emerges from it into an ordinary medium, undergoing double reflexion at the surface where it emerges. In fact, the conditions (20) and (21) hold good whether the ordinary medium is the first or the second; and in the latter case, as well as in the former, it may be shown that the condition (22) is fulfilled, and that the theorem above mentioned is true.

the plane of incidence, the transversals are all perpendicular to that plane. Taking $2\sin i_1$ to represent the length of the incident or reflected ray, the proportional length of the refracted ray is $2\sin i_2$, and the projections of these lengths on the plane of $y_0 z_0$ are $2\sin i_1 \cos i_1$ and $2\sin i_2 \cos i_2$, or $\sin 2i_1$ and $\sin 2i_2$. The transversals applied at the extremities of the rays are not altered by being projected on the plane of $y_0 z_0$; therefore the moments of the incident, reflected, and refracted transversals, projected on this plane, are represented by the quantities $\tau_1 \sin 2i_1 - \tau'_1 \sin 2i_1$, and $\tau_2 \sin 2i_2$ respectively. Equating the last moment to the sum of the other two, and the refracted transversal to the sum of the other two transversals, we get

$$(\tau_1 - \tau'_1) \sin 2i_1 = \tau_2 \sin 2i_2, \qquad \tau_1 + \tau'_1 = \tau_2;$$

and thence

$$\tau'_1 = \tau_1 \frac{\tan (i_1 - i_2)}{\tan (i_1 + i_2)}, \qquad \tau_2 = \tau_1 \frac{\sin 2i_1}{\sin (i_1 + i_2) \cos (i_1 - i_2)}. \tag{33}$$

This case has been considered by Fresnel. The relative magnitudes of the incident and reflected transversals, as given by him, are in accordance* with the formulæ (32) and (33); but with respect to the refracted transversals, his results do not agree with the formulæ.

Sect. VI.—Preservation of *Vis Viva*—Theorem of the Polar Plane—Conclusion.

Returning to the general question, if we resolve the transversals parallel to the axes of x_0, y_0, z_0, and equate the sums of the parallel components in one medium to the corresponding

---

* There is, however, a difference as to the relative directions of the incident and reflected transversals. When the second medium is the denser, and the incidence is perpendicular, these transversals, according to the present theory, have the same direction, but according to Fresnel they have opposite directions.

sums in the other, we get the three conditions

$$(\tau_1 \cos \theta_1 + \tau'_1 \cos \theta'_1) \cos i_1 = \tau_2 \cos \theta_2 \cos i_2 + \tau'_2 \cos \theta'_2 \cos i''_2,$$

$$\tau_1 \sin \theta_1 + \tau'_1 \sin \theta'_1 = \tau_2 \sin \theta_2 + \tau'_2 \sin \theta'_2, \qquad (34)$$

$$(\tau_1 \cos \theta_1 - \tau'_1 \cos \theta'_1) \sin i_1 = \tau_2 \cos \theta_2 \sin i_2 + \tau'_2 \cos \theta'_2 \sin i''_2.$$

A fourth condition is supplied by the first of the equations (31), in which equation we have to write

$$\cos a_1 = \sin \theta_1 \cos i_1, \qquad \cos a'_1 = - \sin \theta'_1 \cos i_1,$$

and to substitute similar expressions for $\cos a_2$, $\cos a'_2$.

The right line OQ is perpendicular to the transversal τ_2 and to the ray OT. The cosines of the angles a_2, β_2, γ_2 may therefore be found by means of the cosines of the angles which the transversal and the ray make with the axes of x_0, y_0, z_0.

The cosines of the angles which the transversal τ_2 makes with these axes are respectively

$$\cos \theta_2 \cos i_2, \qquad \sin \theta_2, \qquad - \cos \theta_2 \sin i_2.$$

As the plane which passes through the ray and the wave-normal OS is perpendicular to the transversal τ_2, this plane makes with the plane of incidence an angle equal to $90° + \theta_2$ or $90° - \theta_2$. Let a sphere, having its centre at O, be intersected in the points S_0, T_0 by the right lines OS, OT, and in the points X_0, Y_0, Z_0 by the axes of x_0, y_0, z_0; and conceive the points T_0 and Y_0 to be at the same side of the plane x_0, z_0, the spherical angle $T_0 S_0 X_0$ being $90° + \theta_2$, and the spherical angle $T_0 S_0 Z_0$ being $90° - \theta_2$. Let ϵ be the angle which the ray makes with the wave-normal. Then, the angles which the ray makes with the axes of co-ordinates being measured by the arcs $T_0 X_0$, $T_0 Y_0$, $T_0 Z_0$, the cosines of these angles respectively are

$$\sin i_2 \cos \epsilon - \sin \theta_2 \cos i_2 \sin \epsilon, \qquad \cos \theta_2 \sin \epsilon,$$

$$\cos i_2 \cos \epsilon + \sin \theta_2 \sin i_2 \sin \epsilon.$$

Hence, as the transversal is at right angles to the ray, we

have, by Lemma I.,

$$\cos a_2 = \sin i_2 \sin \epsilon + \sin \theta_2 \cos i_2 \cos \epsilon, \qquad \cos \beta_2 = -\cos \theta_2 \cos \epsilon,$$

$$\cos \gamma_2 = \cos i_2 \sin \epsilon - \sin \theta_2 \sin i_2 \cos \epsilon. \tag{35}$$

In like manner, putting ϵ' for the angle which the other re-fracted ray makes with its wave-normal, we have

$$\cos a'_2 = \sin i''_2 \sin \epsilon' + \sin \theta'_2 \cos i''_2 \cos \epsilon', \qquad \cos \beta'_2 = -\cos \theta'_2 \cos \epsilon',$$

$$\cos \gamma'_2 = \cos i''_2 \sin \epsilon' - \sin \theta'_2 \sin i''_2 \cos \epsilon'. \tag{36}$$

If we substitute, in the first of the equations (31), the values just given for $\cos a_2$, $\cos a'_2$, along with the above values of $\cos a_1$, $\cos a'_1$, and attend to the relations

$$r \cos \epsilon = s. \qquad r' \cos \epsilon' = s',$$

$$\sin i_2 = s \sin i_1, \qquad \sin i''_2 = s' \sin i_1, \tag{37}$$

we find, after multiplying all the terms of the equation by $\sin i_1$,

$$(r_1 \sin \theta_1 - r'_1 \sin \theta'_1) \sin i_1 \cos i_1 = r_2 (\sin \theta_2 \sin i_2 \cos i_2$$

$$+ \sin^2 i_2 \tan \epsilon) + r'_2 (\sin \theta'_2 \sin i''_2 \cos i''_2 + \sin^2 i''_2 \tan \epsilon). \tag{38}$$

Joining this equation to the equations (34) we have all the con-ditions that are necessary for the solution of the question.

Multiplying the first of the equations (34) by the third, also the second of these equations by the equation (38), adding the products together, and then dividing by $\sin i_1$, we obtain

$$\mu_1 (r_1^2 - r'_1^2) = \mu_2 r_2^2 + \mu'_2 r'_2{}^2 + M r_2 r'_2, \tag{39}$$

where we have put

$$\mu_1 = \cos i_1, \qquad \mu_2 = s (\cos i_2 + \sin \theta_2 \sin i_2 \tan \epsilon),$$

$$\mu'_2 = s' (\cos i''_2 + \sin \theta'_2 \sin i''_2 \tan \epsilon'),$$

$$M \sin i_1 = \sin (i_2 + i''_2) \{\cos \theta_2 \cos \theta'_2 + \sin \theta_2 \sin \theta'_2 \cos (i_2 - i''_2)\}$$

$$+ \sin \theta'_2 \sin^2 i_2 \tan \epsilon + \sin \theta_2 \sin^2 i''_2 \tan \epsilon'.$$

The last expression may be put under the form

$$M \sin i_1 \sin (i_2 - i''_2)$$

$$= \sin^2 i_2 \{\cos \theta_2 \cos \theta'_2 + \sin \theta_2 \sin \theta'_2 \cos (i_2 - i''_2) \tag{40}$$

$$+ \sin \theta'_2 \sin (i_2 - i''_2) \tan \varepsilon\}$$

$$- \sin^2 i''_2 \{\cos \theta_2 \cos \theta'_2 + \sin \theta_2 \sin \theta'_2 \cos (i_2 - i''_2)$$

$$- \sin \theta_2 \sin (i_2 - i''_2) \tan \varepsilon'\}.$$

Let the axes of x_0, y_0, z_0 make with the direction of OP the angles $a_{//}$, $\beta_{//}$, $\gamma_{//}$, and with the direction of OP' the angles $a'_{//}$, $\beta'_{//}$, $\gamma'_{//}$. The cosines of these angles may be found from the expressions (35) and (36) by supposing ε and ε' to vanish. Therefore

$$\cos a_{//} = \sin \theta_2 \cos i_2, \quad \cos \beta_{//} = - \cos \theta_2, \quad \cos \gamma_{//} = - \sin \theta_2 \sin i_2,$$
$$\cos a'_{//} = \sin \theta'_2 \cos i'_2, \quad \cos \beta'_{//} = - \cos \theta'_2, \quad \cos \gamma'_{//} = - \sin \theta'_2 \sin i''_2. \tag{41}$$

If ω be the angle which OQ makes with OP', and ω' the angle which OQ' makes with OP, so that

$$\cos \omega = \cos a_2 \cos a'_{//} + \cos \beta_2 \cos \beta'_{//} + \cos \gamma_2 \cos \gamma'_{//},$$

$$\cos \omega' = \cos a'_2 \cos a_{//} + \cos \beta'_2 \cos \beta_{//} + \cos \gamma'_2 \cos \gamma_{//},$$

we find, by the formulæ (35), (36), (41),

$$\cos \omega = \cos \varepsilon \{\cos \theta_2 \cos \theta'_2 + \sin \theta_2 \sin \theta'_2 \cos (i_2 - i''_2)$$

$$+ \sin \theta'_2 \sin (i_2 - i''_2) \tan \varepsilon\},$$

$$\cos \omega' = \cos \varepsilon' \{\cos \theta_2 \cos \theta'_2 + \sin \theta_2 \sin \theta'_2 \cos (i_2 - i'_2)$$

$$- \sin \theta_2 \sin (i_2 - i''_2) \tan \varepsilon'\}.$$

Hence, observing the relations (37), we see that the right-hand member of the equation (40) is equal to the quantity

$$\sin^2 i_1 (rs \cos \omega - r's' \cos \omega').$$

But, by the property of the ellipsoid (Lemma IV.), this quantity is zero;* therefore $M = 0$, and the equation (39) becomes

$$\mu_1 \tau_1^2 = \mu_1 \tau_1'^2 + \mu_2 \tau_2^2 + \mu_2' \tau_2'^2. \tag{42}$$

On each ray let a length, representing the velocity with which the light is propagated along it, be measured, as before, from the point O. The distances of the plane of $x_0 \, y_0$ from the extremities of these lengths will be proportional to the coefficients of the squares of the transversals in the preceding equation. For if we take, on the incident or reflected ray, a length equal to unity, its projection on the axis of z_0 will be $\cos i_1$ or μ_1; and if, on the refracted ray OT, we take a length equal to r, its projection on the same axis will be

$$r \, (\cos i_2 \cos \varepsilon + \sin \theta_2 \sin i_2 \sin \varepsilon),$$

which is equal to μ_2. Similarly, the length r', assumed on the other refracted ray, will have its projection equal to μ_2'. The quantities by which the squares of the transversals are multiplied, in the equation (42), are therefore the corresponding ethereal volumes† which we may conceive to be put in motion by the different waves; and as we suppose the density of the ether to be the same in both media, the equation expresses a principle analogous to that of the preservation of *vis viva*.‡

By giving a certain direction to the incident transversal, that is, by polarizing the incident ray in a certain plane, we may make one of the refracted rays disappear. If OT be the ray which remains, we have $\tau_2' = 0$, and the equations (34) and (38) become

---

* The equation $M = 0$ is the same as the equation (VII.) in my former Paper.— *Transactions*, R.I.A., VOL. XVIII. p. 52 (*supra*, p. 112).

† *Ibid.*, p. 48 (*supra*, p. 106).

‡ A similar equation of *vis viva* holds when the light passes out of a crystal into an ordinary medium.

$$(\tau_1 \cos \theta_1 + \tau'_1 \cos \theta'_1) \cos i_1 = \tau_2 \cos \theta_2 \cos i_2,$$

$$\tau_1 \sin \theta_1 + \tau'_1 \sin \theta'_1 = \tau_2 \sin \theta_2,$$

$$(\tau_1 \cos \theta_1 - \tau'_1 \cos \theta'_1) \sin i_1 = \tau_2 \cos \theta_2 \sin i_2, \qquad (43)$$

$$(\tau_1 \sin \theta_1 - \tau'_1 \sin \theta'_1) \sin i_1 \cos i_1$$

$$= \tau_2 (\sin \theta_2 \sin i_2 \cos i_2 + \sin^2 i_2 \tan \varepsilon).$$

In this case, the three transversals are in the same plane, the refracted transversal being the resultant of the other two. Therefore if we find this plane, everything will be determined.

The axes of x_0, y_0, z_0 make, with the incident transversal, angles whose cosines are

$$\cos \theta_1 \cos i_1, \qquad \sin \theta_1, \qquad - \cos \theta_1 \sin i_1,$$

and, with the reflected transversal, angles whose cosines are

$$\cos \theta'_1 \cos i_1, \qquad \sin \theta'_1, \qquad \cos \theta'_1 \sin i_1 \,;$$

therefore, by Lemma I., the cosines of the angles which these axes make with a right line perpendicular to the plane of the transversals are proportional to the quantities

$$\sin (\theta_1 + \theta'_1) \sin i_1, \quad - \cos \theta_1 \cos \theta'_1 \sin 2i_1, \quad \sin (\theta'_1 - \theta_1) \cos i_1.$$

Now from the product of the first and second of the equations (43), combined with the product of the third and fourth, we find, by the help of the relations (37),

$$2\tau_1 \tau'_1 \sin (\theta_1 + \theta'_1) \sin i_1 = \tau_2^2 \tan i_1 \cos \theta_2 \{\sin \theta_2 \cos i_2$$

$$- s^2 (\sin \theta_2 \cos i_2 + \sin i_2 \tan \varepsilon)\}.$$

From the squares of the first and third of those equations we find

$$- 2\tau_1 \tau'_1 \cos \theta_1 \cos \theta'_1 \sin 2i_1 = \tau_2^2 \tan i_1 \cos^2 \theta_2 (s^2 - 1),$$

and from the product of the first and fourth, combined with the product of the second and third,

$$2\tau_1 \tau'_1 \sin (\theta'_1 - \theta_1) \cos i_1 = \tau_2^2 \tan i_1 \cos \theta_2 \{- \sin \theta_2 \sin i_2$$

$$+ s^2 (\sin \theta_2 \sin i_2 - \cos i_2 \tan \varepsilon)\}.$$

In the three equations just found, the left-hand members are proportional, as we have seen, to the cosines of the angles which a right line perpendicular to the plane of the transversals makes with the axes of co-ordinates; and the right-hand members, as appears by the formulæ (35) and (41), are proportional to the quantities

$$\frac{\cos a_{\prime\prime}}{s} - r \cos a_2, \qquad \frac{\cos \beta_{\prime\prime}}{s} - r \cos \beta_2, \qquad \frac{\cos \gamma_{\prime\prime}}{s} - r \cos \gamma_2,$$

which are obviously the differences between the corresponding co-ordinates of the points R and Q. The plane of the transversals is therefore perpendicular to the right line QR, which joins those points.

A plane parallel to the right line TM, and passing through the transversal of the ray OT, is that which I have called the *polar plane* of the ray;[*] and this plane is perpendicular to QR. Therefore, when there is only one refracted ray, the incident and reflected transversals lie in the polar plane of that ray; and their directions being thus determined, the relative magnitudes of the three transversals are known. In this case the incident and reflected transversals are called *uniradial*; and as each refracted ray in turn may be 'made to disappear, there are two uniradial directions in the plane of the incident wave, and two in that of the reflected wave.

When the incident transversal is not uniradial, it may be considered as the resultant of two uniradial transversals, each of which will supply a refracted ray, and will produce a uniradial component of the reflected transversal.

It is needless to extend these deductions further. They have been carried far enough to show that the results of the foregoing theory are in perfect accordance with the laws established in my former Paper on the subject of crystalline reflexion. The theory itself suggests much matter for consideration; but at present we shall confine ourselves to one remark, which may

---

[*] *Transactions*, Royal Irish Academy, Vol. xviii. p. 39 (*supra*, p. 96).

be necessary to prevent any misconception as to the nature of the foundation on which it stands. In this theory, everything depends on the form of the function V ; and we have seen that, when that form is properly assigned, the laws by which crystals act upon light are included in the general equation of dynamics. This fact is fully proved by the preceding investigations. But the reasoning which has been used to account for the form of the function* is indirect, and cannot be regarded as sufficient, in a mechanical point of view. It is, however, the only kind of reasoning which we are able to employ, as the constitution of the luminiferous medium is entirely unknown.

* Since this Paper was read to the Academy, I have found that the form of the function V is more general than it would seem to be from the mode in which it is here deduced ; and I have obtained from it a theory of the Total Reflexion of Light. For a sketch of this theory, *see* the *Proceedings* of the Royal Irish Academy, Vol. ii. p. 96 (*supra*, p. 187).

XV.—ON THE OPTICAL LAWS OF ROCK-CRYSTALS.

[*Proceedings of the Royal Irish Academy*, Vol. i. p. 385.—Read Jan. 13, 1840.]

Professor Mac Cullagh made a communication respecting the optical Laws of Rock-crystal (Quartz).

In a Paper read to the Academy in February 1836, and published in the *Transactions* (Vol. xvii. p. 461),* he had shown how the peculiar properties of that crystal might be explained, by adding to the usual equations of vibratory motion certain terms depending on differential co-efficients of the third order, and containing only one new constant C. This hypothesis, which was very simple in itself, not only involved as consequences all the laws that were previously known, but led to the discovery of a new one—the law, namely, by which the ellipticity of the vibrations depends on the direction of the ray within the crystal. He was not able, however, to account for his hypothesis, nor has it since been accounted for by anyone.

But the theory developed in the Paper which he read at the last meeting of the Academy now enables him to assign, with a high degree of probability, the origin of the additional terms above mentioned, and, if not to account for them mechanically, at least to advance a step higher in the inquiry. In that theory it was supposed (and the supposition holds good in all known crystals, except quartz), that the molecules of the ether vibrate in right lines, the displacements remaining always parallel to each other as the wave is propagated; and it was shown that the function V, by which the motion is determined,

* *Supra*, p. 63.

then depends only on the *relative displacements* of the molecules. But when this is not the case—when, as in quartz, each molecule is supposed to vibrate in a curve—then it is natural to conceive that the function V may depend, not only on the relative displacements, but also on the *relative areas* which each molecule describes about every other more or less advanced in its vibration.   This idea, analytically expressed, introduces a new term v into the value of the function 2V ; and, if the plane of the wave be taken for the plane of xy, it is easy to show that

$$v = C\left(\frac{d\eta}{dz}\frac{d^2\xi}{dz^2} - \frac{d\xi}{dz}\frac{d^2\eta}{dz^2}\right).$$

Now if we integrate by parts the expression

$$\iiint dx\,dy\,dz\,\delta v,$$

so as to get rid of the variations of differential co-efficients, the reduced form of the triple integral will be

$$2\,C \iiint dx\,dy\,dz \left(\frac{d^3\eta}{dz^3}\,\delta\xi - \frac{d^3\xi}{dz^3}\,\delta\eta\right);$$

from which it appears that the quantities

$$C\,\frac{d^3\eta}{dz^3}, \qquad -\,C\,\frac{d^3\xi}{dz^3},$$

are to be added to the usual expressions for the force in the directions of x and y respectively.   These are the very terms in the addition of which the hypothesis before alluded to consists.

XVI.—ON A DYNAMICAL THEORY OF CRYSTALLINE REFLEXION AND REFRACTION.

[*Proceedings of the Royal Irish Academy*, Vol. II. p. 96.—Read May 24, 1841.]

Professor Mac Cullagh read a supplement to his Paper "On a Dynamical Theory of Crystalline Reflexion and Refraction."

In his former Paper on that subject,[*] the author had given the general principles for solving all questions relative to the propagation of light in a given medium, or its reflexion and refraction at the separating surface of two media; but he had applied them only to the common case of waves, which suffer no diminution of intensity in their progress, and in which the vibration may be represented by the sine or cosine of an arc multiplied by a constant quantity. Some months after that Paper was read, it occurred to him that he might obtain new and important results by substituting in his differential equations of motion a more general expression for the integral, that is (as usual in such problems), by making the displacements proportional to the sine or cosine of an arc, multiplied by a negative exponential, of which the exponent should be a linear function of the co-ordinates. Such vibrations would become very rapidly insensible, and would, therefore, be fitted to represent the disturbance which, in the case of *total reflexion*, takes place immediately behind the reflecting surface; and, the laws of this disturbance being thus discovered, the laws of polarization in the totally

* See *Proceedings*, 9th December, 1839 (*supra*, p. 145).

reflected light would also become known, by means of the general formulæ which the author had established for all cases of reflexion at the common surface of two media.

The present supplement is the fruit of these considerations. It contains the complete theory of the new kind of vibrations, not only in ordinary media, but in doubly-refracting crystals; and also the complete discussion of the laws of total reflexion at the first or second surface of a crystal, including, as a particular case, the well-known empirical formulæ of Fresnel for total reflexion at the surface of an ordinary medium.

The existence of vibrations represented by an expression containing a negative exponential as a factor had been recognised by other writers, and was indeed sufficiently indicated by the phenomenon of total reflexion; but it was impossible to obtain the laws of such vibrations, so long as the general equations for the propagation of light were unknown.

The method of deducing these equations was given in the abstract of the author's former Paper;[*] but as they were not there stated, it may be well to transcribe them here. If then we put

$$X = \frac{d\eta}{dz} - \frac{d\zeta}{dy}, \quad Y = \frac{d\zeta}{dx} - \frac{d\xi}{dz}, \quad Z = \frac{d\xi}{dy} - \frac{d\eta}{dx}, \tag{1}$$

and suppose the axes of co-ordinates to be the principal axes of the crystal, the equations in question may be thus written:

$$\left.\begin{aligned}
\frac{d^2\xi}{dt^2} &= c^2 \frac{dZ}{dy} - b^2 \frac{dY}{dz}, \\[1em]
\frac{d^2\eta}{dt^2} &= a^2 \frac{dX}{dz} - c^2 \frac{dZ}{dx}, \\[1em]
\frac{d^2\zeta}{dt^2} &= b^2 \frac{dY}{dx} - a^2 \frac{dX}{dy};
\end{aligned}\right\} \tag{2}$$

and if we further put

$$\xi = \frac{d\eta_1}{dz} - \frac{d\zeta_1}{dy}, \quad \eta = \frac{d\zeta_1}{dx} - \frac{d\xi_1}{dz}, \quad \zeta = \frac{d\xi_1}{dy} - \frac{d\eta_1}{dx}, \tag{3}$$

* See *Proceedings*, 9th December, 1839 (*supra*, p. 157).

they will take the following simple form :

$$\frac{d^2\xi_1}{dt^2} = -a^2 X, \qquad \frac{d^2\eta_1}{dt^2} = -b^2 Y, \qquad \frac{d^2\zeta_1}{dt^2} = -c^2 Z, \qquad (4)$$

in which it is remarkable that the auxiliary quantities ξ_1, η_1, ζ_1, are exactly, for an ordinary medium, the components of the displacement in the theory of Fresnel. In a doubly-refracting crystal, the resultant of ξ_1, η_1, ζ_1 is perpendicular to the *ray*, and comprised in a plane passing through the ray and the wave-normal. Its amplitude, or greatest magnitude, is proportional to the amplitude of the vibration itself, multiplied by the velocity of the ray.

The conditions to be fulfilled at the separating surface of two media were given in the abstract already referred to. From these it follows, that the resultant of the quantities ξ_1, η_1, ζ_1, projected on that surface, is the same in both media ; but the part perpendicular to the surface is not the same ; whereas the quantities ξ, η, ζ, are identical in both. These assertions, analytically expressed, would give five equations, though four are sufficient ; but it can be shown that any one of the equations is implied in the other four, not only in the case of common, but of total reflexion ; which is a very remarkable circumstance, and a very strong confirmation of the theory.

The laws of double refraction, discovered by Fresnel, but not legitimately deduced from a consistent hypothesis, either by himself or any intermediate writer, may be very easily obtained, as the author has already shown, from equations (2), by assuming

$$\xi = p\cos a \sin\phi, \quad \eta = p\cos\beta \sin\phi, \quad \zeta = p\cos\gamma \sin\phi, \qquad (5)$$

where

$$\phi = \frac{2\pi}{\lambda}(lx + my + nz - st);$$

but the new laws, which are the object of the present supplement, are to be obtained from the same equations by making

$$\left.\begin{aligned}
\xi &= \varepsilon(p\cos a \sin\phi + q\cos a' \cos\phi), \\
\eta &= \varepsilon(p\cos\beta \sin\phi + q\cos\beta' \cos\phi), \\
\zeta &= \varepsilon(p\cos\gamma \sin\phi + q\cos\lambda' \cos\phi),
\end{aligned}\right\} \qquad (6)$$

where ϕ has the same signification as before, and

$$\epsilon = e^{-\frac{2\pi r}{\lambda}(fx + gy + hz)};$$

the vibrations being now elliptical, whereas in the former case they were rectilinear. In these elliptic vibrations the motion depends not only on the distance of the vibrating particle from the plane whose equation is

$$lx + my + nz = 0, \tag{7}$$

but also on its distance from the plane expressed by the equation

$$fx + gy + hz = 0 ; \tag{8}$$

and if the constants in the equation of each plane denote the cosines of the angles which it makes with the co-ordinate planes, we shall have λ for the length of the wave, and s for the velocity of propagation ; while the rapidity with which the motion is extinguished, in receding from the second plane, will depend upon the constant r. The constants p and q may be any two conjugate semi-diameters of the ellipse in which the vibration is performed ; the former making, with the axes of co-ordinates, the angles α, β, γ, the latter the angles α', β', γ'.

As vibrations of this kind cannot exist in any medium, unless they are maintained by total reflexion at its surface, we shall suppose, in order to contemplate their laws in their utmost generality, that a crystal is in contact with a fluid of greater refractive power than itself, and that a ray is incident at their common surface, at such an angle as to produce total reflexion. The question then is, the angle of incidence being given, to determine the laws of the disturbance within the crystal.

The author finds that the refraction is still *double*, and that two distinct and separable systems of vibration are transmitted into the crystal. He shows that the surface of the crystal itself (the origin of co-ordinates being upon it at the point of incidence) must coincide with the plane expressed by equation (8), a circumstance which determines the three constants f, g, h. The plane expressed by (7) is parallel to the plane of the refracted wave; and a normal, drawn to it through the origin, lies in the plane of incidence, making with a perpendicular to the face of the crystal an angle ω, which may be called the angle of refraction; so that, if i be the angle of incidence, we have

$$\sin \omega = s \sin i,$$

the velocity of propagation in the fluid being regarded as unity.

To each refracted wave, or system of vibration, corresponds a particular system of values for r, s, ω. These the author shows how to determine by means of the *index-surface* (the reciprocal of Fresnel's wave-surface), which he has employed on other occasions,[*] and the rule which he gives for this purpose affords a remarkable example of the use of the imaginary roots of equations, without the theory of which, indeed, it would have been difficult to prove, in the present instance, that there are two, and only two, refracted waves. Taking a new system of co-ordinates x', y', z', of which z' is perpendicular to the surface of the crystal, and y' to the plane of incidence, while x' lies in the intersection of these two planes; put $y' = 0$ in the equation of the index-surface referred to those co-ordinates, the origin being at its centre; we shall then have an equation of the fourth degree between x' and z', which will be the equation of the section made in the index-surface by the plane of incidence. In this equation put $x' = \sin i$, and then solve it for z'. When i exceeds a certain angle i'', the four values of z' will be imaginary; and if they be denoted by

$$u \pm v \sqrt{-1}, \qquad u' \pm v' \sqrt{-1},$$

each pair will correspond to a refracted system, and we shall have, for the first,

$$\tan \omega = \frac{\sin i}{u}, \qquad s = \frac{\sin \omega}{\sin i}, \qquad r = sv ; \qquad (9)$$

and for the second,

$$\tan \omega' = \frac{\sin i}{u'}, \qquad s' = \frac{\sin \omega'}{\sin i}, \qquad r' = s'v'. \qquad (10)$$

[*] *Transactions* of the Academy, Vols. XVII. and XVIII. (*supra*, pp. 36, 96).

When i lies between i' and a certain smaller angle i''', two of the roots will be real, and two imaginary. The real roots correspond to waves which follow the law of Fresnel; the imaginary roots give a single wave, following the other laws just mentioned.

Lastly, when i is less than i''', all the roots are real, the refraction is entirely regulated by Fresnel's law, and the reflexion by the laws already discovered and published by the author.

If the crystal be uniaxal, and all the values of z' imaginary, the ordinary wave-normal will coincide with the axis of x'; whilst the extraordinary wave-normal and the axis of z' will be conjugate diameters of the ellipse in which the index surface is cut by the plane of incidence.

When $a = b = c$, the crystal becomes an ordinary medium; there is then only single refraction, and the refracted wave is always perpendicular to the axis of x'.

With regard to the ellipse in which the vibrations are performed, it may be worth while to observe, that if it be projected perpendicularly on the plane of incidence, the projected diameters which are parallel to the surface of the crystal and to the wave-plane will, in all cases, be conjugate to each other, and their respective lengths will be in the proportion of r to unity. The vibrations, it is obvious, are not performed in the plane of the wave, though they take place without changing the density of the ether.

The new laws here announced are, properly speaking, laws of double refraction, and are necessary to complete our knowledge of that subject. Between them and the laws of Fresnel a curious analogy exists, founded on the change of real into imaginary constants.

The laws of the total reflexion, which accompanies the new kind of refraction, need not be dwelt upon in this abstract, as nothing is now more easy than to form the equations which contain them. In fact, the difficulties which formerly surrounded the problem of reflexion, even in the simplest cases, have completely disappeared, since the author made known the conditions which must be fulfilled at the separating surface of two media.

In what precedes, it has been supposed that the reflexion and refraction take place at the *first* surface of the crystal, because this is the more difficult and complicated of the two cases into which the question resolves itself. But it will usually happen in practice that a ray which has entered the crystal will suffer total reflexion at the *second* surface, while the new kind of vibration is propagated into the air without. The refracted wave will then be always perpendicular to the axis of x'; the two reflected rays, within the crystal, will be plane-polarized, according to the common law, but they will each undergo a change of phase; and the *vis viva* of the two rays together will be equal to that of the incident ray, the *vis viva* being measured by the square of the amplitude multiplied by the proportional mass.

In conclusion, the author states a mathematical hypothesis by which both the laws of dispersion, and those of the elliptic polarization of rock crystal, may be connected with the laws already developed.

XVII.—NOTES ON SOME POINTS IN THE THEORY OF LIGHT.

[*Proceedings of the Royal Irish Academy*, Vol. II. p. 139.—Read Nov. 8, 1841.]

I.

On a Mechanical Theory which has been proposed for the Explanation of the Phenomena of Circular Polarization in Liquids, and of Circular and Elliptic Polarization in Quartz or Rock-crystal; with Remarks on the corresponding Theory of Rectilinear Polarization.

THE theory of elliptic polarization, which I feel myself called upon to notice, was first stated by M. Cauchy, and has been made the subject of elaborate investigation by other writers. That celebrated analyst, conceiving (though without sufficient reason, as will presently appear) that he had fully explained the known laws of the propagation of *rectilinear* vibrations by the hypothesis that the luminiferous ether, in media transmitting such vibrations, consists of separate molecules *symmetrically* arranged with respect to each of three rectangular planes, and acting on each other by forces which are some function of the distance, was led very naturally to imagine that he would find the laws of *circular* and *elliptic* vibrations, in other media, to be included in the more general hypothesis of an *unsymmetrical* arrangement. Accordingly, in a letter read to the French Academy on the 22nd of February, 1836—a letter to which he attached so much importance that he desired it might not only be published in the *Proceedings*, but also "deposited in the Archives" of that body*—he gave a precise statement of his more extended views, informing the Academy that he had submitted his new theory to calculation, and that, among other remarkable results, he had obtained (with a slight variation or correction) the laws of circular polarization, discovered by Arago, Biot, and Fresnel. Referring to his Memoir on Dispersion, published at Prague, under the title of *Nouveaux Exercices de Mathématiques*, he observes, that the results therein contained may be generalized, by "ceasing to neglect" in the equations of motion [the equations marked (24) in § 2 of that memoir] certain terms which vanish in the case of a symmetrical distribution of the ether. He then goes on to say—

"Nos formules ainsi généralisées représentent les phénomènes de l'absorption de la lumière ou de certains rayons, produite par les verres colorés, la tourmaline, &c., le phenomène de la polarisation circulaire produite par le cristal de roche, l'huile de térébenthine, &c. (*Voir* les expériences de MM. Arago, Biot, Fresnel). Elles servent même à déterminer les conditions et les lois de ces phénomènes; elles montrent que généralement, dans un rayon de lumière polariseé, une molecule d'éther décrit une ellipse. Mais dans certains cas particuliers, cette ellipse se change en une droite, et alors on obtient la polarisation rectiligne." "Enfin le calcul prouve que, dans le cristal de roche, l'huile de térébenthine, &c., la polarisation des rayons transmis parallèlement à l'axe (s'il s'agit du cristal de roche) n'est pas rigoureusement circulaire, mais qu'alors l'ellipse diffère très peu du cercle."

Thus, to say nothing for the present of the questions of dispersion and absorption, it appears that M. Cauchy conceived he had completely accounted for the facts of circular and elliptic polarization, and that he had deduced the formulas "which serve to determine the conditions and laws of these phenomena." But neither in this letter, nor in any subse-

---

See the *Comptes Rendus des Séances de l'Académie des Sciences*, tom. ii. p. 182.

quent version* of his theory, has he given the formulas themselves. Nor has he told us the nature of the calculations by which he was enabled to correct the received opinion, and to prove that the vibrations in a ray transmitted along the axis of quartz, or through oil of turpentine, are not rigorously circular, as Fresnel and others have supposed, but slightly elliptical. Now—to take the case of quartz—if we consider that the vibrations of a ray passing along the axis are in a plane perpendicular to it, and if we admit, as M. Cauchy always does in the case of other uniaxal crystals, that there is a perfect optical symmetry all round the axis, we shall find it hard to conceive on what grounds he could have come to the conclusion that the vibrations of such a ray are performed in an ellipse. For if all planes passing through the axis of the crystal be alike in their optical properties, there will be absolutely nothing to determine the position and ratio of the axes of the ellipse; there will be no reason why its major axis, for example, should lie in one of these planes, rather than in any other. But, whatever may be thought of this case independently of observation, it is manifestly absurd to suppose that the vibrations are elliptical in the case of a ray passing through oil of turpentine, or any other *liquid* possessing the property of rotatory polarization; for, in a liquid, all planes drawn through the ray itself are circumstanced alike. From these simple considerations it is evident that the theory of M. Cauchy is unsound; but a closer examination will show that it is entirely without foundation, and that it is directly opposed to the very phenomena which it professes to explain. To make this appear, however, in the easiest way that the abstruseness of the subject will allow, it will be necessary to

---

* From some statements that have been made within the last few days by Professor Powell (*Phil. Mag.* Vol. xix. p. 374), at the request of M. Cauchy himself, it appears that the latter republished his views about circular and elliptic polarization, in a lithographed memoir of the date of August, 1836; but I do not find that he published, either then or since, the detailed calculations which he seems to have made.

advert to some former researches of my own, which have a direct bearing on the question.

The same day on which M. Cauchy's letter was read to the French Academy, I had the honour of reading to the Royal Irish Academy a Paper "On the Laws of Double Refraction in Quartz"* wherein I showed that everything which we know respecting the action of that crystal upon light is comprised mathematically in the following equations:—

$$\frac{d^2\xi}{dt^2} = A\frac{d^2\xi}{dz^2} + C\frac{d^3\eta}{dz^3},$$

$$\frac{d^2\eta}{dt^2} = B\frac{d^2\eta}{dz^2} - C\frac{d^3\xi}{dz^3},$$

(1)

which differ from the common equations of vibratory motion by the two additional terms containing third differential co-efficients multiplied by the same constant C, this constant having *opposite* signs in the two equations. The quantities ξ and η are, at any time t, the displacements parallel to the axes of x and y, which are supposed to be the principal directions in the plane of the wave, one of them being therefore perpendicular to the axis of the crystal. The constants A and B are given by the expressions

$$A = a^2, \quad B = a^2 - (a^2 - b^2)\sin^2\psi,$$

where a and b are the principal velocities of propagation, ordinary and extraordinary, and ψ is the angle made by the wave-normal (or the direction of z) with the axis of the crystal. The only new constant introduced is C, which, though the peculiar phenomena of quartz depend entirely on its existence, is almost inconceivably small: its value is determined in the Paper just referred to. The equations are there proved to afford a strict geometrical representation of the facts; not only connecting together all the laws discovered by the distinguished observers to whom M. Cauchy refers, and includ-

* See *Transactions*, R. I. A., Vol. XVII. p. 461 (*supra*, p. 63).

ing the subsequent additions for which we are indebted to Mr. Airy, but leading to new results, one of which establishes a relation between two different classes of phenomena, and is verified by the experiments of M. Biot and Mr. Airy. Having, therefore, such conclusive proofs of the truth of these equations, we are entitled to assume them as a standard whereby to judge of any theory; so that any mechanical hypothesis which leads to results inconsistent with them may be at once rejected.

Now I assert that the mechanical hypothesis of M. Cauchy contradicts these equations, and therefore contradicts all the phenomena and experiments which he supposed it to represent. But before we proceed to the proof of this assertion, it may perhaps be proper to remark, that previously to the date of M. Cauchy's communication, and of my own Paper, I had actually tried and rejected this identical hypothesis, and had even gone so far as to reject along with it the whole of M. Cauchy's views about the mechanism of light. For though, in my Paper, I have said nothing of any mechanical investigations, yet, as a matter of course, before it was read to the Academy, I made every effort to connect my equations in some way with mechanical principles; and it was because I had failed in doing so to my own satisfaction, that I chose to publish the equations without comment,* as bare geometrical assumptions, and contented myself with stating orally to the Academy, as I did some months after to the Physical Section of the British Association in Bristol† that a mechanical account of the phenomena still remained a *desideratum* which no attempts of mine had been able to supply. I am not sure that on the first occasion I stated the precise nature of these attempts, though I

---

* The circumstances here related will account for what Mr. Whewell (*History of the Inductive Sciences*, Vol. ii. p. 449) calls the "obscure and oracular form" in which those equations were published. Having, at that time, no good explanation of them to give, I thought it better to attempt none. But in the general view which I have since taken (*see* p. 224 of this volume), they do not offer any peculiar difficulty.

† *See* "Transactions of the Sections," p. 18.

incline to think I did; but I have a distinct recollection of having done so on the second occasion, in reply to questions that were asked me by some Members of the Association.* Now, my first attempt to explain those equations, which was made almost as soon as I discovered them, actually turned upon the very idea which about the same time found entrance into the mind of M. Cauchy— I mean the idea of an unsymmetrical arrangement of the ether. For as it was generally believed, at that period, that the hypothesis of ethereal molecules symmetrically distributed had led, in the hands of M. Cauchy, to a complete theory of rectilinear polarization in crystals,† the notion of endeavouring to account for the phenomena of elliptic polarization, by freeing the hypothesis from any restriction as to the distribution of the ether, would naturally occur to anyone who was thinking on the subject, no less than to M. Cauchy himself. And though, for my own part, I never was satisfied with that theory, which seemed to me to possess no other merit than that of following out in detail the extremely curious, but (as I thought) very imperfect, analogy which had been perceived to exist between the vibrations of the luminiferous medium and those of a common elastic‡ solid (for

* At the period of this meeting, M. Cauchy's letter on Elliptic Polarization had been published for some months; but I was not then aware of its existence. Indeed the letter appears not to have attracted any general notice; for the theory which it contains was afterwards advanced in England as a new one, and M. Cauchy has been lately obliged to assert his prior claim to it, through the medium of Professor Powell.—*See* notes, pp. 196, 202-3.

† *See* his *Exercices de Mathématiques*, Cinquième Année, Paris, 1830, and the *Mémoires de l'Institut*, tom. x. p. 293.

‡ The analogy was suggested by the hypothesis of transversal vibrations, which, when viewed in its physical bearing, was considered by Dr. Young to be "perfectly *appalling* in its consequences," as it was only to *solids* that a "lateral resistance" tending to produce such vibrations had ever been attributed. (*Supplement to the Encyclopædia Britannica*, Vol. vi. p. 862, Edinburgh, 1824.) He admits, however, that the question, whether fluids may not "transmit impressions by lateral adhesion, remains completely open for discussion, notwithstanding the apparent difficulties attending it." As far as I am aware, Fresnel always regarded the ether as a *fluid*. M. Poisson affirms that it *must* be so regarded, and attributes its apparent peculiarities to the immense rapidity of its vibrations, which does not

it is usual to regard such a solid as a rigid system of attracting
or repelling molecules, and M. Cauchy has really done nothing
more than transfer to the luminiferous ether both the constitution of the solid and differential formulas of its vibration), still
I should have been glad, in the absence of anything better, to
find my equations supported by a similar theory, and their form
at least countenanced by the like mechanical analogy. Besides,
I recollected that Fresnel himself, in his Memoir on Double Refraction, had indicated a "helicoidal arrangement," or something
of that sort, as a probable cause of circular polarization* and as
this was an hypothesis of the same kind as the other, only not so
general, I was prepared to find that the supposition of an arbitrary
arrangement, whatever might be thought of its physical reality,
would lead to equations *of the same form* as those which I had
assumed.   Upon trial, however, the very contrary proved to be
the case; for though it was possible to obtain additional terms, containing differential co-efficients of the third order, multiplied by
the same constant C, yet this constant always came out with
the *same* sign in both equations, whereas a *difference* of sign
was *essential* for the expression of the phenomena. I had no
sooner arrived at this result than I perceived it to be fatal to
the theory of M. Cauchy, and to afford a demonstration of its
insufficiency, not only in the particular application which I had
made of it, but in all its applications.   For the hypothesis

allow the law of equal pressure to hold good in the state of motion (*Annales de
Chimie*, tom. xliv. p. 432). M. Cauchy calls the ether a fluid, though he treats it
as a solid. My own impression is, that the ether is a medium of a peculiar kind,
differing from all ponderable bodies, whether solid or fluid, in this respect, that it
absolutely refuses, in any case, to change its density, and therefore propagates to
a distance transversal vibrations *only;* while ordinary elastic fluids transmit only
normal vibrations, and ordinary solids admit vibrations of both kinds. This hypothesis also includes the supposition that the density of the ether is unchanged by
the presence of ponderable matter. As to M. Cauchy's *third ray*, with vibrations
nearly normal to the wave, there is no reason to believe that it has even the
faintest existence; but it is necessarily introduced by his identification of the
vibrations of light with those of an indefinitely extended elastic solid.

* *Mémoires de l'Institut*, tom. vii. p. 73.

which I used was, in fact, identical with that theory, in the most general form of which it is susceptible, when unrestricted by any particular supposition as to the arrangement of the ethereal molecules; and therefore the fundamental conception of the theory could not be true, as it not merely failed to explain a large and most remarkable class of phenomena—those of circular and elliptical polarization—but absolutely excluded them, and left no room for their existence. It followed from this, that the mechanical explanation, which the same theory was supposed to have given, of the phenomena of rectilinear polarization and double refraction in crystals, could not be well founded: indeed, as I have said, I had always distrusted it, and that for various reasons, of which one has been already mentioned, and another was suggested by the forced relations which M. Cauchy had found it necessary to establish among the constants of his theory, and by which he had *compelled*, as it were, his complicated formulas to assume the appearance of an agreement (though, after all, a very imperfect one) with the simple laws of Fresnel.

Such were the conclusions at which I arrived, and the reflections which they forced upon me, nearly six years ago. They have been frequently mentioned in conversation to those who took an interest in such matters, and their general tenor may be gathered from what I have elsewhere written;* but I did not think it worth while to publish them in detail, because it seemed probable that juster notions would prevail in the course of a few years, and that the ingenious speculations to which I have alluded would gradually come to be estimated at their proper value. But from whatever cause it has arisen— whether from the real difficulties of the subject, or the extreme vagueness of the ideas that most persons are content to form of it, or from deference to the authority of a distinguished mathematician—certain it is that the doctrines in question have not only been received without any expression of dissent, but have been eagerly adopted, both in this country and abroad, by

* *Transactions, R. I. A.*, Vol. xviii. p. 68 (*supra*, p. 129).

a host of followers; and even the extraordinary error, which it is my more immediate object to expose, has been continually gaining ground up to the very moment at which I write, and has at last begun to be ranked among the elementary truths of the undulatory theory of light. Notwithstanding my unwillingness, therefore, to be at all concerned in such discussions, I do not think myself at liberty to remain silent any longer. There are occasions on which every consideration of this kind must give way to a regard for the interests of science.

To show that the principles of M. Cauchy contradict, instead of explaining, the phenomenon of elliptic polarization, let us take the axes of co-ordinates as before; and let us suppose, for the sake of simplicity, and to avoid his *third ray*, that the normal displacements vanish. Then his fundamental equations take the form

$$\frac{d^2\xi}{dt^2} = \Sigma f \Delta \xi + \Sigma h \Delta \eta,$$

$$\frac{d^2\eta}{dt^2} = \Sigma g \Delta \eta + \Sigma h \Delta \xi,$$

(2)

where f, g, h are quantities depending on the law of force and the mutual distances of the molecules.* If, therefore,

---

* I have not thought it necessary to transcribe the original equations of M. Cauchy, which are rather long. He has presented them in different forms; but the system marked (16) at the end of § 1 of his *Memoir on Dispersion*, already quoted, is the most convenient, and it is the one which I have here used. The directions of the co-ordinates being arbitrary, I have supposed the axis of z to be perpendicular to the wave-plane. Then, on putting $\zeta = 0$, $\Delta \zeta = 0$, in order to get rid of the normal vibration, the last equation of the system becomes useless, and the other two are reduced to the equations (2), given above; the letters f, g, h, being written in place of certain functions depending on the mutual actions of the molecules. It will be proved, further on, that this simplification does not at all affect the argument. As the directions of x and y still remain arbitrary, I have made them parallel to the axes of the supposed elliptic vibration.

It may be right to observe, for the sake of clearness, that, when the medium is arranged symmetrically, it is always possible to take the directions of x and y such that the two sums depending on the quantity h may disappear from the equations (2), and then the vibrations are rectilinear. But when the arrangement is unsymmetrical, this is no longer possible.

we assume that each molecule describes an ellipse, the axes of which are parallel to those of x and y; that is to say, if we make

$$\xi = p \cos \phi, \quad \eta = q \sin \phi,$$

$$\phi = \frac{2\pi}{\lambda} (st - z),$$

(3)

and consequently,

$$\Delta \xi = p \,(\sin 2\theta \sin \phi - 2 \sin^2 \theta \cos \phi),$$

$$\Delta \eta = - q \,(\sin 2\theta \cos \phi + 2 \sin^2\theta \sin \phi),$$

where $\theta = \dfrac{\pi \Delta z}{\lambda}$, we shall find, by substituting these values in the equations (2), which must hold good independently of ϕ,

$$s^2 = A' + C'k, \quad s^2 = B' - \frac{C'}{k},$$

(4)

$$\Sigma f \sin 2\theta - 2k \,\Sigma h \sin^2\theta = 0,$$

$$\Sigma g \sin 2\theta + \frac{2}{k} \,\Sigma h \sin^2\theta = 0,$$

The equations (2) are precisely the same as those which have been employed by Mr. Tovey and by Professor Powell, the latter of whom, in his lately published work, entitled, "*A General and Elementary View of the Undulatory Theory, as applied to the Dispersion of Light, and other Subjects,*" has dwelt at great length on the theory of elliptic polarization which they have been supposed to afford, and which he regards as a most important accession to the Science of Light. Professor Powell has also made some communications on the subject to the British Association, and has written two Papers about it in the *Philosophical Transactions* (1838, p. 253: and 1840, p. 157), besides several others in the *Philosophical Magazine*. He, however, always attributed this theory of elliptic polarization to Mr. Tovey, until his attention was directed, by a letter from M. Cauchy, to some investigations of the latter which he had not previously seen (*Phil. Mag.* Vol. xix. p. 374). Mr. Tovey set out with the principles of M. Cauchy, and therefore naturally struck into the same track, in pursuit of the same object, apparently quite unconscious that anyone had preceded him. It was, indeed, an obvious reflection, that these principles, when generalized to the utmost, ought to include, not only the laws of elliptic polarization, but (as really has been thought by M. Cauchy and his followers) of dispersion and absorption, and, in short, of all the phenomena of optics.

wherein $k = \dfrac{q}{p}$ expresses the ratio of the semiaxes of the elliptic vibration, and

$$A' = \frac{\lambda^2}{2\pi^2}\, \Sigma f \sin^2\theta, \qquad B' = \frac{\lambda^2}{2\pi^2}\, \Sigma g \sin^2\theta,$$

$$C' = \frac{\lambda^2}{4\pi^2}\, \Sigma h \sin 2\theta.$$

Equating the two values of s^2, we get, for the determination of k, the following quadratic :—

$$k^2 + \frac{A' - B'}{C'}\, k + 1 = 0. \tag{5}$$

Now making the substitutions (3) in equations (1), page 197, we have

$$s^2 = A - \frac{2\pi}{\lambda}\, Ck, \qquad s^2 = B - \frac{2\pi}{\lambda}\, \frac{C}{k}, \tag{6}$$

and thence

$$k^2 - \frac{\lambda}{2\pi C}\, (A - B)\, k - 1 = 0, \tag{7}$$

a result which is perfectly inconsistent with the former, since the two roots of (5) have the *same sign*, if they are not imaginary, while those of (7) have *opposite signs*, and cannot be imaginary. If, therefore, one equation agrees with the phenomena, the other must contradict them. The last equation indicates that, in the double refraction of quartz, the two elliptic vibrations are always *possible*, and performed in *opposite* directions, which is in accordance with the facts; whereas the equation (5), deduced from M. Cauchy's theory, would inform us that the vibrations of the two rays are either *impossible* or in the *same* direction.*

To apply the results to a particular instance, let us conceive a circularly polarized ray passing along the axis of quartz, or through one of the rotatory liquids, such as oil of

---

* This conclusion, which shows that M. Cauchy's Theory is in direct opposition to the phenomena, might have been obtained without any reference to the equations (1). But these equations are necessary in what follows.

turpentine; the position of the co-ordinates x and y, in the plane of the wave, being now, of course, arbitrary. In each of these cases we have $k = \pm 1$, and $A = B = a^2$, so that the value of s^2 in equation (6) is expressed by the constant a^2, *plus* or *minus* a term which is inversely proportional to the wave-length λ; the sign of this term depending on the direction of the circular vibration. Now it will not be possible to obtain a similar value of s^2 from the formulas (4), unless we suppose $A' = B' = a^2$, since it is only in the expansion of C' that a term inversely proportional to λ can be found; but on this supposition the formulas are inconsistent with each other, nor can they be reconciled by any value of k. Indeed, when $A' = B'$, the equation (5) give $k = \pm \sqrt{-1}$. Thus it appears that circular vibrations, such as are known to be propagated along the axis of quartz, and through certain fluids, cannot possibly exist on the hypothesis of M. Cauchy. It was probably some partial perception of this fact that caused M. Cauchy to assert that the vibrations, in these cases, are not exactly circular, but in some degree elliptical—a supposition which, if it were at all conceivable, which we have seen it is not (p. 196), would be at once set aside by what has just been proved; for no assumed value of k, whether small or great, will in any way help to remove the difficulty.

But this is not all. Rectilinear vibrations are excluded as well as circular; for we cannot suppose $k = 0$ in the equations (4), so long as the quantity C', resulting from the hypothesis of unsymmetrical arrangement, has any existence. Thus the inconsistency of that hypothesis is complete, and the equations to which it leads are utterly devoid of meaning.

The foregoing investigation does not differ materially from that which I had recourse to in the beginning of the year 1836. To render the proof more easily intelligible, and to get rid of M. Cauchy's "third ray," which has no existence in the nature of things, I have suppressed the normal vibrations; a procedure which is not, in general, allowable on the principles of M. Cauchy. It will readily appear, however, that this simplification still leaves the demonstration perfectly rigorous in the case of circular vibrations, and does not affect its force when the vibrations are elliptical. For in the rotatory fluids it is obvious that the normal vibrations, supposing such to exist, must, by reason of the symmetry which the fluid constitution requires, be independent of the transversal vibrations, and separable from them, so that the one kind of vibrations may be supposed to vanish when we wish merely to determine the laws of the other. The equations (2) are, therefore, quite exact in this case; and they are also exact in the case of a ray passing along the axis of quartz, since such a ray is not experimentally distinguishable from one transmitted by a rotatory fluid, and its vibrations must consequently be subject to the same kind of symmetry. In these two cases, therefore, it is *rigorously* proved that the values of k, which ought to be equal to *plus* and *minus* unity, are imaginary, and equal to $\pm \sqrt{-1}$. And if we now take the most general case with regard to quartz, and suppose that the ray, which was at first coincident with the axis of the crystal, becomes gradually inclined to it, the values of k must evidently continue to be imaginary, until such an inclination has been attained that the two roots of equation (5) become possible and equal, in consequence of the increased magnitude of the co-efficient of the second term. Supposing the last term of that equation to remain unchanged, this would take place when the co-efficient of k (without regarding its sign) became equal to the number 2, and the values of k each equal to unity, both values being positive or both negative. The vibrations which before were impossible would, at this inclination, suddenly become possible; they would be *circular*, which is the exclusive property of vibrations transmitted along the axis; and they would have the same direction in both rays, which is not a property of any vibrations that are known to exist. At greater inclinations the vibrations would be elliptical, but they would still have the same direction in the two rays. These results would not be sensibly altered by regarding the equation (5) as only approximate in the case of rays inclined to the axis; for the last term of that equation, if it does not remain the same, can never differ much from unity; since it must become exactly equal to unity, *whatever* be the direction of the ray, when the crystalline structure is supposed to disappear, and the medium to become a rotatory fluid.

That a theory involving so many inconsistencies should have been advanced by a person of M. Cauchy's reputation would, perhaps, appear very extraordinary, if we did not recollect that it was unavoidably suggested by the general principles which he had previously adopted, and which were supposed, not merely by himself, but by the scientific world generally, to have already afforded the only satisfactory explanation of the laws of double refraction in the common and well-known case where the vibrations are rectilinear. This supposed explanation was obtained, as has been said, by restricting the application of M. Cauchy's principles to the hypothesis of a vibrating medium arranged symmetrically, in which case it was shown that the vibrations were necessarily rectilinear; and of course the removal of this restriction was the only way in which it was possible, on those principles, to account for the existence of circular and elliptical vibrations. Accordingly, when M. Cauchy perceived that, on the hypothesis of unsymmetrical arrangement, the existence of rectilinear vibrations became impossible, and that of elliptic vibrations, generally speaking, possible, he found it very easy to persuade himself that he had obtained a new proof of the correctness of his views, and a new and most important application of the fundamental equations by which his general principles were analytically expressed. To have supposed otherwise would have been to admit that his general principles were false. If the elliptical or *quasi*-circular vibrations which he was now contemplating were not capable of being identified with those which had been recognized in the phenomena presented by quartz and the rotatory fluids—if their laws were essentially or very considerably different—his theory would be inconsistent with a wide range of well-known facts, and, notwithstanding its so-called explanations of other laws, should be finally abandoned. Under these circumstances, therefore, he very naturally supposed that his new results *must* be in complete harmony with the phenomena discovered by M. Arago, and analyzed so successfully by MM. Biot and Fresnel; although, had he taken the precaution of acquiring such a clear notion of the phenomena as would have enabled him to translate them into analytical language, he must have perceived that they were entirely opposite to his results, and that this opposition furnished an argument which swept away the very foundations of his theory. For, if the constitution of the luminiferous medium were such as M. Cauchy supposes, the well-known phenomena of circular and elliptic polarization would, as we have seen, be absolutely impossible.

Thus the argument which overturns the particular theory of elliptical polarization destroys at the same time all the other optical theories of M. Cauchy, because they are all built on the principles which we have now *demonstrated* to be false. But though the principles of M. Cauchy are now, for the first time, formally refuted, they were objected to, on general grounds, so long ago as the year 1830, by a person whose opinion, on a question of mechanics, ought to have had considerable weight. This was M. Poisson, who, having deduced from the equations of motion of an elastic solid the consequence that such a body admitted vibrations perpendicular to the direction of their propagation, thought it right to remark that this conclusion could not be supposed to account for transversal vibrations in the theory of light, because (as he expressed himself) "the same equations of motion could not possibly apply to two systems [of molecules] so essentially different from each other" as the ethereal fluid and an elastic solid.*—(See the *Annales de Chimie*, tom. xliv.

---

* As the theory of M. Cauchy (*Mém. de l'Institut*, tom. x.) had been communicated to the Academy of Sciences some months before the period (October, 1830) at which M. Poisson wrote, there can be no doubt that M. Poisson's remark was directed against that theory, though he did not expressly mention it.

p. 432). The remark, however, did not meet with much attention from mathematicians, who were, perhaps, not disposed to scrutinize too closely any hypothesis which gave transversal vibrations as a result. Besides, the hypothesis appeared to go much further, as it offered *primâ facie* explanations of a great variety of phenomena; it was one to which calculation could be readily applied, and therefore it naturally found favour with the calculator; and as to M. Poisson's objection, it was easily removed by a change of terms, for when the elastic *solid* was called an " elastic *system*," there was no longer anything startling in the announcement that the motions of the ether are those of such a system. The hypothesis was therefore embraced by a great number of writers in every part of Europe, who reproduced, each in his own way, the results of M. Cauchy, though sometimes with considerable modifications. Every day saw some new investigation purely analytical—some new mathematical research uncontrolled by a single physical conception—put forward as a " mechanical theory " of double refraction, of circular polarization, of dispersion, of absorption; until at length the Journals of Science and Transactions of Societies were filled with a great mass of unmeaning formulas. This state of things was partly occasioned by the great number of " disposable " constants entering into the differential equations of M. Cauchy and their integrals; for it was easy to introduce, among the constants, such relations as would lead to any desired conclusion; and this method was frequently adopted by M. Cauchy himself. Thus, in his theory of double (or rather triple) refraction, given in the works already cited (p. 145), he supposes three out of his nine constants to vanish, and assumes, among the other six, three very strange and improbable relations, by means of which each of the principal sections of his wave-surface (considering only two out of its three sheets) is reduced to the circle and ellipse of Fresnel's law; and the three principal sections being thus *forced* to coincide, it would not be very surprising if the two sheets were found to coincide in every part with the wave-surface of Fresnel. The coincidence, however, is only approximate; but M. Cauchy is so far from being embarrassed by this circumstance, that he does not hesitate to regard his own theory as rigorously true, and that of Fresnel as bearing to it, in point of accuracy, the same relation which the elliptical theory of the planets, in the system of the world, bears to that of gravitation.* Nor is he at all embarrassed by the supernumerary ray belonging to the third sheet of his wave-surface; he assumes at once that such a ray exists, though it was never seen, and promises, for the satisfaction of philosophers, to make known the means of ascertaining its existence.† But he afterwards contented himself with observing that as its vibrations are in the direction of propagation they probably make no impression on the eye, and he then gave it the name of the "invisible ray."‡

In these investigations, the suppositions which M. Cauchy had made respecting the constants led to the result that the vibrations of a polarized ray are *parallel* to its plane of polarization; but in the year 1836 he changed his opinion on this point, and then, by reinstating the constants that he had before supposed to vanish, and establishing proper relations amongst them and the rest, he arrived at the conclusion that the vibrations are *perpendicular* to the plane of polarization.§ All his other results, of course, underwent some corresponding change; and it is this new theory which must now be regarded as rigorous, while that of Fresnel is to be looked on as approximate. But it is needless to say, that if the accuracy of Fresnel's law of double refraction is to be disputed, it must be on much better grounds than these; and the results of M. Cauchy are certainly too far removed from that law to have any chance of being consonant with truth. Although, for example, his new views respecting the direction of the vibra-

* *Mémoires de l'Institut*, tom. x. p. 313.
† *Ibid.* p. 305.
‡ *Nouveaux Exercices*, p. 40.
§ *Comptes Rendus*, tom. ii. p. 342.

tions agree, in a general way, with those of Fresnel, there is yet, in one particular, an important difference between them; for, according to Fresnel, the vibrations are always exactly in the surface of the wave, while, according to M. Cauchy (in his old theory as well as the new), they are only so in ordinary media. In a biaxal crystal he finds—and this is one of the ways in which the "invisible ray" manifests its influence—that the direction of vibration, in each of the two rays that are visible, is inclined at a certain angle to the wave-plane; but this angle, though small, is by no means inconsiderable, as M. Cauchy seems to intimate, overlooking the fact, which appears from his own equations, that it is of the same order of magnitude as the quantities on which the double refraction depends. It is true, the deviation measured by this angle cannot, if it exists, be directly observed in the refracted light; but its indirect effects on *reflected* light ought to be very great, since the action of the crystal on a ray reflected at its surface differs from that of an ordinary medium by a quantity of the same order merely as the aforesaid angle; and as the problem of crystalline reflexion has been already solved* on the supposition (which is an essential one in the solution) that the vibrations are *exactly* in the plane of the wave, it is highly improbable, considering the complex nature of the question, that it will be solved, in any satisfactory way, on a supposition so different as that which is required by the theory of M. Cauchy. However, as the laws of such reflexion are now well known, by means of the solution alluded to, it is possible that M. Cauchy may, as in the case of double refraction, succeed in deducing the same laws, or, if not the same, what may seem to be more exact laws, from certain principles † of his own, helped out, if need be,

---

* *Transactions*, Royal Irish Academy, Vol. xviii., p. 31 (*supra*, p. 87).

† In applying these principles to the question of reflexion and refraction at the surface of an *ordinary* medium (*Comptes Rendus*, tom. ii. p. 348), M. Cauchy has arrived at the singular conclusion, that light may be greatly increased by refraction through a prism, at the same time that it is almost totally reflected within it. Supposing the refracting angle of the prism to be very little less than the angle of

by proper relations among his constants; especially if, to allow greater scope for such relations, the number of constants be increased by the hypothesis of two coexisting systems of molecules, an hypothesis which M. Cauchy has already considered with his usual generality, but without making any precise application of it.*

Perhaps one cause why M. Cauchy's views on the subject of double refraction have met with such general acceptance may be found in the fact, that a theory setting out from the

total reflexion for the substance of which it is composed, a ray incident perpendicularly on one of the faces will emerge, making a very small angle with the other face; and as the reflexion at the latter face is nearly total, it is self-evident that the intensity of the emergent light, as compared with that of the incident, must be very small. M. Cauchy, however, finds by an elaborate analysis that a prodigious multiplication of light ["*une prodigieuse multiplication de a lumière*"] takes place, the emergent ray being nearly six times more intense than the incident when the prism is made of glass, and nearly nine times when the prism is of diamond. This result was, in a general way, actually verified experimentally by himself and another person; so easy it is, in some cases, to see anything that we expect to see. Had the result been true, it would have been a very brilliant discovery indeed; for then we should have been able, by a simple series of refractions, to convert the feeblest light into one of any intensity we pleased; but the very absurdity of such a supposition should have taught M. Cauchy to distrust both his theory and his experiment. Far from doing so, however, he considers the fact to be perfectly established, and to afford a new argument against the system of emission. "Ici," says he, "un rayon, réfléchi en totalité, est de plus transmis avec accroissement de lumière; ce qui est un nouvel argument contre le système d'émission." The system of emission has at least this advantage, that by no possible error could such a conclusion be deduced from it. For if all the particles of light be reflected, certainly none of them can be refracted.

The truth is, that M. Cauchy mistook the measure of intensity in the hypothesis of undulations, supposing it to be proportional simply to the square of the amplitude of vibration; whereas it is really measured by the *vis viva*, or by that square multiplied by the quantity of ether put in motion, a quantity which in the present case is evanescent, since the corresponding volumes of ether, moved by the ray within in the prism and by the emergent ray, are to each other as the sine of twice the angle of the prism to the sine of twice the very small angle which the emergent ray makes with the second face of the prism. The intensity of the emergent light is therefore very small, as it ought to be, though the amplitude of its vibrations is considerable.

* *Exercices d'Analyse et de Physique Mathématique*, tom. i. p. 33.

same principles, and leading, by the same relations among constants, to formulas identical in every respect with his earlier results, was advanced independently, and nearly at the same time, by M. Neumann of Königsberg.* A coincidence so remarkable would be looked upon, not unreasonably, as a strong argument in favour of the theory; though it must be allowed that, in the effort to extend the knowledge of any subject, there is a tendency in different minds to adopt the same errors respecting it, as well as the same truths; a fact of which we have seen other examples in the course of the present article.

According to M. Neumann,† the "third ray," not being perceived as light, must manifest its existence as radiant heat, or as a chemical power, or as some other agent ["*als strahlende Wärme, oder chemisch wirkend, oder als irgend ein anderes Agens*"] and he thinks that the nature of this ray will be more easily investigated, if the laws of *reflexion* shall be deduced from the aforesaid theory. But we have seen that the laws of reflexion are, to all appearance, at variance with the theory, and they take no account whatever of the third ray. Besides, the discoveries which have been made of late years respecting the polarization of radiant heat, and the strong analogies that have been traced between it and light, amount to a demonstration that its vibrations are transversal, and of course essentially different from those of the supposed third ray, which are normal, or nearly so. There is every reason to believe that the vibrations of the chemical rays are also transversal; and we may confidently assert, that the three species of rays—those of light and heat, and the chemical rays—are produced not only by vibrations of the same medium, but by the same kind of vibrations, propagated with nearly the same velocities. If, therefore, the third ray of MM. Cauchy and Neumann has any existence, it must be referred to "some other agent," the nature of which it is impossible to conjecture.

Enough has now been said to show that the optical theory

* Poggendorff's *Annals*, Vol. xxv. p. 418.
† *Ibid.* p. 454.

which we have examined, and which has passed current in the scientific world for a considerable period, is quite inadequate to explain the leading phenomena of light, and that it is based upon principles which are altogether inapplicable to the subject. M. Cauchy states, in the memoir so often quoted,* that the first application which he had made of his principles was to the theory of *sound*, and that the formulas which he had deduced from them agreed remarkably well with the experiments of Savart and others on the vibrations of elastic solids. As I have already intimated, it is in the solution of such questions (which, however, have long been familiar to mathematicians) that the fundamental equations of M. Cauchy may be most advantageously employed; and had he pursued his researches in this direction, his labours would doubtless have been attended with more success, and with greater benefit to science.

II.—*On Fresnel's Formula for the Intensity of Reflected Light, with Remarks on Metallic Reflexion.*

When Mr. Potter discovered, by experiment, 'that more light is reflected by a metal at a perpendicular incidence than at any oblique incidence (at least as far as 70°), the fact was looked upon, by himself and others, as contrary to all received theories; and certainly the universal opinion, up to that time, was, that the intensity of reflexion always increases with the incidence. It may therefore be worth while to remark, that the formula given by Fresnel for reflexion at the surface of a transparent body, though not of course applicable, except in a very rude way, to the case of metals, would yet lead us to expect, for highly refracting bodies, as the metals are supposed to be, precisely such a result as that obtained by Mr. Potter. For when the index of refraction exceeds the number $2 + \sqrt{3}$, or the tangent of 75°, the expression for the intensity of reflected light will be found to have a *minimum* value at a certain angle of in-

---

* *Mem. de l'Institut*, tom. x. p. 294.

cidence; while for all less values of the refractive index the intensity will be least at the perpendicular incidence.

Let i and i' be the angles of incidence and refraction, and put

$$M = \frac{\sin i}{\sin i'}, \quad \mu = \frac{\cos i}{\cos i'};$$

then if I be the intensity of the reflected light, when common light is incident, Fresnel's expression

$$1 = \tfrac{1}{2}\left\{ \frac{\sin^2(i-i')}{\sin^2(i+i')} + \frac{\tan^2(i-i')}{\tan^2(i+i')} \right\},$$

in which the intensity of the incident light is taken for unity, may be put under the form

$$I = \frac{\left(\dfrac{1}{\mu}-\mu\right)^2 + \left(\dfrac{1}{M}-M\right)^2}{\left(\dfrac{1}{\mu}+\mu+\dfrac{1}{M}+M\right)^2},$$

which has a minimum value when

$$\mu + \frac{1}{\mu} = M + \frac{1}{M} - \frac{8}{M + \dfrac{1}{M}};$$

the value of I being in that case

$$I = \frac{\left(M-\dfrac{1}{M}\right)^2 - 4}{2\left(M-\dfrac{1}{M}\right)^2} = \frac{\left(M+\dfrac{1}{M}\right)^2 - 8}{2\left(M+\dfrac{1}{M}\right)^2 - 8},$$

and the corresponding angle of incidence being given by the formula

$$\sin i = \frac{\sqrt{M}\,\sqrt[4]{\epsilon^2-1}}{\epsilon + \sqrt{\epsilon^2-1}}, \quad \text{where } \epsilon = \tfrac{1}{4}\left(M+\frac{1}{M}\right).$$

Since $\mu + \dfrac{1}{\mu}$ cannot be less than 2, it is easy to see that, when there is a minimum, $M + \dfrac{1}{M}$ cannot be less than 4, and therefore M cannot be less than $2 + \sqrt{3}$, or 3·732.

As an example, let $M + \dfrac{1}{M} = 6$. Then, at a perpendicular incidence, one-half the incident light will be reflected. The minimum will be when $i = 65°\ 36'$, and at this angle only $\frac{7}{16}$ of the incident light will be reflected. The value here assumed for the refractive index is that which Sir J. Herschel* assigns to mercury; but if my ideas be correct, it is far too low for that metal.

The only person who supposes that the refractive index of a metal is not a large number is M. Cauchy. It has always been held as a maxim in optics, that the higher the reflective power of any substance, the higher also is its refractive index. But M. Cauchy completely reverses this maxim; for, as I have elsewhere shown,† it follows from his theory that the most reflective metals are the least refractive, and even that the index of refraction, which for transparent bodies is always greater than unity, may for metals descend far below unity. Thus, according to his formula, the index of refraction for pure silver is the fraction $\frac{1}{4}$, so that the dense body of the silver actually plays the part of a very rare medium with respect to a vacuum. It appears to me that such a result as this is quite sufficient to overturn the theory from which it is derived. The formulas, however, which he gives for the intensity of the reflected light, are identical with the empirical expressions which I had given long before, and are at least approximately true.

In framing my own empirical theory,‡ two suppositions relative to the value of the refractive index presented themselves. Putting M for the *modulus*, and χ for the *characteristic*, I had to choose between the values $M \cos \chi$ and $\dfrac{M}{\cos \chi}$. The latter value is that which I adopted; the former, which is M. Cauchy's, was

---

* *Treatise on Light*, Art. 594.

† *Comptes Rendus*, tom. viii. p. 964; *vid.* note at the end of this volume.

‡ See *Proceedings*, Vol. i. p. 2 (*supra*, p. 58).

rejected, because I saw that it would lead to the result above mentioned.

Another result of M. Cauchy's, which he has given twice in the *Comptes Rendus*,* requires to be noticed. When a polarized ray is reflected by a metal, the phase of its vibration is altered; and if the incidence be oblique, the change of phase is different, according as the light is polarized in the plane of incidence, or in the perpendicular plane. But when the ray is reflected at a perpendicular incidence, it is manifest that the change is a constant quantity, whatever be the plane of polarization. In fact, the distinction between the plane of incidence and the perpendicular plane no longer exists, and the phenomena must be the same in all planes passing through the ray. Yet M. Cauchy, in the two places above quoted, asserts it to be a consequence of his theory, that in this case the alterations of phase are different for two planes of polarization at right angles to each other, and that the difference of the alterations amounts to half an undulation. The same singular hypothesis had been previously made by M. Neumann,† whom M. Cauchy appears to have followed; but M. Neumann has since admitted it to be erroneous.‡

* Tom. ii. p. 428, and tom. viii. p. 965.
† Poggendorff's *Annals*, Vol. xxvi. p. 90.
‡ *Ibid.* Vol. xl. p. 513.

XVIII.—ON THE PROBLEM OF TOTAL REFLEXION.

[*Proceedings of the Royal Irish Academy*, Vol. ii.—Read November 30, 1841.]

PROFESSOR MAC CULLAGH communicated to the Academy a very simple geometrical rule, which gives the solution of the problem of *total reflexion*, for ordinary media, or for uniaxal crystals.

First, let the total reflexion take place at the common surface of two ordinary media, as between glass and air, and let it be proposed to determine the incident and reflected vibrations, when the refracted vibration is known. It is to be observed, that the refracted vibration (which is in general elliptical) cannot be arbitrarily assumed; for, as may be inferred from what has been already stated,* it must be always similar to the section of a certain cylinder, the sides of which are perpendicular to the plane of incidence, and the base of which is an ellipse lying in that plane, and having its major axis perpendicular to the reflecting surface, the ratio of the major to the minor axis being that of unity to the constant r. The value of r, as determined by the general rule in p. 191, is

$$r = \sqrt{1 - \frac{1}{n^2 \sin^2 i}},$$

where i is the angle of incidence, and n the index of refraction out of the rarer into the denser medium. The ellipse is greatest

---

* *Proceedings* of the Academy, Vol. ii. p. 102 (*supra*, p. 192).

for a particle at the common surface of the media; and for a particle situated in the rarer medium, at the distance z from that surface, its linear dimensions are proportional to the quantity $e^{-\frac{2\pi rz}{\lambda}}$; so that for a very small value of z the refracted vibration becomes insensible.

Now, taking any plane section of the aforesaid cylinder to represent the refracted vibration for a particle situated at the common surface of the two media, let OP and OQ be the semi-axes of the section, and let them be drawn, with their proper lengths and directions, from the point of incidence O; through which point also let two planes be drawn to represent the incident and reflected waves. Then conceive a plane passing through the semiaxis OP, and intersecting the two wave-planes, to revolve until it comes into the position where the semiaxis makes equal angles with the two intersections; and in this position let the intersections be made the sides of a parallelogram, of which the semiaxis OP is the diagonal. Let OA and OA', which are of course equal in length, denote these two sides. Make a similar construction for the other semiaxis OQ, and let OB, OB', which are also equal, denote the two sides of the corresponding parallelogram. Then will the incident vibration be represented by the ellipse of which OA and OB are conjugate semidiameters, and the reflected vibration by the ellipse of which OA' and OB' are conjugate semidiameters. And the correspondence of *phase* in describing the three ellipses will be such that the points A, A', P will be simultaneous positions, as also the points B, B', Q.

The same construction precisely will answer for the case of total reflexion at the surface of a uniaxal crystal, which is covered with a fluid of greater refractive power than itself. It is to be applied successively to the ordinary and extraordinary refracted vibrations, and we thus get the *uniradial* incident and reflected vibrations, or rather the ellipses which are similar to them. And as any incident vibration may be resolved into two which shall be similar to the uniradial ones, we can find the reflected vibration which corresponds to it, by compounding the uniradial reflected vibrations.

It may be well to mention that, in a uniaxal crystal, the plane of the extraordinary refracted vibration is always perpendicular to the axis, and therefore the ellipse in which the vibration is performed may be easily determined by the remark in p. 192. The plane of the ordinary vibration has no fixed position in the crystal; but if we conceive the auxiliary quantities ξ_1, η_1, ζ_1 (p. 188), to be compounded into an ellipse (as if they were displacements), the plane of this auxiliary ellipse will be perpendicular to the axis of the crystal.

Whether the preceding very simple construction, for finding the incident and reflected vibrations by means of the refracted vibration, extends also to the case of *biaxal* crystals, is a point which has not yet been determined, on account of the complicated operations to which the investigation leads, at least when attempted in any way that obviously suggests itself.

XIX.—ON THE DISPERSION OF THE OPTIC AXES, AND OF THE AXES OF ELASTICITY, IN BIAXAL CRYSTALS.

[*From the Philosophical Magazine*, Vol. XXI., October, 1842.]

In the last number of the *Philosophical Magazine* (p. 228), there appeared an extract from the *Proceedings* of the Royal Irish Academy, containing a notice of a memoir which I had the honour of reading to that body on the 24th of May, 1841; and in the concluding paragraph of the notice a brief allusion is made to a "mathematical hypothesis" by which I had connected the laws of dispersion and those of the elliptic polarization of rock-crystal with the other laws that were there announced. My present object is to indicate the development of that hypothesis, with reference more particularly to the subject of dispersion in crystals, and to communicate a very simple result which I have lately had occasion to obtain from it. The result is remarkable as embracing and explaining a class of intricate phenomena which hitherto have not been connected with any theory, or rather have stood in opposition to all theories; I mean the phenomena of the dispersion of the optic axes, and of the axes of elasticity (as they are called) in biaxal crystals.

The name of axes of elasticity was given by Fresnel to three rectangular directions, which, according to his theory, exist in every crystallized medium, and which are distinguished by the property, that if a particle of the medium be slightly displaced in the direction of any one of them, the elastic force thereby called into play will act precisely in the line of the dis-

placement. These directions coincide with the axes of the
ellipsoid by which he constructs his wave-surface; and the position of the axes being thus fixed, it is only their *lengths* that
can be supposed to vary for the differently coloured rays.
Such is the view taken by Fresnel with regard to crystalline
dispersion, and it is obviously the only view that his theory
admits. Succeeding theorists, in their numerous attempts to
deduce Fresnel's beautiful laws from dynamical principles, have
always been obliged to assume that the medium is symmetrically arranged with respect to three rectangular planes; and
as, in this hypothesis, the axes of elasticity, or of optical symmetry, necessarily coincide with those of symmetrical arrangement, their directions are fixed, as before, independently of
colour.

From these principles it follows that the optic axes for different colours all lie in the same plane, namely, the plane of
the greatest and least axes of the ellipsoid, and that they are
equally inclined to each of the latter axes, so that the angle
made by any pair, to whatever colour they belong, is always
bisected by the same right line. This was accordingly, for a
long time, believed to be the case; and the earlier experiments
of Sir J. Herschel,* which are appealed to by Fresnel, as well
as the observations of Sir David Brewster, seemed to establish
it as a general law.   But it was afterwards discovered by Sir J.
Herschel that, in *borax*, the optic axes for different colours lie
in different planes inclined at very sensible angles to each
other; and the same discovery was made about the same time
(1832) by M. Nörrenberg. The latter observer further ascertained, that even when the optic axes all lie in the same plane
there are cases, as in sulphate of lime, wherein their angles are
not bisected by the same right line. These facts, and others of
a like nature that have been since observed, show the falsehood
of the supposition that the lines called the axes of elasticity
have always the same directions whatever be the colour of the

------

* *Phil. Trans.* 1820.

light; they are inconsistent with all received notions, and contradict every theory that has been hitherto proposed. No person, as far as I am aware, has even attempted to explain them.

But in the theory which I have constructed to represent the laws of the action of crystallized bodies upon light, and which has already brought so much within its grasp, the phenomena in question do not offer any difficulty whatever: on the contrary, they are of a kind that would naturally be looked for, antecedently to experiment. For, in this theory, I make no hypothesis as to the constitution of the ether, or the arrangement of its molecules; nor any hypothesis, like that of Fresnel, respecting the mechanical signification of the axes of elasticity. The existence of three rectangular axes possessing peculiar properties is not a principle, but a result, of theory : their directions are determined by conditions perfectly analogous to those which determine the principal axes of an ellipsoid from its general equation ; and these directions are functions of certain quantities which are constant when differentials of the second and subsequent orders are neglected, but which vary when these are taken into account. The differentials of higher orders introduce terms depending on the wave-length ; and thus the *directions*, as well as the *lengths*, of the principal lines depend on the colour of the light, or, to speak more accurately, on the length of the wave.

All this will be easily understood if we recur to the first principles of the theory. According to these, everything depends on the form assigned to the function V in the general dynamical equation

$$\iiint dx\,dy\,dz \left(\frac{d^2\xi}{dt^2}\,\delta\xi + \frac{d^2\eta}{dt^2}\,\delta\eta + \frac{d^2\zeta}{dt^2}\,d\zeta\right) = \iiint dx\,dy\,dz\,\delta V,$$

from which the motion of the ether is deduced. In my first memoir on the subject (read to the Academy on the 9th of December, 1839), I showed that when differentials of the first order only are preserved, the function V—which may perhaps with propriety be called the *potential*, since the motion of the system is potentially, or virtually, included in it—is a function of the second degree, composed of the three quantities X, Y, Z, which are connected with the displacements ξ, η, ζ, by the following relations :—

$$X = \frac{d\eta}{dz} - \frac{d\zeta}{dy}, \quad Y = \frac{d\zeta}{dx} - \frac{d\xi}{dz}, \quad Z = \frac{d\xi}{dy} - \frac{d\eta}{dx}.$$

To show this, I make use simply of the consideration that the motion must be such as to satisfy the condition

$$\frac{d\xi}{dx} + \frac{d\eta}{dy} + \frac{d\zeta}{dz} = 0;$$

which seems to be characteristic of the vibrations of light. But the same condition allows us to suppose that the potential contains not only the quantities X, Y, Z, but their differential coefficients of any order with respect to the co-ordinates. This supposition, however, is too general, and requires to be limited by other considerations. Now the most natural restriction which can be imposed consists in the assumption that the quantities of all orders are formed on the same type, those of any order being derived from the preceding in the same way that the quantities X, Y, Z are derived from ξ, η, ζ : there are particular reasons also which go to strengthen this hypothesis, and have led me to adopt it. Putting therefore

$$X_1 = \frac{dY}{dz} - \frac{dZ}{dy}, \quad Y_1 = \frac{dZ}{dx} - \frac{dX}{dz}, \quad Z_1 = \frac{dX}{dy} - \frac{dY}{dx};$$

$$X_2 = \frac{dY_1}{dz} - \frac{dZ_1}{dy}, \quad Y_2 = \frac{dZ_1}{dx} - \frac{dX_1}{dz}, \quad Z_2 = \frac{dX_1}{dy} - \frac{dY_1}{dx},$$

and so on, I suppose the potential to be a function of the second degree, composed of all the quantities X, Y, Z, X_1, Y_1, Z_1, X_2, Y_2, Z_2, &c. ; and this is the "mathematical hypothesis" alluded to in the beginning of this article. The hypothesis occurred to me more than three years ago (June, 1839), but I did not venture to communicate it to the Academy until the date of my second memoir (May, 1841); and even then I had not studied it with the attention which I now conceive it merits. It was only very lately, in fact, in some conversations which I had with M. Babinet during a short visit to Paris, that my attention was strongly drawn to the subject of dispersion in crystals, particularly the dispersion of the axes of elasticity. My thoughts then naturally reverted to the hypothesis which I have mentioned, and since my return I have found that it affords a complete explanation of all the phenomena.*

I have also found that it gives the general law, extended to biaxal crystals, of that elliptic and circular polarization which has hitherto been detected only in quartz and in certain fluids; while for the case of rectilinear polarization it gives a law (very possibly a true one) more general than that of Fresnel, but quite as elegant, and differing very slightly from it. The hypothesis, therefore, is still too general for our present purpose. To make it include only those crystals to which the law of Fresnel is rigorously applicable, the alternate derivatives X_1, Y_1, Z_1, X_3, Y_3, Z_3, &c., must be supposed to vanish in the function which represents the potential. Then, the axes of coordinates having any fixed directions within the crystal, the axes of elasticity will be the principal axes of an ellipsoid represented by an equation of the form

$$Ax^2 + By^2 + Cz^2 + 2Dyz + 2Exz + 2Fxy = 1,$$

in which *each* of the six coefficients—the first, for example—expresses a series of the form

$$A_0 + \frac{A_1}{\lambda^2} + \frac{A_2}{\lambda^4} + \frac{A_3}{\lambda^6} + \&\text{c.,}$$

where λ denotes the wave-length, and all the other quantities

* I am indebted, for my information on the subject, to a short article, drawn up by MM. Quetelet and Babinet, in the *Bulletin* of the Royal Academy of Brussels, Vol. II. p. 150; as also to Poggendorff's *Annals*, Vol. XXVI. p. 309; Vol. XXXV. p. 81.

are constant. The ellipsoid itself is the reciprocal of that ellipsoid by which the wave-surface is constructed, and its semiaxes are the three principal indices of refraction. As λ is supposed to vary, not only the lengths but the directions of the principal axes vary, and thus we have a different wave-surface for every different wave-length *within* the crystal.

The optic axes are perpendicular to the circular sections of the above ellipsoid, and describe, in general, two fragments of a cone, the equation of which may be found by supposing λ to be variable in the equation of the ellipsoid. But only very particular cases have been hitherto observed, and I shall not stop to discuss them.

J. Mac Cullagh.

Trin. Coll., Dublin, *September*, 1842.

XX.—ON THE LAW OF DOUBLE REFRACTION.

[*From the Philosophical Magazine*, Vol. xxi., 1842].

HAVING mentioned, in an article * which I sent a few days ago for insertion in the *Philosophical Magazine*, that I had been led, in following out an hypothesis, to a law of double refraction more general than that of Fresnel, I think it may be well to state very briefly the nature of that law, and to point out the difference between it and the law of Fresnel, especially as I have since observed that the difference is one of a very extraordinary kind, and one which, if it has a real existence (a question which experiment only can decide), may serve to account for phenomena that have seemed hitherto inexplicable.

I have said, in the article referred to, that when the potential V, which is a function of the second degree, is supposed to contain only the squares and products of the derivatives X, Y, Z, X_2, Y_2, Z_2, X_4, &c., we get the law of Fresnel, as well as the law of crystalline dispersion; but if we make the more general, and apparently the more natural supposition, that it contains also the squares and products of the alternate derivatives X_1, Y_1, Z_1, X_3, Y_3, Z_3, &c., then we get, of course, a different law. Now I find that there will still be two optic axes for each colour, and that the two directions of vibration in a given wave-plane will have the same relation to them as be-

* "On the Dispersion of the Optic Axes, and of the Axes of Elasticity, in Biaxal Crystals" (*supra*, p. 221).

fore; while the difference of the squares of the two velocities of propagation will continue proportional to the product of the sines of the angles which the wave normal makes with the optic axes; but the *sum* of the squares of these velocities will be increased or diminished by a quantity proportional to the square of a perpendicular let fall from the centre on the tangent plane of a certain very small ellipsoid, this tangent plane being supposed parallel to the wave. Such is the general result for biaxal crystals; but its bearing will be best perceived by taking the case of a uniaxal crystal, wherein the law of Fresnel reduces itself to that of Huyghens.

In this case the wave-surface will, instead of the sphere and spheroid of Huyghens, consist of two ellipsoids touching each other at the extremities of a common diameter, which coincides with the axis of the crystal; one ellipsoid differing slightly from a sphere, the other slightly from a spheroid. Neither of the rays will be refracted according to the ordinary law, nor will the wave-surface be symmetrical round the axis. As the law of refraction is unsymmetrical, that of reflexion will be so likewise, and thus we may perhaps obtain an explanation of the extraordinary phenomena observed by Sir David Brewster in reflexion at the common surface of oil of cassia and Iceland spar.

It will no doubt appear strange to call in question the accuracy of the Huyghenian law, which is generally considered to be established beyond dispute by the experiments of Wollaston and Malus. But the fact is, that no exact experiments have ever been made on the refraction of the ordinary ray. Neither of those philosophers seems to have entertained any suspicion that the ordinary law might be inapplicable to it; they both took for granted that it followed the law of Snellius. But their results seem to be quite consistent with the supposition that the ordinary index, for rays passing in different directions through Iceland spar, may vary in the third place of decimals, perhaps even in the second. The experiments of Rudberg throw no light upon the question, for it happens, oddly enough, that though he had two prisms in every other case, he used only one of Iceland spar : he could not therefore compare the velocities of rays passing in different directions. On comparing his numbers, however, with those of Wollaston and Malus, there is, as Sir David Brewster has observed,* a "surprising discrepancy," so great indeed as to be quite "alarming." After remarking the difficulty of finding any explanation of it, Sir David concludes that it must arise from the different refractive powers possessed by different specimens. But though this cause must operate in some degree, we cannot tell to what extent it is effective, and the discrepancy may notwithstanding be occasioned, in a great measure, by a deviation from the Huyghenian law. The whole question must therefore be reopened, and the ordinary indices for the fixed lines of the spectrum must be determined by means of different prisms cut out of the *same piece* of Iceland spar.

Whatever the result may be—whether it shall confirm the law of Huyghens, or show that another must be substituted for it—it will at least be useful for science, by removing the uncertainty in which the subject is at present involved.

* *Phil. Mag.*, S. 3, Vol. i. p. 8.

Trin. Coll., Dublin, *Sept.* 24, 1842.

XXI.—ON THE LAWS OF METALLIC REFLEXION, AND ON THE MODE OF MAKING EXPERIMENTS UPON ELLIPTIC POLARIZATION.

[*Proceedings of the Royal Irish Academy*, Vol. ii. p. 376.—Read, May 8, 1843.]

SEVERAL years ago, as the Academy are aware, I made an attempt to investigate the laws according to which light is reflected at the surface of metals, and I then proposed certain formulæ which represented, with sufficient accuracy, all the facts and experiments which I was able to collect upon the subject.* But in order to test these formulæ satisfactorily, it was necessary to obtain measurements far more exact than any that had previously been made; and for this end I devised an instrument, which was constructed for me by Mr. Grubb, and of which a brief description has been given in the *Proceedings*.† I regret to say, however, that nothing of much consequence has yet been done with the instrument. Some preliminary trials of its performance were indeed made in the summer of 1837, and the results of one of these shall presently be given; but an accidental strain which it suffered, while I was preparing to undertake a series of experiments, caused me to discontinue the observations at the time; and being then obliged to superintend the printing of my essay on the "Laws of Crystalline Reflexion and Refraction,"‡ my attention was drawn afresh to this latter

---

* See the *Proceedings* of the Academy, Vol. i. p. 2, October, 1836 (*supra*, p. 58); *Transactions*, Vol. xviii. p. 71, note (*supra*, p. 133).

† Vol. i. p. 159 (*supra*, p. 138).

‡ *Transactions* R. I. A. (*supra*, p. 87).

subject, respecting which some new questions suggested themselves, which I thought it right to discuss in notes appended to the essay. I was not afterwards at leisure to take up the experimental inquiry, until the beginning of the year 1839, when I began to think of putting the instrument in order for that purpose. The strain which it had suffered rendered some slight alterations necessary; and I now resolved to make additions to it also, with the view of operating upon the fixed lines of the spectrum, as a few trials had convinced me that measures sufficiently precise could not be obtained without employing light of definite refrangibility. I wished, moreover, to take the opportunity which the nature of the proposed experiments presented, of verifying the theory of Fresnel's rhomb, or rather of verifying, by means of the rhomb, the formulæ which Fresnel has given for computing the effects of total reflexion, when it takes place at the common surface of two ordinary media. I wrote therefore to Munich for several articles which I wanted; among others, for a set of rhombs cut at different angles, out of different kinds of glass. But while I was waiting for these some months elapsed, and in the meantime I got sight of a new theory, which, from its connexion with my former researches, possessed more immediate interest, and the pursuit of which, in conjunction with other studies and various engagements, caused me again to suspend the inquiry respecting the laws of metallic reflexion. I allude to the " Dynamical Theory of Crystalline Reflexion and Refraction," communicated to the Academy in December, 1839.* This was followed soon after by a general " Theory of Total Reflexion,"† founded on the same principles. The latter theory, forming a new department of physical optics, and involving the solution of questions not previously attempted, was *analytically* complete when it was communicated to the Academy in May, 1841 ; but its *geometrical* development has since required my attention from time to time, and has not yet been brought to that degree of simplicity of which it appears to

* *Proceedings*, VOL. I. p. 374, (*supra*, p. 145).
† *Ibid.* VOL. II. p. 96 (*supra*, p. 187).

be susceptible.* Indeed I have found that, in this instance, the geometrical laws of the phenomena are by no means obvious interpretations of the equations resulting from the analytical solution of the problem ; and in endeavouring to verify such supposed laws I have often been led to algebraical calculations of so complicated a nature that it has been impracticable to bring them to any conclusion, and I have been obliged, from mere weariness, to abandon them altogether. On returning, however, to the investigation, after perhaps a long interval of time, I have usually perceived some mode of eluding the calculations, or of directly deducing the geometrical law; and, when the theory comes to be published in its final form, no trace of these difficulties will probably appear.

From the causes above mentioned, combined with frequent absence from Dublin, the researches which I had entered upon, respecting the action of metals upon light, have been hitherto interrupted ; and as it may still be some time before they are resumed, I venture, in the meanwhile, to submit to the Academy the results already spoken of, which were obtained on the first trial of the instrument, and which afford the best data that can yet be had for comparison with theory.

The results, it must be confessed, are those of very rough experiments, made one evening (about the month of July, 1837) in company with Mr. Grubb, before I had received the instrument from his hands, and merely with the view of showing him, when it was finished, the kind of phenomena that I proposed to observe with it, and the mode of observing them. But the instrument was so far superior (in workmanship at least) to any apparatus previously employed for this sort of experiments, that it was impossible, without great negligence in using it, not to obtain measures of considerable accuracy. I did not, however, at the time, set much value on these measures, because I expected shortly to possess a series of observations made with every possible precaution; but having chanced to preserve the paper on which they were noted down, I was tempted, a few

* *Proceedings*, Vol. ii. p. 174 (*supra*, p. 218).

days ago, to try how far they agreed with my formulæ; and the agreement turns out to be so close, that I think myself justified in publishing them. Besides, it will be curious hereafter to compare them with more careful measurements.

Before we proceed, however, to the details of the experiments, it may be well to give the formulæ in a state fitted for immediate application. The light incident on the metal being polarized in a certain plane, let a denote the azimuth of this plane, or the angle which it makes with the plane of incidence; and as the reflected light will be elliptically polarized, or, in other words, will perform its vibrations in ellipses all similar and equal to each other, as well as similarly placed, put θ for the angle which either axis of any one of these ellipses makes with the plane of incidence, and let β be another angle, such that its tangent may represent the ratio of one axis of the ellipse to the other. Then when the optical constants M and χ (of which I suppose the first to be a number greater than unity, and the second an angle less than 90°) are known for the particular metal, the angles θ and β may be computed for any value of a, at any given angle of incidence, by the following formulæ:

$$\tan 2\theta = \frac{(v' - v) \sin 2a}{2f + (v' + v) \cos 2a},$$

(A)

$$\sin 2\beta = \frac{2g \sin 2a}{v' + v + 2f \cos 2a},$$

in which f and g are constant quantities given by the expressions

$$f = \left(M - \frac{1}{M}\right) \cos \chi, \quad g = \left(M + \frac{1}{M}\right) \sin \chi,$$

(B)

and v, v' are quantities depending on the angle of incidence i, in the following way. Let i' be an angle such that

$$\frac{\sin i}{\sin i'} = \frac{M}{\cos \chi},$$

(C)

and put

$$\frac{\cos i}{\cos i'} = \mu, \tag{D}$$

then will

$$\nu = \frac{1}{\mu} - \mu, \qquad \nu' = \frac{f^2 + g^2}{\nu}. \tag{E}$$

The angles θ and β are given by immediate observation with the instrument; and from their values at any incidence, and for any azimuth a of the plane of primitive polarization, we can find the constants M and χ, which we may afterwards use to calculate the values of θ and β for all other incidences and azimuths, in order to compare them with the observed values. It is indifferent, in the formulæ, whether θ be referred to the major or the minor axis of the elliptic vibration, as also whether $\tan \beta$ be the ratio of the minor to the major axis, or the reciprocal of that ratio; but in what follows we shall suppose θ to be the inclination of the plane of incidence to that axis, which, when a is 45° or less, is always the major axis; and β shall be supposed less than 45°, in order that its tangent may represent the ratio of the minor axis to the major.

When the azimuth a is equal to 45°, the formulæ (A) become

$$\tan 2\theta = \frac{\nu' - \nu}{2f}, \quad \sin 2\beta = \frac{2g}{\nu' + \nu}; \tag{F}$$

from which we may deduce the remarkable relation

$$\frac{\tan 2\beta}{\cos 2\theta} = \frac{g}{f}, \tag{G}$$

showing that, in the case supposed, the ratio of $\tan 2\beta$ to $\cos 2\theta$ is independent of the angle of incidence. In the experiments which I made with Mr. Grubb this azimuth was always 45°; and the following Table contains the results of observation compared with those obtained by calculation from formulæ (F). The experiments were made upon a small disk of speculum metal; and in the calculations I have taken

$$M = 2 \cdot 94, \ \chi = 64° \ 25'.$$

Angle of Incidence.	Value of θ.		Value of β.	
	Observed.	Calculated.	Observed.	Calculated.
65°	27° 55′	27° 53′	28° 0′	28° 0′
70	15 41	15 44	33 7	33 1
75	− 8 46	− 9 16	34 10	34 6
80	− 30 15	− 29 25	27 0	26 53
84	− 37 22	− 37 25	16 47	17 17

The light used in these observations was that of a candle placed at a short distance, and was admitted through small apertures at the ends of the tubes.*   The Nicol's prism in the first tube having been secured in a position in which its principal plane was inclined 45° to the plane of incidence, and the two arms having been set at the proper angle with the surface of the metal, the Fresnel's rhomb and the Nicol's prism in the second tube were moved simultaneously, until the image of the candle became as faint as possible.   Had light perfectly homogeneous been employed, the image could·have been made to vanish altogether; but instead of vanishing, it became highly coloured; and our rule in observing was to make the blue at one side of it, and the red at the other, equally vivid, so as to get results which should belong, as nearly as possible, to the mean ray of the spectrum.   When this was done, the angles θ and β (subject, however, to certain corrections which will be hereafter explained) were respectively read off from the divided circles belonging to the rhomb and the prism.   The observations were made at large incidences, because it is within the last thirty degrees of incidence that the phenomena go through their most rapid changes.

If we now cast our eyes on the above Table, making due allowance for the uncertainty arising from the *dispersion* of the metal, we shall be struck with the agreement between the calculated and observed numbers.   The differences are greatest in

* *See* the description of the instrument in the *Proceedings*, Vol. I. p. 159 (*supra*, p. 138).

the last two observations, which, however, were really the first ;
for the observations were made in the inverse order of the incidences, and their accuracy may have improved as they went on
However that may be, the differences are quite within the
limits of the errors of observation ; and they are actually less
than those which Fresnel found to exist between calculation
and experiment in the much simpler case of reflexion at the
surface of a transparent ordinary medium, when he proceeded
to verify the formula which he had discovered for computing
the effect of such reflexion.*

It may seem extraordinary that these experiments should
have been in my possession for nearly six years before I became
aware of their close agreement with my formulæ ; but the fact
is, that I did not regard them with much interest, because
from the circumstances in which they were made, I did not expect more than a general accordance with theory. And even
now I am in no haste to infer the absolute exactitude of the
formulæ, though they are found to represent the phenomena
so well. It was far more allowable to infer that the formula of
Fresnel was exact in the case just mentioned, though it appeared
to represent the phenomena less perfectly. For, to say nothing
of the small number of our experiments, the present is a much
more complicated case, and the phenomena depend on two constants instead of one, so that the formulæ might be slightly
altered, and yet perhaps continue to agree very well with rough
experiments. Where there is only one constant this is not so
probable. Again, there is one of the quantities in the preceding
formulæ which may be greatly altered without producing more
than a slight effect on the values of θ and β. This quantity is
the ratio of sin i to sin i', which, according to the value in formula (c), is a number so large as to make the angle i' always
small, so that its cosine never differs much from unity ; and
therefore if the above ratio were taken equal to any other large
number, the value of μ in formula (D) would remain nearly the

---

* *See* the Table which he has given in the *Annales de Chimie*, tom. xviii.
p. 314.

same, and consequently the values of θ and β would be but slightly changed.

It is with regard to the value of μ as a function of the incidence that I entertain the greatest doubts, and if any defect shall be found in the formulæ I think it will be here. The relations (c) and (d), from which μ may be deduced in terms of i, were not indeed adopted without strong reasons; but I am not entirely satisfied with them; because, when we reverse the problem, and seek to determine the constants M and χ from the observed values of θ and β at a given incidence, the results are rather complicated and involved, though the approximate determination is easy enough. As the formulæ are in a great measure built upon conjecture, we must not be disposed to receive them without the strongest experimental proofs; and it will certainly require experiments of no ordinary accuracy to decide some of the questions which may be raised respecting them.

When plane-polarized light is incident on a metal, if its vibrations be resolved in directions parallel and perpendicular to the plane of incidence, the effect of the reflexion is to change unequally the phases of the resolved vibrations; and it may be useful to have the formulæ which express the difference of phase after reflexion, and the ratio of the amplitudes of vibration. Put ϕ for the difference of phase; and supposing, for simplicity, the incident light to be polarized in an azimuth of 45°, let σ be an angle less than 45°, such that tan σ may represent the ratio of the reflected amplitudes respectively perpendicular and parallel to the plane of incidence; then we shall have

$$\text{tn } \phi = \frac{2g}{v' - v}, \quad \cos 2\sigma = \frac{2f}{v' + v}; \qquad \text{(H)}$$

from which we may infer that

$$\sin \phi \tan 2\sigma = \frac{g}{f}, \qquad \text{(I)}$$

or that the product on the left side of the last equation is independent of the angle of incidence. It is to be observed that the relations (G) and (I) are independent of the value of μ, and may hold good though that value should require to be changed.

All the preceding formulæ are merely mathematical consequences of those which I published long ago in the *Transactions*[*] of the Academy. The formulæ which I had previously given in the *Proceedings*,[†] are slightly different, and, I think, less likely to be exact, because they are less simple, and do not lead to any of the remarkable relations which may be deduced from the others.

Having had occasion, in the course of the few experiments which I made with the instrument before mentioned, to study the nature of Fresnel's rhomb, which constitutes an important part of it, I shall here describe the method which must be followed in order to obtain true results, when the rhomb is employed in observations on light elliptically polarized. A ray in which the vibrations are supposed to be elliptical is given, and what we want is to determine the ratio of the axes of the elliptic vibration, and their directions with respect to a fixed plane passing through the ray; in other words, to determine the angles which we have denoted by β and θ in the case of a ray reflected from a metal. For this purpose the ray is admitted perpendicularly to the surface at one end of the rhomb, and after having suffered two total reflexions within, passes out perpendicularly to the surface at the other end. Then causing the rhomb to revolve about the ray, we shall find two positions of it in which the emergent light will be the plane-polarized, these positions being readily indicated by a Nicol's prism interposed between the rhomb and the eye; for such a prism, by being turned round the ray, can make the light totally disappear when it is plane-polarized, but not otherwise. These two positions of the rhomb will be exactly 90° from each other; in one of them the principal plane of the rhomb (the plane of reflexion within it) will be parallel to the major axis of the elliptic vibration, and the angle which it makes with the plane of incidence on the metal will be equal to θ: while in the same position the angle which the principal plane makes with the plane of polarization of the emergent ray (as given by the Nicol's prism) will be equal to β. In the other position, the principal plane will be parallel to the minor axis of the elliptic vibration, and the corresponding angles will be equal to $90° - \theta$ and $90° - \beta$ respectively. This, however, proceeds on the supposition that the rhomb is exact. When it is not so, which is of course the proper supposition, and a very necessary one in the experiments with which we are concerned, there will still be, generally speaking, two positions of it in which the emergent ray will be plane-polarized, or in which a disappearance of the light may be produced by the Nicol's prism; but these positions will no longer be $90°$ from each other, nor will the principal plane, in either of them, coincide with an axis of the elliptic vibration. If we now measure the angles between the different planes as before, and denote them by θ', β' in the first position, and by $90° - \theta''$, $90° - \beta''$ in the second, we shall find that θ' and θ'' are unequal, but we shall have β' equal to β''. The values of θ and β will then be given by the formulæ

$$\frac{\theta' + \theta''}{2}, \quad \cos 2\beta = \frac{\cos 2\beta'}{\cos (\theta' - \theta'')}. \tag{K}$$

The error of the rhomb may easily be found. Supposing the vibrations to be resolved in directions parallel and perpendicular to its principal plane, the rhomb is intended to produce a difference of $90°$ between the phases of the resolved vibrations, or to alter by that amount the difference of phase which may already exist; but the effect really produced is usually different from $90°$, and this difference, which I call ϵ, is the error of the rhomb. The value of ϵ is given by the formula

$$\tan \epsilon = \frac{\sin (\theta' - \theta'')}{\tan 2\beta}; \tag{L}$$

and as the error of the rhomb is a constant quantity, we have thus an equation of condition which must always subsist between the angles $\theta' - \theta''$ and β. For any given rhomb the sine of the first of these angles is proportional to the tangent of twice the second, and therefore $\theta' - \theta''$ constantly increases as β increases towards 45°, that is, as the axes of the elliptic vibration approach to equality. When β is equal to $45° - \frac{1}{2}\epsilon$, we have $\theta' - \theta'' = 90°$; and for values of β still nearer to 45°, the value of $\sin(\theta' - \theta'')$ becomes greater than unity, that is to say, it becomes impossible, by means of the rhomb, to reduce the light to the state of plane-polarization. This is a case that may easily happen with an ordinary rhomb in making experiments on the light reflected from metals; because at a certain incidence, and for a certain azimuth of the plane of primitive polarization, the reflected light will be circularly polarized.

The rhomb which I used in the experiments tabulated above was made by Mr. Dollond, and was perhaps as accurate as rhombs usually are; it was cut at an angle of $54\frac{1}{2}°$, as prescribed by Fresnel. Its error was about 3°, and the value of $\theta' - \theta''$, at the incidence of 75°, was about 7°. But in another rhomb, also procured from Mr. Dollond, and cut at the same angle, the value of $\theta' - \theta''$, under the same circumstances, was about 20°, and the value of ϵ was therefore about 8°. The angle given by Fresnel was calculated for glass of which the refractive index is 1·51; and the errors of the rhombs are to be attributed to differences in the refractive powers of the glass. I was not at all prepared to expect errors so large as these when I began to work with the rhomb, and they perplexed me a good deal at first, until I found the means of taking them into account, and of making the rhomb itself serve to measure and to eliminate them. The value of the rhomb as an instrument of research is much increased by the circumstance that it can thus determine its own effect, and that it is not at all necessary to adapt its angle exactly to the refractive index of the glass. It may also be remarked, that this circumstance affords a method of directly and accurately testing the truth of the formulæ which. Fresnel has given for the case of total reflexion at the separating surface of two ordinary media; for we have only to measure the angle of the rhomb and the refractive index of the glass, and to compute, by Fresnel's formula, the alteration which the rhomb ought to produce in the difference between the phases of the resolved vibrations; which alteration of phase we may then compare with that deduced, by means of the formulæ (K) and (L), from direct experiment.

If, in each position of the rhomb, we measure the angle which the plane of polarization of the emergent ray makes with the plane of incidence on the metal, and call the two angles respectively γ', γ'', we shall have

$$\gamma' = \theta' - \beta', \qquad \gamma'' = \theta'' + \beta', \qquad \text{(M)}$$

and therefore

$$\gamma' + \gamma'' = \theta' + \theta'' = 2\theta, \qquad 2\beta' = \gamma'' - \gamma' + \theta' - \theta''; \qquad \text{(N)}$$

from which it appears that if the rhomb were perfectly exact, that is, if θ' and θ'' were equal to each other, the angle θ would be half the sum of γ', γ'', and the angle β half their difference. It would then be sufficient to measure the angles γ' and γ'', in order to get θ and β accurately. And if the rhomb were erroneous, the true value of θ would still be half the sum of γ', γ''; but the true value of β would not be discoverable without measuring the angles θ', θ'', by the help of which it can be deduced from the second of formulæ (N), combined with the second of formulæ (K). Nor can we discover whether the rhomb is erroneous or not, without measuring the angles θ', θ''; and therefore as these angles *must* be measured in any case, the former method of determining θ and β is to be preferred.

In making experiments on elliptically polarized light, a plate of mica, or any other doubly-refracting crystal, placed perpendicular to the ray, may be used instead of Fresnel's rhomb. If the thickness of the crystalline plate be such that the interval between the two rays which emerge from it is equal to the fourth part of the length of a wave, for light of a given refrangibility, the plate will, for such light, perform all the functions of the rhomb; the principal plane of the rhomb being represented by the plane of polarization of one of the emergent rays. But unless the light be perfectly homogeneous, this method is liable to great inaccuracy in practice, since the effect of the plate in producing or altering the difference of phase between the two rays which interfere on their emergence from it is inversely proportional to the length of a wave, and will therefore be extremely different for light of different colours, and will change very perceptibly even within the limits of the same colour. It is true, the effect of the rhomb always varies with the colour of the light: but this variation is trifling compared with that which exists in the other case. It was for this reason that I employed the rhomb in my experiments, instead of a crystalline plate. The apparatus, however, is much simplified by using such a plate; and if any one chooses to do so, and to work with homogeneous light, he must take care to follow, in every respect, the directions which I have given for conducting experiments with the rhomb. The two cases are precisely similar; and if it be necessary not to neglect the errors of the rhomb, it is certainly not less necessary to take into account those which may arise from a want of accuracy in the thickness of the plate, considering how difficult it is to make the thickness correspond exactly to the particular ray which we wish to observe.

I have been induced to enter into these particulars, respecting the mode of making experiments on elliptic polarization, because the subject is one which has not hitherto been studied; nor does it seem to have occurred to anyone that any precaution was requisite beyond that of getting the rhomb cut as nearly as possible at the proper angle, or the crystalline plate made as nearly as possible of the proper thickness. This, indeed, was quite sufficient for ordinary purposes. For example, light polarized in a plane inclined 45° to the principal plane of the rhomb or of the plate, would, as far as the eye could judge, be circularly polarized after passing through either of them. Notwithstanding a certain error in the angle of the one, or in the thickness of the other, such light would, when analyzed by a rhomboid of Iceland-spar, give two images always sensibly equal in intensity. But an error which could not be at all detected in this way might produce a very great effect in such experiments as those upon the metals, and, for the purpose of comparison with theory, might render them entirely useless, if in the first method of observing we relied upon one set of observations, taking (suppose) the values of θ' and β' for the true values of θ and β; or if, in the second method, we contented ourselves with merely measuring the angles γ' and γ''.

The necessity of attending to the foregoing rules and remarks will appear from an examination of the experiments of M. de Senarmont, published in the *Annales de Chimie.** In these very elaborate experiments, which were made upon light reflected at various incidences from steel and speculum metal, the author followed a plan similar to that which I have adopted, and which, in a general way, I had previously sketched in the *Proceedings* † of the Academy. There was this difference, however, that he used a plate of mica instead of Fresnel's rhomb. Now as he worked with common white light, the use of the mica plate must have rendered two kinds of errors unavoidable. In the first place, it would be impossible always to take the observations for the same ray of the spectrum; and next, as a consequence of this, the thickness of the plate would be generally inexact for the particular ray to which the observations happened to correspond. If the thickness of the plate were exact for a certain ray, it would be very sensibly inexact even for the neighbouring parts of the spectrum; and as the part of the spectrum to which the observations belonged was continually changing, the results obtained for different incidences and azimuths would not be comparable with each other, even though, in each separate case, the error of the plate were allowed for and eliminated. The values of θ, however, as determined by M. de Senarmont, would be correct, so far as *this* error is concerned; those of β alone would be erroneous. For the values of θ were determined in two ways: by measuring the angles

θ', θ'', and taking their sum for 2θ; also by measuring the angles γ', γ'', and taking their sum for the same quantity. Now each of these methods gives a true value of θ, because by the preceding formulæ we have $2\theta = \theta' + \theta'' = \gamma' + \gamma''$; and this accounts for the agreement, shown by the tables of M. de Senarmont, between the values* of 2θ obtained by these different methods. But the values of β were deduced from the angles γ', γ'', by simply making their difference equal to 2β; and we see by the second of formulæ (N) that, when the plate is not of the proper thickness, this value of 2β is erroneous by the whole amount of the angle $\theta' - \theta''$, the difference between β' and β being supposed so small that it may be neglected. As M. de Senarmont proceeded on the common assumption that when the thickness of the plate has been adjusted to that part of the spectrum to which the observations are intended to refer, it may afterwards, through the whole series of experiments, be regarded as exact, he necessarily conceived θ' and θ'' to be the same angle; and it was on the principle of taking an average between two measures of the same quantity that he made the supposition $2\theta = \theta' + \theta''$, which happened to be correct. When therefore he found θ' and θ'' to be different, he of course looked upon the difference as merely an error of observation, which it would be superfluous to tabulate. Not having the values of this difference, therefore, we have not the means of immediately correcting the values of 2β. But as observations were made for several azimuths at each angle of incidence, we may use the values of θ to determine those of β; for when at any incidence (except that of maximum polarization, where $\theta = 0$ for all azimuths) the values of θ are known for two given values of a, we can deduce the corresponding values of β, without any other theory than that of the composition of vibrations. The values

---

* Or rather the values of $180° + 2\theta$; because the angle ω, the double of which appears in the tables of M. de Senarmont, is equal to $90° + \theta$. The angles which he calls γ_1 and γ_2 are equal to $90° + \gamma''$ and $90° + \gamma'$ respectively. It therefore comes to the same thing, whether the one set of angles or the other is supposed to be measured. The letter β has the same signification in both notations.

of β so deduced must indeed be expected to be very inaccurate, partly because of errors in the observed values of θ, partly because the observations in different azimuths do not answer to the same ray of the spectrum; but they will be accurate enough to show the great amount of the error committed by neglecting the difference $\theta' - \theta''$. For example, putting θ_0 and β_0 for the values of θ and β when $a = 45°$, M. de Senarmont gives, at the incidence of 60° upon steel, $2\theta_0 = 64° 15'$ (taking the mean of his two determinations), and for the azimuths 55°, 30°, 25°, he gives 2θ equal to 88° 5′, 37° 2′, and 29° 36′ respectively. Combining these values of 2θ in succession with that of $2\theta_0$, we get for $2\beta_0$ the series of values 32° 38′, 33° 28′, 34° 30′; the differences between which are to be attributed to the causes above stated. The mean value of $2\beta_0$ thus found is 33° 32′; while its value, as given by M. de Senarmont, is only 28° 41′. The difference 4° 51′ is the value of $\theta' - \theta''$, which, divided by the tangent of $2\beta_0$, gives 7° 19′ for the mean value of ϵ, the error of the mica plate corresponding to that part of the spectrum which was observed at the incidence of 60°.

At incidences nearer the angle of maximum polarization the errors are probably much greater. Beyond that angle they again diminish, and in some cases they almost vanish. Thus, at the incidence of 85° upon steel, with the value of $2\theta_0$ and the value of 2θ corresponding to $a = 20°$, we get, by computation, a value of $2\beta_0$, which differs only by a few minutes from that given by M. de Senarmont. Nearly the same thing happens at the same incidence when we take $a = 25°$. In these cases, therefore, the results belong to that particular ray for which the thickness of the plate was exact.

The observations of M. de Senarmont on speculum metal were not carried beyond the incidence of 60°. He states that he was unable to observe at higher incidences, on account of the uncertainty arising from the *dispersion* of the metal; but though this cause operated in some degree, his embarrassment must have been really occasioned by the increasing magnitude of the difference $\theta' - \theta''$, as he approached the angle of maximum polarization ; that difference being perhaps twice as great as in the case of steel. My own experiments on speculum metal were all made, as has been seen, at incidences *greater* than 60°.

The experiments of M. de Senarmont do not at all agree with the formulæ; and therefore I have been obliged to analyze his method of observation, and to show that it could not lead to correct results. It is to be regretted that his method was defective, as the zeal and assiduity which he has displayed in the inquiry would otherwise have put us in possession of a large collection of valuable data.

I shall conclude by saying a few words respecting the intensity of the light reflected by metals. The formulæ for computing this intensity have been given in the *Transactions* of the Academy, in the place already referred to; but they may be here stated in a form better suited for calculation. If we suppose ψ and ψ' to be two angles, such that

$$\cot \psi = \frac{M}{\mu}, \qquad \cot \psi' = M\mu, \tag{o}$$

and then take two other angles ω, ω', such that

$$\cos \omega = \sin 2\psi \cos \chi, \qquad \cos \omega' = \sin 2\psi' \cos \chi, \tag{p}$$

we shall have

$$\tau = \tan \tfrac{1}{2}\omega, \qquad \tau' = \tan \tfrac{1}{2}\omega', \tag{q}$$

where τ is the amplitude of the reflected rectilinear vibration, when the incident light is polarized in the plane of incidence, and τ' is the amplitude of the reflected vibration when the incident light is polarized perpendicularly to that plane; the amplitude of the incident vibration being in each case supposed to be unity. Hence when common light is incident, if its intensity be taken for unity, the intensity I of the reflected light will be given by the formula

$$I = \tfrac{1}{2} \left(\tan^2 \tfrac{1}{2}\omega + \tan^2 \tfrac{1}{2}\omega' \right). \tag{r}$$

If with the values of M and χ determined by my experiments we compute, by the last formula, the intensity of reflexion for speculum metal at a perpendicular incidence, in which case $\mu = 1$, we shall find $I = \cdot583$. This is considerably lower than the estimate of Sir William Herschel, who, in the *Philosophical Transactions* for 1800 (p. 65), gives $\cdot673$ as the measure of the reflective power of his specula. The same number, very nearly, results from taking the mean of Mr. Potter's observations.* It might seem therefore that the formula is in fault; but I am inclined to think that the metal which I employed had really a low reflective power. Its angle of maximum polarization was certainly much less than that of the speculum metal used by Sir David Brewster,† who states the angle to be 76°, whereas in my experiments it was only about $73\frac{1}{2}°$; and any increase in this angle, by increasing the value of M, raises the reflective power. On the other hand, the maximum value of β (when $a = 45°$) was greater than that given by Sir David Brewster, namely, 32°; and any increase in β tends also to increase the reflective power. Now it is not unreasonable to suppose that the highest values of both angles may be most nearly those which belong to the best specula; and accordingly, if we take 76° for the incidence of maximum polarization, and retain the maximum value of β, namely, 34° 37′, which results from my experiments, we shall get $M = 3\cdot68$, $\chi = 66°\ 16′$, and the value of I at the perpendicular incidence will come out equal to $\cdot662$, which scarcely differs from the number given by Herschel.

It is clear from what precedes that the optical constants are different for different specimens of speculum metal, and this is no more than we should expect, from the circumstance that the metal is a compound, and therefore liable to vary in its optical properties from variations in the proportion of its constituents; but I am disposed to believe that the same thing is generally true, though of course in a less degree, of the simple metals; so that in order to render the comparison satisfactory, the measures of intensity should always be made on the same spe-

* *Edinburgh Journal of Science*, New Series, Vol. iii. p. 280.
† *Philosophical Transactions*, 1830, p. 324.

cimen which has furnished the values of M and χ. There is one metal, however, with respect to which there can be no doubt that the experiments of different observers are strictly comparable, when it is pure, and at ordinary temperatures—I mean mercury. For this metal Sir David Brewster states the angle of maximum polarization to be 78° 27′, and the maximum value of β, when $a = 45$°, to be 35°; from which I find $M = 4{\cdot}616$, $\chi = 68$° 13′, and, at the perpendicular incidence, $I = {\cdot}734$. Now Bouguer observed the quantity of light reflected by mercury, but not at a perpendicular incidence. His measures were taken at the incidences of 69° and 78½°, for the first of which he gives, by two different observations, ·637 and ·666; for the second, by two observations, ·754 and ·703, as the intensity of reflexion.* If we make the computation from the formula, with the above values of M and χ, we find the quantities of light reflected at these two incidences to be, as nearly as possible, equal to each other, and to seven-tenths of the incident light, the intensity of reflexion being a minimum at an intermediate incidence; and if we suppose these quantities to be really equal at the incidences observed by Bouguer, we must take the mean of all his numbers, which is ·69, as the most probable result of observation. This result differs but little from one of the two numbers given by him at each incidence, and scarcely at all from the result of calculation.

The angle at which the intensity of reflexion is a minimum, when common light is incident, may be found from the formula

$$\left(M + \frac{1}{M}\right)\left(\mu + \frac{1}{\mu}\right) = \left(M - \frac{1}{M}\right)\sqrt{(f^2 + g^2)} - 4\cos\chi, \qquad \text{(s)}$$

which gives the values of μ, and thence that of i. This incidence for mercury is, by calculation, 75° 15′, and the minimum value of I is ·693, which is less than its value at a perpendicular incidence by about one-eighteenth of the latter. According to the formulæ, the reflexion is always total at an incidence of 90°.

* *See* his *Traité d'Optique sur la Gradation de la Lumière:* Paris, 1760; pp. 124, 126.

XXII.—ON THE ATTEMPT LATELY MADE BY M. LAURENT TO EXPLAIN, ON MECHANICAL PRINCIPLES, THE PHENOMENON OF CIRCULAR POLARIZATION IN LIQUIDS.

[*Abstract of a Communication addressed to the* BRITISH ASSOCIATION, *in the year* 1843. *Report*, p. 7.]

THE Author showed that this attempt had not succeeded. M. Laurent supposes the particles of the luminiferous ether not to be simply material points, but to have dimensions which are not insensible when compared with their distances; and on this hypothesis he deduces a system of differential equations, the integrals of which he conceives to represent the phenomenon in question. The integrals given by M. Laurent are, however, altogether erroneous, though this circumstance was not noticed by M. Cauchy in the remarks and comments which he made on M. Laurent's Memoir. The true integrals of these equations (supposing the equations to be correctly deduced) were shown by Professor MacCullagh to indicate motions of the ether which do not correspond to the observed phenomenon. The account of M. Laurent's theory, with M. Cauchy's remarks upon it, will be found in the eighteenth volume of the *Comptes Rendus* of the Academy of Sciences of Paris.

XXIII.—ON TOTAL REFLEXION.

Proceedings of the Royal Irish Academy, Vol. iii. p. 49.—Read, January 13, 1845.

Professor Mac Cullagh made a communication on the subject of Total Reflexion.

In the case of total reflexion the vibrations which take place in the rarer medium are in general elliptical, and when this medium is a crystal, the equations by which the ellipse of vibration is determined are very complicated. The projection of this ellipse upon the plane of incidence may, however, be easily found by the remark in p. 12 of the present volume; the projecting cylinder is therefore known, and as the ellipse of vibration is a section of this cylinder, the question of determining the ellipse is reduced to that of determining its plane. For this purpose Mr. Mac Cullagh gave the following rule. Having constructed the ellipsoid of *indices* (that whose axes are parallel to the axes of elasticity, and inversely proportional to the three principal velocities of propagation in the crystal), let its two planes of circular section intersect the aforesaid cylinder. The curves of intersection will be ellipses, which shall be supposed to have a common centre O in the axis of the cylinder. Let OP, OP' be the greater semiaxes of these ellipses, and OQ, OQ' the less semiaxes; the lengths of the two former being denoted by p, p', and the lengths of the two latter by q, q'. Join the extremities P, P' of the greater semiaxes, and the extremities Q, Q' of the less semiaxes; and divide each of the right lines PP', QQ', in the ratio of $\sqrt{p^2 - q^2}$ to $\sqrt{p'^2 - q'^2}$. Then a plane drawn through the centre O and the two points of division will be the plane of vibration. In the application of this rule some precautions are to be observed, but they need not here be insisted on.

The foregoing rule was deduced (in the year 1843) from the general equations by a peculiar use of imaginary quantities, after the author had several times tried in vain to obtain a geometrical interpretation of those equations by considerations of a more obvious and ordinary kind. This use of imaginaries is founded on a remarkable theorem relative to the ellipse, by which it appears, that the *plane* of an ellipse and its *species* (that is, the directions and the ratio of its axes) may be expressed by two imaginary constants, just as the direction of a right line in space is expressed by two real constants. By means of this theorem—which it is unnecessary to repeat, as it has been published in the *University Calendar**—we may find such properties of elliptical vibrations as are analogous to those of rectilinear vibrations; and it was in this way that the above rule was discovered. It is analogous (though it scarcely appears so at first sight) to the rule by which, in the theory of Fresnel, the direction of rectilinear vibrations is determined, when the plane of the wave is given.

---

* "Examination Papers" of the year 1842, p. lxxxiv.   [The theorem is as follows:—

Given an ellipse in space, the origin of co-ordinates being taken at the centre. Let the points x, y, z, x', y', z', be the extremities of conjugate diameter. Then the imaginary quantities

$$\frac{y + y'\sqrt{-1}}{x + x'\sqrt{-1}}, \qquad \frac{z + z'\sqrt{-1}}{x + x'\sqrt{-1}}$$

are constant for every system of conjugate diameters.]

PART II.
—
GEOMETRY.

I.—GEOMETRICAL THEOREMS ON THE RECTIFICATION OF THE CONIC SECTIONS.

[*Transactions of the Royal Irish Academy*, Vol. xvi. p. 79.—Read, June 21, 1830.]

Lemma 1.   Let T and t be two points indefinitely near each other on any given curve AT, and let tangents at T and t meet in the points P and p any other given line MN, straight or curved, and draw Pq perpendicular to tp; then the difference between the arc AT and the tangent TP will exceed or fall short of the difference between the arc At and the tangent tp by a quantity which is ultimately to pq in a ratio of equality.

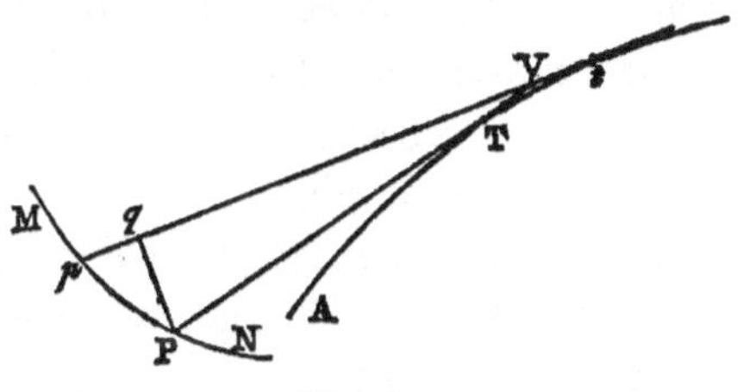

Fig. 1.

For the increment of TP, or the difference of TP and tp, is ultimately equal to the sum of pq, VT, and Vt (V being the intersection of pt and PT produced); and Tt, or the increment of the arc AT, is ultimately equal to the sum of VT and Vt; therefore the difference of the increments is ultimately equal to pq.   Whence the proposition is manifest.

PROBLEM.—*To find the Length of the Arc of a Parabola.*

Let F be the focus and A the vertex of a parabola AT: draw AK perpendicular to AF, and let a tangent at the point T meet it in P: take p indefinitely near to P, and let Fp

intersect PT in q: then since FP and Fp are perpendicular to the tangents PT and pt, it follows (by the preceding lemma) that Pq is ultimately equal to the increment of the difference between the arc AT and the tangent TP. With the centre F and semiaxis FA describe the equilateral hyperbola GAH, and bisect the angles AFP, AFp by the straight lines FL, Fl. Then (since the square of the radius vector of an equilateral hyperbola is inversely as the cosine of twice the angle which it makes with the axis) the square of LF will be equal to $AF \times PF$; and because the angle LFl is half the angle PFq, there-

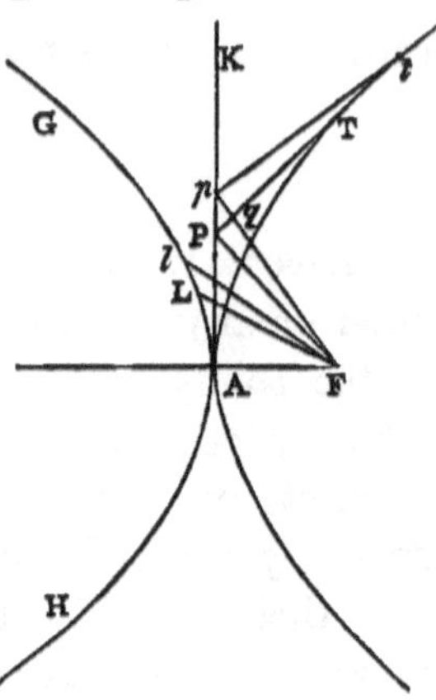

Fig. 2.

fore the area LFl will be equal to one-fourth of the rectangle under AF and Pq.

Hence the hyperbolic sector AFL is equal to one-fourth of the rectangle under AF and the difference between the parabolic arc AT and the tangent TP.

Lemma 2. If on either axis of an ellipse a semicircle be described, of which CD and CH are two radii at right angles to each other, and if DN and HM be drawn perpendicular to the axis aA, and meeting the ellipse in E and L; then CE and CL will be conjugate semidiameters.

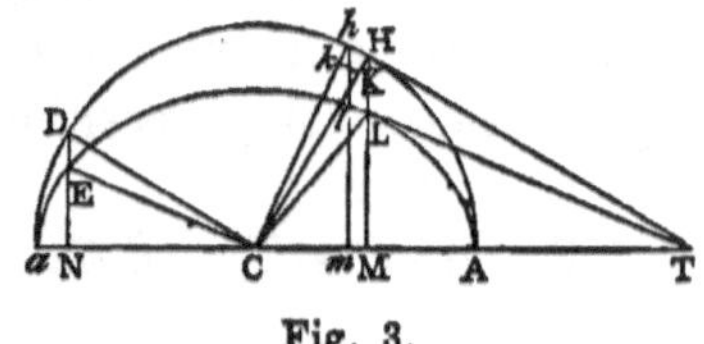

Fig. 3.

For tangents at H and L will meet in a point T in Aa produced; the triangles HMT and DNC will be similar, and DN and HM will be similarly divided in E and L; therefore CE and TL will be parallel, and consequently CE and CL will be conjugate semidiameters.

Lemma 3. Take in the ellipse a point l indefinitely near to L, and draw through it mh parallel to MH; join Ch, and with the centre C and a radius equal to CE describe the arc Kk

meeting CH and Ch in K and k: then Kk will be ultimately equal to Ll.

For $Ll : Hh :: LT : HT :: CE : CD :: CK : CH :: Kk : Hh$. Therefore $Ll = Kk$.

Lemma 4.   If the semiaxes AC and BC of an ellipse be equal to the sum and difference of the sides PQ, QR, of a triangle PQR,

and if the angle BCD be equal to half the contained angle PQR (ADa being the semicircle on Aa); then, DEN being drawn perpendicular to Aa, CE will be

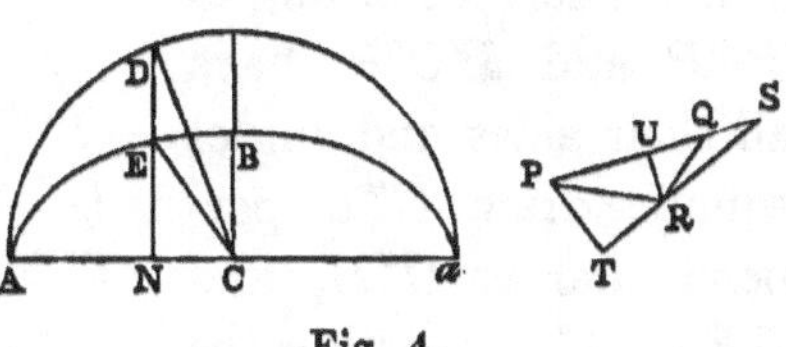

Fig. 4.

equal to the base PR.   Take QU and QS equal to QR; then PS and PU will be equal to AC and CB, and the angle CDN to TSP; therefore drawing PT perpendicular to TS, DN and NC will be equal to TS and TP.   But URS being a right angle, UR is parallel to PT, and therefore $TS : TR :: PS : PU :: AC : BC :: DN : EN$; but $TS = DN$, therefore $TR = EN$; and since $PT = CN$, it follows that $PR = CE$.

THEOREM.

Let AT and $A'T'$ be an ellipse and hyperbola, the semiaxis (CA or $C'A'$) of either being equal to ($C'F'$ or CF) the distance between the focus and centre of the other; and let tangents at the points T and T' meet in P and P' the circles described on the axes, so that $FP = F'P'$: let

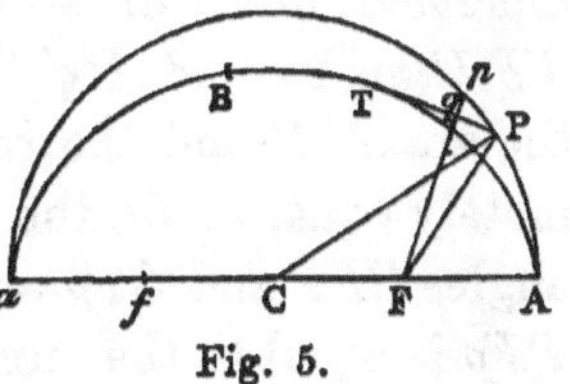

Fig. 5.

also $a''\, B''\, A''$ be another ellipse whose semiaxes ($A''\, C''$ and $B''\, C''$) are equal to aF and FA, and take in its circumference a point L so that the semidiameter conjugate to that passing through L may be equal to FP or $F'P'$; then will the excess of the ellip-

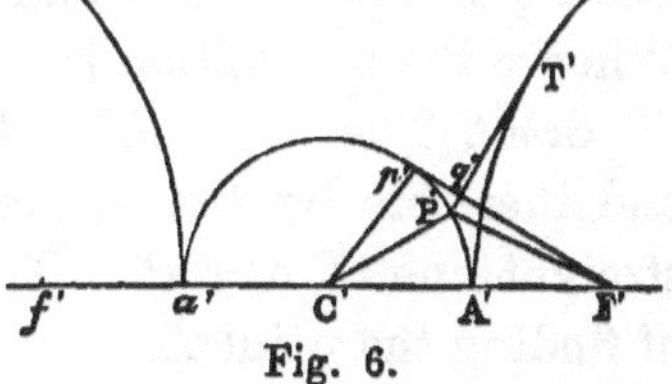

Fig. 6.

tic arc AT above its tangent TP be greater than the excess of the hyperbolic arc $A'T'$ above its tangent $T'P'$, by twice the elliptic arc $A''L$.

Take the point L so that when the ordinate MLH is drawn to meet in H the semicircle described on the axis, the angle

$HC''M$ may be equal to half the angle PCF (or $P'C'F'$, for the triangles PCF and $P'C'F'$ have all their sides and angles equal); draw $C''D$ perpendicular to $C''H$, and DE to $A''a''$, meeting the

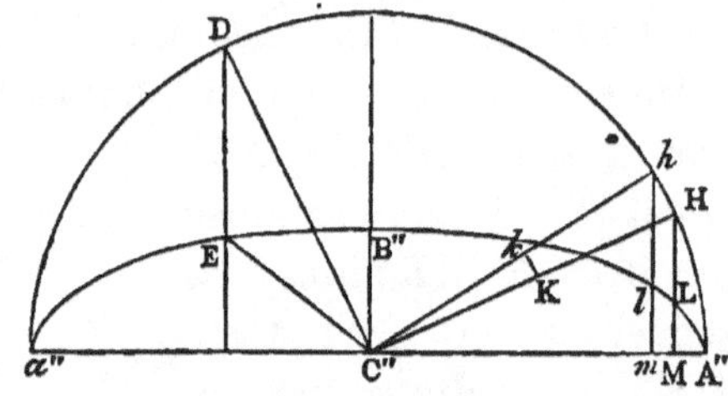

Fig. 7.

ellipse in E; then, by *lem.* 2, $C''E$ will be conjugate to $C''L$, and by *lem.* 4 it will be equal to FP, since the angle $B''C''\dot{D}$ is equal to $HC''M$, and is therefore half of PCF, whilst the semi-axes $C''A''$, $C''B''$, are the sum and difference of PC and CF. Hence the point L thus found is that required by the enunciation. Take p, p', h, indefinitely near to P, P', H, and similarly related to each other; let Fp and Fp' intersect TP and $T'P'$ in q and q', and with the centre C'' and a radius equal to $C''E$ describe the evanescent arc Kk. Then FP, $F'P'$ are always perpendicular to TP, $T'P'$, and therefore Pq is ultimately the increment of the difference between the arc AT and the tangent TP (*lem.* 1.) and $P'q'$ the increment of the difference between the arc $A'T'$ and the tangent $T'P'$; also by *lem.* 3. Kk is ultimately equal to Ll, the increment of the arc $A''L$. Now the angles CFP and CFp are equal to $C'P'F'$ and $C'p'F'$; therefore PFp is equal to the sum of $P'F'p'$ and $P'C'p$, or to $P'F'p'$ with twice $HC''h$: but FP, $F'P'$, and $C''K$ are all equal, and therefore Pq is equal to $P'q'$ and twice Kk, or to $P'q'$ and twice Ll. Whence the proposition is manifest.

Schol. The angle $B''C''H$ is half the angle fCP or $f'C'P'$, and therefore by *lem.* 4, the semidiameter $C''L$ is equal to the straight line fP or $f'P'$. This gives another and easier method of finding the point L.

Hence every arc of a hyperbola may be found by means of

two elliptic arcs. This beautiful theorem was discovered by Landen, and is now for the first time demonstrated geometrically; but the manner in which it is stated by him and by succeeding writers differs from the above, and is much more complicated. The different forms under which they have presented it may be easily deduced from the preceding, by means of the theorem of Fagnani, of which a geometrical demonstration was first given in vol. ix. of the *Transactions* of the Royal Irish Academy, by the Lord Bishop of Cloyne.

December 23, 1829.

II.—ON THE SURFACES OF THE SECOND ORDER.

[*Proceedings of the Royal Irish Academy*, Vol. ii. p. 446.—Read Nov. 30, 1843.]

THERE is hardly any geometrical theory which more requires to be studied, or which promises to reward better whatever thought may be bestowed upon it, than that of the surfaces of the second order. My attention was drawn to it, many years ago, by the consideration of mechanical and physical questions. In the dynamical problem of the Rotation of a Solid body, and in the investigation of the properties of the Wave-Surface of Fresnel, I found, so long since as the year 1829, that the ellipsoid could be employed with very great advantage; while the discussion of these questions, but especially of the former,* suggested properties of the ellipsoid and its kindred surfaces which I might not otherwise have perceived. In this manner I was led to consider systems of confocal surfaces, and thence to notice the focal curves, which I discovered to be analogous, in the theory of the surfaces of the second order, to the foci in that of the plane conic sections. That theory now began to interest me on its own account, and, guided by analogy, I struck out the leading properties possessed by the surfaces in relation to their focal curves; but the interference of other matters prevented me from continuing the inquiry. I had done enough, however, in this

---

* The Theory of Rotation, here spoken of, was completed in the year 1831; but, from causes which need not be mentioned at present, it was not published. The investigations relative to Fresnel's Wave-Surface will be found in the *Transactions* of the Royal Irish Academy, Vol. xvi. p. 65; Vol. xvii. p. 241. *See also* Vol. xxi. p. 32, of the same *Transactions*.

and other parts of the theory, to open new views respecting it; and the results at which I had arrived seemed so fitted for instruction, that, when I was appointed Professor of Mathematics in the University, I made them the subject of the first lectures which I gave in that capacity, in the beginning of the year 1836. Next year the heads of these lectures were communicated to this Academy, in a Paper of which a very short abstract appeared in the *Proceedings.** The subject soon became a favourite one among the more advanced students in the University, who are, for the most part, excellent geometers, and in the present Article very little will be found which is not well known amongst them; very little, indeed, which was not communicated to the Academy on the occasion just mentioned, or which may not be gathered, in the shape of detached questions, out of the Examination Papers published in the *University Calendar*. But as nothing has yet been published on the subject in a connected form, except the brief notice in the *Proceedings* of the Academy, and as mathematicians in other countries attach some importance to researches of this kind, and appear to be in quest of certain principles which are familiar to us here, it seems proper to collect together the chief results that have already been obtained, in order that persons wishing to pursue these speculations may be better able to judge where their inquiries should begin, and in what direction further progress is most likely to be made.

PART I.—GENERATION OF SURFACES OF THE SECOND ORDER.

§ 1. The different species of surfaces of the second order are obtained, as is usually shown in elementary treatises, by the discussion of the general equation of the second degree among three co-ordinates; but it is necessary that we should also be able to derive these surfaces from a common geometrical origin, if we would bring them completely within the grasp of geometry. Now as the different conic sections may (with the

* *Proceedings* of the Royal Irish Academy, VOL. I. p. 89.

exception of the circle), be described *in plano* by the motion of a
point whose distance from a given point bears a constant ratio
to its distance from a given right line,* it is natural to suppose
that there must be some analogous method by which the surfaces of the second order may be generated in space.   Accordingly I have sought for such a method, and I have found that
(with certain analogous exceptions) every surface of the second
order may be regarded as the locus of a point whose distance
from a given point bears a constant ratio to its distance from a
given right line, provided the latter distance be measured parallel to a given plane; this plane being, in general, oblique to
the right line.   The given point I call, from analogy, a *focus*,
and the given right line a *directrix;* the given plane may be
called a *directive plane*, and the constant ratio may be termed
the *modulus*.

To find the equation of the surface so defined, let the axis
of z be parallel to the directrix; let the plane of xy pass through
the focus, and cut the directrix perpendicularly in Δ, the co-
ordinates being rectangular, and their origin arbitrarily assumed
in that plane; and let the axis of y be parallel to the intersection of the plane xy with the directive plane, the angle between
the two planes being denoted by ϕ.   Then if we put x_1, y_1 for
the co-ordinates of the focus, and x_2, y_2 for those of the point Δ,
while the co-ordinates of a point S upon the surface are denoted
by x, y, z, the distance of this last point from the focus will be
the square root of the quantity

$$(x - x_1)^2 + (y - y_1)^2 + z^2 \, ;$$

and if a plane drawn through S, parallel to the directive plane,
be conceived to cut the directrix in D, the distance SD will be
the square root of the quantity

$$(x - x_2)^2 \sec^2\phi + (y - y_2)^2 \, ;$$

* This method of describing the conic sections is due to the Greek geometers.
It is given by Pappus at the end of the Seventh Book of his *Mathematical Collec-
tions.*

so that, m being the modulus, the locus of the point S will be a surface of the second order, represented by the equation

$$(x - x_1)^2 + (y - y_1)^2 + z^2 = m^2 \{(x - x_2)^2 \sec^2\phi + (y - y_2)^2\}, \quad (1)$$

which, by making

$$A = 1 - m^2 \sec^2\phi, \qquad B = 1 - m^2,$$

$$G = m^2 x_2 \sec^2\phi - x_1, \qquad H = m^2 y_2 - y_1, \qquad (2)$$

$$K = m^2 (x_2^2 \sec^2\phi + y_2^2) - x_1^2 - y_1^2,$$

may be put under the form

$$Ax^2 + By^2 + z^2 + 2Gx + 2Hy = K, \qquad (3)$$

showing that the plane of xy is one of the principal planes of the surface, and that the planes of xz and yz are parallel to principal planes.

Before we proceed to discuss this equation it may be well to observe, that as it remains the same when ϕ is changed into $-\phi$, or into $180° - \phi$, the directive plane may have two positions equally inclined to the plane of xy, and therefore equally inclined to the directrix. Indeed it is obvious that, if through the point S we draw two planes making equal angles with the directrix, and cutting it in the points D and D' respectively, the distances SD and SD' will be equal. Every surface described in this way has consequently two directive planes; and as each of these planes is parallel to the axis of y, their intersection is always parallel to one of the axes of the surface. This axis may therefore be called the *directive axis*. The directive planes have a remarkable relation to the surface, as may be shown in the following manner :—

Suppose a section of the surface to be made by a plane which is parallel to one of the directive planes, and which cuts the directrix in D; then the distance of any point S of the section from the focus F will have a constant ratio to its distance SD

from the point D; and, as the locus of a point whose distances from the two points F and D are in a constant ratio to each other is a plane or a sphere, according as the ratio is one of equality or not, it follows that the section aforesaid will be a right line in the one case, and a circle in the other. Hence it appears that all *directive sections*, that is, all sections made in the surface by planes parallel to either of the directive planes, are *right lines* when the modulus is unity, and *circles* when the modulus is different from unity.

Since the equation (3) is not altered by changing the sign of ϕ, or by changing ϕ into its supplement, we may suppose this angle (when it is not zero) to be always positive and less than $90°$; for the supposition $\phi = 90°$ is to be excluded, as it would make the secant of ϕ infinite, and the directive planes parallel to the directrix. In the discussion of the equation there are two leading cases to be considered, answering to two classes of surfaces. The first case, when neither A nor B vanishes, gives the ellipsoid, the two hyperboloids, and the cone; the second, when either or each of these quantities is zero, includes the two paraboloids and the different kinds of cylinders.

§ 2. *First Class of Surfaces.*—When neither A nor B vanishes, we may make both G and H vanish, by properly assuming the origin of co-ordinates. Supposing this done, we have

$$x_1 = m^2 x_2 \sec^2 \phi, \qquad y_1 = m^2 y_2, \qquad (4)$$

the equation of the surface being then

$$A x^2 + B y^2 + z^2 = K, \qquad (5)$$

in which the axes of co-ordinates are of course the axes of the surface. When K is not zero, the surface is an ellipsoid or hyperboloid, having its centre at the origin of co-ordinates; when $K = 0$, the surface is a cone having its vertex at the origin.

Eliminating x_2, y_2 from the value of K, by means of the relations (4), we get

$$K = \frac{A}{1 - A} x_1^2 + \frac{B}{1 - B} y_1^2 ; \qquad (6)$$

and eliminating x_1, y_1 in like manner, we get

$$K = A\,(1 - A)\,x_2{}^2 + B\,(1 - B)\,y_2{}^2\,; \qquad (7)$$

from which expressions it appears that, everything else remaining, the focus and directrix may be changed without changing the surface described. For in order that the surface may remain unchanged, it is only necessary that K should remain constant, since A and B are supposed constant. This condition being fulfilled, the focus may be any point F whose co-ordinates x_1, y_1 satisfy the equation (6), and Δ (the foot of the directrix) may be any point whose co-ordinates x_2, y_2 satisfy the equation (7); it being understood, however, that when one of these points is chosen, the other is determined. The locus of F (supposing K not to vanish) is therefore an ellipse or a hyperbola,* which may be called the *focal curve*, or the *focal line;* and the locus of Δ is another ellipse or hyperbola, which may be called the *dirigent* curve or line : the centre of each curve is the centre of the surface, and its axes coincide with the axes of the surface which lie in the plane of xy. Moreover, as the quantities $1 - A$ and $1 - B$ are essentially positive, the two curves are always of the same kind, that is, both ellipses, or both hyperbolas ; and when they are hyperbolas, their real axes have the same direction. The directrix, remaining always parallel to the axis of z, describes a cylinder which may be called the *dirigent cylinder.*

Since, by the relations (4), the corresponding co-ordinates of F and Δ have always the same sign, these points either lie within the same right angle made by the axes of x and y, or lie on the same axis, at the same side of the centre. And as these relations give

$$x_2 - x_1 = \frac{A}{1 - A}\,x_1, \qquad y_2 - y_1 = \frac{B}{1 - B}\,y_1, \qquad (8)$$

it is easy to see that the right line ΔF is a normal to the focal

---

* In the *Proceedings* of the Academy, Vol. i. p. 90, it was stated inadvertently that " if we confine ourselves to the central surfaces, the locus of the foci will be an ellipse."

curve ; for the quantities $x_2 - x_1$ and $y_2 - y_1$ are proportional to the cosines of the angles which that right line makes with the axes of x and y respectively, while the values just given for these quantities are, in virtue of the equation (6), proportional to the cosines of the angles which the normal to the focal curve at the point F makes with the same axes.

It may also be shown, that if the directrix prolonged through Δ intersects a directive plane in a certain point, and if a right line drawn through F, parallel to the directrix, intersect the same plane in another point, the right line joining those points will be a normal to the curve described in that plane by the first point.

§ 3. To find in what way the focal and dirigent curves are connected with the surface, let the equations (5), (6), (7) (when K does not vanish), be put under the forms

$$\frac{x^2}{P} + \frac{y^2}{Q} + \frac{z^2}{R} = 1, \tag{9}$$

$$\frac{x_1^2}{P_1} + \frac{y_1^2}{Q_1} = 1, \qquad \frac{x_2^2}{P_2} + \frac{y_2^2}{Q_2} = 1, \tag{10}$$

so that the quantities P, Q, R may represent the squares of the semiaxes of the surface, and P_1, Q_1, P_2, Q_2 the squares of the semiaxes of the curves, these quantities being positive or negative, according as the corresponding semiaxes are real or imaginary.   Then we have

$$P = \frac{K}{A}, \qquad Q = \frac{K}{B}, \qquad R = K,$$

$$P_1 = P\,(1 - A), \qquad Q_1 = Q\,(1 - B), \tag{11}$$

$$P_2 = \frac{P}{1 - A}, \qquad Q_2 = \frac{Q}{1 - B};$$

whence it follows that

$$P_1 P_2 = P^2, \qquad Q_1 Q_2 = Q^2, \tag{12}$$

and also that

$$P_1 = P - R, \qquad Q_1 = Q - R. \tag{13}$$

From equations (12) we see that P_1 and P_2 have always the same sign, as also Q_1 and Q_2; and that, neglecting signs, the semiaxes of the surface are mean proportionals between the corresponding semiaxes of the focal and dirigent curves. These curves are therefore reciprocal polars with respect to the section made in the surface by the plane of xy; and it would be easy to show that the points F and Δ are reciprocal points, or that a tangent applied at one of them to the curve which is its locus has the other for its pole.

The focal curve, when we know in which of the principal planes it lies, is determined by the conditions (13); and as it depends on the relative magnitudes of the quantities P, Q, R, it will be convenient to distinguish the axes of the surface, with relation to these magnitudes. Supposing, therefore, the quantities P, Q, R to be taken with their proper signs, as they are in the equation (9), that axis to which the greatest of them (which is always positive) refers shall be called the *primary* axis; and that to which the quantity algebraically least has reference shall be termed the *secondary* axis; while the quantity which has an intermediate algebraic value shall mark the *middle* or *mean* axis. Then, since P_1 and Q_1 will be negative, if R be the greatest of the quantities aforesaid, the focal curve cannot lie in the plane of the mean and secondary axes. Its plane must therefore pass through the primary axis: it will be the plane of the primary and mean axes, if R be the least of the three quantities; but the plane of the primary and secondary axes, if R be the intermediate quantity. In the former case the curve will be an ellipse, in the latter a hyperbola; and we shall extend the name of focal curves to both the curves so determined, though it may happen that only one of them can be used in the generation of the surface by the *modular method*, as the method of which we are treating may be called, from its employment of the modulus. A focal curve which can be so used shall be distinguished as a *modular focal;* but each focal, whether modular or not, shall be supposed to have a dirigent curve and a dirigent cylinder connected with it by the relations

Since $P_1 - Q_1 = P - Q$, the foci of a focal curve are the same as those of the principal section in the plane of which it lies, and they are therefore on the primary axis of the surface. It will sometimes contribute to brevity of expression, if we also give the name of primary to the major axis of an ellipse and to the real axis of a hyperbola. We may then say that the primary axes of the surface and of its two focal curves are coincident in direction ; and that (as is evident) the foci of either curve are the extremities of the primary axis of the other.

If K be supposed to approach gradually to zero, while A and B remain constant, the focal and dirigent ellipses will gradually contract, and the focal and dirigent hyperbolas will approach to their asymptotes, which remain fixed. When K actually vanishes, the surface becomes a cone; the two ellipses are each reduced to a point coinciding with the vertex of the cone, and each hyperbola is reduced to the pair of right lines which were previously the asymptotes. The dirigent cylinder, in the one case, is narrowed into a right line; in the other case it is converted into a pair of planes, which we may call the *dirigent planes* of the curve.

§ 4. We have now to show how the different kinds of surfaces belonging to the first class are produced, according to the different values of the modulus and other constants concerned in their generation.

I. When m is less than $\cos \phi$, the quantities A, B, K, P, Q, R are all positive, and Q is intermediate in value between P and R. The surface is therefore an ellipsoid, and its mean axis is the directive. As the quantities $1 - A$ and $1 - B$ are always positive, the focal and dirigent curves are ellipses.

Here we cannot suppose K to vanish, as the surface would then be reduced to a point.

When $\phi = 0$, that is, when the directive planes coincide with each other, and therefore with a plane perpendicular to the directrix, so that SD is the shortest distance of the point S from the directrix, the surface is a spheroid produced by the revo-

lution of an ellipse round its minor axis, and the focal and dirigent curves are circles.

II. When m is greater than unity; A and B are negative;
and if K be finite, it is also negative; whence P and Q are positive, and K is negative. Also, supposing ϕ not to vanish, Q
is greater than P. The surface is therefore a hyperboloid of
one sheet, with its real axes in the plane of xy; and the directive axis is the primary. The focal and dirigent curves are
ellipses. But when $\phi = 0$, the surface is that produced by the
revolution of a hyperbola round its imaginary axis, and the
focal and dirigent* are circles.

If $K = 0$, which implies, since A and B have the same sign,
that x_1, y_1, x_2, y_2 are each zero, the surface is a cone having the
axis of z for its internal axis; and the focal and dirigent are
each reduced to a point. The focus and directrix are consequently unique; the focus can only be the vertex of the cone;
the directrix can only be the internal axis; and the directrix
therefore passes through the focus. The directive axis, which
coincides with the axis of y, is one of the external axes; that
one, namely, which is parallel to the greater axes of the elliptic
sections made in the cone by planes perpendicular to its internal
axis. This is on the supposition that ϕ is finite; for, when
$\phi = 0$, the cone becomes one of revolution round the axis of z.

III. When m is greater than $\cos \phi$, but less than unity, we
have A positive and B negative, and the species of the surface
depends on K. It is inconsistent with these conditions to suppose $\phi = 0$, and therefore the surface cannot, in this case, be one
of revolution. The value of K may be supposed to be given
by the formula

$$K = \frac{1-A}{A}(x_2 - x_1)^2 + \frac{1-B}{B}(y_2 - y_1)^2, \qquad (14)$$

which contains only the relative co-ordinates of the focus and
the foot of the directrix, and is a consequence of the equations
(6) and (7).

---

* When the term *dirigent* stands alone, it is understood to mean a dirigent *line*.

1°. If K is a positive quantity, the surface is a hyperboloid of one sheet, with its secondary axis in the direction of x; the primary axis, as before, in the directive, but the focal and dirigent are now hyperbolas.

2°. If K is a negative quantity, the surface is a hyperboloid of two sheets, having its primary axis coincident with that of x. The secondary axis is the directive; the focal and dirigent are hyperbolas.

3°. If $K = 0$, the surface is a cone, having the axis of x for its internal axis; the directive axis being, as before, that external axis to which the greater axes of the elliptic sections, made by planes perpendicular to the internal axis, are parallel. The axis of z is the other external axis, which may be called the *mean axis* of the cone, because it coincides with the mean axis of any hyperboloid to which the cone is asymptotic. As A and B have different signs, it is evident, from the equations (6) and (7), that the focal and dirigent are each a pair of right lines passing through the vertex, each pair making equal angles with the internal axis. Two planes, each of which is drawn through the mean axis and a dirigent line, are the dirigent planes of the cone.

The corresponding focal and dirigent lines are those which lie within the same right angle made by the internal and directive axes; and since by the equations (6) and (8) the value of K may be written

$$K = x_1 (x_2 - x_1) + y_1 (y_2 - y_1),$$

we see that, as K now vanishes, the right line joining corresponding points F and Δ upon these lines is perpendicular to the focal line. Of the two sides of the cone which are in the plane xy, one lies between each focal and its dirigent; and it may be inferred from the equations, that the tangents of the angles which the internal axis makes with a focal line, with one of these sides of the cone, and with a dirigent line, are in continued proportion, the proportion being that of the cosine of ϕ to unity. And hence it follows, that these two sides of the cone, with a focal line and its dirigent, cut harmonically any right line which crosses them.

§ 5. From this discussion it appears, that the ellipsoid and the hyperboloid of two sheets can be generated modularly, each in one way only, the modular focal being the ellipse for the former, and the hyperbola for the latter; but that the hyperboloid of one sheet can be generated in two ways, each of its focals being modular, and each focal having its proper modulus. The cone also admits two modes of generation,* in one of which, however, the focus is limited to the vertex of the cone, and the directrix to its internal axis. But when the hyperboloid of one sheet, or the cone, is a surface of revolution, it has only one mode of modular generation. In cases of double generation, the directive planes of course remain the same, as they have a fixed relation to the surface. A modular focal, it may be observed (and the remark applies equally to surfaces of the second class), is distinguished by the circumstance that it does not intersect the surface. The only exception to this rule are the focal lines of the cone, which pass through its vertex. A focal which is not modular may be called *umbilicar*, because it intersects the surface in the umbilics; an umbilic being a point on the surface where the tangent plane is parallel to a directive plane. Thus the focal hyperbola of the ellipsoid, and the focal ellipse of the hyperboloid of two sheets, are umbilicar focals, and pass through the umbilics of these surfaces; but the hyper-

---

* The double generation of the cone, when its vertex is the focus, may be proved synthetically by the method indicated in the Examination Papers of the year 1838, p. xlvi. (published in the *University Calendar* for 1839). Supposing the cone to stand on a circular base (one of its directive sections), and to be circumscribed by a sphere, the right lines joining its vertex with the two points where a diameter perpendicular to the plane of the base intersects the sphere, will be its internal and mean axes. Then if P be either of these points, V the vertex, C the point where the axis PV cuts the plane of the base, and B any point in the circumference of the base, the triangles PVB and PBC will be similar, since the angles at V and B are equal, and the angle at P is common to both triangles; therefore BV will be to BC as PV to PB, that is, in a constant ratio. It is not difficult to complete the demonstration, when the focus is supposed to be any point on one of the focal lines.

boloid of one sheet has no umbilics, and accordingly both its focals are modular, and neither of them intersects the surface. The umbilicar focals and dirigents have properties which shall be mentioned hereafter.

An umbilicar focal and the principal section whose plane coincides with that of the focal are curves of different kinds, the one being an ellipse when the other is a hyperbola; but a modular focal is always of the same kind with the coincident section of the surface, being an ellipse, a hyperbola, or a pair of right lines, according as the section is an ellipse, a hyperbola, or a pair of right lines; and when the section is reduced to a point, so likewise is the modular focal.

The plane of a modular focal always passes through the directive axis. When the directive axis is the primary, as in the hyperboloid of one sheet, both focals are modular. But in the ellipsoid and the hyperboloid of two sheets, where the primary axis is not directive, only one of the focals can be modular. The plane of an umbilicar focal is always perpendicular to the directive axis; and therefore, when that axis is the primary, there is no umbilicar focal.*

When the surface is doubly modular, the two moduli m, m' are connected by the relation

$$\frac{\cos^2\phi}{m^2} + \frac{\sin^2\phi}{m'^2} = 1 ; \qquad\qquad (16)$$

---

* If the first of the equations (10), when P_1 and Q_1 are both negative, be supposed to express an imaginary focal, there will, in a central surface, be three focals, two modular and one umbilicar; the two modular focals being in the principal planes which pass through the directive axis, and the umbilicar focal in the remaining principal plane. Then, when we know which of the axes is the directive axis, we know which of the three focals is imaginary, because the plane of the imaginary focal is perpendicular to the primary axis. A modular focal may be imaginary, and yet have a real modulus; this occurs in the hyperboloid of two sheets. In the ellipsoid, the imaginary focal has an imaginary modulus. In all cases the two moduli are connected by the relation (16).

It will appear hereafter that the vertex of the cone is an umbilicar focus. The cone has therefore three focals, none of which is imaginary; but two of them are single points coinciding with the vertex.

where ϕ is the angle made by a directive plane with the plane of the focal to which the modulus m belongs. One modulus is greater than unity; the other is less than unity, but greater than the cosine of the angle which the plane of the corresponding focal makes with a directive plane. In the hyperboloid of one sheet, the less modulus is that which belongs to the focal hyperbola. In the cone, the less modulus belongs to the focal lines. Of the two moduli of a cone, that which belongs to the focal lines may be termed the *linear modulus;* and the other, to which only a single focus corresponds, may be called the *singular modulus.*

§ 6. *Second Class of Surfaces.*—In this class of surfaces, one of the quantities A, B vanishes, or both of them vanish.

I. When $m = \cos \phi$, and ϕ is not zero, A vanishes, but B does not; and the surface is either a paraboloid or a cylinder.

1°. If the surface is a paraboloid, we may suppose the origin of co-ordinates to be at its vertex, in which case both H and K vanish, and we have the relations

$$G = x_2 - x_1, \qquad y_1 = y_2 \cos^2 \phi,$$
$$x_2^2 + y_2^2 \cos^2 \phi - x_1^2 - y_1^2 = 0 ; \tag{17}$$

the equation of the surface being

$$y^2 \sin^2 \phi + z^2 + 2Gx = 0, \tag{18}$$

which shows that the paraboloid is elliptic, having its axis in the direction of x, and the plane of xy for that of its greater principal section. From the relations (17) we obtain the following:

$$y_1^2 \tan^2 \phi + 2Gx_1 + G^2 = 0,$$
$$y_2^2 \sin^2 \phi \cos^2 \phi + 2Gx_2 - G^2 = 0 ; \tag{19}$$

from which we see that the focal and dirigent curves are parabolas, having their axes the same as that of the surface; and their vertices equidistant from the vertex of the surface, but at opposite sides of it. The cavity of each curve is turned in the same direction as that of the section xy. The focus of the focal parabola is the focus of the section xy, and its vertex is the focus of the section xz of the surface; its parameter being the difference of the parameters of these two sections. The parameter of the section xy is a mean proportional between the parameters of the focal and dirigent parabolas.

2°. If the surface is a cylinder, we may make G and H vanish, by taking the origin on its axis. We then have

$$x_2 = x_1, \qquad y_1 = y_2 \cos^2\phi,$$

$$K = y_1^2 \tan^2\phi = y_2^2 \sin^2\phi \, \cos^2\phi; \qquad (20)$$

the equation of the cylinder, which is elliptic, being

$$y^2 \sin^2\phi + z^2 = K. \qquad (21)$$

Here the focal and dirigent are each a pair of right lines parallel to the axis of the cylinder, and passing through the foci and directrices of a section perpendicular to the axis. The corresponding focal and dirigent lines lie at the same sides of the axis.

II. When $m = 1$, and ϕ is not zero, B vanishes, but A does not.

1°. If the surface is a paraboloid, and the origin of co-ordinates at its vertex, the quantities G and K vanish; and the equation of the surface becomes

$$x^2 \tan^2\phi - z^2 = 2Hy, \qquad (22)$$

and we have the relations

$$H = y_2 - y_1, \qquad x_1 = x_2 \sec^2\phi,$$

$$x_2^2 \sec^2\phi + y_2^2 - x_1^2 - y_1^2 = 0. \qquad (23)$$

The paraboloid is therefore hyperbolic, its axis being that of y, which is also the directive axis; and as the tangent of ϕ may have any finite value, the plane of xy, which is that of the focal curve, may be either of the principal planes passing through the axis of the surface. The relations (23) give

$$x_1^2 \sin^2\phi - 2Hy_1 - H^2 = 0,$$

$$x_2^2 \tan^2\phi \sec^2\phi - 2Hy_2 + H^2 = 0,$$

(24)

for the equations of the focal and dirigent, which are therefore parabolas, having their axes the same as those of the surface, and their concavities turned in the same direction as that of the section xy; their vertices being equidistant from the vertex of the surface, and at opposite sides of it. The focus of the focal parabola is the focus of the section xy, and its vertex is the focus of the section yz, its parameter being the sum of the parameters of these two sections. The parameter of the section xy is a mean proportional between the parameters of the focal and dirigent parabolas.

2°. If the surface is a cylinder, and the origin on its axis, G and H vanish, and we have

$$x_1 = x_2 \sec^2\phi, \qquad y_1 = y_2,$$

$$- K = x_1^2 \sin^2\phi = x_2^2 \tan^2\phi \sec^2\phi\,;$$

(25)

the equation of the cylinder, which is hyperbolic, being

$$x^2 \tan^2\phi - z^2 = - K.$$

(26)

The focal and dirigent are each a pair of right lines parallel to the axis of the cylinder; the corresponding lines passing through a focus and the adjacent directrix of any section perpendicular to the axis. The directive planes are parallel to the asymptotic planes of the cylinder.

In this case, if $K = 0$, the surface is reduced to two directive planes, and the focal and dirigent to the intersection of these planes.

III. When $m = 1$, and $\phi = 0$, both A and B vanish, and the surface is the parabolic cylinder. If, as is allowable, we suppose G and K to vanish, the equation of the cylinder becomes

$$z^2 + 2Hy = 0, \tag{27}$$

and we have

$$H = y_2 - y_1, \qquad x_1 = x_2,$$

$$x_2^2 + y_2^2 - x_1^2 - y_1^2 = 0; \tag{28}$$

whence

$$y_1 = -\tfrac{1}{2}H, \qquad y_2 = \tfrac{1}{2}H. \tag{29}$$

The focal and dirigent are each a right line parallel to the axis of x, the former passing through the focus, the latter meeting the directrix of the parabolic section made by the plane of yz. The plane of xy is the directive plane.

§ 7. We learn from this discussion that, among the surfaces of the second class, the hyperbolic paraboloid is the only one which admits a twofold modular generation; the modulus, however, being the same for both its focals. In the elliptic paraboloid the modular focal is restricted to the plane of that principal section which has the greater parameter; we shall therefore suppose a parabola to be described in the plane of the other principal section, according to the law of the modular focals; the law being, that the focus of the parabola shall be the focus of the principal section in the plane of which the parabola lies, and its vertex the focus of the principal section in the perpendicular plane. The parabola so described will have its concavity opposed to that of the surface; it will cut the surface in the umbilics, and will be its umbilicar focal, the only such focal to be found among the surfaces of the second class. We shall of course suppose further, that this focal has a dirigent parabola connected with it by the same law as in the other cases, the vertices of the focal and dirigent being equidistant from that of the surface and at opposite sides of it, while the parameter of the dirigent is a third proportional to the parameters of the focal and of the principal section in the plane of which the curve lies. The two focals of a paraboloid are so related, that the focus of the one is the vertex of the other. The cylinders have no other focals than those which occur above.

§ 8. In this, as in the first class of surfaces, the right line $F\Delta$, joining a focus F with the foot of its corresponding directrix, is perpendicular to the focal line; and the focal and dirigent are reciprocal polars with respect to the section xy of the surface. These properties are easily inferred from the preceding results; but, as they are general, it may be well to prove them generally for both classes of surfaces. Supposing, therefore, the origin of co-ordinates to be anywhere in the plane of xy, and writing the equation of the surface in the form

$$(x - x_1)^2 + (y - y_1)^2 + z^2 = L(x - x_2)^2 + M(y - y_2)^2, \qquad (30)$$

which, when identified with (3), gives the relations

$$A = 1 - L, \qquad B = 1 - M,$$
$$G = Lx_2 - x_1, \qquad H = My_2 - y_1, \qquad (31)$$
$$K = Lx_2^2 + My_2^2 - x_1^2 - y_1^2,$$

we find, by differentiating the values of the constants G, H, and K,

$$Ldx_2 = dx_1, \qquad Mdy_2 = dy_1,$$
$$Lx_2\,dx_2 + My_2\,dy_2 - x_1\,dx_1 - y_1\,dy_1 = 0. \qquad (32)$$

Hence we obtain

$$(x_2 - x_1)\,dx_1 + (y_2 - y_1)\,dy_1 = 0; \qquad (33)$$

an equation which expresses that the right line joining the points F and Δ is perpendicular to the line which is the locus of the point F.

Again, the equation of the section xy of the surface being

$$Ax^2 + By^2 + 2Gx + 2Hy = K, \qquad (34)$$

the equation of the right line which is, with respect to this section, the polar of a point Δ whose co-ordinates are x_2, y_2, is

$$(Ax_2 + G)x + (By_2 + H)y = K - Gx_2 - Hy_2; \qquad (35)$$

but the relations (31) give

$$Ax_2 + G = x_2 - x_1, \qquad By_2 + H = y_2 - y_1,$$
$$K - Gx_2 - Hy_2 = x_1(x_2 - x_1) + y_1(y_2 - y_1); \qquad (36)$$

and hence the equation (35) becomes

$$(x_2 - x_1)(x - x_1) + (y_2 - y_1)(y - y_1) = 0, \qquad (37)$$

which, as is evident from (33), is the equation of a tangent applied to the focal at the point F corresponding to Δ. This shows that the focal and dirigent are reciprocal polars with respect to the section xy, and that in this relation, as well as in the other, the points F and Δ are corresponding points.

Supposing F′ and Δ′ to be two other corresponding points on the focal and dirigent, if tangents applied to the focal at F and F′ intersect each other in T, the point T will be the pole of the right line $\Delta\Delta$′ with respect to the section xy, as well as the pole of the right line FF′ with respect to the focal; and hence if any right line be drawn through T, and if P be the pole of this right line with respect to the section, and N its pole with respect to the focal, the points P and N will be on the right lines $\Delta\Delta$′ and FF′ respectively. Now it is useful to observe that the distances $\Delta\Delta$′ and FF′ are always similarly divided (both of them internally or both of them externally) by the points P and N, so that we have ΔP to Δ′P as FN to F′N. This property may be proved directly by means of the foregoing equations; or it may be regarded as a consequence of the following theorem:—If through a fixed point in the plane of two given conics having the same centre, or of two given parabolas having their axes parallel, any pair of right lines be drawn, and their poles be taken with respect to each curve, the distance between the poles relative to one curve will be in a constant ratio to the distance between the poles relative to the other curve.* In fact, the poles of the right lines TF, TF′, with respect to the focal, are F, F′; and their poles with respect to the section xy are Δ, Δ′; therefore, since the focal and the section xy may be taken for the given curves, and the point T

---

for the fixed point, the ratio of FF′ to ΔΔ′ is the same as the ratio of FN to ΔP, or of F′N to Δ′P; and consequently the distances FF′ and ΔΔ′ are similarly divided in the points N and P.

§ 9. In the equation (30), considered as equivalent to the equation (1), the constants L and M are both positive; but the properties which have been deduced from the former equation are independent of this circumstance, and equally subsist when one of these constants is supposed to be negative (for they cannot both be negative). This leads us to inquire what surfaces the equation (30) is capable of representing when the constants L and M have different signs; as also, for a given surface, what lines are traced in the plane of xy by points F and Δ, of which x_1, y_1, and x_2, y_2 are the respective co-ordinates. After the examples already given, this question is easily discussed, and the result is, that the only surfaces which can be so represented are the ellipsoid, the hyperboloid of two sheets, the cone, and the elliptic paraboloid—that is to say, the umbilicar surfaces together with the cone; and that, for an umbilicar surface, the locus of F is the umbilicar focal, and therefore the locus of Δ is the corresponding dirigent; while for the cone the points F and Δ are unique, coinciding with each other and with the vertex of the cone. A geometrical interpretation of this case is readily found; for as L and M have different signs, the right-hand member of the equation (30), if M be the negative quantity, is the product of two factors of the form

$$f(x - x_2) + g(y - y_2), \qquad f(x - x_2) - g(y - y_2),$$

in which f and g are constant; and these factors are evidently proportional to the distances of a point whose co-ordinates are x, y, z, from two planes whose equations are

$$f(x - x_2) + g(y - y_2) = 0, \quad f(x - x_2) - g(y - y_2) = 0,$$

which planes always pass through a directrix, and are inclined at equal and constant angles to the axis of x or of y. Therefore, if F be the focus which belongs to this directrix, the square of the distance of F from any point of this surface is in a constant ratio to the rectangle under the distances of the latter point from the two planes. And these planes are directive planes; because, if a section parallel to one of them be made in the surface, the distance of any point of the section from the other plane will be proportional to the square of the distance of the same point from the focus; and, as the locus of a point, whose distance from a given plane is proportional to the square of its distance from a given point, is obviously a sphere, it follows that the section aforesaid is the section of a sphere, and consequently a circle; which shows that the plane to which the section is parallel is a directive plane. Thus,* the square of the

---

* In attempting to find a geometrical generation for the surfaces of the second order, one of the first things which I thought of, before I fell upon the modular method, was to try the locus of a point such that the square of its distance from a given point should be in a constant ratio to the rectangle under its distances from two given planes; but when I saw that this locus would not represent all the species of surfaces, I laid aside the discussion of it. Some time since, however, Mr. Salmon, Fellow of Trinity College, was led independently, in studying the modular method, to consider the same locus; and he remarked to me, what I had not previously observed, that it offers a property supplementary, in a certain sense, to the modular property; that when the surface is an ellipsoid, for example, the given point or focus is on the focal hyperbola, which the modular property leaves empty. This remark of Mr. Salmon served to complete the theory of the focals, by indicating a simple geometrical relation between a non-modular focal and any point on the surface to which it belongs.

In a memoir " On a new method of Generation and Discussion of the Surfaces of the second Order," presented by M. Amyot to the Academy of Sciences of Paris, on the 26th December, 1842, the author investigates this same locus, conceiving it to involve that property in surfaces which is analogous to the property of the focus and directrix in the conic sections; and the importance attached to the discovery of such analogous properties induced M. Cauchy to write a very detailed report on M. Amyot's memoir, accompanied with notes and additions of his own (*Comptes rendus des Séances de l'Académie des Sciences*, tom. xvi. pp. 783–828, 885–890; April, 1843); and also occasioned several discussions, principally between M. Poncelet and M. Chasles, relative to that Memoir (*Comptes rendus*, tom. xvi. pp. 829, 938, 947, 1105, 1110). But the property involved in this locus cannot be said to afford a method of generation of the surfaces of the second order, since it applies only to some of the surfaces, and gives an ambiguous result even where it does apply. It is therefore not at all analogous to the aforesaid general property of the conic sections, and moreover it was not new when M. Amyot brought it

distance of any point of the surface from an umbilicar focus bears a constant ratio to the rectangle under the perpendicular distances of the same point from two directive planes drawn through the directrix corresponding to that focus; and it is easy to see that this ratio, the square root of which we shall denote by μ, is equal to $L - M$, or, neglecting signs, to the sum of the numerical values of L and M. Of course, if the distances from the directive planes, instead of being perpendicular, be measured parallel to any fixed right line, the ratio will still be constant, though different. For example, if the fixed right line for each plane be that which joins the corresponding umbilic with either focus of the section xy, the ratio

forward. Mr. Salmon had in fact proposed it for investigation to the students of the University of Dublin, at the ordinary Examinations in October, 1842; and it was published, towards the end of that year, in the *University Calendar* for 1843, some months before the date of M. Cauchy's report, by which the contents of M. Amyot's memoir were first made known. The parallelism of the two given planes to the circular sections of the surface is also stated in the *Calendar ;* but this remarkable relation is not noticed by M. Amyot, nor by M. Cauchy (*see* the " Examination Papers" of the year 1842, p. xlv., quest. 17, 18; in the *Calendar* for 1843). It is scarcely necessary to add, that the analogue which M. Amyot and other mathematicians have been seeking for, and which was long felt to be wanting in the theory of surfaces of the second order, is no other than the modular property of these surfaces, which appears to be not yet known abroad. M. Poncelet insists much on the importance of extending the signification of the terms *focus* and *directrix*, so as to make them applicable to surfaces; and he supposes this to have been effected, for the first time, by M. Amyot. These terms, however, applied in their true general sense to surfaces, had been in use, several years before, among the mathematical students of Dublin, as may be seen by referring to the *Calendar* ("Examination Papers" of the year 1838, p. c. 1839, p. xxxi.).

The locus above mentioned, being co-extensive with the umbilicar property, does not represent any surface which can be generated by the right line, except the cone. To remedy this want of generality, M. Cauchy proposes to consider a surface of the second order as described by a point, the square of whose distance from a given point bears a constant ratio either to the rectangle under its distances from two given planes, or to the sum of the squares of these distances. This enunciation, no doubt, takes in both kinds of focals, and all the species of surfaces; but the additional conception is not of the kind required by the analogy in question, nor has it any of the characters of an elementary principle. For the given planes, according to M. Cauchy's idea, do not stand in any simple or natural relation to the surface; and besides there is no reason why, instead of the sum of the squares

of the square to the rectangle will be the square of the number m sec ϕ, where m is the modulus, and ϕ the angle which the primary axis makes with a directive plane.

When the umbilicar property is applied to the cone, the vertex of which is, as we have seen, to be regarded as an umbilicar focus, having the directive axis for its directrix, it indicates that the product of the sines of the angles which any side of the cone makes with its two directive planes is a constant quantity.

It is remarkable that the vertex of the cone affords the only instance of a focal point which is at once modular and umbilicar, as well as the only instance of a focal point which is doubly modular. This union of properties it may be conceived to owe to the circumstance that the cone is the asymptotic limit of the two kinds of hyperboloids. For if a series of hyperboloids have the same asymptotic cone, and their primary axes be indefinitely diminished, they will approach indefinitely to the cone; and, in the limit, the focal ellipse and hyperbola of the hyperboloid of one sheet will pass into the vertex and the focal lines of the cone, thus making the vertex doubly modular; while the focal ellipse of the hyperboloid of two sheets will also be contracted into the vertex, and will make that point umbilicar.

of the distances from the given planes, we should not take the sum after multiplying the one square by any given positive number, and the other square by another given positive number; nor is there any reason why we should not take other homogeneous functions of these distances. This conception would therefore be found of little use in geometrical applications; while the modular principle, on the contrary, by employing a simple ratio between two right lines, both of which have a natural connexion with the surface, lends itself with the greatest ease to the reasonings of geometry. Indeed the whole difficulty, in extending the property of the directrix to surfaces of the second order, consisted in the discovery of such a ratio inherent in all of them—a ratio having nothing arbitrary in its nature, and for which no other of equal simplicity can be substituted.

It may be proper to mention that the term *modulus*, which I have used for the first time in the present Paper, with reference to surfaces of the second order, has been borrowed from M. Cauchy, by whom it is employed, however, in a signification entirely different. Several other new terms are also now introduced, from the necessity of the case.

When the two directive planes coincide, and become one directive plane, the umbilicar property is reduced to this, that the distances of any point in the surface from the point F and from the directive plane are in a constant ratio to each other; and therefore the surface becomes one of revolution round an axis passing through F at right angles to that plane; the point F being a focus of the meridional section, or the vertex if the surface be a cone. When the directive planes are supposed to be parallel, but separated by a finite interval, we get the same class of surfaces of revolution, with the addition of the surface produced by the revolution of an ellipse round its minor axis; the point F being still on the axis of revolution, but not having any fixed relation to the surface.

§ 10. If in the equation (30) we supposed the right-hand member to have an additional term containing the product of the quantities $x - x_2$ and $y - y_2$, with a constant coefficient, all the foregoing conclusions regarding the geometrical meaning of that equation would remain unchanged, because the additional term could always be taken away by assigning proper directions to the axes of x and y. If, after the removal of this term, the coefficients of the squares of the aforesaid quantities were both positive, the locus of F would be a modular focal of the surface expressed by the equation; but if one coefficient were positive and the other negative, the locus of F would be an umbilicar focal. The equation in its more general form is evidently that which we should obtain for the locus of a point S, such that the square of its distance SF from a given point F should be a given homogeneous function of the second degree of its distances from two given planes; the plane of xy being drawn through F perpendicular to the intersection of these planes, and x_2, y_2 being the co-ordinates of any point on this intersection, while x_1, y_1 are the co-ordinates of F. The point F might be any point on one of the focals of the surface described by S; the intersection of the two planes (supposing them always parallel to fixed planes) being the corresponding directrix.

These considerations may be further generalized, if we remark that the equation of any given surface of the second order may be put under the form

$$(x-x_1)^2+(y-y_1)^2+(z-z_1)^2 = L\,(x-x_2)^2+M(y-y_2)^2+N(z-z_2)^2$$
$$+L'\,(y-y_2)\,(z-z_2)+M'\,(x-x_2)\,(z-z_2)+N'(x-x_2)\,(y-y_2), \qquad (38)$$

where L, M, N, L', M', N' are constants, and x_1, y_1, z_1 are conceived to be the co-ordinates of a certain point F, and x_2, y_2, z_2 the co-ordinates of another point Δ. The constants L', M', N' may, if we please, be made to vanish by changing the directions of the axes of co-ordinates; and when this is done, the new co-ordinate planes will be parallel to the principal planes of the surface. Then, by proceeding as before, it may be shown that, without changing the surface, we are at liberty, under certain conditions, to make the points F and Δ move in space. The conditions are expressed geometrically by saying that the two surfaces, upon which these points must be always found, are reciprocal polars with respect to the given surface, the points F and Δ being, in this polar relation, corresponding points; and that the surface which is the locus of F is a surface of the second order, *confocal* with the given one, it being understood that confocal surfaces are those which have the same focal lines. The surface on which Δ lies is therefore also of the second order, and the right line ΔF is a normal at F to the surface which is the locus of this point. Moreover, if through the point Δ three or more planes be drawn parallel to fixed planes, and perpendiculars be dropped upon them from any point S whose co-ordinates are x, y, z, the right-hand member of the equation (38) may be conceived to represent a given homogeneous function of the second degree of these perpendiculars; and the given surface may therefore be regarded as the locus of a point S, such that the square of the distance SF is always equal to that function.

§ 11. In the enumeration of the surfaces capable of being generated by the modular method, we miss the five following

varieties, which are contained in the general equation of the
second degree, but are excluded from that method of generation by reason of the simplicity of their forms—namely, the
sphere, the right cylinder on a circular base, and the three
surfaces which may be produced by the revolution of a conic
section (not a circle) round its primary axis.* These three
surfaces are the prolate spheroid, the hyperboloid of two sheets,
and the paraboloid of revolution; and the circumstance, that
the foci of the generating curves are also foci of the surfaces,
renders it easy to investigate their focal properties.† In point
of simplicity, the excepted surfaces are to the other surfaces of
the second order what the circle is to the other conic sections,
the circle being, in like manner, excepted from the curves
which can be generated by the analogous method *in plano;*
and the geometry of the five excepted surfaces may therefore
be regarded as comparatively elementary. These five surfaces
were, in fact, studied by the Greek geometers,‡ and, along with
the oblate spheroid and the cone, they make up all the surfaces
of the second order with which the ancients were acquainted.
Except the cone, the surfaces considered by them are all of
revolution; and there is only one surface of revolution, the
hyperboloid of one sheet, which was not noticed until modern
times. This surface is mentioned (under the name of the
hyperbolic cylindroid) by Wren,§ who remarks that it can
be generated by the revolution of a right line round another
right line not in the same plane. As to the general conception
of surfaces of the second order, the suggestion of it was reserved
for the algebraic geometry of Descartes. In that geometry the

* The case of two parallel planes is also excluded, but it is not here taken into
account. The case of two parallel right lines is in like manner excluded from the
corresponding generation of lines of the second order.

† A Paper by M. Chasles, on these surfaces of revolution, will be found in the
"Memoirs," of the Academy of Brussels, tom. v. (An. 1829).

‡ The hyperboloid of two sheets, and the paraboloid of revolution, were known
by the name of *conoids.* Archimedes has left a treatise on Conoids and Spheroids,
as well as a treatise on the Sphere and Cylinder.

§ In the *Philosophical Transactions* for the year 1669, p. 961.

curves previously known as sections of the cone are all expressed by the general equation of the second degree between two co-ordinates; and hence it occurred to Euler* about a century ago, to examine and classify the different kinds of surfaces comprised in the general equation of the second degree among three co-ordinates. The new and more general forms thus brought to light have since engaged a large share of the attention of geo-meters; but the want of some other than an algebraic principle of connexion has prevented any great progress from being made in the investigation of such of their properties as do not im-mediately depend on transformations of co-ordinates. This want the modular method of generation perfectly supplies, by evolving the different forms from a simple geometrical concep-tion, at the same time that it brings them within the range of ideas familiar to the ancient geometry, and places their relation to the conic sections in a striking point of view.

It may be well to remark that the excepted surfaces are *limits* of surfaces which can be generated modularly, as the circle is the limit of the ellipse in the analogous generation of the conic sections. Thus the sphere is the limit of an oblate spheroid, one of whose axes remains constant, while its focal circle is indefinitely diminished; and the right circular cylinder is the limit of an elliptic cylinder, whose focal lines are con-ceived to approach indefinitely to coincidence with each other and with the axis of the cylinder, while one of the axes of the principal elliptic section remains constant. In these cases the dirigent lines, along with the directrices, move off to infinity. The other three excepted surfaces correspond to the supposition $\phi = 90°$, which was excluded in the discussion of the general equation (1). For if we make $m \sec \phi = n$, the quantity which constitutes the right-hand member of that equation may be written

$$n^2 (x - x_2)^2 + n^2 (y - y_2)^2 \cos^2 \phi;$$

and if we suppose n to remain finite and constant, while ϕ

* *See his Introductio in Analysin Infinitorum*, p. 373. Lausanne, 1748.

approaches to 90°, and m indefinitely diminishes, this quantity will approach indefinitely to $n^2 (x - x_2)^2$, which will be its limiting value when $\phi = 90°$. But $x - x_2$ is the distance of the point S from a fixed plane intersecting the axis of x perpendicularly at the distance x_2 from the origin of co-ordinates; and therefore, in the limit, the equation expresses that the distances of any point S of the surface, from the focus F and from this fixed plane, are to each other as n to unity, that is, in a constant ratio, which is a common property of the three surfaces in question. This property also belongs to the right cone, but the right cone does not rank among the excepted surfaces.

§ 12. We have seen that, when the modulus is unity, any plane parallel to either of the directive planes intersects the surface in a right line; whence it follows, that through any point on the surface of a hyperbolic paraboloid two right lines may be drawn which shall lie entirely in the surface. The plane of these right lines is of course the tangent plane at that point, and therefore every tangent plane intersects the surface in two right lines. This is otherwise evident from considering that the sections parallel to a given tangent plane are similar hyperbolas, whose centres are ranged on a diameter passing through the point of contact, and whose asymptotes, having always the same directions, are parallel to two fixed right lines which we may suppose to be drawn through that point. For as the distance between the plane of section and the tangent plane diminishes, the axes of the hyperbola diminish; and they vanish when that distance vanishes, the hyperbola being then reduced to its asymptotes. The tangent plane therefore intersects the surface in the two fixed right lines aforesaid. The same reasoning, it is manifest, will apply to any other surface of the second order which has hyperbolic sections parallel to its tangent planes; and therefore the hyperboloid of one sheet, which is the only other such surface,* is also intersected in two

---

* The double generation of these two surfaces by the motion of a right line has been long known. It appears to have been discovered and fully discussed by some of the first pupils of the Polytechnic School of Paris. This mode of generation had,

right lines by any of its tangent planes. These right lines are usually called the *generatrices* of the surface.

From what has been said, it appears that the generatrices of the hyperbolic paraboloid, and the asymptotes of its sections (all its sections, except those made by planes parallel to the axis, being hyperbolas), are parallel to the directive planes. The generatrices of the hyperboloid of one sheet, and the asymptotes of its hyperbolic sections, are parallel to the sides of the asymptotic cone; because any section of the hyperboloid is similar to a parallel section of the asymptotic cone; and when the latter section is a hyperbola its asymptotes are parallel to two sides of the cone.

Part II.—Properties of Surfaces of the Second Order.

§ 1. In the preceding part of this Paper it has been necessary to enter into details for the purpose of communicating fundamental notions clearly. In the following part, which will contain certain properties of surfaces of the second order, we shall be as brief as possible; giving demonstrations of the more elementary theorems, but confining ourselves to a short statement of the rest.

Many consequences follow from the principles already laid down.

Through any directrix of a surface of the second order let a fixed plane be drawn cutting the surface, and let S be any point of the section. If the directrix and its focus F be modular, and if a plane always parallel to the same directive plane be conceived to pass through S and to cut the directrix in D, the directive distance SD will be always parallel to a given right line, and will therefore be in a constant ratio to the perpendicular distance of S from the directrix. This perpendicular distance will

however, been remarked by Wren, with regard to the hyperboloid of revolution. It does not seem to have been observed, that the existence of rectilinear generatrices is included in the idea of hyperbolic sections parallel to a tangent plane.

consequently bear a given ratio to SF, the distance of the point S from the focus. And the same thing will be true when the directrix and focus are umbilicar, because the perpendicular distance of the point S from the directrix will be in a constant ratio to its distance from each directive plane drawn through the directrix.

The fixed plane of section will in general contain another directrix parallel to the former, and belonging to the same focal; and it is evident that the perpendicular distance of S from this other directrix will be in a given ratio to its distance SF′ from the corresponding focus F′, the ratio being the same as in the former case. Hence, according as the point S lies between the two directrices, or at the same side of both, the sum or difference of the distances SF and SF′ will be constant.

If the plane of section pass through either of the foci, as F, this focus and its directrix will manifestly be the focus and directrix of the section. In this case the plane of section will be perpendicular to the focal at F. And if the surface be a cone, the point F being anywhere on one of its focal lines, the distance of the point S from the directrix will be in a constant ratio to its perpendicular distance from the dirigent plane which contains the directrix, and therefore this perpendicular distance will be in a given ratio to the distance SF. Now, calling V the vertex of the cone, and taking SV for radius, the perpendicular distance aforesaid is the sine of the angle which the side SV of the cone makes with the dirigent plane; and SF, which is perpendicular to VF, is the sine of the angle SVF. Consequently the sines of the angles which any side of a cone makes with a dirigent plane and the corresponding focal line are in a given ratio to each other.]

§ 2. Conceive a surface of the second order to be intersected in two points S, S′ by a right line which cuts two parallel directrices in the points E, E′, and let F, F′ be the foci corresponding respectively to these directrices. The perpendicular distances of the points S, S′ from the first directrix and from the second are to each other as the lengths SE, S′E, SE′, S′E′

respectively, and therefore the ratios of FS to SE, of FS′ to S′E, of F′S to SE′, and of F′S′ to S′E′, are all equal.

Hence, the right line FE bisects one of the angles made by the right lines FS and FS′; and the right line F′E′ bisects one of the angles made by F′S and F′S′.

When the points S, S′ are at the same side of E, the angle supplemental to SFS′ is that which is bisected by the right line FE. Now if the point S be fixed, and S′ approach to it indefinitely, the angle SFE will approach indefinitely to a right angle. Therefore if a right line touching the surface meet a directrix in a certain point, the distance between this point and the point of contact will subtend a right angle at the focus which corresponds to the directrix. And if a cone circumscribing the surface have its vertex in a directrix, the curve of contact will be in a plane drawn through the corresponding focus at right angles to the right line which joins that focus with the vertex.

When the surface intersected by the right line SS′ is a cone, suppose this line to lie in the plane of the focus F and its directrix, that is, in the plane which is perpendicular at F to the focal line VF (the vertex of the cone being denoted, as before, by V); the angles made by the right lines FE, FS, FS′, are then the same as the angles made by planes drawn through VF and each of the right lines VE, VS, VS′; and the last three right lines are the intersections of a plane VSS′ with the dirigent plane on which the point E lies, and with the surface of the cone. Therefore if a plane passing through the vertex of a cone intersect its surface in two right lines, and one of its dirigent planes in another right line, and if a plane be drawn through each of these right lines respectively and the focal line which belongs to the dirigent plane, the last of the three planes so drawn will bisect one of the angles made by the other two. And hence, if a plane touching a cone along one of its sides intersect a dirigent plane in a certain right line, and if through this right line and the side of contact, respectively, two planes be drawn intersecting each other in the focal line which corresponds to the dirigent plane, the two planes so drawn will be at right angles to each other.

Let a right line touching a surface of the second order in S meet two parallel directrices in the points E, E′, and let F, F′ be the corresponding foci. Then the triangles FSE and F′SE′ are similar, because the angles at F and F′ are right angles, and the ratio of FS to SE is the same as the ratio of F′S to SE′. Therefore the tangent EE′ makes equal angles with the right lines drawn from the point of contact S to the foci F, F′. When the surface is a cone, let the tangent be perpendicular to the side VS which passes through the point of contact; the angles FSE and F′SE′ are then the angles which the tangent plane VEE′ makes with the planes VSF and VSF′, because the right line FE is perpendicular to the plane VSF, and the right line F′E′ is perpendicular to the plane VSF′. Therefore the tangent plane of a cone makes equal angles with the planes drawn through the side of contact and each of the focal lines.

Supposing a section to be made in a surface of the second order by a plane which cuts any directrix in the point E, if the focus F belonging to this directrix be the vertex of a cone having the section for its base, the right line FE will be an axis of the cone. For if through FE any plane be drawn cutting the base of the cone in the points S, S′, one of the angles made by the sides FS, FS′ which pass through these points will always be bisected by the right line FE; and this is the characteristic property of an axis.

§ 3. Two surfaces of the second order being supposed to have the same focus, directrix, and directive planes, so that they differ only in the value of the modulus m, or of the umbilicar ratio μ (*see* Part I. § 9): let a right line passing through any point E of the directrix cut one surface in the points S, S′, and the other in the points S_0, S_1, and conceive right lines to be drawn from all these points to the common focus F. Since, if ratios be expressed by numbers, the ratio of FS to SE (or of FS′ to S′E) is to the ratio of FS_0 to S_0E (or of FS_1 to S_1E) as the value of m for the one surface is to its value for the other, when the focus is modular, or as the value of μ for the one surface is to its value for the other when the focus is umbilicar, the sines of the angles EFS_0 and EFS (or of the angles EFS_1 and EFS') are in a constant proportion to each other, because these sines are proportional to those ratios. And since the right line FE bisects the angles SFS' and S_0FS_1, both internally or both externally, in which case the angles SFS_0 and $S'FS_1$ are equal or else one internally and the other externally, in which case the angles SFS_0 and $S'FS_1$ are supplemental, it is easy to infer from the constant ratio of the aforesaid sines, that in the first case the product, in the second case the ratio of the tangents of the halves of the angles SFS_0 and $S'FS_0$ (or of the halves of the angles SFS_1 and $S'FS_1$) is a consequent quantity.

If the point S' approximate indefinitely to S, the right line passing through these points will approach indefinitely to a tangent. Therefore when two surfaces are related as above, if a right line passing through any point E of their common directrix intersect one surface in the points S_0, S_1, and touch the other in the point S, the chord S_0S_1 will subtend a constant angle at the common focus F, and this angle will be bisected, either internally or externally, by the right line FS drawn from the focus to the point of contact. And the angle EFS being then a right angle, the cosine of the angle SFS_0 or SFS_1 will be equal to the ratio of the less value of m or μ to the greater.*

§ 4. Among the surfaces of the second order, the only one which has a point upon itself for a modular focus is the cone the vertex of which is such a focus, related either to the internal or to the mean axis as directrix. In the latter relation the vertex belongs to the series of foci which are ranged on the focal lines. To see the consequence of this, let V be the vertex of the cone, and VW its mean axis perpendicular to the plane of the focal lines. On one of the focal lines and its dirigent assume any corresponding points F and Δ, and let ΔD be the directrix passing through Δ. Then if a directive plane, drawn through any point S of the surface, cut this directrix in D and the mean

<hr>

* *See* Exam. Papers, An. 1839, p. xxxi., questions 9, 10. These and some of the preceding theorems were originally stated with reference to modular foci only. They are now extended to umbilicar foci.

axis in W, the ratio of SF to SD will be expressed by the linear modulus, as will also the ratio of VF to WD, since V is a point of the surface, and WD is equal to the directive distance of V from $\triangle$D. But since V is a focus to which the mean axis is directrix, the ratio of SV to SW is expressed by the same modulus. Thus the triangles SVF and SWD are similar, the sides of the one being proportional to those of the other. Therefore the angle SVF is equal to the angle SWD ; that is to say, the angle which the side VS of the cone makes with the focal line VF is equal to the angle contained by two right lines WD and WS, of which one is the intersection of the directive plane with the dirigent plane VWD corresponding to VF, and the other is the intersection of the directive plane with the plane VWS passing through the mean axis and the side VS of the cone.

Hence it appears that the sum of the angles (properly reckoned) which any side of the cone makes with its two focal lines is constant. For if F′ be a point on the other focal line, and D′ the point where the directrix corresponding to F′ is intersected by the same directive plane SWD, it may be shown, as above, that the angle SVF′ is equal to the angle SWD′, that is, to the angle made by the right line WS with the right line WD′, in which the directive plane intersects the dirigent plane corresponding to VF′. Conceiving therefore the points F, F′, S, and with them the points D, D′, to lie all on the same side of the principal plane which is perpendicular to the internal axis, the right line WS will lie between the right lines WD and WD′, and the sum of the angles SVF and SVF′ will be equal to the angle DWD′, which is a constant angle, being contained by the right lines in which a directive plane intersects the two dirigent planes of the cone. This constant angle will be found to be equal, as it ought to be, to one of the angles made by the two sides of the cone which are in the plane of the focal lines, namely, to the angle within which the internal axis lies.

If we conceive the cone to have its vertex at the centre of a sphere, and the points F, F′, S to be on the surface of this sphere, the arcs of great circles connecting the point S with each of the fixed points F, F' will have a constant sum. The curve formed by the intersection of the sphere and the cone may therefore, from analogy, be called a *spherical ellipse*, or, more generally, a *spherical conic*, because, by removing one of its foci F, F' to the opposite extremity of the diameter of the sphere, the difference of the arcs SF and SF' will be constant, which shows that the spherical curve is analogous to the hyperbola as well as to the ellipse. Either of these plane curves may, in fact, be obtained as a limit of the spherical curve when the sphere is indefinitely enlarged, according as the diameter along which the enlargement takes place, and of which one extremity may be conceived to be fixed while the other recedes indefinitely, coincides with the internal or with the directive axis of the cone. The fixed extremity becomes the centre of the limiting curve, which is an ellipse in the first case, and a hyperbola in the second.

The great circle touching a spherical conic at any point makes equal angles with the two arcs of great circles which join that point with the foci, because the sum of these arcs is constant. This is identical with a property already demonstrated relative to the tangent planes of the cone. Indeed it is obvious that the properties of the cone may also be stated as properties of the spherical conic, and this is frequently the more convenient way of stating them.

§ 5. If the sides of one cone be perpendicular to the tangent planes of another, the tangent planes of the former will be perpendicular to the sides of the latter. For the plane of two sides of the first cone is perpendicular to the intersection of the two corresponding tangent planes of the second cone ; and as these two sides approach indefinitely to each other, their plane approaches to a tangent plane, while the intersection of the two corresponding tangent planes of the second cone approaches indefinitely to a side of the cone. Thus any given side of the one cone corresponds to a certain side of the other ; and any side of either cone is perpendicular to the plane which touches the other along the corresponding side. This reasoning applies to cones of any kind.

Two cones so related may be called *reciprocal cones.* When one is of the second order, it will be found that the other is also of the second order, and that, in their equations relative to their axes, which are obviously parallel or coincident, the coefficients of the squares of the corresponding variables are reciprocally proportional, so that the equations

$$Px^2 + Qy^2 + Rz^2 = 0, \qquad \frac{x^2}{P} + \frac{y^2}{Q} + \frac{z^2}{R} = 0, \tag{1}$$

express two such cones which have a common vertex. These cones have the same internal axis, but the directive axis of the one coincides with the mean axis of the other, and it may be shown from the equations that the directive planes of the one are perpendicular to the focal lines of the other. The two curves in which these cones are intersected by a sphere, having its centre at their common vertex, are reciprocal spherical conics. In general, two curves traced on the surface of a sphere may be said to be reciprocal to each other, when the cones passing through them, and having a common vertex at the centre of the sphere, are reciprocal cones. Any given point of the one curve corresponds to a certain point of the other, and the great circle which touches either curve at any point is distant by a quadrant from the corresponding point of the other curve.

By means of these relations any property of a cone of the second order, or of a spherical conic, may be made to produce a reciprocal property. Thus, we have seen that the tangent plane of a cone makes equal angles with two planes passing through the side of contact and through each of the focal lines; therefore, drawing right lines perpendicular to the planes, and planes perpendicular to the right lines here mentioned, we have, in the reciprocal cone, a side making equal angles with the right lines in which the directive planes of this cone are intersected by a plane touching it along that side. It is therefore a property of the cone, that the intersections of a tangent plane with the two directive planes make equal angles with the side of contact; a property which it is easy to prove without the aid of the reciprocal cone.

The two directive sections drawn through any point S of a given surface of the second order may, when they are circles, be made the directive sections of a cone, and this may obviously be done in two ways. Each of the two cones so determined will be touched by the plane which touches the given surface at the point S, because the right lines which are tangents to the two circular sections at that point are tangents to each cone as well as to the given surface; therefore the side of contact of each cone bisects one of the angles made by these two tangents; and hence the two sides of contact are the principal directions in the tangent plane at the point S, that is, they are the directions of the greatest and least curvature of the given surface at that point; for these directions are parallel to the axes of a section made in the surface by a plane parallel to the tangent plane, and the axes of any section bisect the angles contained by the right lines in which the plane of section cuts the two directive planes.

§·6. It has been shown that the sum of the angles which any side of a cone makes with its focal lines is constant. Hence we obtain the reciprocal property,* that the sum of the angles (properly reckoned) which any tangent plane of a cone makes with its two directive planes is constant. This property may be otherwise proved as follows :—

Through a point assumed anywhere in the side of contact

---

* This property, and that to which it is reciprocal, as well as some other properties of the cone, were, together with the idea of reciprocal cones and of spherical conics, suggested by my earliest researches connected with the mechanical theory of rotation and the laws of double refraction. I was not then aware that the focal lines of the cone had been previously discovered, nor that the spherical conic had been introduced into geometry. Indeed all the properties of the cone which are given in this Paper were first presented to me in my own investigations. Its double modular property, related to the vertex as focus, was one of the propositions in the theory of the rotation of a solid body, and was used in finding the position of the axis of rotation within the body at a given time. But the modular property common to all the surfaces of the second order was not discovered until some years later.

let two directive planes be drawn. As the circles in which the cone is cut by these planes have a common chord, they are circles of the same sphere; and a tangent plane applied to this sphere, at the aforesaid point, coincides with the tangent plane of the cone, because each tangent plane contains the tangents drawn to the two circles at that point. The common chord of the circles is bisected at right angles by the principal plane which is perpendicular to the directive axis, and therefore that principal plane contains the centres of the two circles and the centre of the sphere. Now the acute angle made by a tangent plane of a sphere with the plane of any small circle passing through the point of contact is evidently half the angle subtended at the centre of the sphere by a diameter of that circle; therefore the acute angles, which the common tangent plane of the cone and of the sphere above mentioned makes with the planes of the directive sections, are the halves of the angles subtended at the centre of the sphere by the diameters of the sections. But the diameters which lie in the principal plane already spoken of, and are terminated by two sides of the cone, are chords of the great circle in which that plane intersects the sphere; and the halves of the angles which they subtend at its centre are equal to the angles in the greater segments of which they are the chords, and consequently equal to the two adjacent acute angles of the quadrilateral which has these chords for its diagonals. Hence, as two opposite angles of the quadrilateral are together equal to two right angles, it follows that the four angles of the quadrilateral represent the four angles, the obtuse as well as.the acute angles, which the tangent plane of the cone makes with the planes of the directive sections; the two angles of the quadrilateral which lie opposite to the same diagonal being equal to the acute and obtuse angles made by the tangent plane with the plane of the section of which that diagonal is the diameter.

Thus any two adjacent angles of the quadrilateral may be taken for the angles which the tangent plane of the cone makes with the directive planes. If we take the two adjacent angles which lie in the same triangle with the angle κ contained by the two sides of the cone that help to form the quadrilateral, the sum of these two angles will be equal to two right angles diminished by κ; and if we take the two remaining angles of the quadrilateral, their sum will be equal to two right angles increased by κ; both which sums are constant. But if we take either of the other pairs of adjacent angles, the difference of the pair will be constant, and equal to κ.

The same conclusion may be deduced as a property of the spherical conic. Let a great circle touching this curve be intersected in two points, one on each side of the point of contact, by the two directive circles, that is, by two great circles whose planes are directive planes of the cone which passes through the conic and has its vertex at the centre of the sphere. Since the right lines in which the tangent plane of a cone intersects the directive planes are equally inclined to the side of contact, the arc intercepted between the points where the tangent circle of the conic intersects the directive circles is bisected in the point of contact; therefore, either of the spherical triangles whose base is the tangent arc so intercepted, and whose other two sides are the directive circles, has a constant area; because, if we suppose the tangent arc to change its position through an indefinitely small angle, and to be always terminated by the directive circles, the two little triangles bounded by its two positions and by the two indefinitely small directive arcs which lie between these positions, will have their nascent ratio one of equality, so that the area of either of the spherical triangles mentioned above will not be changed by the change in the position of its base. But in each of these triangles the angle opposite the base is constant; therefore the sum of the angles at the base is constant.

From this reasoning it appears that if a spherical triangle have a given area, and two of its sides be fixed, the third side will always touch a spherical conic having the fixed sides for its directive arcs, and will be always bisected in the point of contact.

§ 7. The intersection of any given central surface of the second order with a concentric sphere is a spherical conic, since the cone which passes through the curve of intersection, and has its vertex at the common centre, is of the second order. The cylinder also, which passes through the same curve and has its side parallel to any of the axes of the given surface, is of the second order; and the cone, the cylinder, and the given surface are *condirective*, that is, the directive planes of one of them are also the directive planes of each of the other two. This may be seen from the equations of the different surfaces; for, in general, two surfaces whose principal planes are parallel will be condirective, if, when their equations are expressed by co-ordinates perpendicular to these planes, the differences of the coefficients of the squares of the variables in the equation of the one be proportional to the corresponding differences in the equation of the other.

If any given surface of the second order be intersected by a sphere whose centre is any point in one of the principal planes, the cylinder passing through the curve of intersection, and having its side perpendicular to that principal plane, will be of the second order, and will be condirective with the given surface. This cylinder, when its side is parallel to the directive axis, is hyperbolic; otherwise it is elliptic. If a paraboloid be cut by any plane, the cylinder which passes through the curve of section, and has its side parallel to the axis of the paraboloid, will be condirective with that surface; and it will be elliptic or hyperbolic, according as the paraboloid is elliptic or hyperbolic.*

If two concentric surfaces of the second order be reciprocal polars with respect to a concentric sphere, the directive axis of the one surface will coincide with the mean axis of the other, and the directive planes of the one will be perpendicular to the asymptotes of the focal hyperbola of the other. When one of the surfaces is a hyperboloid, the other is a hyperboloid of the same kind; the asymptotes of the focal hyperbola of each sur-

---

* I have introduced the terms *directive* and *condirective*, as more general than the terms *cyclic* and *biconcyclic* employed by M. Chasles. The latter terms suggest the idea of circular sections, and therefore could not properly be used with reference to the hyperbolic paraboloid, or to the hyperbolic or parabolic cylinder, in each of which surfaces a directive section is a right line.

face are the focal lines of its asymptotic cone; and the two asymptotic cones are reciprocal.

When any number of central surfaces of the second order are confocal, or, more generally, when their focal hyperbolas have the same asymptotes, it is obvious that their reciprocal surfaces, taken with respect to any sphere concentric with them, are all condirective.

§ 8. If a diameter of constant length, revolving within a given central surface, describe a cone having its vertex at the centre, the extremities of the diameter will lie in a spherical conic. And if the cone be touched by any plane, the side of contact will evidently be normal to the section which that plane makes in the given surface, and will therefore be an axis of the section. As the axes of a section always bisect the angles made by the two right lines in which its plane intersects the directive planes of the surface, and as the cone aforesaid has the same directive planes with the given surface, it follows that the right lines in which a tangent plane of a cone cuts its directive planes are equally inclined to the side of contact—a theorem which has been already obtained in another way.

If a section be made in a given central surface by any plane passing through the centre, the cone described by a constant semidiameter equal to either semiaxis of the section will touch the plane of section; for if it could cut that plane, a semiaxis would be equal to another radius of the section. Denoting by r, r' the semiaxes of the section, conceive two cones to be described by the revolution of two constant semidiameters equal to r and r' respectively. These cones are condirective with the given surface, and have the plane of section for their common tangent plane. Supposing that surface to be expressed by the equation

$$\frac{x^2}{P} + \frac{y^2}{Q} + \frac{z^2}{R} = 1, \tag{2}$$

and the directive axis to be that of y, the axis of x will be the internal axis of one cone, say of that described by r, and the axis of z will be the internal axis of the other cone. Let κ be the angle made by the two sides of the first cone which lie in the plane xz, and κ' the angle made by the two sides of the second cone which lie in the same plane ; the former angle being taken so as to contain the axis of x within it, and the latter so as to contain within it the axis of z. Then, considering r, r' as radii of the section xz of the surface, we have obviously

$$\frac{1}{r^2} = \frac{\cos^2\frac{1}{2}\kappa}{P} + \frac{\sin^2\frac{1}{2}\kappa}{R} = \frac{1}{2}\left(\frac{1}{P}+\frac{1}{R}\right) + \frac{1}{2}\left(\frac{1}{P}-\frac{1}{R}\right)\cos\kappa,$$

$$\frac{1}{r'^2} = \frac{\cos^2\frac{1}{2}\kappa'}{R} + \frac{\sin^2\frac{1}{2}\kappa'}{P} = \frac{1}{2}\left(\frac{1}{P}+\frac{1}{R}\right) - \frac{1}{2}\left(\frac{1}{P}-\frac{1}{R}\right)\cos\kappa' ;$$

$$(3)$$

observing that when these formulæ give a negative value for r^2 or r'^2, in which case the surface expressed by the equation (2) must be a hyperboloid, the direction of r or r' meets, not that surface, but the surface of the conjugate hyperboloid expressed by the equation

$$\frac{x^2}{P} + \frac{y^2}{Q} + \frac{z^2}{R} = -1. \qquad (4)$$

Now calling θ and θ' the angles made by the tangent plane of the cones with the directive planes of the given surface, which are also the directive planes of each cone, the angles κ, κ' depend on the sum or difference of θ and θ'. If the latter angles be taken so that their sum may be equal to the supplement of κ, their difference will be equal to κ', and the formulæ (3) will become

$$\frac{1}{r^2} = \frac{1}{2}\left(\frac{1}{P}+\frac{1}{R}\right) - \frac{1}{2}\left(\frac{1}{P}-\frac{1}{R}\right)\cos(\theta+\theta')$$

$$(5)$$

$$\frac{1}{r'^2} = \frac{1}{2}\left(\frac{1}{P}+\frac{1}{R}\right) - \frac{1}{2}\left(\frac{1}{P}-\frac{1}{R}\right)\cos(\theta-\theta'),$$

by which the semiaxes of any central section are expressed in terms of the non-directive semiaxes of the surface, and of the angles which the plane of section makes with the directive planes.*

§ 9. From the centre O of the surface expressed by equation (2) let a right line $O\Sigma$ be drawn cutting perpendicularly in Σ the plane which touches the surface at S. Let σ denote the length of the perpendicular $O\Sigma$, and α, β, γ the angles which it makes with x, y, z. Then

$$\sigma^2 = P \cos^2 \alpha + Q \cos^2 \beta + R \cos^2 \gamma. \tag{6}$$

From this formula it is manifest that, if three planes touching the surface be at right angles to each other, the sum of the squares of their perpendicular distances from the centre will be equal to the constant quantity $P + Q + R$, and therefore the point of intersection of the planes will lie in the surface of a given sphere. If another surface represented by the equation

$$\frac{x^2}{P_0} + \frac{y^2}{Q_0} + \frac{z^2}{R_0} = 1$$

be touched by a plane cutting $O\Sigma$ perpendicularly in Σ_0, and if σ_0 be the length of $O\Sigma_0$, then

$$\sigma_0^2 = P_0 \cos^2 \alpha + Q_0 \cos^2 \beta + R_0 \cos^2 \gamma \; ;$$

and therefore when the two surfaces are confocal, that is, when

$$P - P_0 = Q - Q_0 = R - R_0 = k,$$

we have $\sigma^2 - \sigma_0^2 = k$, which is a constant quantity. Hence, if three confocal surfaces be touched by three rectangular planes, the sum of the squares of the perpendiculars dropped on these planes from the centre will be constant, and the locus of the intersection of the planes will be a sphere.

The focal curves of a given surface are the limits of surfaces confocal with it,† when these surfaces are conceived, by the pro-

---

* See *Transactions* of the Royal Irish Academy, Vol. xxi., as before cited. The formulæ (5) were first given, for the case of the ellipsoid, by Fresnel, in his Theory of Double Refraction, *Mémoires de l'Institut*, tom. vii., p. 155.

† It was by this consideration, arising out of the theorems given in this and the next section about confocal surfaces, that I was led to perceive the nature of the

gressive diminution of their mean or secondary axes, to become flattened, and to approach more and more nearly to·a plane passing through the primary axis. And it will appear hereafter, that if a *bifocal right line*, that is, a right line passing through both focal curves, be the intersection of two planes touching these curves, those two planes will be at right angles to each other. Therefore the locus of the point where a tangent plane of a given central surface is intersected perpendicularly by a bifocal right line is a sphere. The primary axis of the surface is evidently the diameter of this sphere.

Hence we conclude that the locus of the point where a tangent plane of a paraboloid is intersected perpendicularly by a bifocal right line is a plane touching the paraboloid at its vertex. For a paraboloid is the limit of a central surface whose primary axis is prolonged indefinitely in one direction, and a plane is the corresponding limit of the sphere described on that axis as diameter. As this consideration is frequently of use in deducing properties of paraboloids from those of central surfaces, it may be well to state it more particularly. It is to be observed, then, that the indefinite extension of the primary axis at one extremity may take place according to any law which leaves the other extremity always at a finite distance from a given point, and gives a finite limiting parameter to each of the principal sections of the surface which pass through that axis. The simplest supposition is, that one extremity of the axis and the adjacent foci of those two principal sections remain fixed, while the other extremity and the other foci move off, with the centre, to distances which are conceived to increase without limit. Then, at any finite distances from the fixed points, the focal curves approach indefinitely to parabolas, as do also all sections of the surface which pass through the primary axis, while the surface itself approaches indefinitely to a paraboloid; so that the limit

focal curves, and the analogy between their points and the foci of conics. And I regarded that analogy as fully established when I found (in March or April, 1832) that the normal at any point of a surface of the second order is an axis of the cone which has that point for its vertex and a focal for its base.

of the central surface is a paraboloid having parabolas for its focal curves. The limit of an ellipsoid, or of a hyperboloid of two sheets, is an elliptic paraboloid, having one of its focals modular and the other umbilicar, like each of the central surfaces from which it may be derived ; and the limit of a hyperboloid of one sheet is a hyperbolic paraboloid, having, like that hyperboloid, both its focals modular.

§ 10. Let the plane touching at S the surface expressed by equation (2) intersect the axis of x in the point X, and let the normal applied at S intersect the planes yz, xz, xy, in the points L, M, N respectively. Since the section made in the surface by a plane passing through OX and the point S has one of its axes in the direction of OX, it appears, by an elementary property of conics, that the rectangle under OX and the co-ordinate x of the point S is equal to the quantity P ; but that co-ordinate is to LS as OΣ or σ is to OX, and therefore the rectangle under σ and LS is equal to P. Similarly the rectangle under σ and MS is equal to Q, and the rectangle under σ and NS is equal to R. Thus the parts of the normal intercepted between the point S and each of the principal planes are to each other as the squares of the semiaxes respectively perpendicular to these planes ; the square of an imaginary semiaxis being regarded as negative, and the corresponding intercept being measured from S in a direction opposite to that which corresponds to a real semiaxis.

The rectangle under σ and the part of the normal intercepted between two principal planes is equal to the difference of the squares of the semiaxes which are perpendicular to these planes. This rectangle is therefore constant, not only for a given surface, but for all surfaces which are confocal with it.

Hence the part of the normal intercepted between two principal planes bears a given ratio to the part of it intercepted between one of these and the third principal plane, whether the normal be applied at any point of a given surface, or at any point of a surface confocal with it.

If therefore normals to a series of confocal surfaces be all

passing through the common centre of the surfaces, because otherwise the parts of any such normal, which are intercepted between each pair of principal planes, would not be in a constant ratio to each other.

The point S being the point at which any of these parallel normals is applied, the plane touching the surface at S is parallel to a given plane; the perpendicular $O\Sigma$ dropped upon it from the centre has a given direction, the plane $OS\Sigma$ is fixed, and the directions of the lines OL, OM, ON, in which the plane intersects the principal planes, are also fixed. And as the angle $O\Sigma S$ is always a right angle, and the normal at S is always parallel to $G\Sigma$, the distance $S\Sigma$ bears a given ratio to each of the distances OL, OM, ON, and therefore also to each of the intercepts MN. Hence, since the rectangle under $O\Sigma$ and any one of these intercepts is constant, the rectangle under $O\Sigma$ and $S\Sigma$ is constant.

Therefore if a series of confocal central surfaces be touched by parallel planes, the points of contact will all lie in one plane, and their locus, in that plane, will be an equilateral hyperbola, having its centre at the centre of the surfaces, and having one of its asymptotes perpendicular to the tangent planes. This hyperbola evidently passes through two points on each of the focal curves, namely the points where the tangent to each curve is parallel to the tangent planes.

If a series of confocal paraboloids be touched by parallel planes, it will be found that the points of contact all lie in a bifocal right line, and that the normals at these points lie in a plane parallel to the axis of the surfaces; so that the part of any normal which is intercepted by the two principal planes is constant. This theorem may be proved from the two following properties of the paraboloid :—1. A normal being applied to the surface at the point S, the segments of the normal, measured from S to the points where it intersects the planes of the two principal sections, are to each other inversely as the parameters of these sections. 2. Supposing the axis x to be that of the surface, the difference between the co-ordinates x of the point S and of the point where the normal meets the plane of the principal sections, is equal to the semiparameter of the other principal section.

§ 11. Let a tangent plane, applied at any point S of a surface of the second order, intersect the plane of one of its focals in the right line Θ, and let P be the foot of the perpendicular dropped from S upon the latter plane. The pole of the right line Θ, with respect to the principal section lying in this plane, is the point P. Let N be its pole with respect to the focal. Then if T be any point of the right line Θ, the polar of this point with respect to the section will pass through P, and its polar with respect to the focal will pass through N ; and if the former polar intersect the dirigent curve in Δ, Δ′, and the latter intersect the focal in F, F′, the points F, F′ will correspond respectively to the points Δ, Δ′, and the distances ΔΔ′ and FF′ will be similarly divided by the points P and N (*see* Part I. § 8). But since the point S is in the plane of the two directrices which pass through Δ and Δ′, the lengths ΔP and Δ′P, which are the perpendicular distances of S from the directrices, are proportional to the lengths FS and F′S. Therefore FN is to F′N as FS is to F′S, and the right line NS bisects one of the angles made by the right lines FS and F′S. And as this holds wherever the point T is taken on the right line Θ, that is, in whatever direction the right line FF′ passes through the point N, it follows that the right line NS is an axis of the cone which has the point S for its vertex and the focal for its base. Further, if FF′ intersect Θ in the point Q, we have FN to F′N as FQ is to F′Q, because N is the pole of Θ with respect to the focal ; therefore FQ is to F′Q as FS is to F′S, and hence the right line QS also bisects one of the angles made by FS and F′S. The right lines NS and QS are therefore at right angles to each other ; and as the latter always lies in the tangent plane, the former must be perpendicular to that plane.

Consequently the normal at any point of a surface of the second order is an axis of the cone which has that point for its vertex and either of the focals for its base.

It is known that when two confocal surfaces intersect each

other, they intersect everywhere at right angles ; and that through any given point three surfaces may in general be described, which shall have the same focal curves. If three confocal surfaces pass through the point S, the normal to each of them at S is an axis of each of the cones which stand on the focals and have S for their common vertex. The normals to the three surfaces are therefore the three axes of each cone.

If the points at which a series of confocal surfaces are touched by parallel planes be the vertices of cones having one of the focals for their common base, each of these cones will have one of its axes perpendicular to the tangent planes. Therefore when an axis of a cone which stands on a given base is always parallel to a given right line, the locus of the vertex is an equilateral hyperbola or a right line, according as the base is a central conic or a parabola.

§ 12. A system of three confocal surfaces intersecting each other consists of an ellipsoid, a hyperboloid of one sheet, and a hyperboloid of two sheets, if the focals be central conics ; but it consists of two elliptic paraboloids and a hyperbolic paraboloid, if the focals be parabolas. In the central system, the ellipsoid has the greatest primary axis, and the hyperboloid of two sheets the least ; and the focal which is modular in one of these surfaces is umbilicar in the other. The asymptotic cones of the hyperboloids are confocal, the focal lines of each cone being the asymptotes of the focal hyperbola. In the system of paraboloids, the two elliptic paraboloids are distinguished by the circumstance that the modular focal of the one is the umbilicar focal of the other.

The curve in which two confocal surfaces intersect each other is a line of curvature of each, as is well known ;* and a series of lines of curvature on a given surface are found by making a series of confocal surfaces intersect it.

Now if a series of the lines of curvature of a given surface be projected on one of its directive planes by right lines parallel

---

* *See* Dupin's *Développements de Géométrie.*

to either of its non-directive axes, the projections will be a series
of confocal conics ; and when the surface is umbilicar, the foci
of all these conics will be the corresponding projections of the
umbilics.*   When the surface is not umbilicar, its directive axis
will be parallel to the primary axis of the projections.

The same line of curvature has two projections, according as
it is projected by right lines parallel to the one or to the other
non-directive axis.   In the ellipsoid these projections are always
curves of different kinds, the one being an ellipse when the other
is a hyperbola ; but in a hyperboloid the projections are either
both ellipses or both hyperbolas.   In the hyperbolic paraboloid
the projections are parabolas.   In the elliptic paraboloid one
of the projections is always a parabola, and the other is either
an ellipse or a hyperbola.

The corresponding projections of two lines of curvature which
pass through a given point of the surface are confocal conics intersecting each other in the projection of that point, and of
course intersecting at right angles.

§ 13. A *bifocal chord* is a bifocal right line terminated both
ways by the surface.† In a central surface, the length of a
bifocal chord is proportional to the square of the diameter which
is parallel to it ; the square of the diameter being equal to the
rectangle under the chord and the primary axis.

More generally, if a chord of a given central surface touch
two other given surfaces confocal with it, the length of the chord
will be proportional to the square of the parallel diameter of the
first surface, the square of the diameter being equal to the rectangle under the chord and a certain right line $2l$, determined by
the formula

$$l^2 = \frac{PQR}{(P - P')\,(P - P'')},\qquad(7)$$

wherein it is supposed that the equation (2) represents the first

* "Exam. Papers," An. 1838, p. xlvi., question 4 ; p. xcix., question 70.
† The theorems in § 13 are now stated for the first time.

surface, and that P', P'' are the quantities corresponding to P in the equations of the other two surfaces.

In any surface of the second order, the lengths of two bifocal chords are proportional to the rectangles under the segments of any two intersecting chords to which they are parallel.

In the paraboloid expressed by the equation

$$\frac{y^2}{p} + \frac{z^2}{q} = x,$$

if χ be the length of a bifocal chord making the angles β and γ with the axes of y and z respectively, we have

$$\frac{1}{\chi} = \frac{\cos^2 \beta}{p} + \frac{\cos^2 \gamma}{q}. \tag{8}$$

§ 14. At the point S on a given central surface expressed by the equation (2), let a tangent plane be applied, and let k, k' be the squares of the semiaxes of a central section made in the surface by a plane parallel to the tangent plane; each of the quantities k, k' being positive or negative, according as the corresponding semiaxis of the section is real or imaginary, that is, according as it meets the given surface or not. Then the equations* of two other surfaces confocal with the given one, and passing through the point S, are

$$\frac{x^2}{P-k} + \frac{y^2}{Q-k} + \frac{z^2}{R-k} = 1, \quad \frac{x^2}{P-k'} + \frac{y^2}{Q-k'} + \frac{z^2}{R-k'} = 1. \tag{9}$$

The given surface is intersected by these two surfaces respectively in the two lines of curvature which pass through the point S ; the tangent drawn to the first line of curvature at S is parallel to the second semiaxis of the section, and the tangent drawn to the second line of curvature at S is parallel to the first semiaxis of the section.

When two confocal surfaces intersect, the normal applied to

---

* "Exam. Papers," An. 1837, p.c., questions 4, 5, 6 ; An.1838, p. c., questions 71, 72.

one of them at any point S of the line of curvature formed by their intersection lies in the tangent plane of the other, and is parallel to an axis of any section made in the latter by a plane parallel to the tangent plane. Supposing the surfaces to be central, if two normals be applied at the point S, and a diameter of each 'surface be drawn parallel to the normal of the other, the two diameters so drawn will be equal and of a constant length, wherever the point S is taken on the line of curvature; the square of that length being equal to the difference of the squares of the primary axes of the surfaces, and the diameter of the surface which has the greater primary axis being real, while that of the other surface is imaginary. As the point S moves along the line of curvature, each constant diameter describes a cone condirective with the surface to which it belongs; the two cones so described are reciprocal, and the focal lines of the cone which belongs to one surface are perpendicular to the directive planes of the other surface.

When two confocal paraboloids intersect, if normals be applied to them at any point S of their intersection, and a bifocal chord of each surface be drawn parallel to the normal of the other, the two chords so drawn will be equal and of a constant length, wherever the point S is taken in the line of intersection of the surfaces; that constant length being equal to the difference between the parameters of either pair of coincident principal sections.

§ 15. The point S being the common intersection of a given system of confocal surfaces, of which the equations are

$$\frac{x^2}{P} + \frac{y^2}{Q} + \frac{z^2}{R} = 1, \qquad \frac{x^2}{P'} + \frac{y^2}{Q'} + \frac{z^2}{R'} = 1,$$

$$\frac{x^2}{P''} + \frac{y^2}{Q''} + \frac{z^2}{R''} = 1,$$

$$(10)$$

suppose that another surface A confocal with these, and expressed by the equation is circumscribed by a cone having its vertex at S. If the normals applied at S to the given surfaces, taken in the order of the equation (10), be the axes of new rectangular co-ordinates ξ, η, ζ, the equation of the cone, referred to these co-ordinates, will be*

$$\frac{\xi^2}{P - P_0} + \frac{\eta^2}{P' - P_0} + \frac{\zeta^2}{P'' - P_0} = 0. \tag{12}$$

The surfaces of the given system, in the order of their equations, may be supposed to be an ellipsoid, a hyperboloid of one sheet, and a hyperboloid of two sheets; the axes of x, y, z being respectively the primary, the mean, and the secondary axes of each surface. Then P is greater than P', and P' greater than P''.

The normals to the given surfaces are the axes of the cone expressed by the equation (12); and if the surface A be changed, but still remain confocal with the given system, it is obvious from that equation that the focal lines of the circumscribing cone will remain unchanged, since the differences of the quantities by which the squares of ξ, η, ζ are divided are independent of the surface A. As P' is intermediate in value between P and P'', the normal to the hyperboloid of one sheet is always the mean axis of the cone; the focal lines lie in the plane $\xi\zeta$, and their equation is

$$\frac{\xi^2}{P' - P} + \frac{\zeta^2}{P' - P''} = 0, \tag{13}$$

---

* The equation (12) was obtained in the year 1832, and was given at my Lectures in Hilary Term, 1836. The most remarkable properties of cones circumscribing confocal surfaces are immediate consequences of this equation. That such cones, when they have a common vertex, are confocal, their focal lines being the generatrices of the hyperboloid of one sheet passing through the vertex, was first stated by Professor C. G. J. Jacobi, of Königsberg, in 1834 (*see* Crelle's *Journal*, Vol. xii. p. 137). *See* also the excellent work of M. Chasles, published in 1837, and entitled *Aperçu historique sur l'Origine et le Développement des Méthodes en Géométrie*, p. 387. The analogy which exists between the focals of surfaces and the foci of curves of the second order was supposed by M. Chasles to have been pointed out in that work for the first time (*Comptes Rendus*, tom. xvi., pp. 833, 1106); but that analogy had been previously taught and developed in the Lectures just alluded to.

which shows that they are parallel to the asymptotes of a central section made in the hyperboloid of one sheet by a plane parallel to the plane $\xi\zeta$, since the quantities $P' - P$ and $P' - P''$ are (including the proper signs) the squares of the semiaxes of the section which are parallel to ξ and ζ respectively. The focal lines are therefore the generatrices of that hyperboloid at the point S.

When $R_0 = 0$, the equation (12) becomes

$$\frac{\xi^2}{R} + \frac{\eta^2}{R'} + \frac{\zeta^2}{R''} = 0, \tag{14}$$

which is that of the cone standing on the focal ellipse and having its vertex at S. When $Q_0 = 0$, the same equation becomes

$$\frac{\xi^2}{Q} + \frac{\eta^2}{Q'} + \frac{\zeta^2}{Q''} = 0, \tag{15}$$

which is that of the cone standing on the focal hyperbola, and having its vertex at S. The normal to the hyperboloid of one sheet at the point S is the mean axis of both cones; the normal to the ellipsoid is the internal axis of the first cone and the directive axis of the second, while the normal to the hyperboloid of two sheets is the directive axis of the first and the internal axis of the second.

The three surfaces expressed by the equations

$$\frac{\xi^2}{P} + \frac{\eta^2}{P'} + \frac{\zeta^2}{P''} = 1, \qquad\qquad \frac{\xi^2}{Q} + \frac{\eta^2}{Q'} + \frac{\zeta^2}{Q''} = 1,$$

$$\frac{\xi^2}{R} + \frac{\eta^2}{R'} + \frac{\zeta^2}{R''} = 1, \tag{16}$$

are a confocal system, having their centres at S, and being respectively an ellipsoid, a hyperboloid of one sheet, and a hyperboloid of two sheets. They intersect each other in the centre of the system expressed by the equations (10), and their normals at that point are the axes of x, y, z respectively. The relations between the two systems of surfaces are therefore perfectly reciprocal. From the equations (14) and (15) it is manifest that the asymptotic cones of the hyperboloids of one system pass through the focals of the other.

§ 16. The point S being the intersection of a given system of confocal paraboloids whose equations are

$$\frac{y^2}{p} + \frac{z^2}{q} = x + h, \qquad\qquad \frac{y^2}{p'} + \frac{z^2}{q'} = x + h',$$

$$\frac{y^2}{p''} + \frac{z^2}{q''} = x + h'', \tag{17}$$

where $p - p' = q - q' = 4\,(h - h')$, and $p - p'' = q - q'' = 4\,(h - h'')$: suppose that another paraboloid A confocal with these, and expressed by the equation

$$\frac{y^2}{p_0} + \frac{z^2}{q_0} = x + h_0, \tag{18}$$

is circumscribed by a cone having its vertex at S. Then if the normals applied at S to the given system of surfaces, taken in the order of their equations, be the axes of the co-ordinates ξ, η, ζ respectively, the equation of the circumscribing cone will be

$$\frac{\xi^2}{p - p_0} + \frac{\eta^2}{p' - p_0} + \frac{\zeta^2}{p'' - p_0} = 0 ; \tag{19}$$

showing that those normals are the axes of the cone, and that the focal lines of the cone are independent of the surface A, provided it be confocal with the given surfaces. If the hyperbolic paraboloid be the second surface of the given system, the parameter p' will be intermediate in value between p and p'', and the equation of the focal lines of the cone will be

$$\frac{\xi^2}{p' - p} + \frac{\zeta^2}{p' - p''} = 0, \tag{20}$$

which is the equation of a pair of right lines parallel to the asymptotes of a section made in the hyperbolic paraboloid by a plane parallel to the plane $\xi\zeta$, since the quantities $p'-p$ and $p'-p''$ are proportional to the squares of the semiaxes of the section which are parallel to ξ and ζ respectively. The focal lines are therefore the generatrices of the hyperbolic paraboloid at the point S.

Putting p_0 and q_0 alternately equal to zero in the equation (19), we get

$$\frac{\xi^2}{p} + \frac{\eta^2}{p'} + \frac{\zeta^2}{p''} = 0, \qquad \frac{\xi^2}{q} + \frac{\eta^2}{q'} + \frac{\zeta^2}{q''} = 0, \qquad (21)$$

the equations of two cones which have a common vertex at S, the first of them standing on the focal which lies in the plane xz, the second on the focal which lies in the plane xy. The mean axis of each of these cones is the normal at S to the hyperbolic paraboloid; the internal axis of either cone is the normal to the elliptic paraboloid which has the base of that cone for its modular focal.

As the cones which have a common vertex, and stand on the focals of any surface of the second order, are confocal, they intersect at right angles. Therefore when two planes passing through a bifocal right line touch the focals, these planes are at right angles to each other. And as cones which have a common vertex, and circumscribe confocal surfaces, are confocal, two such cones, when they intersect each other, intersect at right angles. Therefore when a right line touches two confocal surfaces, the tangent planes passing through this right line are at right angles to each other.

§ 17. When two surfaces are reciprocal polars* with respect to any sphere, and one of them is of the second order, the other is also of the second order. Let the surface B be reciprocal to the surface A before mentioned, with respect to a sphere of which the centre is S; and suppose R' and R to be any corresponding points on these surfaces. Then the plane which

---

* *Transactions* of the Royal Irish Academy, Vol. xvii. p. 241; "Examination Papers," An. 1841, p. cxxvi., question 4.

touches the surface A at the point R intersects the right line SR′ perpendicularly in a point K, such that the rectangle under SR′ and SK is constant, being equal to the square of the radius of the sphere. Now if the point K approach indefinitely to S, the distance SR′ will increase without limit, the surface B being of course a hyperboloid; and if through S any plane be drawn touching the surface A, a right line perpendicular to this plane will evidently be parallel to a side of the asymptotic cone of the hyperboloid. The asymptotic cone of B is therefore reciprocal to the cone which, having its vertex at S, circumscribes the surface A. Hence, as the directive planes of a hyperboloid are the same as those of its asymptotic cone, it follows that the directive planes of the surface B are perpendicular to the generatrices of the hyperboloid of one sheet, or the hyperbolic paraboloid, which passes through S, and is confocal with the surface A. And this relation between two reciprocal surfaces ought to be general, whatever be the position of the point S with respect to them;* for though it has been deduced by the aid of the circumscribing cone aforesaid, it does not, in its enunciation, imply the existence of such a cone. This conclusion may be verified by investigating the equation of the surface B in terms of the co-ordinates ξ, η, ζ. Suppose ρ to be the radius of the sphere with respect to which the surfaces A and B are reciprocal. Then if A be a central surface expressed by the equation (11), and having ξ_0, η_0, ζ_0 for the co-ordinates of its centre, the surface B will be represented by the equation

$$(P - P_0)\,\xi^2 + (P' - P_0)\,\eta^2 + (P'' - P_0)\,\zeta^2$$
$$= 2\rho^2(\xi_0\xi + \eta_0\eta + \zeta_0\zeta) - \rho^4; \tag{22}$$

but if A be a paraboloid expressed by the equation (18), the equation of B will be

$$(p - p_0)\,\xi^2 + (p' - p_0)\,\eta^2 + (p'' - p_0)\,\zeta^2$$
$$= \rho4^2(\xi\cos\alpha + \eta\cos\beta + \zeta\cos\gamma), \tag{23}$$

where a, β, γ are the angles which the axis of x makes with the axes of ξ, η, ζ respectively. In the first case, the equation (22) shows that the directive planes of B are perpendicular to the right lines expressed by the equation (13); in the second case, the equation (23) shows that the directive planes of B are perpendicular to the right lines expressed by the equation (20).

When the surface A is a paraboloid, and the distance of the point R from its vertex is indefinitely increased, the plane touching the surface at R approaches indefinitely to parallelism with its axis, and the right line SK, perpendicular to that plane, increases without limit. Therefore the surface B passes through the point S, and is touched in that point by a plane perpendicular to the axis of A.

When the point S lies upon the surface A, the co-efficient of the square of one of the variables, in the equation (22) or (23), is reduced to zero, and the surface B is a paraboloid having its axis parallel to the normal applied at S to the surface A. This also appears from considering that when S is a point of the surface A, the normal at that point is the only right line passing through S, which meets the surface B at an infinite distance.

If a series of surfaces be confocal, their reciprocal surfaces, taken with respect to any given sphere, will be condirective.

When the equations of any two condirective surfaces are expressed by co-ordinates perpendicular to their principal planes, the constants in the equations may be always so taken that the differences of the co-efficients of the squares of the variables in one equation shall be equal to the corresponding differences in the other. Then, by subtracting the one equation from the other, we get the equation of a sphere. Therefore when two condirective surfaces intersect each other, their intersection is, in general, a spherical curve. But when the surfaces are two paraboloids of the same species, their intersection is a plane curve.

§ 18. Through any point S of a given surface four bifocal

to be central, let a plane drawn through the centre, parallel to the first plane which touches the surface at S, intersect any one of these right lines. Then the distance of the point of intersection from the point S will always be equal to the primary semi-axis of the surface.*

If through any point S of a given central surface a right line be drawn touching two other given surfaces confocal with it, and if this right line be intersected by a plane drawn through the centre parallel to the plane which touches the first surface at S, the distance of the point of intersection from the point S will be constant, wherever the point S is taken on the first surface. If this constant distance be called l, and the other denominations be the same as in the formula (7), the value of l will be given by that formula.†

---

* "Examination Papers," An. 1838, p. xlvii., question 9.

† In the notes to the last-mentioned work of M. Chasles, on the *History of Methods in Geometry*, will be found many theorems relative to surfaces of the second order. Among them are some of the theorems which are given in the present Paper; but it is needless to specify these, as M. Chasles's work is so well known.

III.—NOTE RELATIVE TO THE COMPARISON OF ARCS OF CURVES, PARTICULARLY OF PLANE AND SPHERICAL CONICS.

[*Proceedings of the Royal Irish Academy*, Vol. ii. p. 446.—Read Nov. 30, 1843.]

THE first Lemma given in my Paper on the rectification of the conic sections[*] is obviously true for curves described on any given surface, provided the tangents drawn to these curves be *shortest lines* on the surface. The demonstration remains exactly the same; and the Lemma, in this general form, may be stated as follows :—

Understanding a tangent to be a shortest line, and supposing two given curves E and F to be described on a given surface, let tangents drawn to the first curve at two points T, t, indefinitely near each other, meet the second curve in the points P, p. Then taking a fixed point A on the curve E, if we put s to denote (according to the position of this point with respect to T) the sum (or difference) of the arc AT and the tangent TP, and $s + ds$ to denote the sum (or difference) of the arc At and the tangent tp, we shall have ds equal to the projection of the infinitesimal arc Pq upon the tangent; that is, if a be the angle which the tangent TP makes with the curve F at the point P, we shall have ds equal to Pp multiplied by the cosine of a.

Now through the points P, p conceive other tangents T′P,

---

[*] *Transactions* of the Royal Irish Academy, Vol. xvi. p. 79 (*supra*, p. 20).

$t'p$ to be drawn, touching the curve E in the points T′, t'; and let s' and ds' have for these tangents the same signification which s and ds have for the former tangents. Supposing the nature of the curve F to be such that it always bisects, either internally or externally, the angle made at the point P by the tangents TP and T′P, it is evident that $ds = \pm ds'$, and therefore either $s + s'$ or $s - s'$ is a constant quantity.

A simple example of this theorem is afforded by the plane and spherical conics. If the curves E and F be two confocal conics, either plane or spherical, and tangents TP, T′P be drawn to F from any point P of E (the tangents being of course right lines when the curves are plane, and arcs of great circles when they are spherical; in both cases shortest lines), it is well known that the angle TPT′ made by the tangents is always bisected by the conic E. The angle is bisected internally or externally according as the conics intersect or not. Hence we have the two following properties* of confocal conics :—

1. When two confocal conics do not intersect, if one of them be touched in the points T, T′ by tangents drawn from any point P of the other, the sum of the tangents TP, T′P will exceed the convex arc TT′ lying between the points of contact, by a constant quantity.

2. When two focal conics intersect in the point A, if one of them be touched in the points T, T′ by tangents drawn from any point P of the other, the difference between the tangents

---

* The first of these properties was originally given for spherical conics by the Rev. Charles Graves, Fellow of Trinity College, in the "notes and additions" to his translation of M. Chasles's Memoirs on Cones and Spherical Conics, p. 77 (Dublin, 1841). Mr. Graves obtained it as the reciprocal of the proposition, that when two spherical conics have the same directive circles, any tangent arc of the inner conic divides the outer one into two segments, each of which has a constant area. Both properties, with the general theorem relative to curves described on any surface and touched by shortest lines, were afterwards given in the *University Calendar*. See "Examination Papers," An. 1841, p. xli., questions 3–6; An. 1842, p. lxxxiii., questions 30–34. These two properties of conics were communicated, in October, 1843, to the Academy of Sciences of Paris, by M. Chasles, who supposed them to be new. *See* the *Comptes Rendus*, tom. xvii. p. 838.

TP, T'P will be equal to the difference between the arcs AT AT'.

These properties give the readiest and most elegant solution of problems concerning the comparison of different arcs of a plane or spherical conic. Any arc being given on a conic, we may find another arc beginning from a given point, which shall differ from the given arc by a right line if the conic be plane, or by a circular arc if the conic be spherical.

IV.—NOTE ON SURFACES OF THE SECOND ORDER.

[*Proceedings of the Royal Irish Academy*, Vol. III. p. 429.—Read April 12, 1847.]

LET a surface A of the second order be represented by the equation

$$\frac{x^2}{P_0} + \frac{y^2}{Q_0} + \frac{z^2}{R_0} = 1,$$

its primary axis being that of x. Through a given point S whose co-ordinates are x', y', z', conceive three surfaces confocal with A to be described, and let P, P', P'', be the squares of their primary semiaxes. Then if normals drawn to these surfaces respectively at the point S be the axes of a new system of co-ordinates ξ, η, ζ, and if we put

$$P - P_0 = k, \quad P' - P_0 = k', \quad P'' - P_0 = k'', \quad \frac{x'^2}{P_0} + \frac{y'^2}{Q_0} + \frac{z'^2}{R_0} \quad f,$$

the equation of the surface A, referred to the new co-ordinates, will be

$$\frac{\xi^2}{k} + \frac{\eta^2}{k'} + \frac{\zeta^2}{k''} = (f-1)\left(\frac{\xi_0\xi}{k} + \frac{\eta_0\eta}{k'} + \frac{\zeta_0\zeta}{k''} - 1\right)^2, \qquad (a)$$

where ξ_0, η_0, ζ_0 are the co-ordinates of its centre.

From the form of this equation it is evident that, if the surface be intersected by the plane whose equation is

$$\frac{\xi_0\xi}{k} + \frac{\eta_0\eta}{k'} + \frac{\zeta_0\zeta}{k''} = 1, \qquad (b)$$

Y

it will be touched along the curve of intersection by the cone whose equation is

$$\frac{\xi^2}{k} + \frac{\eta^2}{k'} + \frac{\zeta^2}{k''} = 0. \qquad (c)$$

This mode of deducing, in its simplest form, the equation of a cone circumscribing a surface of the second order, is much easier than the direct investigation by which the equation (c) was originally obtained.

Let a right line passing through S intersect the plane expressed by the equation (b), in a point whose distance from S is equal to ϖ, while it intersects the surface A in two points, P and P', the distance of either of which from S is denoted by ρ. Let the surface B, represented by the equation

$$\frac{\xi^2}{k} + \frac{\eta^2}{k'} + \frac{\zeta^2}{k''} = f - 1, \qquad (d)$$

be intersected by the same right line in a point whose distance from S is equal to r, the distance r being, of course, a semidiameter of this surface. Then it is obvious that the equation (a) may be written

$$\frac{1}{r^2} = \left(\frac{1}{\varpi} - \frac{1}{\rho}\right)^2,$$

so that, if ρ and ρ' represent the distances SP and SP' respectively, we have

$$\frac{1}{\rho} = \frac{1}{\varpi} + \frac{1}{r}, \qquad \frac{1}{\rho'} = \frac{1}{\varpi} - \frac{1}{r}; \qquad (e)$$

and therefore

$$\frac{1}{\rho} - \frac{1}{\rho'} = \frac{2}{r}. \qquad (f)$$

This result is useful in questions relating to attraction. For if A be an ellipsoid, every point of which attracts an external point S with a force varying inversely as the *fourth* power of the distance, and if the point S be the vertex of a pyramid, one of whose sides is the right line SPP', and whose transverse section, at the distance unity from its vertex, is the indefinitely small area ω, the portion PP' of the pyramid will attract the point S, in the direction of its length, with a force expressed by the quantity

$$\left(\frac{1}{\rho} - \frac{1}{\rho'}\right)\omega, \quad \text{or} \quad \frac{2\omega}{r};$$

and putting θ for the angle which the right line SP makes with the axis of ξ, the attraction in the direction of ξ will be

$$\frac{2\omega \cos \theta}{r}. \tag{g}$$

Now, supposing the axis of ξ to be normal to the confocal ellipsoid described through S, it will be the primary axis of the surface B, which will be a hyperboloid of two sheets; and the surface being symmetrical round this axis, it is easy to see, from the expression for the elementary attraction, that the whole attraction of the ellipsoid will be in the direction of ξ. Therefore when the force is inversely as the fourth power of the distance, the attraction of an ellipsoid on an external point is normal to the confocal ellipsoid passing through that point.

Hence we infer, that if U be the sum of the quotients found by dividing every element of the volume of an ellipsoid by the cube of its distance from an external point, the value of U will remain the same, wherever that point is taken on the surface of an ellipsoid confocal with the given one.

The question of the attraction of an ellipsoid, when the law of force is that of the inverse square of the distance, has been treated by Poisson, in an elegant but very elaborate memoir, presented to the Academy of Sciences in 1833.* In the preceding year I had obtained the theorems just mentioned, by considering the law of the inverse fourth power; and, as well as I remember, they were deduced exactly as above, by setting out from the equation (a). But I did not then succeed in applying

---

* *Mémoires de l'Institut*, tom. xiii.

the same method to the case where the law of force is that o
nature, probably from not perceiving that, in this case, the ellip
soid ought to be divided (as Poisson has divided it) into concen
tric and similar shells.   This application requires the following
theorem, which is easily proved :—

Supposing A' to be another ellipsoid, concentric, similar, and
similarly placed with A; let the right line SPP' intersec
it in the points p and p', respectively, adjacent to P and P'
then if the direction of that right line be conceived to vary, the
rectangle under Pp and $P'p$ (or under Pp' and $P'p'$) will be to
the rectangle under SP and SP' in a constant ratio.

Denoting the constant ratio by m, and combining this theo·
rem with the formula (f), we have

$$\frac{Pp \times P'p}{PP'} = \frac{mr}{2}. \qquad (h)$$

Now let the two surfaces A and A' be supposed to approach indefinitely near each other, so as to form a very thin shell, then
ultimately $P'p$ will be equal to PP', and we shall have

$$Pp = P'p' = \frac{mr}{2},$$

where m is indefinitely small. Therefore if the point S, external
to the shell, be the vertex of a pyramid whose side is the right
line SP, and whose section, at the unit of distance from the
vertex, is ω, the attraction of the two portions Pp and $P'p'$ of
this pyramid, which form part of the shell, will be equal to $mr\omega$.
Hence it appears, as before, on account of the symmetry of the
surface B round the axis of ξ, that the whole attraction of the
shell on the point S is in the direction of that axis, and consequently (as was found by Poisson) in the direction of the internal axis of the cone whose vertex is S, and which circumscribes
the shell.

To find the whole attraction of the shell, the expression

$$mr\omega \cos\theta \qquad (i)$$

must be integrated.   Let ϕ be the angle which a plane, passing through SP and the axis of ξ, makes with the plane $\xi\eta$, then

$$\omega = \sin\theta\, d\theta\, d\phi$$

$$\frac{1}{r} = \sqrt{\left(\frac{\cos^2\theta}{k} + \frac{\sin^2\theta\,\cos^2\phi}{k'} + \frac{\sin^2\theta\,\sin^2\phi}{k''}\right)} \frac{1}{\sqrt{f-1}}.$$

When these values are substituted in (i), that expression may be readily integrated, first with respect to θ, and then with respect to ϕ.

It is evident that, by the same substitutions, the expression (g) may be twice integrated.

An investigation similar to the preceding has been given by M. Chasles, for the case in which the force varies inversely as the square of the distance.*   He uses a theorem equivalent to the formula (f), but deduces it in a different way.

From what has been proved it follows that, if V be the sum of the quotients found by dividing every element of the shell by its distance from an external point S, the value of V will be the same wherever that point is taken on the surface Σ of an ellipsoid confocal with the surface A of the shell.

Let Σ' be another ellipsoid confocal with A, and indefinitely near the surface Σ.   The normal interval between the two surfaces Σ and Σ', at any point S on the former, will be inversely as the perpendicular dropped from the common centre of the ellipsoids on the plane which touches Σ at S.   Hence, supposing the point S to move over the surface Σ, that perpendicular will vary as the attraction exerted by the shell on the point S, when the force is inversely as the square of the distance, or as the attraction exerted by the whole ellipsoid A on the point S, when the force is inversely as the fourth power of the distance.

When the point S is on the focal hyperbola, the integrations, by which the actual attraction is found in either case, are simplified, for the surface B is then one of revolution round the axis of ξ, and its semidiameter r is independent of the angle ϕ.

* *Mémoires des Savants Etrangers*, tom. ix.

From the expression for the attraction of a shell we can find, by another integration, the attraction of the entire ellipsoid when the law of force is that of nature. And thus the well-known problem of the integral calculus, in which it is proposed to determine directly the attraction of an ellipsoid on an external point, without employing the theorem of Ivory to evade the difficulty, is solved in what appears to be the simplest manner.

PART III.

—

ROTATION.

I.—ON THE ROTATION OF A SOLID BODY ROUND A FIXED POINT; BEING AN ACCOUNT OF THE LATE PROFESSOR MAC CULLAGH'S LECTURES ON THAT SUBJECT.* COMPILED BY THE REV. SAMUEL HAUGHTON, FELLOW OF TRINITY COLLEGE, DUBLIN.

[*Transactions of the Royal Irish Academy*, Vol. XXII. p. 139.—Read April 23, 1849.]

I.—Composition of Rotations.

Let O be the intersection of two axes of rotation, OR, OR′; and let the magnitudes of the rotations be represented by ω, ω'; then the motion impressed upon the body by these two rotations will be the same as the motion produced by a single rotation round an axis, which is represented in magnitude and position by the diagonal of the parallelogram formed by ω, ω'. For, draw through any point I of the body a plane perpendicular to the line OI, and project upon this plane the parallelogram formed by ω, ω'; the sides of this parallelogram will be $\omega \sin$ ROI and $\omega' \sin$ R′OI. Now the velocities impressed upon the

---

* This Essay—"On the Rotation of a Solid Body round a Fixed Point,"—has been compiled from my notes of Professor Mac Cullagh's Lectures, delivered in the Hilary Term of the year 1844, in Trinity College. A short account of some of the results contained in it was published by Professor Mac Cullagh himself, in the *Proceedings* of the Royal Irish Academy.† As it has appeared to many of Mr. Mac Cullagh's friends desirable that a somewhat more detailed account of his researches in this subject should be published, I have, in accordance with this desire, drawn up and presented to the Academy an account of his Lectures on Rotation. I have endeavoured to arrange the subject in a systematic order, and to give the results proved by him during the course of the Lectures, carefully excluding all theorems and proofs of theorems, which were not originally given by him, as here stated.—Samuel Haughton.

† Vol. II. pp. 520, 542.

point I by the rotations ω and ω' are $OI.\omega$ sin ROI and $OI.\omega'$ sin R'OI; and the directions of these velocities are perpendicular to the sides of the projected parallelogram. Hence, if this parallelogram be turned in its plane through 90°, its sides will represent in magnitude and direction the actual velocities: the resultant of these velocities is perpendicular to the projection of the diagonal of the parallelogram (ω, ω'): this projection, turned round through 90°, will represent the actual velocity, which is therefore the same in magnitude and direction as would be produced by a single rotation represented by the diagonal of (ω, ω'). Hence rotations may be resolved along three rectangular axes by the same laws as couples, and they must be counted positive when the motion produced is from z to x, x to y, y to z, and *vice versâ*.

II.—LINEAR VELOCITIES PRODUCED BY A GIVEN ROTATION.

Let the origin of co-ordinates be assumed on the axis of rotation, and let the magnitude of the rotation and of its components be represented by (ω, p, q, r): the velocity of any point (x, y, z) is in a direction perpendicular to the plane containing the axis of rotation and the point (x, y, z); and its magnitude is represented by the area of the triangle whose angles are situated at the origin, the point (x, y, z), and the point (p, q, r). Hence, the components of the linear velocity are represented by the projections of this triangle on the co-ordinate planes. These projections are

$$u = qz - ry ;$$
$$v = rx - pz ; \qquad (1)$$
$$w = py - qx.$$

III.—To represent geometrically the Moments of Inertia of a Body with respect to Axes drawn through a Fixed Point.

The moment of inertia of a body with respect to any axis (a, β, γ) is

$$M = A' \cos^2 a + B' \cos^2 \beta + C' \cos^2 \gamma - 2L' \cos \beta \cos \gamma$$
$$- 2M' \cos a \cos \gamma - 2N' \cos a \cos \beta \, ;$$

where

$$A' = \int (y^2 + z^2) \, dm, \qquad L' = \int yz \, dm \, ;$$
$$B' = \int (x^2 + z^2) \, dm, \qquad M' = \int xz \, dm \, ;$$
$$C' = \int (x^2 + y^2) \, dm, \qquad N' = \int xy \, dm.$$

Assume $M = \dfrac{\mu}{r^2}$; μ being the mass of the body, and r a distance measured on the line (a, β, γ), and construct the ellipsoid whose equation is

$$A'x^2 + B'y^2 + C'z^2 - 2L'yz - 2M'xz - 2N'xy = \mu \, ; \qquad (2)$$

then it is evident that the moments of inertia of the body with respect to axes passing through the fixed point are represented by the squares of the reciprocals of the radii vectores of this ellipsoid. Assume $A = \mu a^2$, $B = \mu b^2$, $C = \mu c^2$, and let the axes of co-ordinates be the axes of the ellipsoid; its equation will thus become

$$a^2 x^2 + b^2 y^2 + c^2 z^2 = 1 \, ; \qquad (3)$$

and the equation of the reciprocal ellipsoid will be

$$\frac{x^2}{a^2} + \frac{y^2}{b^2} + \frac{z^2}{c^2} = 1. \qquad (4)$$

This latter ellipsoid may be called the ellipsoid of gyration, as the perpendiculars on its tangent planes represent the radii of gyration ; this is evident from the consideration, that these perpendiculars are reciprocal to the radii vectores of the ellipsoid (3). In fact, the moment of inertia with respect to any axis will be represented by the formula

$$M = (a^2 \cos^2 a + b^2 \cos^2 \beta + c^2 \cos^2 \gamma)\, \mu = \mu P^2 = \frac{\mu}{R'^2};\qquad (5)$$

(R, P) denoting the radius vector and perpendicular on tangent plane of the ellipsoid (4); and (R', P') the corresponding lines in the ellipsoid (3).

IV.—To find the Magnitude, Position, and Direction of the Statical Couple produced by the Centrifugal Forces.

If from any point (x, y, z) of the body, a perpendicular be let fall on the axis of rotation (a, β, γ), the centrifugal force will be represented by the product of the square of the angular velocity and this perpendicular : the corresponding elementary statical couple will be found by multiplying the centrifugal force by the distance from the foot of the perpendicular to the origin, which is represented by the quantity $(x \cos a + y \cos \beta + z \cos \gamma)$. The components of the elementary couple will be proportional to the projections of the triangle formed by the lines before mentioned. The components of the elementary couples must be integrated for the entire extent of the body, and the integrals thus found will be the components of the couple produced by centrifugal force: the expressions are as follows :

$$\omega^2 (x \cos a + y \cos \beta + z \cos \gamma)(z \cos \beta - y \cos \gamma)\, dm ;$$

$$\omega^2 (x \cos a + y \cos \beta + z \cos \gamma)(x \cos \gamma - z \cos a)\, dm ;$$

$$\omega^2 (x \cos a + y \cos \beta + z \cos \gamma)(y \cos a - x \cos \beta)\, dm .$$

If the axes of co-ordinates be principal axes, these expressions, when integrated, will become

$$\omega^2 \cos \beta \cos \gamma\, (B - C) = qr\, (B - C) ;$$

$$\omega^2 \cos a \cos \gamma\, (C - A) = pr\, (C - A) ;\qquad (6)$$

$$\omega^2 \cos a \cos \beta\, (A - B) = pq\, (A - B) :$$

p, q, r being the components of the angular velocity ω. The position of the resultant couple may be expressed by means of the ellipsoid (4). If a tangent plane be drawn to this ellipsoid at the point (x, y, z), and perpendicular to the line (a, β, γ), it may be easily shown that the projections of the triangle formed by the radius vector and perpendicular are represented by the quantities

$$\cos \beta \cos \gamma \, (b^2 - c^2), \quad \cos a \cos \gamma \, (c^2 - a^2), \quad \cos a \cos \beta \, (a^2 - b^2):$$

these three expressions multiplied by $\mu \omega^2$ will produce the quantities used in (6). Hence it appears that the couple produced by the centrifugal forces lies in the plane of the radius vector and perpendicular to a tangent plane of the ellipsoid (4); the tangent plane being perpendicular to the axis of rotation. Also, the magnitude of the resultant couple is proportional to the triangle formed by the radius vector and perpendicular.

The differential equations of motion commonly used in the solution of this problem may be deduced immediately from equations (6). In fact, as the axes of co-ordinates are axes of permanent rotation, the increment of angular velocity round each axis will be equal to the statical couple of the applied forces (including centrifugal forces), divided by the moment of inertia round that axis. The statement of this fact, in analytical language, will give the equations of motion :

$$A \frac{dp}{dt} = (B - C)\, qr + L\,;$$

$$B \frac{dq}{dt} = (C - A)\, pr + M\,; \tag{7}$$

$$C \frac{dr}{dt} = (A - B)\, pq + N:$$

(L, M, N) being the components of the applied statical couple.

The *position* and *magnitude* of the couple produced by the centrifugal forces are easily found by the method which has been just given; but the *direction* will be found more readily by taking more particular axes of co-ordinates. Let the axis of rotation be the axis OZ, and the plane of radius vector and perpendicular be the co-ordinate plane XOZ. In the accompanying figure OR′ and OP′ are the radius vector and perpendicular of the ellipsoid (2), and OR, OP the radius vector and perpendicular of the ellipsoid (4), which is reciprocal to the former; the rotation is positive, in the direction indicated by the arrow. As the rotation is round the axis of z, it is

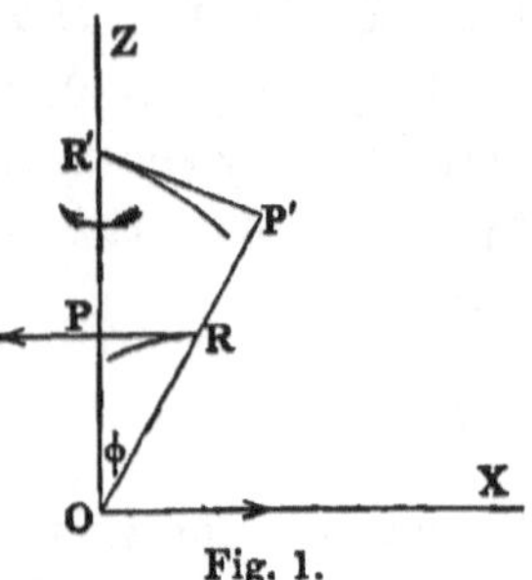

Fig. 1.

easy to see that the statical couple produced by centrifugal force will have for components, round the axes of x and y respectively, the quantities $\omega^2\!\int yz\,dm$, $\omega^2\!\int xz\,dm$ taken with their proper sign; *i. e.* the components are $\pm\,\omega^2 L'$, $\pm\,\omega^2 M'$; L', M' being coefficients in the equation of the ellipsoid

$$A'x^2 + B'y^2 + C'z^2 - 2L'yz - 2M'xz - 2N'xy = \mu.$$

The tangent plane to this ellipsoid, applied at the point (x, y, z), will be

$$(A'x - M'z - N'y)\,x' + (B'y - N'x - L'z)\,y' + (C'z - L'y - M'x)\,z' = \mu.$$

At the point R′ the tangent plane will be perpendicular to the plane XOZ, and will be found by making $x = 0$, $y = 0$, and destroying the coefficient of y' in the preceding equation. These conditions give us $L' = 0$, which proves that the statical couple produced by centrifugal force lies altogether in the plane XOZ. The equation of the tangent plane is the same as the equation of the line R′P′, and is

$$C'z' - M'x' = -\frac{\mu}{z}.$$

Hence we obtain

$$\tan\phi = -\frac{M'}{C'}.$$

The value of the centrifugal couple is $\omega^2 M'$, which is found from the preceding equation by replacing C' and $\tan \phi$ by their values μP^2, and $\dfrac{Q}{P}$; Q being the line RP.

We thus obtain finally the centrifugal couple lying in the plane XOZ, and expressed by the equation

$$\omega^2 \!\int xz\, dm = - \mu \omega^2 PQ. \tag{8}$$

It thus appears that the centrifugal couple lies in the plane of radius vector and perpendicular, is proportional to the area of the triangle ROP, and has a direction opposite to the direction of rotation.

V.—To find the Relation between the Plane of Principal Moments and the Axis of Rotation at any Instant.

The motion of the body at any instant consists of a rotation of a certain magnitude round a certain axis; this rotation might be produced by an impulsive couple of a determinate magnitude and direction. The statical impulsive couple thus conceived is the couple of principal moments. Let this couple be represented by G, and act round the axis OR (fig. 1, p. 334); then the corresponding axis of rotation will be the perpendicular OP, and the relation between G and ω may be thus found:—Let the axes of co-ordinates be the axes of the ellipsoid (4), the radius vector being determined by the angles (λ, μ, ν), and the axes of rotation by the angles (a, β, γ). From mechanical considerations we obtain the equations

$$G \cos \lambda = Ap = \mu \omega\, a^2 \cos a\,;$$

$$G \cos \mu = Bq = \mu \omega\, b^2 \cos \beta\,;$$

$$G \cos \nu = Cr = \mu \omega\, c^2 \cos \gamma.$$

Hence we obtain

$$\frac{\cos \lambda}{\cos \nu} = \frac{a^2 \cos a}{c^2 \cos \gamma}, \quad \frac{\cos \mu}{\cos \nu} = \frac{b^2 \cos \beta}{c^2 \cos \gamma}, \tag{9}$$

$$\omega = \frac{G}{\mu PR} = \frac{G \cos \phi}{\mu P^2}.$$

The first two of these equations prove that the axis of rotation is the perpendicular on tangent plane of the ellipsoid, and the last equation gives the magnitude of the rotation in terms of the impressed couple and quantities determined by the nature of the body itself. Equations (9) are true, whatever be the forces acting on the body; if no forces act, G will be fixed in magnitude and position in space, by the principle of conservation of areas, but will change its position in the body, the axis of rotation accompanying it, and changing its position both in the body and in space. -

VI.—Rotation produced by Centrifugal Force; particular Properties of the Motion when no Forces act.

The axis of rotation produced by the centrifugal couple always lies in the plane of principal moments. This theorem may be thus proved: Let the radius vector and perpendicular be drawn, which coincide with the axis of principal moment and axis of rotation at any instant; a line perpendicular to the plane of radius vector and perpendicular is the axis of centrifugal couple; this line and the original radius vector are axes of the section of the ellipsoid made by their plane: at the point where the axis of the centrifugal couple pierces the ellipsoid let a tangent plane be applied; the perpendicular let fall on this tangent plane is the axis of rotation produced by centrifugal forces. From the construction it is evident that the plane of the second radius vector and perpendicular is perpendicular to the axis of G; hence the axis of the centrifugal couple and the axis of rotation produced by it always lie in the plane of principal moment. Two important corollaries follow from the theorem just demonstrated, in the case where no forces act:—First, the component of angular velocity round the axis of primitive impulse is constant during the motion. Secondly, the radius vector which coincides with the axis of G is of constant length during the motion. The first theorem is obvious; for as the axis of rotation produced by centrifugal force is always perpendicular to the axis of G, it cannot alter the rotation round that axis. The second theorem follows from equation (9), from which we deduce

$$\omega \cos \phi = \frac{G}{\mu R^2}. \qquad (10)$$

The left-hand member of this equation is constant by the preceding theorem; and G is constant, since there is no external force; therefore R is constant.

As the axis of G is fixed in space, and the line R is constant, it is evident that the axis of G will describe in the body the cone of the second degree, determined by the intersection of the ellipsoid (4) with the sphere whose radius is R. The equation of this cone is

$$\frac{R^2 - a^2}{a^2}\, x^2 + \frac{R^2 - b^2}{b^2}\, y^2 + \frac{R^2 - c^2}{c^2}\, z^2 = 0. \qquad (11)$$

As the axis of principal moments describes this cone in the body, it is accompanied by the axis of rotation, which is always the corresponding perpendicular on tangent plane of the ellipsoid. The cone described by the axis of rotation might be found thus. Let tangent planes be applied to the ellipsoid along the spherical conic in which the cone (11) cuts the ellipsoid. From the centre let fall perpendiculars on these tangent planes; the locus of these perpendiculars is the required cone.

VII.—The Axis of principal Moments is fixed in Space.

This is evident from D'Alembert's principle, but may be shown by geometrical considerations in the particular case under consideration. The axis varies in position in the body, in consequence of the centrifugal couple, which must be compounded with the impressed couple at each instant. Referring to equation (8), the value of the centrifugal couple is $- \mu \omega^2 P Q dt$, the principal moment being $G = \mu \omega P R$ (*vid.* (9)). Hence the angle through which the axis of principal moments shifts in an element of time is $-\dfrac{\omega Q dt}{R}$: this angle, multiplied by the constant radius vector, will give the elementary motion on the spherical conic traced by the axis of principal moment on the surface of the ellipsoid : this motion is therefore $-\omega Q dt$; but in the same time the point of the body which coincides with the point where the axis of moments pierces the spherical conic will describe the angle $+\omega Q dt$ in consequence of the angular rotation. Hence the axis of moments will remain fixed in space, and will move in the body with a velocity proportional to the tangent of the angle between the radius vector and perpendicular, the motion being in a direction opposite to the direction of the rotation. This is evident from the consideration that $Q\omega = P\omega \tan \phi$, $P\omega$ being constant and equal to $\dfrac{G}{\mu R}$ (*vid.* (9)).

VIII.—To find the Motion of the principal Axis in the Body.

First Method.

The point of the principal axis of moments, which is situated at the distance R from the centre, moves on the spherical conic which has been determined. Let this point be projected on the three co-ordinate planes ; then, since the spherical conic is projected into a conic section, the movement of the axis of moments is reduced to the movement of a point on a conic section, according to a law which must be determined. The radius vector describes an elementary triangle in the surface of the cone (11) : let the projections of this triangle on the co-ordinate planes be (dA_1, dA_2, dA_3) ; we obtain easily

$$\frac{dA_1}{dt} = y\frac{dz}{dt} - z\frac{dy}{dt}, \quad \frac{dA_2}{dt} = z\frac{dx}{dt} - x\frac{dz}{dt}, \quad \frac{dA_3}{dt} = x\frac{dy}{dt} - y\frac{dx}{dt}.$$

Substituting in these equations the values of the velocities given by (1), we obtain

$$\frac{dA_1}{dt} = P\omega\,\frac{R^2 - a^2}{a^2}\,x = (R^2 - a^2)\,p\,;$$

$$\frac{dA_2}{dt} = P\omega\,\frac{R^2 - b^2}{b^2}\,y = (R^2 - b^2)\,q\,; \qquad (12)$$

$$\frac{dA_3}{dt} = P\omega\,\frac{Q^2 - c^3}{c^2}\,z = (R^2 - c^2)\,r.$$

These equations prove that the *areolar velocity* of the projection on a co-ordinate plane varies as the ordinate to that plane. By means of the method of quadratures, we may determine from equations (12) the position of the projections of the principal axis at any instant, and hence deduce the position of the axis itself.

Second Method.

If the spherical conic be projected on a cyclic plane of the ellipsoid of gyration, by lines parallel to x and z, the projections will be two concentric circles, and the corresponding projections will lie on the same ordinate SII′ (fig. 2). The inner circle will belong to the projection parallel to x, if R be greater than b, and will belong to the projection parallel to z if R be less than b; and if R be equal to b, the two circles will coincide with each other and with the

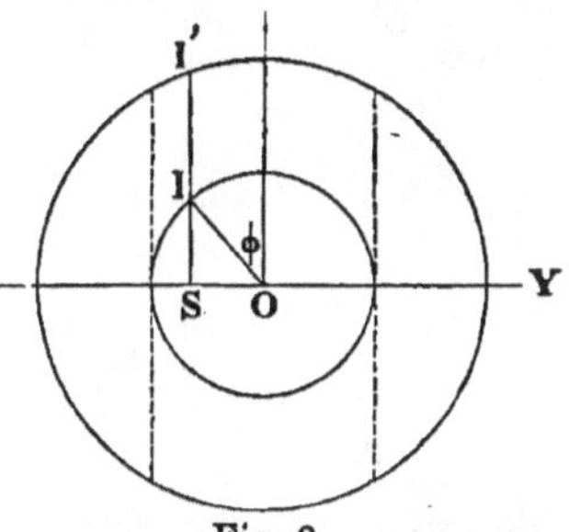

Fig. 2.

spherical conic, which in this case becomes the circular section of the ellipsoid. The projected point will revolve round the circumference of the inner circle, and will vibrate on the circumference of the outer circle between the dotted lines. It is evident that the mean axis of the ellipsoid OY lies in the plane of the figure. Let SI and SI′ be equal to ρ, ρ', and let C, C' denote the radii of the two circles: the velocities of the projections in the circles will evidently be

C and C' having the values

$$C = b\sqrt{\left(\frac{a^2 - R^2}{a^2 - b^2}\right)}, \quad C' = b\sqrt{\left(\frac{R^2 - c^2}{b^2 - c^2}\right)}.$$

The value of $\dfrac{dy}{dt}$ deduced from (1) is

$$\frac{dy}{dt} = P\omega\left(\frac{1}{c^2} - \frac{1}{a^2}\right)zx = P\omega\left(\frac{1}{c^2} - \frac{1}{a^2}\right)\rho\rho'\sin\theta\cos\theta.$$

θ being the angle made by the plane of the circular section with the plane (x, y),

$$\sin\theta = \frac{c}{b}\sqrt{\left(\frac{a^2 - b^2}{a^2 - c^2}\right)}, \quad \cos\theta = \frac{a}{b}\sqrt{\left(\frac{b^2 - c^2}{a^2 - c^2}\right)}.$$

Introducing these values of $\dfrac{dy}{dt}$, $\sin\theta$ and $\cos\theta$, and for $P\omega$ its

value $\dfrac{G}{\mu R}$, we obtain finally for the velocities

$$V = \frac{G}{\mu}\sqrt{\left\{\left(\frac{1}{R^2} - \frac{1}{a^2}\right)\left(\frac{1}{c^2} - \frac{1}{b^2}\right)\right\}}\,\rho' = K\rho';$$

$$V' = \frac{G}{\mu}\sqrt{\left\{\left(\frac{1}{R^2} - \frac{1}{c^2}\right)\left(\frac{1}{a^2} - \frac{1}{b^2}\right)\right\}}\,\rho = K'\rho. \tag{13}$$

The velocity of each projection, therefore, varies as the ordinate of the other. This theorem enables us to find a simple expression for the time. Using the angle (ϕ) marked in fig. 2, we obtain

$$\frac{Cd\phi}{dt} = K\sqrt{(C'^2 - C^2\sin^2\phi)};$$

(ϕ, C, K) belonging to the projection parallel to axis of x. If (ψ, C', K') be the corresponding quantities for the other projection, we obtain also

or, since it is easily seen that $\dfrac{K}{K'} = \dfrac{C}{C''}$, we obtain finally

$$K'dt = \frac{d\phi}{\sqrt{\left(1 - \dfrac{C'^2}{C''^2}\sin^2\phi\right)}}\,;$$

$$Kdt = \frac{d\psi}{\sqrt{\left(1 - \dfrac{C'^2}{C^2}\sin^2\psi\right)}}.$$

$$(14)$$

The motion of the principal axis of moments is, therefore, expressed by an elliptic function of the first kind.

The motion of the axis of moments is determined by the magnitude of the radius vector of the ellipsoid, which is the axis of the original couple impressed upon the body ; if this radius vector be greater than the mean axis of the ellipsoid, the corresponding spherical conic will have the axis of x for its internal axis ; and if the radius be less than the mean axis, the axis of z will be the internal axis of the conic ; in no case will the mean axis be the internal axis of the spherical conic. If the radius R be nearly equal to either the greatest or least semi-axis, the expression (14) for the time may be integrated. Let R be nearly equal to the greatest semi-axis. The first of the equations (14) belongs to the interior circle, which is of small dimensions in the case supposed ; the second equation expresses the vibratory motion of the projection, through a small arc of the outer circle, which will have a radius much greater than the inner circle ; we may, therefore, suppose the angle ψ to be equal to its sine.

Multiplying both sides of the equation by $\dfrac{C'}{C}$ we obtain.

$$\frac{C'K}{C}dt = Kdt\,\frac{\dfrac{C'}{C}d\psi}{\sqrt{\left(1 - \dfrac{C'^2}{C^2}\psi^2\right)}}.$$

Hence

$$\frac{C'\psi}{C} = \sin\,(K't + A).$$

$$(15)$$

If T_0 denote the time of a complete oscillation or revolution of the axis of moments about the axis of x, and T_r the time of a revolution of the body round the axis of x, the following relation between these two periods may be readily deduced from (15) :

$$T_0 = T_r \frac{bc}{\sqrt{\{(a^2 - b^2)\ (a^2 - c^2)\}}}. \tag{16}$$

If the axis of moments, and consequently the axis of revolution, be situated near the axis of greatest or least inertia, it will always continue near this axis ; if, however, it be situated near the mean axis, the movement of the body will be determined by the following construction :—Let the two cyclic planes of the ellipsoid be drawn through the mean axis; they will divide the ellipsoid into two regions, in one of which is situated the axis of maximum inertia, and in the other the axis of minimum inertia. The spherical conic described by the axis of principal moments will have the first or second of these axes for its internal axis, according as R is greater or less than the mean axis. If the axis of principal moments lie in one of the cyclic planes, the spherical conic becomes a circle, and its two projections become identical with itself (fig. 2, p. 339) ; the expressions (14) are reduced to the form

$$Kdt = \frac{d\phi}{\cos \phi} ;$$

which when integrated gives

$$Kt + A = \log \cot \left(\frac{\pi}{4} - \frac{\phi}{2}\right) ;$$

or,

$$\cot \left(\frac{\pi}{4} - \frac{\phi}{2}\right) = \cot \left(\frac{\pi}{4} - \frac{\phi_0}{2}\right) \epsilon^{Kt} ; \tag{17}$$

ϕ_0 being the value of ϕ corresponding to $t = 0$, and K being expressed by the following quantity :

$$K = \frac{G}{\mu} \frac{\sqrt{\{(a^2 - b^2)\ (b^2 - c^2)\}}}{b^2 ac}.$$

It is evident from the equation (17) that the axis of moments will coincide with the mean axis of inertia at the end of an infinite time.

IX.—To find the Position of the Body in Space at the End of any given Time.

First Method.

The radius vector of the ellipsoid of gyration, which is perpendicular to the plane containing the axes of principal moment and of rotation, always lies in the plane of principal moment, and describes in that plane areas proportional to the time.

Let OG, OΩ be the axes of principal moment and of rotation; OR′, OΩ′, the axes of centrifugal couple and of corresponding rotation; the plane ΩOΩ′ will contain the two successive positions of the axis of rotation. Let OI be the position of the axis of rotation at the end of the time δt; then δu will be equal to the angle described in the fixed plane by the line OR′. Let $R′$ and $P′$ be the radius vector and perpendicular corresponding to the centrifugal couple and its axis of rotation. The following relations are evident from the figure:

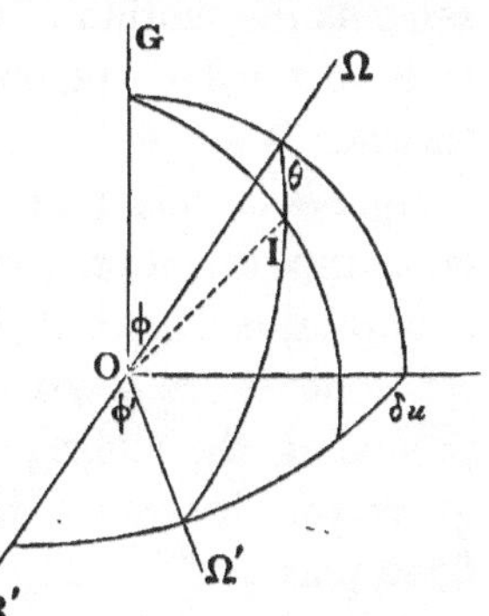

Fig. 3.

$$\frac{\omega}{\omega'} = - \frac{\sin \Omega'OI}{\sin \Omega OI} = \frac{\cos \phi'}{\sin \phi \delta u} ;$$

because

$$\sin \Omega'OI = \frac{\cos \phi'}{\sin \theta}, \quad \sin \Omega OI = \frac{\sin \phi \delta u}{\sin \theta} ;$$

but, from mechanical considerations,

$$\frac{\omega}{\omega'} = - \frac{P'R'}{PR\omega \sin \phi \delta t}; \quad \text{because} \quad \omega = \frac{G}{\mu PR}, \quad \omega' = - \frac{G\omega \sin \phi \delta t}{\mu P'R'}.$$

Hence, by equating the geometrical and mechanical expression, we obtain

$$- R'^2 \delta u = \omega PR \delta t = \frac{G}{\mu} \delta t. \tag{18}$$

The position of the body in space is thus reduced to quadratures; but the problem may be solved more readily in the following manner.

Second Method.

The axis of principal moments, appearing to move in a direction opposite to the rotation, describes in the body the cone whose equation has been given (11). If the cone reciprocal to this cone be described, one of its sides will lie in the fixed plane, and the whole motion of the body in space will be the same as the motion of this cone, which partly slides and partly rolls on the fixed plane, the sliding motion being uniform. This theorem is evident by resolving the angular velocity ω into two components, one round the axis of principal moments, and the other in a direction perpendicular to this, round the side of the reciprocal cone, which is in contact with the fixed plane. These components are $\omega \cos \phi$ and $\omega \sin \phi$; $\omega \cos \phi$ being constant and producing the sliding motion, while $\omega \sin \phi$ represents the angular velocity round the side of the cone in contact with the fixed plane. The angle described by the side of the reciprocal cone in the fixed plane at the end of a given time is, therefore, the algebraic sum of two angles, one of which is proportional to the time, and the other is the angle described in the cone in consequence of the rotation $\omega \sin \phi$, and is, therefore, measured by the arc of a spherical conic. The position of the body at the end of the time t is thus found:—determine by equation (14) the position of the axis of principal moments in the cone (11); the corresponding position of the component axis of rotation in the reciprocal cone is therefore known. Hence the angle described in the time t in the fixed plane is

$$\Theta = \int \omega \cos \phi\, dt \pm \int \frac{ds}{R} = \omega \cos \phi . t \pm \frac{s}{R}. \qquad (19)$$

The equation of the reciprocal cone is

In (19) the positive or negative sign must be used according as R is less or greater than the mean axis of the ellipsoid ; this is evident from the composition of rotations, and from the consideration that in the former case the axis of rotation falls inside the cone (11), while in the latter case it falls outside.

X.—To find a Point, if any, in a given Axis of Rotation, which being fixed, the Axis will be permanent.

Let R′R″ (fig. 4) be the given axis, round which the body revolves with a rotation expressed by ω ; describe the ellipsoid of gyration round the centre of gravity O, and draw OP′ parallel to R′R″.

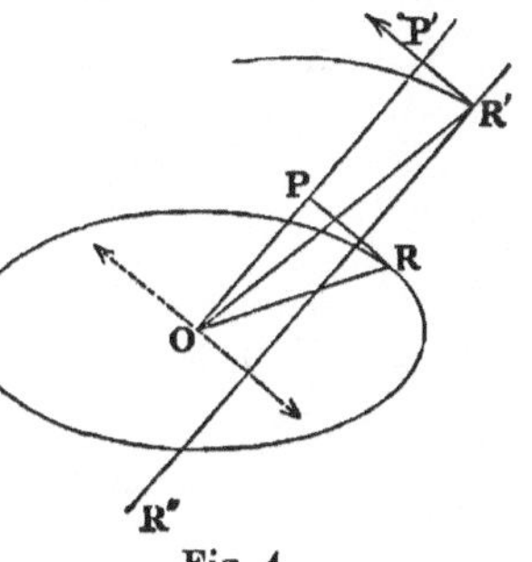

Fig. 4.

The centrifugal force $\omega^2 r\,dm$ at any point (x, y, z) may be resolved into two components, $\omega^2 \rho\,dm$ and $\omega^2 \cdot \mathrm{R'P'} \cdot dm$; r and ρ denoting the distances of the point from the axes R′R″ and OP′ respectively ; the effect of the rotation round R′R″ is therefore the same as an equal rotation round OP′, together with a number of parallel and equal forces applied to each point of the body. The rotation round OP′ produces a centrifugal couple represented by $-\mu\omega^2 \cdot \mathrm{OP} \cdot \mathrm{PR}$ (*vid.* (8)); or, determining the point R′ by the condition $\mathrm{OP} \cdot \mathrm{PR} = \mathrm{OP'} \cdot \mathrm{P'R'}$, the centrifugal couple is $-\mu\omega^2 \cdot \mathrm{OP'} \cdot \mathrm{P'R'}$. The resultant of the parallel forces is a force applied at the centre of gravity, acting in the direction parallel to R′P′, and equal to $\mu\omega^2 \cdot \mathrm{R'P'}$. Comparing this with the centrifugal couple, it is evident that the forces at O destroy each other, and, therefore, the total result of the rotation round R′R″ is to produce a force acting at the point R′, which has been just determined. If this point be fixed, the axis R′R″ will be a permanent axis of rotation. The condition by which the point R′ is found is, that the triangle OR′P′ is equal to and in the same plane with the triangle ORP : hence, if an ellipsoid confocal to the ellipsoid of gyration be described through the point R′, it will be perpendicular to the line R′R″. The general construction for permanent axes is, therefore, the following:—Let the ellipsoid of gyration be described, and confocal ellipsoids : any line which pierces one of these ellipsoids at right angles is a permanent axis of rotation for the point of intersection.

the nature of the surface or of the magnitude of the sphere; the only things supposed being that all the lines drawn from P meet the surface again but once, and that no part of it passes beyond a plane through P at right angles to PQ.

With respect to the limit of the quantity V'', it is obvious that if a hemisphere be described from P'' as a centre, with a radius equal to the greatest difference δ between the lines Pp, $P'p'$, the solid $P''p''$ will lie wholly within this hemisphere, and consequently V'' will be less than the value of V for the hemisphere, that is, less than $\pi\delta^2$; for here all the little pyramids from the centre have the same length δ, and their bases are spread over the hemispherical surface; wherefore $V'' = 2\pi \times \frac{1}{2}\delta^2 = \pi\delta^2$. All this is independent of anything but the supposition just mentioned.

If now PQ be supposed to be a spheroid of any sort, slightly differing from the sphere $P'Q'$, and such that the line PQ, perpendicular to the surface at P, passes nearly through the centre, then all the differences, of which δ is the greatest, being of the first order, the quantity V'', which is less than $\pi\delta^2$, will be of the second order; and therefore neglecting, as Laplace has done, the quantities of that order, we get the theorem in question.

It may be well to apply the general theorem to the simple case in which the first solid is a sphere of the radius a', because both Lagrange and Ivory have used this case to show that the reasonings of Laplace are incorrect. In this instance, then, the surface described by the point p'' is that of a sphere whose radius is the difference between a and a'; and the values of V, V', V'', and A, are $\frac{4}{3}\pi a'^2$, $\frac{4}{3}\pi a^2$, $\frac{4}{3}\pi (a' - a)^2$ and $\frac{4}{3}\pi a'$ respectively.

Substituting these values in the equation $V + V' - V'' = 2aA$, and omitting the common factor $\frac{4}{3}\pi$, the resulting equation

$$a'^2 + a^2 - (a' - a)^2 = 2aa'$$

ought to be identical; and so it manifestly is.

November, 1831.

II.—ON THE ATTRACTION OF ELLIPSOIDS, WITH A NEW DEMONSTRATION OF CLAIRAUT'S THEOREM, BEING AN ACCOUNT OF THE LATE PROFESSOR MAC CULLAGH'S LECTURES ON THOSE SUBJECTS. COMPILED BY GEORGE JOHNSTON ALLMAN, LL.D., OF TRINITY COLLEGE, DUBLIN.

[*Transactions of the Royal Irish Academy*, Vol. XXII. p. 379.—Read June 13, 1853.]

PROPOSITION I.

If P be any point on the surface of an ellipsoid, and PC_1 be drawn perpendicular to an axis OC, and an ellipsoid be described through C_1 concentric, similar, and similarly placed to the given ellipsoid; then the component of the attraction of the given ellipsoid on P in a direction parallel to OC is equal to the attraction of the inner ellipsoid on the point C_1.

This theorem is an extension of that given by Mac Laurin[*] relating to the attraction of a spheroid on a point placed on its surface. It may, moreover, be established by means of the same geometrical proposition from which MacLaurin deduced his theorem.

Through the point P let a chord PP′ of the given ellipsoid be drawn parallel to the axis OC. Now, suppose both ellipsoids to be divided into wedges by planes parallel to each other, and passing respectively through this chord and the parallel axis of the inner; and suppose the wedges to be divided into pyramids, the common vertex of one set being at P, and of the other at C_1.

---

[*] *De caus. Phys. Flux. et Refl. Maris*, sect. 3; or see Airy's Tract on the *Figure of the Earth*, Prop. 8.

Observing that any two of these parallel planes cut the two surfaces in similar ellipses, such that the semi-axis of one is equal to the parallel ordinate of the other, it is easy to see that

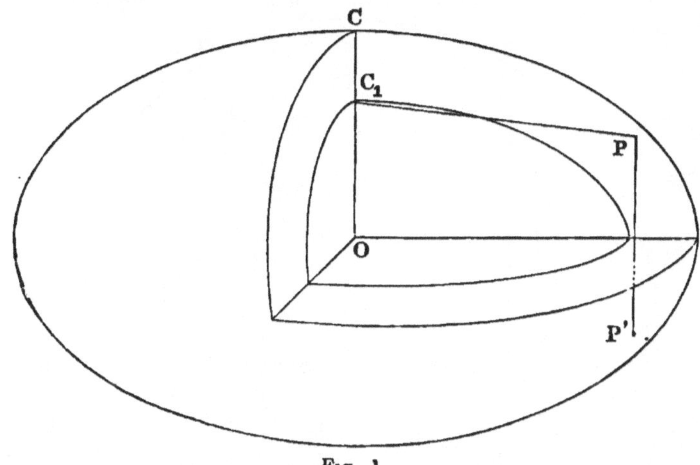

Fig. 1.

the reasoning employed by Mac Laurin may be used to establish the truth of the theorem stated above.

PROPOSITION II.

*To calculate the Attraction of an Ellipsoid on a Point placed at the extremity of an Axis.**

Let the semi-axes of the ellipsoid be a, b, c, where $a > b > c$, and let the point on which it is required to find the attraction be C (Fig. 1), the extremity of the least axis.

Suppose the ellipsoid to be divided by a series of cones of revolution which have a common vertex C and a common axis CC', C' being the vertex of the ellipsoid opposite to C; it will be sufficient to find an expression for the attraction of the part of the ellipsoid contained between two consecutive conical surfaces, whose semi-angles are θ and $\theta + d\theta$ respectively. Suppose now the part of the ellipsoid between two consecutive cones to be divided into

* *Proceedings* of the Royal Irish Academy, Vol. III. p. 367.

elementary pyramids with a common vertex C. Let CP be one of these elementary pyramids, whose solid angle is ω; let PQ be drawn perpendicular to CC'; from the centre O draw a radius

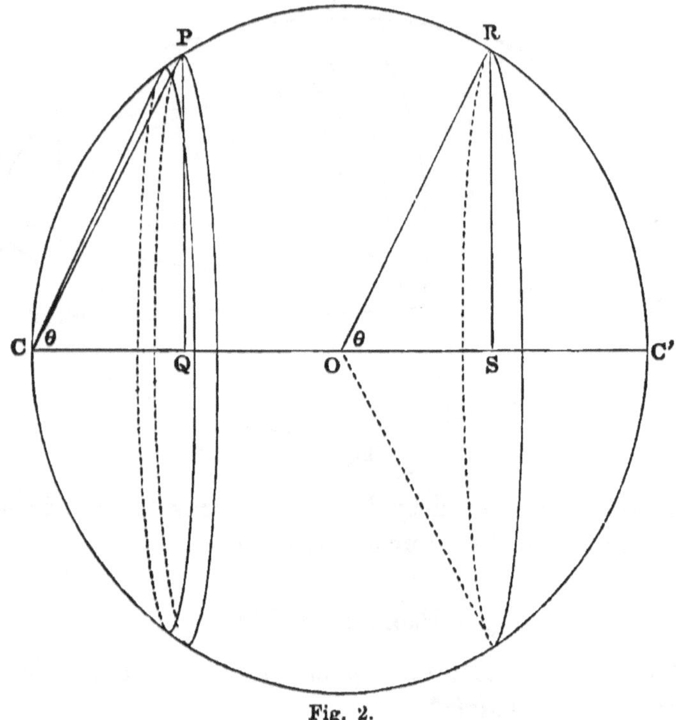

Fig. 2.

vector OR parallel to CP, and from the extremity R let fall a perpendicular RS on the axis CC'.

Now the attraction of the elementary pyramid CP on the material point μ, placed at its vertex $= \mu f \rho \omega . \text{CP}$; and the component of this attraction in the direction of the axis is

$$\mu f \rho \omega . \text{CQ} = 2\mu f \rho \omega . \frac{\overline{\text{OR}}^2 \cos^2 \theta}{c}.$$

Now suppose the radius vector OR to revolve around the axis OC', then the attraction on the point C of the portion of the ellipsoid bounded by the two cones of revolution, whose semi-angles are θ and $\theta + d\theta$ respectively, since it is made up of the components in the direction CC' of the attractions of all the elementary pyramids CP, is

$$\frac{2\mu f\rho}{c} \cos^2\theta . \Sigma (\overline{OR}^2 \omega) = \frac{2\mu f\rho}{c} \cos^2\theta \, d\theta . \Sigma (\overline{OR}^2 d\phi),$$

$d\phi$ being the angle between two consecutive sides of the cone generated by the revolution of OR.

But $\Sigma (\overline{OR}^2 d\phi)$ is equal to twice the superficial area of the part of this cone which is enclosed within the ellipsoid. Moreover, the projection on the plane ab of this portion of the surface of the cone is an ellipse, whose semi-axes are $r_1 \sin\theta$, $r_2 \sin\theta$, and whose area is $\pi r_1 r_2 \sin^2\theta$, r_1 and r_2 being the maximum and minimum values of OR : the superficial area of the portion of the cone within the ellipsoid is therefore $\pi r_1 r_2 \sin\theta$.

Hence it follows that

$$\Sigma (\overline{OR}^2 d\phi) = 2\pi r_1 r_2 \sin\theta.$$

The attraction on the point C of the part of the ellipsoid contained between the two cones of revolution, whose common vertex is at C, and whose semi-angles are θ and $\theta + d\theta$ respectively, is therefore

$$\frac{4\pi\mu f\rho}{c} \cos^2\theta \, d\theta . r_1 r_2 \sin\theta,$$

where

$$\frac{1}{r_1} = \sqrt{\left(\frac{\cos^2\theta}{c^2} + \frac{\sin^2\theta}{a^2}\right)}, \quad \text{and} \quad \frac{1}{r_2} = \sqrt{\left(\frac{\cos^2\theta}{c^2} + \frac{\sin^2\theta}{b^2}\right)}.$$

On substituting these values, the expression given above becomes

$$4\pi\mu f\rho \, \frac{abc \cos^2\theta \sin\theta \, d\theta}{\sqrt{(a^2 \cos^2\theta + c^2 \sin^2\theta)} \sqrt{(b^2 \cos^2\theta + c^2 \sin^2\theta)}}.$$

Hence the attraction of the solid ellipsoid on the point C at the extremity of the least axis is

$$4\pi\mu f\rho \int_0^{\frac{\pi}{2}} \frac{abc \cos^2\theta \sin\theta \, d\theta}{\sqrt{(a^2 \cos^2\theta + c^2 \sin^2\theta)} \sqrt{(b^2 \cos^2\theta + c^2 \sin^2\theta)}}.$$

Let $\cos \theta = u$, this expression becomes

$$4\pi\mu f\rho \int_0^1 \frac{abc\, u^2\, du}{\sqrt{\{c^2 + u^2 (a^2 - c^2)\}} \, \sqrt{\{c^2 + u^2 (b^2 - c^2)\}}}. \qquad (1)$$

In the same way it may be shown that the attraction of the ellipsoid on a point μ placed at the extremity of the mean axis is

$$4\pi\mu f\rho \int_0^1 \frac{abc\, u^2\, du}{\sqrt{\{b^2 + u^2 (c^2 - b^2)\}} \, \sqrt{\{b^2 + u^2 (a^2 - b^2)\}}} ;$$

and on a point at the extremity of the greatest axis,

$$4\pi\mu f\rho \int_0^1 \frac{abc\, u^2\, du}{\sqrt{\{a^2 + u^2 (b^2 - a^2)\}} \, \sqrt{\{a^2 + u^2 (c^2 - a^2)\}}}.$$

It will be seen in a subsequent proposition, that these three expressions are not independent of each other, the values of the three attractions in question being connected by an equation.

Proposition III.

*To give Geometrical Representations of the Attraction of an Ellipsoid on Points placed at the extremities of its least and mean Axes.**

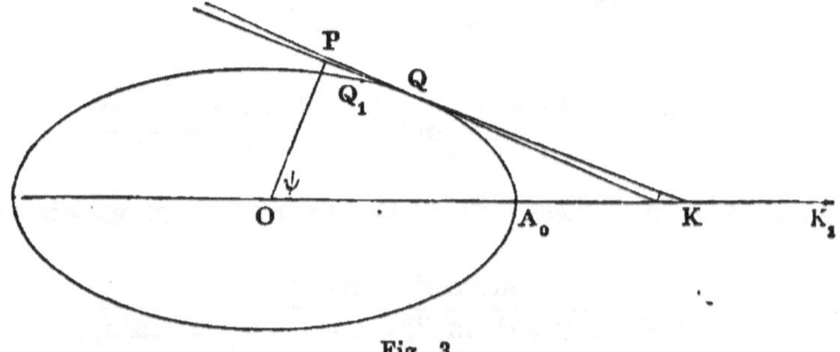

Fig. 3.

On the greater axis OA_0 of the focal ellipse assume a point K_1 such that $OK_1 = \dfrac{b}{c}\, OA_0$; from the point K_1 draw a tangent

* *Proceedings* of the Royal Irish Academy, Vol. iii. p. 367.

K_1Q_1 to the focal ellipse, and let $T = \tan K_1Q_1 - \text{arc } A_0Q_1$; then the attraction of the ellipsoid on the particle μ placed at the extremity C of the least axis is

$$\frac{4\pi\,\mu f \rho\, abc^2}{(a^2 - c^2)\,(b^2 - c^2)}\; T. \tag{2}$$

For let a point K (see fig. 3) be assumed on the greater axis OA_0 of the focal ellipse, such that

$$OK = \frac{OA_0}{c}\,\sqrt{\{c^2 + u^2\,(b^2 - c^2)\}}\;;$$

from K let a tangent KQ be drawn to the focal ellipse, and let OP be the perpendicular let fall from O and KQ; then ψ denoting the angle A_0OP,

$$\overline{OK}^2 . \cos^2\psi = \frac{a^2 - c^2}{c^2}\,\{c^2 + u^2\,(b^2 - c^2)\} . \cos^2\psi.$$

Moreover,

$$\overline{OK}^2 . \cos^2\psi = \overline{OP}^2 = (a^2 - c^2)\cos^2\psi + (b^2 - c^2)\sin^2\psi.$$

Equating these values, and solving for $\sin^2\psi$, we get

$$\sin^2\psi = \frac{(a^2 - c^2)\,u^2}{c^2 + u^2\,(a^2 - c^2)}.$$

Now

$$d . (\tan KQ - \text{arc } A_0Q) = \sin\psi\,d . OK^*$$

$$= \frac{(a^2 - c^2)\,(b^2 - c^2)}{c}\,\frac{u^2\,du}{\sqrt{\{c^2 + u^2\,(a^2 - c^2)\}}\,\sqrt{\{c^2 + u^2\,(b^2 - c^2)\}}}.$$

By comparing this expression with (1), given in the last proposition, it appears that the attraction on the point C of the portion of the ellipsoid contained between the two conical surfaces whose semi-angles are θ and $\theta + d\theta$, respectively, is

$$\frac{4\pi\mu f\rho\, abc^2}{(a^2 - c^2)\,(b^2 - c^2)}\, d . (\tan KQ - \text{arc } A_0Q).$$

---

* *Transactions* of the Royal Irish Academy, Vol. XVI. p. 79. *Proceedings* of the Royal Irish Academy, Vol. II. p. 507 (*supra*, p. 255).

Now, in order to obtain the attraction of the whole ellipsoid on the point C, we have to integrate the expression given above between the limits $u = 0$ and $u = 1$, or $OK = OA_0$ and $OK = OK_1$; from which it appears that its value is

$$\frac{4\pi\mu f\rho\, abc^2}{(a^2 - c^2)\,(b^2 - c^2)}\, T.$$

It is easy to see that the attraction of the part of the ellipsoid contained within the conical surface, whose semi-angle θ is equal to the angle $\cos^{-1} u$, is

$$4\pi\mu f\rho\, \frac{abc^2}{(a^2 - c^2)\,(b^2 - c^2)}\,(T - t), \tag{3}$$

where $t = \tan KQ - \text{arc } A_0Q$.

To represent the attraction on a point μ placed at the extremity of the mean axis, assume on the transverse OA_0 of the focal hyperbola a point K_1 such that $OK_1 = OA_0\,\dfrac{c}{b}$, and from K_1 draw a tangent K_1Q_1 to the hyperbola, and let $T = \tan K_1Q_1 - \text{arc } A_0Q_1$; then the attraction of the ellipsoid on the point μ is

$$- 4\pi\mu f\rho\, \frac{ab^2c}{(a^2 - b^2)\,(c^2 - b^2)}\, T. \tag{4}$$

To prove this, assume a point K such that

$$OK = \frac{OA_0}{b}\,\sqrt{\{b^2 + u^2\,(c^2 - b^2)\}};$$

from K draw a tangent KQ to the hyperbola, and from O let fall a perpendicular OP on this tangent; then if $\psi = $ angle A_0OP,

$$\sin^2\psi = \frac{(a^2 - b^2)\,u^2}{b^2 + u^2\,(a^2 - b^2)}.$$

Hence, by following a method similar to that used in finding the representation of the attraction on a point at the extremity of the least axis, the expression given above may be easily obtained.

The attractions C, B of the ellipsoid on points placed at the extremity of the least and mean axes are thus represented by means of arcs of the focal ellipse and hyperbola respectively. In consequence of the third focal conic of the ellipsoid being imaginary, no direct geometrical representation can be given for the attraction A on a point placed at the extremity of its greatest axis. It will, however, be found, as was intimated above, that a simple relation exists between the three attractions, which enables us to represent this last by means of arcs of both focal conics.

The relation alluded to is

$$\frac{A}{a} + \frac{B}{b} + \frac{C}{c} = 4\pi\mu f\rho.^{*} \tag{5}$$

This can be easily proved by the help of the following geometrical theorem :—

If from the extremities A, B, C of the three axes of an ellipsoid three parallel chords Ap, Bq, Cr, be drawn, and if these chords be projected each on the axis from whose extremity it is drawn, then the sum of these three projections, $A\alpha$, $B\beta$, $C\gamma$, divided respectively by the lengths of the axes AA′, BB′, CC′, on which they are measured, will be equal to unity.

Now conceive three chords Ap, Ap', Ap'', to be drawn from A, making each with the other two very small angles, and so forming a pyramid with a very small vertical solid angle ω; and from B and C let two systems of chords Bq, Bq', Bq'', and Cr, Cr', Cr'', be drawn, each system forming a very small pyramid whose three edges are parallel to the three edges Ap, Ap', Ap'', of the pyramid which has its vertex at A.

The attractions of the three pyramids, reduced each to the direction of the axis passing through its vertex, will be equal to $\mu f\rho\omega . A\alpha$, $\mu f\rho\omega . B\beta$, $\mu f\rho\omega . C\gamma$ respectively; and, therefore, the sum of those attractions divided respectively by the lengths of the axes will be

$$\mu f\rho\omega \left(\frac{A\alpha}{AA'} + \frac{B\beta}{BB'} + \frac{C\gamma}{CC'} \right) = \mu f\rho\omega.$$

* *Proceedings* of the Royal Irish Academy, Vol. ii. p. 525.

Let pyramids thus related be indefinitely multiplied, and the ellipsoid will be simultaneously exhausted from the three points A, B, C.

Hence the sum of the whole attractions at A, B, C, divided respectively by the lengths of the corresponding axes, will be $2\pi\mu f\rho$, or,

$$\frac{A}{a} + \frac{B}{b} + \frac{C}{c} = 4\pi\mu f\rho.$$

PROPOSITION IV.

To find an expression for the potential V of a system of particles at a point M, whose distance from the centre of gravity of the system is very great compared with the mutual distances of the particles.

It is proved by Poisson,[*] that if the origin of co-ordinates be at the centre of gravity of the system

$$V = \frac{M}{r'} + \frac{3}{2r'^5}\,\Sigma\,(xx' + yy' + zz')^2\,dm - \frac{1}{2r'^3}\,\Sigma\,(x^2 + y^2 + z^2)\,dm,$$

x', y', z' being the co-ordinates of the distant point, and r' its distance from the origin. Let now the principal axes at that centre be taken as axes of co-ordinates; then, since

$$\Sigma xy\,dm = 0, \quad \Sigma xz\,dm = 0, \quad \Sigma yz\,dm = 0\,;$$

$$V = \frac{M}{r'} + \frac{3}{2r'^5}\,\Sigma\,(x^2 x'^2 + y^2 y'^2 + z^2 z'^2)\,dm - \frac{1}{2r'^3}\,\Sigma\,(x^2 + y^2 + z^2)\,dm.$$

Hence, if A, B, C be the three principal moments of inertia, and I the moment of inertia of the system round OM,

$$V = \frac{M}{r'} + \frac{1}{2r'^3}\,(A + B + C - 3I). \tag{6}$$

* *Mecanique*, tom. i. p. 178.

Proposition V.

A system of material particles attracts a point **M**, *whose distance from the centre of gravity* O *of the attracting system is very great compared with the mutual distances of the particles; then if a tangent plane be drawn to the " ellipsoid of gyration,"* perpendicular to* OM, *the whole attraction lies in the plane* OST, *where* S *is the point in which this tangent plane intersects* OM, *and* T *its point of contact with the ellipsoid.*

Let a, β, γ be the direction angles of OT ; a', β', γ' of OM ; and a_1, β_1, γ_1 of TS ; and a_0, β_0, γ_0 of the normal to the

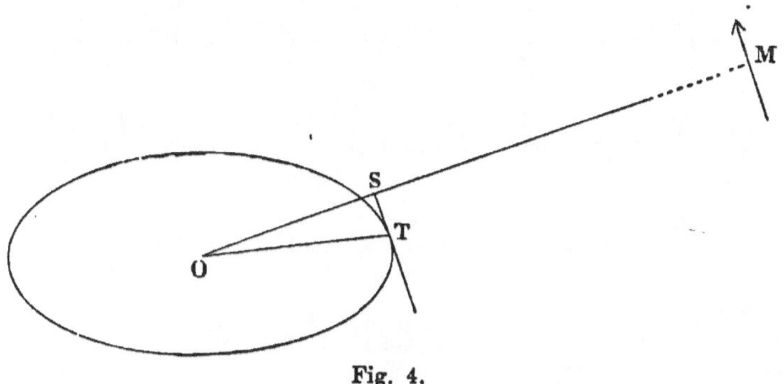

Fig. 4.

plane OST ; and let OS, OT and the angle SOT, be denoted by p, r, and ϕ respectively. It will be sufficient to prove that the component Q of the attraction in the direction of the normal to the plane OST is zero.

We shall first find the components X, Y, Z, of the attraction in the directions of the axes, and thence deduce the value of Q.

---

* The centre of this ellipsoid is at the centre of gravity ; its axes are in the directions of the principal axes, and their lengths are determined by the equations

$$Ma^2 = A, \quad Mb^2 = B, \quad Mc^2 = C.$$

This ellipsoid is used by Professor Mac Cullagh in his " Theory of Rotation ": *see* Rev. S. Haughton's Account of Professor Mac Cullagh's Lectures on that subject, *Transactions* R. I. A., Vol. xxii. p. 139 (*supra*, p. 329).

Now,

$$X = -\frac{dV}{dx'} = \frac{M}{r'^2}\cos\alpha' + \frac{3}{2r'^4}(A+B+C-3I)\cos\alpha' + \frac{3}{2r'^3}\frac{dI}{dx'},$$

$$Y = -\frac{dV}{dy'} = \frac{M}{r'^2}\cos\beta' + \frac{3}{2r'^4}(A+B+C-3I)\cos\beta' + \frac{3}{2r'^3}\frac{dI}{dy'},$$

$$Z = -\frac{dV}{dz'} = \frac{M}{r'^2}\cos\gamma' + \frac{3}{2r'^4}(A+B+C-3I)\cos\gamma' + \frac{3}{2r'^3}\frac{dI}{dz'};$$

but,

$$\frac{dI}{dx'} = \frac{2(A-I)\cos\alpha'}{r'}; \quad \frac{dI}{dy'} = \frac{2(B-I)\cos\beta'}{r'}; \quad \frac{dI}{dz'} = \frac{2(C-I)\cos\gamma'}{r'}.$$

Hence we have

$$X = \frac{M}{r'^2}\cos\alpha' + \frac{3}{2r'^4}(A+B+C-5I)\cos\alpha' + \frac{3A\cos\alpha'}{r'^4},$$

$$Y = \frac{M}{r'^2}\cos\beta' + \frac{3}{2r'^4}(A+B+C-5I)\cos\beta' + \frac{3B\cos\beta'}{r'^4}, \quad (7)$$

$$Z = \frac{M}{r'^2}\cos\gamma' + \frac{3}{2r'^4}(A+B+C-5I)\cos\gamma' + \frac{3C\cos\gamma'}{r'^4}.$$

Now,

$$Q = X\cos\alpha_0 + Y\cos\beta_0 + Z\cos\gamma_0;$$

but,

$$\sin\phi\,\cos\alpha_0 = \cos\beta\,\cos\gamma' - \cos\gamma\,\cos\beta,$$

$$\sin\phi\,\cos\beta_0 = \cos\gamma\,\cos\alpha' - \cos\alpha\,\cos\gamma',$$

$$\sin\phi\,\cos\gamma_0 = \cos\alpha\,\cos\beta' - \cos\beta\,\cos\alpha';$$

The following relations, moreover, exist :

$$a^2\cos\alpha' = rp\,\cos\alpha, \quad b^2\cos\beta' = rp\,\cos\beta, \quad c^2\cos\gamma' = rp\,\cos\gamma : \quad (8)$$

hence, by substitution, we have

$$\cos\alpha_0 = \frac{b^2-c^2}{pr\sin\phi}\cos\beta'\cos\gamma', \quad \cos\beta_0 = \frac{c^2-a^2}{pr\sin\phi}\cos\gamma'\cos\alpha',$$

$$\cos\gamma_0 = \frac{a^2-b^2}{pr\sin\phi}\cos\alpha'\cos\beta'.$$

Substituting these values for $\cos a_0$, $\cos \beta_0$, $\cos \gamma_0$, in the expression for Q, and observing that

$$\cos a' \cos a_0 + \cos \beta' \cos \beta_0 + \cos \gamma' \cos \gamma_0 = 0,$$

we get

$$Q = \frac{3M}{r'^4} \frac{a^2(b^2-c^2)+b^2(c^2-a^2)+c^2(a^2-b^2)}{pr \sin \phi} \cos a' \cos \beta' \cos \gamma' = 0. \quad (9)$$

Proposition VI.

The same things being supposed, to find the other Components of the Attraction, namely R in the direction of the centre of gravity MO, and P in the transverse direction TS.

To find R; ·

$$R = X \cos a' + Y \cos \beta' + Z \cos \gamma';$$

$$\therefore R = \frac{M}{r'^2} + \frac{3}{2r'^4}(A + B + C - 5I) + \frac{3I}{r'^4},$$

or

$$R = \frac{M}{r'^2} + \frac{3}{2r'^4}(A + B + C - 3I). \quad (10)$$

To find P;

$$P = X \cos a_1 + Y \cos \beta_1 + Z \cos \gamma_1;$$

but,

$$\sin \phi \cos a_1 = \cos a' \cos \phi - \cos a,$$

$$\sin \phi \cos \beta_1 = \cos \beta' \cos \phi - \cos \beta,$$

$$\sin \phi \cos \gamma_1 = \cos \gamma' \cos \phi - \cos \gamma.$$

Substituting for $\cos a$, $\cos \beta$, $\cos \gamma$ their values from (8), we get

$$\cos a_1 = - \frac{a^2 - p^2}{pr \sin \phi} \cos a', \quad \cos \beta_1 = - \frac{b^2 - p^2}{pr \sin \phi} \cos \beta',$$

$$\cos \gamma_1 = - \frac{c^2 - p^2}{pr \sin \phi} \cos \gamma'.$$

Substituting these values of $\cos a_1$, $\cos \beta_1$, $\cos \gamma_1$, and observing that

$$\cos a' \cos a_1 + \cos \beta' \cos \beta_1 + \cos \gamma' \cos \gamma_1 = 0,$$

we have

$$P = - \frac{3M}{r'^4} \frac{p^2(r^2-p^2)}{pr\sin\phi} = -\frac{3M}{r'^4} pr \sin\phi\;;$$

or,

$$P = -\frac{3M}{r'^4} OS \times ST. \tag{11}$$

The negative sign indicates* that the force P acts in the direction TS, *i.e.* from the radius vector towards the perpendicular of the ellipsoid of gyration. If the force P be resolved into three others in the direction of the axes, it is evident from the values given in Proposition V. for X, Y, Z, that these components are

$$\frac{3(A-I)}{r'^4}\cos a', \qquad \frac{3(B-I)}{r'^4}\cos\beta', \qquad \frac{3(C-I)}{r'^4}\cos\gamma'.\dagger \tag{12}$$

---

* The direction of the force P, which Professor Mac Cullagh determines by the interpretation of the negative sign, may be very clearly seen from the following considerations. This force exists in every case where the three principal moments of inertia of the system at O are not all equal, that is, when the ellipsoid of gyration is not a sphere. The greatest axis of that ellipsoid is manifestly towards that part of the body in which there is a deficiency of attracting matter. If we now consider the position of a perpendicular on a tangent plane of an ellipsoid with relation to the corresponding radius vector, we shall find that it always lies away from the greatest axis. But the transverse force has been shown to be in the plane of radius vector and perpendicular. Therefore, the direction of the transverse force, being towards the preponderating matter, must be from T to S.

† The results given by Professor Mac Cullagh in Propositions V. and VI. may be otherwise obtained, and, perhaps, with greater facility, by introducing the consideration of the *statical moment* of the attracting force. *

If the three principal moments of inertia were equal to each other, then the whole attraction would be in the direction of the centre of gravity, and its magnitude would be

$$\frac{M}{r'^2}.$$

In general, however, the attracting mass will be of an irregular shape ; there will exist then, in addition to the principal part of the attraction, which will be central, a transverse force which will tend to cause a motion of rotation about the centre of gravity.

The components of the moment of this transverse force in the three principal planes are

$$x'Y - y'X, \quad y'Z - z'Y, \quad z'X - x'Z;$$

* See Rev. R. Townsend, in the " Dublin University Examination Papers," 1849, p. 51.

Proposition VII.

An Ellipsoid is composed of ellipsoidal strata of different densities and of variable but small ellipticities ; to find the Components, central and transverse, of its Attraction on an external point.

The values found in the last Proposition for the components of the attraction of any mass on a very distant point will be found to hold in the present case, whatever be the position of the attracted point. In order to show this, we shall first prove it for a homogeneous ellipsoid of small ellipticities. Such an ellipsoid being given, another confocal with it can be constructed so small, that the distance to the attracted point may be

---

but from (7),

$$x'Y - y'X = - \frac{3(A - B)}{r'^3} \cos \alpha' \cos \beta' = - \frac{3M}{r'^3} (a^2 - b^2) \cos \alpha' \cos \beta',$$

$$y'Z - z'Y = - \frac{3(B - C)}{r'^3} \cos \beta' \cos \gamma' = - \frac{3M}{r'^3} (b^2 - c^2) \cos \beta' \cos \gamma',$$

$$z'X - x'Z = - \frac{3(C - A)}{r'^3} \cos \gamma' \cos \alpha' = - \frac{3M}{r'^3} (c^2 - a^2) \cos \gamma' \cos \alpha'.$$

Now it is well known, that

$$\tfrac{1}{2}(a^2 - b^2) \cos \alpha' \cos \beta', \quad \tfrac{1}{2}(b^2 - c^2) \cos \beta' \cos \gamma', \quad \tfrac{1}{2}(c^2 - a^2) \cos \gamma' \cos \alpha',$$

are the areas of the projections of the triangle OST on the principal planes. Hence it follows that the resultant moment lies in the plane of the radius vector OT and the perpendicular OS to the corresopnding tangent plane of the ellipsoid of gyration ; the tangent plane being perpendicular to OM. It appears, also, that the magnitude of the resultant moment is

$$- \frac{3M}{r'^3} \text{OS} \times \text{ST},$$

and therefore that the transverse component of the attraction

$$P = - \frac{3M}{r'^4} \text{OS} \times \text{ST}.$$

Or, the values of the central force and the moment of the transverse force may be obtained directly from the expression (6) for the potential V. This function is of such a nature, that its differential coefficient with relation to any line (the sign being changed) is equal to the resolved part of the attraction in that direction ; and the differential coefficient with relation to any angle (the sign being changed as

regarded as very great, compared with the axes of this ellipsoid. The components of the attraction of this small ellipsoid on the distant point are given by the expressions (10) and (11): now as the attractions of two confocal ellipsoids on an external point are in the same direction, and proportional to their masses: the components of the attraction of the proposed ellipsoid will, therefore, be

$$R = \frac{M}{r'^2} + \frac{3}{2r'^4}\,\frac{M}{M_1}\,(A_1 + B_1 + C_1 - 3I_1),$$

$$P = -\frac{3M}{r'^4}\,S_1 \times OS_1T_1 ;$$

the letters with suffixes referring to the small ellipsoid.

The attracting ellipsoids being confocal, their ellipsoids of gyration are confocal also; hence it follows that

$$\frac{M}{M_1}\,(A_1 + B_1 + C_1 - 3I_1) = A + B + C - 3I,$$

and

$$OS_1 \times S_1T_1 = OS \times ST.$$

---

before) gives the component in the plane of that angle of the moment of the attractive force.

Hence,

$$R = -\frac{dV}{dr'} = \frac{M}{r'^2} + \frac{3}{2r'^4}\,(A + B + C - 3I),$$

since

$$\frac{dI}{dr'} = 0.$$

Again, if N be the component of the moment of the attractive force round OZ,

$$N = -\left(x'\,\frac{d}{dy'} - y'\,\frac{d}{dx'}\right)V ;$$

but

$$\left(x'\,\frac{d}{dy'} - y'\,\frac{d}{dx'}\right)F(x'^2 + y'^2) = 0 \text{ where } F \text{ is any function ;}$$

$$\therefore N = \frac{3}{2r'^3}\left(x'\,\frac{d}{dy'} - y'\,\frac{d}{dx'}\right) = \frac{3}{2r'^3}\left(x'\,\frac{d}{dy'} - y'\,\frac{d}{dx'}\right)\left(\frac{Ax'^2 + By'^2 + Cz'^2}{r'^2}\right) ;$$

$$\therefore N = -\frac{3\,(A - B)}{r'^3}\,(\cos \alpha' \cos \beta').$$

The two other components of the moment may be similarly obtained. The remainder of the proof is the same as in the former part of this note.

It appears, from this, that the central and transverse components of the attraction of a solid ellipsoid of uniform density, and whose ellipticities are small, on any external point whatever, are given by the same formulæ as the corresponding components of the action of any mass on a distant point.

Now it is a property of moments of inertia, that they are *subtractive*, that is, the difference of the moments of inertia of two masses with relation to any axis is equal to the moment of inertia of the difference of those masses with relation to the same axis. And the values at which we have arrived for the central force, and for the three components of the transverse force, contain in each term either a mass or a moment of inertia in the first power, and therefore, these values also are subtractive. Hence the two components of the attraction of a homogeneous mass contained between two concentric and coaxal ellipsoids of small ellipticities, are given by formulæ (10) and (11). Now suppose an ellipsoidal mass to be composed of strata bounded by ellipsoids of different but small ellipticities, each stratum being homogeneous throughout its extent, while the density varies from one stratum to another according to any law; then, since those formulæ hold for the action of each stratum separately, and since the terms of which they are made up are in their nature *additive*, they hold for the entire mass.*

Proposition VIII.

An oblate Spheroid is composed of spheroidal strata of different densities and of variable but small ellipticities; to find the Components of its Attraction on any external point.

The expressions given in the last Proposition for R and P become simplified in this case. Let OZ be the axis of revolution, and let λ denote the angle which OM makes with the plane

---

* See Professor Mac Cullagh, in the "Dublin University Examination Papers," 1833, p. 268.

XY ; then since A and B are equal, we have

$$I = A \cos^2 \lambda + C \sin^2 \lambda ;$$

and therefore

$$A + B + C - 3I = (C - A)(1 - 3 \sin^2 \lambda) ;$$

also

$$M\,\text{OS} \times \text{OT} = (A - C) \sin \lambda \cos \lambda.$$

Substituting these values in the expressions for R and P, we have

$$R = \frac{M}{r'^2} + \frac{3}{2} \frac{C - A}{r'^4} (1 - 3 \sin^2 \lambda), \tag{13}$$

$$P = 3 \frac{C - A}{r'^4} \cos \lambda \sin \lambda. \tag{14}$$

The direction of the force P is towards the plane of the equator ; this appears from the shape of the "ellipsoid of gyration," which in this case is a prolate surface of revolution.

Proposition IX.—Clairaut's Theorem.

Whatever be the law of variation of the Earth's density at different distances from the centre, if the ellipticity of the surface be added to the ratio which the excess of the polar above the equatorial gravity bears to the equatorial gravity, their sum will be $\dfrac{5}{2} q$, where q is the ratio of the centrifugal force at Equator to equatorial gravity.

For suppose the attracted point M to be on the surface of the earth, which is known to be an oblate spheroid of small ellipticity. Then, from the principles of Hydrostatics, since the tangential force is zero, we have

$$R \cos \theta - P \sin \theta - \omega^2 r \cos \lambda \cos (\theta - \lambda) = 0, \tag{15}$$

where ω denotes the angular velocity, and θ the angle which the tangent to the meridian through the attracted point makes with the radius vector. Developing $\cos (\theta - \lambda)$ and arranging, we obtain

$$(R - \omega^2 r \cos^2 \lambda) \cos \theta = (P + \omega^2 r \cos \lambda \sin \lambda) \sin \theta. \tag{16}$$

But, from the property of the elliptic section made by the plane of the meridian, we have

$$\cot \theta = \frac{e^2 \sin \lambda \cos \lambda}{1 - e^2 \cos^2 \lambda} = 2\epsilon \sin \lambda \cos \lambda, \quad q. \, p.,$$

where e is the excentricity and ϵ the ellipticity of this ellipse.

Substituting in (16) this value of $\cot \theta$, and the values of R and P from (13) and (14), the equation of equilibrium becomes

$$\left\{ \frac{M}{r^2} + \frac{3}{2} \frac{C-A}{r^4} (1 - 3 \sin^2 \lambda) - \omega^2 r \cos^2 \lambda \right\} 2\epsilon \sin \lambda \cos \lambda$$

$$= \left(3 \frac{C-A}{r^4} + \omega^2 r \right) \sin \lambda \cos \lambda,$$

or, approximately,

$$\left\{ \frac{M}{a^2} + \frac{3}{2} \frac{C-A}{a^4} (1 - 3 \sin^2 \lambda) - \omega^2 a \cos^2 \lambda \right\} 2\epsilon = 3 \frac{C-A}{a^4} + \omega^2 a.$$

If we neglect quantities of the second order, this equation becomes

$$\frac{2\epsilon M}{a^2} = 3 \frac{C-A}{a^4} + \omega^2 a. \qquad (17)$$

We have thus arrived at a relation which enables us to express the unknown quantity $C - A$, in terms of quantities which are all known, and, therefore, to eliminate the former from any other equation in which it may occur.

Now let R_e and R_p denote the equatorial and polar attractions respectively; we have from the general value of R (13),

$$R_e = \frac{M}{a^2} + \frac{3}{2} \frac{C-A}{a^4},$$

$$R_p = \frac{M}{c^2} - 3 \frac{C-A}{c^4} ;$$

but

$$c = a (1 - \epsilon) \therefore \frac{1}{c^2} = \frac{1}{a^2} (1 + 2\epsilon) \text{ and } \frac{1}{c^4} = \frac{1}{a^4} (1 + 4\epsilon)$$

$$\therefore R_p = \frac{M}{a^2} + \frac{2M\epsilon}{a^2} - 3 \frac{C-A}{a^4}.$$

But

$$G_p = R_p \text{ and } G_e = R_e - \omega^2 a;$$

$$\therefore\ G_p - G_e = \frac{2\varepsilon M}{a^2} - \frac{9}{2}\frac{C-A}{a^4} + \omega^2 a.$$

Eliminating $\dfrac{C-A}{a^4}$ by means of equation (17), we get

$$\frac{G_p - G_e}{G_e} = -\,\varepsilon + \frac{5}{2}\frac{\omega^2 a}{G_e};$$

or

$$\frac{G_p - G_e}{G_e} + \varepsilon = \frac{5}{2}q. \tag{18}$$

SUPPLEMENT.

EGYPTIAN CHRONOLOGY.

I.—ON THE CHRONOLOGY OF EGYPT.

[*Proceedings of the Royal Irish Academy*, Vol. i., p. 66.—Read April 24, 1837.]

In this Paper the author endeavours to ascertain the names of the Egyptian sovereigns who were contemporary with Moses. For this purpose he finds it necessary to determine the interval between two celebrated epochs—the reign of Menes and the Exodus of the Israelites. He conceives that the former epoch is fixed by the "old chronicle" at the distance of 443 years from the beginning of a cynic (or canicular) cycle; and he thinks it strange that this simple meaning should not have occurred to chronologists, who have universally supposed the "cynic cycle" of the old chronicle to be a series of demi-god kings who derived that appellation from the dog-headed Anubis. The canicular cycle is a well-known period of 1460 years, which the Egyptians seemed to have used for computing time, as we sometimes use the Julian period. One of these cycles commenced in the year 2782 before the Christian era; and if we reckon 443 years in advance, we shall have the year B. C. 2339 for the commencement of the reign of Menes. This date agrees well with the computation of Josephus, who says that the interval from Menes to Solomon was upwards of 1300 years. Again, we are told by Clemens of Alexandria, that the Exodus of the Israelites took place 345 years before the beginning of a canicular cycle. This is evidently the cycle which commenced B. C. 1322; and hence we have B. C. 1667 for the date of the Exodus. The interval between Menes and the Exodus was, therefore, about 670 years.

If, now, we take the catalogue of Eratosthenes, which commences with Menes, we shall find, at the distance of 670 years from Menes, a king named Achescus Ocaras, who reigned only one year; preceded by a king named Apappus, who reigned a hundred years, and succeeded by queen Nitocris, who reigned six years. Mr. Mac Cullagh thinks that Apappus is the king in whose reign Moses was born; that Ocaras is he who pursued the Israelites to the Red Sea; and that Nitocris is the famous queen mentioned by Herodotus. It may be objected that Eratosthenes gives us the succession of Theban kings, whereas the Pharaohs of the Mosaic history reigned in Lower Egypt; but it is remarkable that the three sovereigns mentioned above are found in Manetho's dynasties among those who reigned at Memphis; and it is singular that these are the only sovereigns (except Menes and his immediate successor) in which the dynasties of Manetho and the catalogue of Eratosthenes agree. All the other names are different. Of course the predecessors of Apappus, at Thebes and at Memphis, were different; and thus we can easily understand how there arose up at Memphis "a new king who knew not Joseph." It would appear, in fact, that Apappus was of a Theban family, and that he succeeded, for some reason or another, to the throne of Lower Egypt. He was only six years old (as we learn from Manetho) when he came to the throne; and it is natural to suppose that his chief advisers, as he grew up, were the courtiers who accompanied the young king from his own country to Memphis, and who knew nothing of Joseph, and cared nothing for his people. Accordingly, when Apappus arrived at manhood he issued an order that every male child of the Hebrews should be destroyed, lest they should grow too numerous for the Egyptians; and, under these circumstances, Moses was born in the twenty-first year of his reign, and was saved by the king's young daughter, a girl about ten years old. About the sixtieth year of Apappus, Moses was obliged to fly to the land of Midian, for having killed an Egyptian; and when at length the king of Egypt died—"after many days," as it is in the original—Moses returned in the beginning of the reign of Ocaras, before whom were performed those signs and wonders which prepared the way for the departure of the Israelites. On the night of the Passover, the king lost his first-born, perhaps his only son ; and this may be the reason that he was succeeded by his sister Nitocris. The short reign of Ocaras (a single year) might be explained by supposing he was drowned in the Red Sea ; but as there is nothing in the sacred narrative which obliges us to admit that the king perished in this manner, we may adopt the account of Herodotus, that he was murdered by his subjects. We may imagine that some of his nobles remained with Pharaoh on the shore ; and that when they saw the sea return and swallow up all that had gone in after the Israelites, they murdered the king, whose obstinacy had brought such calamities on his people, and then placed his sister Nitocris on the throne. As Nitocris was the daughter of Apappus, there is nothing to prevent us from supposing that the queen, now ninety years old, was the princess who had saved the infant Moses. Weary of her life, she lived only to avenge her brother. For this purpose, says Herodotus, she constructed a large subterranean chamber, to which, when it was finished, she invited the principal agents in her brother's death ; and there, by the waters of the Nile admitted through a secret canal, they were drowned in the midst of the banquet. The queen then threw herself into a room filled with ashes, where she perished.

II.—ON THE CATALOGUE OF EGYPTIAN KINGS, WHICH IS USUALLY KNOWN BY THE NAME OF THE *LATERCULUM* OF ERATOSTHENES.

[*Proceedings of the Royal Irish Academy*, Vol. ii. p. 366.—Read January 9, 1843.]

THIS Catalogue, which the distinguished mathematician and philosopher whose name it bears drew up by command of Ptolemy Euergetes, contains a long series of kings who reigned at Thebes in Upper Egypt, and has been preserved to us in the *Chronographia* of Georgius Syncellus, a Greek monk of the eighth century. It is a document which has been made much use of by chronologers; by some of whom (as by Sir John Marsham for example, who calls it " *venerandissimum antiquitatis monumentum*"), it has been reckoned of the very highest authority; but it is extremely corrupt in the latter part, owing to the carelessness with which it was transcribed either by Syncellus himself or his immediate copyists. The writers on Egyptian antiquities have in consequence been much perplexed in settling the chronology of the reigns in which the errors exist, and the attempts that have been made to remove the confusion have only served to increase it. It was the object of the author to restore the document to its original state, and he showed that this might be effected, with complete certainty, by a proper attention to the manuscripts of Syncellus. Of these only two are known: one has been used by Father Goar, the first editor of the *Chronographia* (Paris, 1652); the other, which is a much better one, has been collated by Dindorf, the second and latest editor. Dindorf's edition was published at Bonn, in the year 1829, as part of the *Corpus Scriptorum Historiæ Byzantinæ*, and on its first appearance Mr. Mac Cullagh had satisfied himself as to the original readings of the Catalogue, and had seen how to account for the errors which, probably from Syncellus's own negligence, had crept into it; but he did not publish his conclusions at the time, thinking that similar considerations could not fail to occur to some of the numerous writers who were then giving their especial attention to such subjects. This, however, has not been the case. Chronologers have continued to follow in the footsteps of Goar, a man of little learning, and of no critical sagacity, who corrected the Catalogue most injudiciously, and whose corrections, strange to say, are left without any remark by Dindorf. Thus Mr. Cory, in his *Ancient Fragments*, a work much referred to, merely transcribes Goar's list; and Mr. Culli- more, in attempting to reconcile ancient authors with each other and with the monuments, has adopted an hypothesis respecting the identity of two sovereigns which is not tenable when the true version of the Catalogue is known. Even in Goar's edition, however, there was quite enough to have led a person of ordi- nary judgment to the correct readings of the Catalogue, though perhaps they could not be said to be absolutely certain without the additional light obtained from that of Dindorf.

The Catalogue in question professes to contain the names of thirty-eight sovereigns, with the years of their reigns; the whole succession occupying, as is stated, a period of 1076 years; but it is only in the last eight reigns that the errors and inconsist- encies occur. The thirty-second prince is called Stamenemes β, that is, Stamenemes the Second, though there is, at present, no other of that name in the list; and the beginning of his reign— as appears from the years of the world, which Syncellus has annexed according to the Constantinopolitan reckoning—follows the termination of the preceding one by an interval of twenty-six years. Jackson, in his *Chronological Antiquities*, is positive that this prince is called the Second by a mistake, and adds the years that are wanting to the reign of his predecessor, as Goar had previously done. In the first part of this view all authors, without exception, are agreed, though they do not explain how a mistake, so very odd, could have originated; but the learned Marsham—who, having adopted the short chronology of the Hebrew Bible, is so hard pressed to find room for the Egyptian dynasties that he is obliged to begin the reign of Menes the very year after the Deluge—is glad to omit the twenty-six years altogether, thus reducing the sum of all the reigns to 1050 years, contrary to what is expressly stated by Syncellus. The natural inference from the state of the MSS. is, however, simply this: that the thirty-second king was Stamenemes I., that he reigned twenty-six years, and was succeeded by Stamenemes II. We may easily conceive that the eye of the transcriber, deceived by the identity of names, passed over the first, and rested on the second, thus occasioning the error. Indeed there can now be no doubt that this was the fact; because, in the MS. marked (B) by Dindorf, the next king is numbered as the thirty-fourth, the next but one as the thirty-fifth, and so on; which shows that a name had dropped out, and this name could be no other than that of Stamenemes I., who must have filled the vacant interval, and must consequently have reigned the number of years that has been assigned to him.

As neither Goar nor any other writer perceived this omission, the successor of Stamenemes II. has always been reckoned as the thirty-third in the list, and the next following as the thirty-fourth, &c. But as one error begets another, the omission was compensated by the insertion of an anonymous king, who is placed thirty-sixth in the list, with a reign of fourteen years; the insertion being necessary to complete the number (thirty-eight) which the Catalogue ought to contain. And, by a further error, these fourteen years are taken out of the reign of the thirty-seventh sovereign, who ought to have nineteen years instead of the five that have been hitherto assigned to him. This last error was occasioned by an ignorant correction of a mistake which is found in both the MSS., and which therefore probably arose from the carelessness of Syncellus himself. The thirty-seventh king and his predecessor are stated to have begun to reign in the same year of the world, and to have reigned the same number of years (five). Now from what goes before it is plain that both these numbers belong to the thirty-sixth king; and from the year of the world in which the thirty-eighth and last king began to reign, it is clear that the thirty-seventh reigned nineteen years. The mistake in the MSS. is one which might easily be made by a thoughtless writer; for the Catalogue is given in detached portions—a few reigns at a time—separated by a great quantity of other matter, and the name of the thirty-sixth king ends one of these portions, while that of the thirty-seventh begins another; so that, not having both before his eyes at the same moment, a person so careless as Syncellus might, without being conscious of it, attach the same reign and date to the two names, by transcribing twice over the same line of numbers in the Catalogue which he was copying; the whole of which Catalogue, in all likelihood, he had previously drawn up in a tabular form, with the years of the world annexed according to his own chronology, that it might be ready, as any portion of it was wanted, for immediate transference to his pages. Such seems to be the natural account of the matter; but, as usual, it does not occur to Goar, who takes the opportunity, which the confusion affords him, of foisting in his supplementary king between the two last mentioned, giving each of these five years, as in the MS., by which means he obtains room for him; while on the other hand he alters the year of the world attached to the thirty-seventh king, so as to make it suit his hypothesis.

The following is a view of the last eight reigns, as they appear to have stood in the original document, compared with the erroneous list of Goar. The years of the world are omitted, as being of no importance, except so far as they are useful in the preceding argument.

<table>
<tr><td colspan="4">I. Goar's List.</td><td colspan="4">II. Corrected List.</td></tr>
<tr><td></td><td></td><td></td><td>Years.</td><td></td><td></td><td></td><td>Years.</td></tr>
<tr><td>31.</td><td>*Peteathyres* reigned</td><td></td><td>42</td><td>31.</td><td>*Peteathyres*</td><td>reigned</td><td>16</td></tr>
<tr><td>32.</td><td>*Stamenemes*</td><td>,,</td><td>23</td><td>32.</td><td>*Stamenemes* I.</td><td>,,</td><td>26</td></tr>
<tr><td>33.</td><td>*Sistosichermes*</td><td>,,</td><td>55</td><td>33.</td><td>*Stamenemes* II.</td><td>,,</td><td>23</td></tr>
<tr><td>34.</td><td>*Maris*</td><td>,,</td><td>43</td><td>34.</td><td>*Sistosichermes*</td><td>,,</td><td>55</td></tr>
<tr><td>35.</td><td>*Siphoas*</td><td>,,</td><td>5</td><td>35.</td><td>*Maris*</td><td>,,</td><td>43</td></tr>
<tr><td>36.</td><td>Anonymous</td><td>,,</td><td>14</td><td>36.</td><td>*Siphoas*</td><td>,,</td><td>5</td></tr>
<tr><td>37.</td><td>*Phruoro*</td><td>,,</td><td>5</td><td>37.</td><td>*Phruoro*</td><td>,,</td><td>19</td></tr>
<tr><td>38.</td><td>*Amuthartæus*</td><td>,,</td><td>63</td><td>38.</td><td>*Amuthartæus*</td><td>,,</td><td>63</td></tr>
</table>

The interval of time which has been shown to belong to the first Stamenenes, and which was added by Goar to the reign of Peteathyres, is differently disposed of by Mr. Cullimore, in a chronological table which he has given in the second volume of the Transactions of the Royal Society of Literature. His object being to compare the lists of Eratosthenes, Manetho, &c., with the supposed hieroglyphical series, he makes Saophis, the fifteenth in Eratosthenes' Catalogue, the same as a king whose name is read Phrathek Osirtesen ; but the forty-third year of the latter is mentioned on the monuments, whereas Saophis has only twenty-nine years in the Catalogue. To escape from this difficulty, therefore, Mr. Cullimore adds the unappropriated interval to the reign of Saophis, thus giving him fifty-five years instead of twenty-nine. But it now appears that such a supposition is altogether inadmissible, and consequently the two personages in question cannot be identified—a circumstance which proves that there is some fault in Mr. Cullimore's assumptions, and that his other conclusions, at least in this part of his Table, cannot be relied on.

The corrections here given do not interfere with the inferences drawn by Professor Mac Cullagh from the Catalogue of Eratosthenes in a former Paper on Egyptian Chronology (Proceedings of the Royal Irish Academy, vol. i., p. 66),* because the

---

* *Supra*, p. 373.

portion of the Catalogue with which he was there concerned terminates with the reign of Queen Nitocris, the twenty-second in the list. The corrections, indeed, though not hitherto published, were made long before the date (April, 1837) of that Paper, but not before he had adopted the hypothesis therein proposed, as an answer to the old and ever-recurring question—Who were the Egyptian sovereigns that were contemporary with Moses ? For it was in consequence of this hypothesis, which had suggested itself to him at a very early period, that he was led to examine the Catalogue minutely, in order to discover whether his chronology was affected by its errors.

Having been led to refer to his hypothesis, Mr. Mac Cullagh took occasion to observe that, in the interval which had elapsed since it was published, he had not met with any facts that were opposed to it : on the contrary, the more he considered it, the more he was inclined to believe in its reality ; though it was entirely different from every other that had been proposed, either by modern chronologers or by the early Fathers of the Church, in their manifold attempts to connect the narrative of Moses with the remaining fragments of Egyptian history. The hypothesis, indeed, is the *only* one which, while it gives a probable date for the Exodus, also satisfies what Mr. Mac Cullagh conceives to be the necessary conditions of the question ; namely, a very long reign—of at least eighty years—during which the Israelites were persecuted, succeeded by a very short one— apparently not more than a year—during which their deliverance was wrought ; and it is interesting in itself, on account of the remarkable connexion which it establishes between sacred and profane history, and the highly dramatic character of the events which are thus, for the first time, brought into view.

THE END.